PRAISE

Nora Roberts Land
"Ava's story is witty and charming."
—Barbara Freethy #1 *NYT* bestselling author

Selected by *USA Today* as one of the Best Books of the year alongside Nora Roberts' *Dark Witch* and Julia Quinn's *Sum of all Kisses*.

"If you like Nora Roberts type books, this is a must-read."
—Readers' Favorite

Country Heaven
"If ever there was a contemporary romance that rated a 10 on a scale of 1 to 5 for me, this one is it!"
—The Romance Reviews

"*Country Heaven* made me laugh and cry...I could not stop flipping the pages. I can't wait to read the next book in this series." —Fresh Fiction

Country Heaven Cookbook
"Delicious, simple recipes... Comfort food, at its best."
—Fire Up The Oven Blog

The Bridge to a Better Life
Selected by *USA Today* as one of the Best Books of the Summer.

"Miles offers a story of grief, healing and rediscovered love." —USA Today

"I've read Susan Mallery and Debbie Macomber...but never have I been so moved by the books Ava Miles writes." —Booktalk with Eileen Reviews

The Gate to Everything
"The constant love...bring a sensual, dynamic tension to this appealing story." —Publisher's Weekly

More Praise For Ava

The Chocolate Garden
"On par with Nicholas Sparks' love stories."
—Jennifer's Corner Blog

"A must-read...a bit of fairy magic...a shelf full of happiness."
—Fab Fantasy Fiction

The Promise of Rainbows
"This is a story about grace, faith and the power of both..."
—The Book Nympho

French Roast
"Ms. Miles draws from her experience as an apprentice chef...and it shows...I loved {the} authenticity of the food references, and the recipes...looked divine." —BlogCritics

The Holiday Serenade
"This story is all romance, steam, and humor with a touch of the holiday spirit..." —The Book Nympho

The Town Square
"Ms. Miles' words melted into each page until the world receded around me..." —Tome Tender

The Park of Sunset Dreams
"Ava has done it again. I love the whole community of Dare Valley..." —Travel Through The Pages Blog

The Goddess Guides Series
"Miles' series is an **exquisite exploration** of internal discomfort and courage, allowing you to reclaim your divine soul and fully express your womanhood."
—Dr. Shawne Duperon, Project Forgive Founder, Nobel Peace Prize Nominee

"The Goddess Guides are a **world changer**. Well done, Ava." —International Bestseller Kate Perry aka Kathia Zolfaghari, Artist & Activist

Also by Ava Miles

Fiction

The Dare Valley Series

Nora Roberts Land

French Roast

The Grand Opening

The Holiday Serenade

The Town Square

The Park of Sunset Dreams

The Perfect Ingredient

The Bridge to a Better Life

The Calendar of New Beginnings

Home Sweet Love

The Moonlight Serenade

Daring Brides

The Dare River Series

Country Heaven

Country Heaven Song Book

Country Heaven Cookbook

The Chocolate Garden

The Chocolate Garden:
A Magical Tale (Children's Book)

Fireflies and Magnolias

The Promise of Rainbows

The Fountain of Infinite Wishes

The Patchwork Quilt of Happiness

Dare Valley Meets Paris Billionaire Mini-Series
The Billionaire's Gamble
The Billionaire's Courtship
The Billionaire's Secret
The Billionaire's Return

The Goddess Guides to Being a Woman
Goddesses Decide
Goddesses Deserve The G's
Goddesses Love Cock
Goddesses Cry and Say Motherfucker
Goddesses Don't Do Drama
Goddesses Are Sexy
Goddesses Eat
Goddesses Are Happy
Goddesses Face Fear

Other Non-Fiction
The Happiness Corner: Reflections So Far
Home Baked Happiness

The Patchwork Quilt of Happiness

The Dare River Series

Ava Miles

Copyright 2018, Ava Miles

All rights reserved.

No part of this book may be reproduced or transmitted in any form by any means—graphic, electronic or mechanical—without permission in writing from the author, except by a reviewer who may quote brief passages in a review.

This is a work of fiction. All of the characters, organizations, and events portrayed in this novel are either the products of the author's imagination or are used fictionally.

ISBN-13: 978-1-940565-96-5
www.avamiles.com
Ava Miles

Dedication

*To every child who's ever been abandoned.
You are precious. And you are loved.*

*And to my divine entourage, who helps me see the
bigger picture and go for it, every day.*

Acknowledgements

My heartfelt thanks to the special people in my life who support my efforts:

Team Ava, who rocks my world.

Dr. Richa Thapa, goddess extraordinaire, for connecting me to Dr. Kristin Homburg, who provided insights from child psychology for this story.

All the quilters on my Facebook page who provided so much help and feedback and sent me notes. I can't name you all, but a few people deserve special mention for their extra help, including Char Scott and Jenny Anderson. I did my best to capture this incredible craft, and if I got something wrong, all I can say is, "Oops."

T.F. For being my patchwork quilt of happiness.

Chapter 1

Showing up on her long-lost half-sister's doorstep might just be the stupidest plan Sadie McGuiness had ever drummed up.

If they knew, her mama would likely tear up, her brother might sigh like an exasperated elephant, and her sisters were liable to pitch a three-alarm fit. But she couldn't help it.

Their family didn't seem complete without her.

Sadie's eyes were glued to the yellow front door of the blue-gray A-frame home. She'd been inside her car for a spell, fighting nerves, weighing whether she was plumb crazy or downright brave. In her Sunday sermons, Mama always said you chose love first, last, and always. Well, Sadie was choosing love. Big time. She just hoped everyone else would see it that way. Right now she figured she had a fifty-fifty chance of upsetting someone. For her, those weren't *terrible* odds.

When she'd learned she had another sister out there, she'd prayed on it something fierce. Her daddy's affair, if you could call it that, with a teenage girl, Skylar Watkins, had ruined their family, but none of the fault could be laid at her sister's door. She hadn't asked to be born as a child out of wedlock to a then-married man.

Armed with new confidence, Sadie had done a simple online search to find her sister. The ease with which she'd found her seemed like its own kind of sign. Even more surprising, she'd been living right under their noses in Nashville.

Paige Watkins.

She was only a year younger than Sadie. Being the youngest of the four McGuiness siblings, it was weird to think she was someone else's older sister. Paige was married now and went by Paige Bradshaw. She was on Facebook and everything, and Sadie's heart had simply exploded like a shaken bottle of soda pop upon discovering she had a niece—a cute-as-a-button seven-year-old named Haley.

That had cinched her decision to make first contact.

She gripped the door handle. Good sense caused her to pause and check her makeup in her compact. While it was late August, the weather was still as hot as Hades, and her hair was on the frizzy side thanks to the infernal humidity of a Tennessee summer. She wet her finger and smoothed it back. Her lipstick still looked fresh. She was presentable. It had taken her the better part of an hour to pick out the dress she was wearing—a casual yet elegant yellow sundress with a halter-top.

She wanted to look nice without appearing like she was trying too hard.

Then she laughed at herself. Who was she kidding?

Her ankle turned when she opened the car door, and she winced. Her hands started to sweat, and she couldn't think of what to do with them, so she clutched her large purse under her arm and focused on walking to the door. *One step, two steps, three steps*, she counted. The door beckoned, and when she arrived on the porch, the sight of a kid's purple bicycle peppered with glitter had her tearing up. This was why she was being all brave-like. These people were *family*.

When she knocked, she ran through the script she'd prepared. When the door opened, a sandy-haired handsome man stood there smiling. He had a strong jaw and captivating baby blues. Wowza. Who *was* this man? She'd seen pictures of Mark Bradshaw on Facebook, and this wasn't him. Yet he seemed familiar.

"Hi," he said. "Have you come to save me?"

She laughed. "Ah...do you need saving? My mama is a preacher, and she could help with that."

His mouth pursed like he was fighting laughter. "Not that kind of saving, but when I saw you standing in the door, I figured you couldn't be a salesman."

He was flirting with her. "No...I...I'm here to invite Paige to a—"

There was a scurrying sound in the other room, and he looked over his shoulder. "Jess, *Haley*. You'd better not be getting into Paige's china cabinet." Turning back to Sadie, he added, "Sorry, please come inside. It's hot out. Give me a second to check on the girls. Haley and Jess wanted to have a princess banquet in the dining room. Usually we're over at my house after school, but Haley got a new toy, so they decided to play here instead."

Sadie took a breath as he darted off. Now that she'd had a moment to deal with the surprise of someone unexpected answering the door, she did recognize this guy. He'd been in one of the photos on Facebook with Paige and her family, although his name escaped her.

"Man, those girls are going to be the death of me," he said when he returned to the hall. "Okay, let's start again. I'm Riley Thomson, Paige and Mark's next-door neighbor. And you are?"

"I'm Sadie," she replied. Better to keep the McGuiness name out of things until she saw her sister and explained things. It wouldn't do to spill her secret to the neighbor before she even saw Paige.

His eyes traveled over her face, and he smiled again.

"I like that name. It suits you. Now, you said something about inviting Paige to something. Sorry, I get kid brain whenever I babysit, and my mind still thinks it's summer. I pick them up after school since Paige and Mark don't come home until five-thirty."

"Oh, I see," she responded, glancing down at her watch. After quite a bit of thought, she'd decided to come a little after five o'clock, thinking it would give her sister enough of a window before dinner so as to not be rude.

"I'm not really the babysitter, by the way," Riley said, causing her to look up. "I mean…I've got a job and all. I'm a comic book artist."

Sadie felt her eyebrow rise. This wasn't going at all like she'd expected. She was totally off her game now, not to mention completely unprepared to interact with an attractive man. "That's…wonderful."

"Your tone suggests you aren't into comics," he said, bending slightly at the waist and putting an arm on the entryway table.

A candlestick started to topple, and Sadie rushed forward to catch it. He turned his head to see what he'd done and ended up bumping the table more. Sadie caught the candlestick, but there was another crash. Riley muttered something under his breath and bent down to pick up a wooden sign that had fallen to the floor.

He held it out, smiling sheepishly, his face red. "*Welcome*," he said, reading the sign.

"Daddy, did you break something?" Sadie heard a little girl call out. There was a scurrying of feet, and then the same little girl heaved out a dramatic sigh. "Goodness, you're fit to be tied about Haley and me breaking Ms. Bradshaw's china, and here you are messing with her things. Hi, I'm Jess, this klutz's daughter. This is my bestest friend ever, Haley."

The two little girls had on princess gowns. Jess' had blue polka dots and white puffy sleeves. Haley's was purple, and since her bike was the same color, Sadie figured it was likely her favorite color. Her niece's hair was brown and longer than it had been in the pictures online, crowned with a slightly crooked tiara. The little girl smiled, showing the McGuiness dimples, and Sadie felt her heart tighten.

"Hello," she said softly, coughing to clear the emotion in her throat. "I'm Sadie."

"That's a nice name, and I like your dress," Jess said, taking the sign from her father's hand and putting it back on the table. "What do you want?"

"Jess!" Riley cried out. "Don't be rude. Ms.... Ah, Sadie wanted to invite Haley's mama to something. She was just getting around to that."

"Jess is what my daddy calls a plain-speaking woman," Haley said. "He likes that about her."

Sadie felt a smile stretch across her face. "I like women who speak their minds too."

"Then you came to the right house," Jess said. "My dad wants me to be my own superhero. He writes and draws comics. Did he tell you?"

Sadie nodded at the formidable four-foot person who was now pushing sandy blond curls back from her forehead. That hair was identical to Riley's. Was he married? She made sure to check out his left hand. The absence of a wedding ring oddly excited her.

"What were you inviting my mama to?" Haley asked. "If it's church, we already attend."

"That's nice to hear," Sadie responded. "I was going to invite your mama to join my quilting class. We're making quilts for babies in the NICU."

"What's that?" Jess asked.

"It's a part of the hospital where they treat babies who are born sickly or a bit on the small side," Riley said.

Then he shifted his gaze back to Sadie, seeming to weigh her with those blue eyes. To her surprise, the intensity made her want to lean toward him rather than away.

"So, you're a quilter. That's its own form of art."

"You mean like a blanket?" Haley asked.

"Yes, kinda," Sadie said, oddly relieved to divert her attention from Riley and his powerful gaze. "I use small pieces of cloth and form patterns with them."

"Do you have any pictures of them?" Jess asked.

"Well, yes. I also brought one of the baby quilts I made."

She dug into her purse and pulled out the small quilt. Riley and the girls stepped closer as she unfolded it and held it up. She'd brought it as a sample to show her sister in the hopes it might convince her to join the quilting group. Part of her also hoped the quilt would tell Paige a bit about who she was as a person. She wasn't always able to express herself with words as fluently as she could with fabric.

"Wow!" the girls said with awe in their voices.

"That's beautiful," Riley said, sounding just as taken with it. "I love your use of color. The golden tones make the moon and stars feel three-dimensional, and the light blue background—"

"Dad!" Jess cried. "He's a total art geek sometimes, but I love him."

"Thanks," Riley said dryly, making Sadie laugh.

"Can we touch it?" Haley asked.

"Sure," she said, eyeing their hands, which seemed clean.

"It's so soft," Haley said, brushing the fabric with the tips of her fingers. "And pretty."

"Well, I just love it!" Jess announced. "You've got talent. Do you have pictures of your other quilts?"

Sadie reached into her purse for her phone. She saw a text from her sister, Susannah, and felt a pinch of guilt. Oh, she hoped her family wasn't going to pitch a fit when they heard what she'd done. Her sisters and brother thought they knew what was best for everyone, but in this case, her heart told her they weren't right. Ignoring the text, she pulled up her photos.

Jess snatched her phone from her and began to scroll through them while Haley leaned in closer to see.

"Sorry," Riley said. "Kids these days. They love phones. Ah...Jess, please give Ms. Sadie back her phone and let her show you—"

"Dad! You've got to see this one. It's made for a princess." Jess held the phone up to her dad, and Sadie caught sight of the quilt she'd made for her niece, Annabelle.

"That quilt is fit for a princess," Sadie said. "My niece chose the colors and some of the fabric. We designed it together." For a five-year-old, Annabelle had had strong opinions about how it was supposed to come together.

"I love the stars and the unicorn!" Jess said. "Dad, I want a princess quilt."

"Me too!" Haley clapped her hands. "Do you have a store where my mama and daddy can buy one?"

"No, I don't," she answered, shaking her head. "Well, I sell some at the craft store I work at."

"You should use Etsy," Jess said. "You can sell anything there. You're missing a great opportunity. Dad sells artwork on there and does pretty good."

Riley gave his daughter a pained look. "Girls, Ms. Sadie doesn't need advice on where to sell her quilts."

"But I want one of these, Dad," Jess said, "and my birthday is right around the corner."

"In March," Riley drawled.

"Besides, you're always saying something that's made by hand is better. Like one of your drawings."

"My kid is quite the entrepreneur," Riley said, putting his hand on her shoulder. "Ah… If you'd like to wait until Paige gets home, you're welcome to. Can I get you something to drink?"

"You should stay," Jess told her, handing back her phone. "Ms. Bradshaw needs to see this so she can buy Haley a princess quilt. Plus, my dad likes you. See you later."

The little girl winked, took Haley's hand, and together they ran out of the room.

Sadie rested her phone against her thigh, a little embarrassed to look at Riley.

"My daughter usually isn't a matchmaker," he said quietly. "I'm sorry if she embarrassed you."

His tone had completely shifted from exasperated to quietly intent.

"No, she didn't embarrass me," Sadie said, feeling her face turn red in complete contrast to her answer.

"Well, I'm embarrassed," Riley said, pointing to himself. "But since my daughter put it out there, I'll be blunt. I would like to get to know you better. I'm a single dad, and I work at home. Pretty women don't just land on my doorstep—or my neighbor's doorstep—every day."

He stopped then and studied her. Sadie's heart sped up at his regard. She looked back at him. Those eyes were the same shade of dark cerulean she favored in her quilts. His hair was nice and thick and needed a trim. He was easily a foot taller than her, which put him at over six feet. And there was no denying she liked the way he filled out his simple green T-shirt.

His smile was slow but enthralling. "Would you want to go out for dinner with me sometime?"

"I...yes."

She couldn't help herself. She didn't meet many men like him either, what with working at the craft store and spending so much time with her family and at church. Some of the single men at church were cute and kind, and several of them had asked her out, but they all seemed to have the same unrealistic expectations about preachers' kids. The ones she'd gone out with had perceived her as some goody two-shoes who never swore or danced or drank. They wanted a saint and not a woman, and that had bored her to tears.

It had become quite a conundrum. She wanted a guy who went to church who valued what she did, but the right one hadn't materialized, which was why she hadn't been in a serious relationship since college. She'd thought her college boyfriend had valued her, but in the end, he'd only wanted her to be his version of a *good* woman.

And there was something else that had stood in her way, something she didn't much like to talk about. In the back of her mind, she was always trying to look into a man's heart to see if he could up and leave his family like her daddy had left them.

Even though she'd just met Riley, he'd liked her quilts and he was here taking care of his daughter. Big points for her.

"That would be nice," she felt compelled to add after the pause between them.

Then a door slammed, and Sadie jumped. What had she just done? She'd come here to meet her sister, not make a date. What would Paige think of her?

"Haley! Mama and Daddy are home!"

Riley took a step closer and dug out something from his pocket. "Here's my card with my cell on it. Before I embarrass myself in front of my friends, what's your number? You can just tell me. I have a good memory."

She repeated her number to him, her eyes peeled on the hallway, where the girls' delighted giggles now mixed with adult laughter.

Riley's hand brushed hers as he fitted his card in her palm. "I'll call you later tonight," he said, his eyes dancing with delight. "Jess! Let's go. I've got to get dinner on."

The little girl came running down the hall. "I am so getting a princess quilt," she told her father.

"We'll talk about it."

"Nice to meet you, Ms. Sadie," the little girl said.

"Yes," Riley spoke quietly beside her. "It was nice to meet you, Sadie."

The way his voice dipped should have been scandalous, but it felt...nice. Too bad he likely wouldn't call her once he learned the truth. She gave him a half smile, keeping her gaze on the hallway.

The handsome, dark-haired man she'd seen in Paige's Facebook photos appeared, hand in hand with Haley. His suit was garnished with a pink and white-striped tie, and somehow that eased Sadie. Only truly confident men could wear pink.

"My daughter says we have a visitor—one that makes princess quilts."

"I'm going to run before the girls gang up on me again." Riley held up his hand. "Later, man."

The newcomer waved, Riley and Jess left, and just like that Sadie was left alone with the people she'd come to meet.

Haley skipped toward her, dragging her dad. "Wait until you see the princess quilt, Daddy. It even has a unicorn on it."

The man had an amused smile on his face when they reached her. "So you're the quilt maker the girls were going on about. I'm Mark Bradshaw."

"I'm Sadie—"

"McGuiness," a woman said, punctuated by a gasp somewhere down the hall.

She looked toward the voice, and almost reeled from the woman's similarities to Susannah.

"You're Sadie McGuiness," Paige said, covering her mouth with her hand.

"McGuiness?" Sadie heard Mark say over the roar in her ears.

What? Paige knew about her? "How do you—?"

"You know my mama?" Haley asked, interrupting her.

Sadie couldn't seem to reply. The only thing she seemed capable of doing was stare at this woman who looked so familiar.

"Why didn't you say so? Mama, she wants you to make quilts for sick babies in the hospital. You've just gotta do it. Daddy always says to give back and this way you can ask her to show you how to make me a princess quilt."

Sadie shook herself and looked down at Haley with what she hoped passed for a smile. It wasn't the little girl's fault that her mama had known about them and done nothing to reach out. Okay, she probably had her reasons, and Sadie reminded herself it would not be productive to jump to conclusions.

"I'd like to give you the quilt I brought to show your mama. You and Jess can use it for your dolls. Is that okay?"

Her half-sister glanced her way, her face white. She seemed incapable of responding too.

Right. No conclusions.

"Oh, can I really have it?" Haley asked. "Mama, wait until you see it! There are gold stars and a moon on it, and it's the prettiest color blue. I wish I'd had it as a baby. Sadie, show her!"

"Haley," Mark said, putting his hand on their daughter's shoulder, "why don't you run over to Jess' house for a little while? You two can play while your mama and I talk to Ms. Sadie here. Tell Mr. Thomson I'll be over to get you in a bit."

Haley looked at her and then at Sadie. "Oh, adult stuff. But Dad, can I accept Ms. Sadie's present or not?"

"That's for your mama to decide," Mark said, meeting Paige's eyes.

Sadie held her breath, waiting for the outcome of their silent discussion. She told herself it wouldn't hurt her feelings if Paige refused the gift, but she knew it wasn't true. Learning her sister knew about them—and had likely known for some time—changed everything.

"Mama?" Haley asked, a strong note of determination in her voice mixed in with a politeness Sadie respected. "Please. It's so beautiful."

"Honey, go on over to Jess' now," Paige said, finally walking forward.

Sadie wondered if her sister had been scared to get closer to her, to see any similarities in their faces or builds.

"All right," Haley said with a dramatic sigh. "Bye, Ms. Sadie. I hope you come back and show me more princess quilts."

The little girl hugged Mark's leg and then opened the front door and ran out.

"Riley and Jess live next door," Mark explained, clearing his throat. "The girls run back and forth all the time. Keyless entry and all. Well…"

Mark looked at Paige again, and she knew what he was asking his wife. *Do you want to talk to your sister now that she's on our doorstep?*

The urge to cut and run was strong. "I'm so sorry to have…" Sadie blurted out. "I was going to tell you who I was. I didn't realize…you already knew about me. Us."

Paige's face seemed to fall, as if she only now realized that knowledge had been hurtful.

"It's just… We only learned about you last month, and I couldn't stop thinking about you. It wasn't fair what happened to you—to any of us. I prayed about it, and I just had to come meet you. It didn't feel right not to know you."

When tears sprang into her sister's eyes, Sadie felt a modicum of relief. She wasn't the only one upset here.

"I was going to tell you who I was and invite you to my quilting class. We're making quilts for babies in the NICU, you see, and I thought…I thought we might get to know each other. No pressure. In a casual setting." Her sharp intake of breath echoed in the foyer. "For a good cause and all."

Mark took a step toward her and grabbed her sister's hand. The silence seemed to lengthen, and Sadie found herself praying in her head. *Please say yes.*

"Why don't you come into the kitchen with us and have a cup of tea?" Paige finally managed to say in a rasp.

Sadie felt her lip tremble, and it took her a long minute to say, "That would be wonderful. Thank you."

Mark still hadn't released her sister's hand, and Sadie found herself admiring the strength they radiated as a couple. She knew a solid marriage when she saw it.

"Follow me, Sadie," Mark said, gesturing to the left.

Sadie sniffed, wishing she could dig into her purse for a tissue. Since that seemed too obvious, she went in the direction he'd indicated. Paige took a couple of shaky breaths and followed with her husband.

In the kitchen, Mark kissed Paige's cheek oh-so-sweetly before letting go of her hand and crossing to the stove to make them all tea. Paige walked over to the kitchen table and pointed to a chair. Sadie slowly sank into it. Something about the woman's valiant attempt at a smile shot straight to her heart. It was like looking at one of her other sisters in a moment of distress, the gesture an attempt to be kind in the midst of so much hurt.

"I never expected to meet you," Paige whispered.

Her honesty made Sadie look down in her lap for a moment before gathering the courage to look at her sister. "I realize that now. How long have you known about us?"

Paige lifted a shoulder, as if embarrassed. "Since I was a little girl. My mama said we had to go away because my daddy's family didn't like me. She was always lying about things. She claimed she was his second wife and his kids didn't like us. She said…a lot of things that weren't true. We don't talk anymore, and I'm sure you can guess why."

"Oh my God," Sadie said, letting the first tears fall

down her face. "I'm so sorry. That's an awful thing to tell someone. It wasn't that we didn't like you! We didn't know about *you*. Our mama...she was trying to protect us from what happened."

"I can certainly understand your mama's position," Paige said, nodding. "I would have felt the same way. We—Mark and I—do our best to protect Haley from the truth about my family. Thankfully, he's a guidance counselor and knows a thing or two about how to handle family issues like...the ones I grew up with. It's like having an in-house expert pro bono."

Paige looked over at her husband, who was standing by the tea kettle like a sentry. How wonderful that they'd found each other. While Sadie barely knew the CliffsNotes version of Paige's childhood, it certainly hadn't been happy. It broke Sadie's heart to think of the pain her sister had endured, the pain they'd *all* endured.

She finally reached into the purse she realized she was still clutching and pulled out a packet of tissues. "Excuse me. I've been trying to be...circumspect about all of this emotion I seem to be having..."

Her voice trailed off. Paige didn't seem to be aware of her in that moment. Her eyes were fixed on her husband. He was pouring the boiling water into cups, and she rose to help him carry them to the table. He laid his hand on her arm, and Paige shook her head as if telling him she was okay. Then she covered the hand resting on her own.

I love you, she mouthed.

I love you, Mark mouthed back.

Sadie felt her heart expand as she watched them. Then Mark turned and picked up what looked like a sampler box of tea while Paige brought the cups over.

"What can we offer you, Sadie?" Mark asked. "We have just about every tea in here."

"Chamomile would be great if you have it," Sadie said, hoping it would help calm her over-sensitive nervous system. "Thank you for being so kind to me. After hearing what your mama told you, I'm surprised you didn't throw me out the front door. I...worried you might."

"We're usually not violent," Mark joked, giving Sadie a gentle smile. "Plus, it was pretty brave of you to come see Paige. I can tell it was a shock to you and your siblings."

Since that was an understatement, Sadie simply nodded. "Yes, it...felt like the end of the world, but Mama always says there's the promise of rainbows."

Paige selected a citrus lime tea bag and dunked it in her water. "That's a nice turn of phrase."

Silence descended as they all made their tea. Paige seemed to stir in the sugar more vigorously than needed. Sadie racked her mind for what to say. Oh, this was so hard.

"Maybe you should show us this quilt Haley was so excited about," Mark suggested.

Yes, she could work with that! Sadie set her teacup down too fast, and water sloshed over the side. "Oops, I'm so clumsy."

Paige picked up some napkins and together they cleaned up the mess. "Don't worry about it. Please, I'd like to see your quilt, Sadie."

It was the first time her sister had said her name out loud—and it felt odd to hear it somehow. Calling someone by their name meant something, and they both knew it was significant. Sadie's mouth lifted at the corners, realizing it was Paige's way of reassuring her, and she reached into her large gold purse. As she unfolded the quilt, she noted Paige's eyes filling with tears—another encouraging sign.

The little blanket was meant to be pure magic, from the soft baby blue swatches to the golden moon and stars. But it was the phrase in the corner of the blanket that had inspired Sadie to bring it tonight. "Precious One" was what she wanted to call her sister.

When the tears in Paige's eyes spilled down her face and she made no move to brush them aside, Sadie knew on some level she'd understood the message.

"I'd like to join your quilting group, Sadie," her sister finally said softly. "If you still want me to. And I'd be... honored if you still wanted to give this beautiful quilt to me. I mean, my daughter."

When her sister clutched the corner of the quilt, Sadie gave her a teary smile. "Oh, that's...that's...just wonderful...Paige."

Mark smiled and picked up his teacup. "I've never seen anything more beautiful."

Although Sadie couldn't be sure, she thought Mark might be talking about more than the quilt.

Chapter 2

For a man who'd never much thought about having kids, Riley had fallen hard for his daughter. How could he not have? He pushed back the strand of hair covering Jess' cheek, picked her up, and wrapped her in a blanket, gazing at her sweet heart-shaped face.

The sight of his sleepy daughter every morning pretty much rocked his world.

And he was in an especially good mood this morning because Sadie had agreed to go out with him Friday night. He'd called her after Jess had gone to bed, the feeling in his gut both excited and nervous.

They hadn't talked long, but he had a good feeling about her—one he hadn't had in a long time. His trust in the opposite sex had gotten messed up, but he finally felt ready to start looking for a serious relationship again. Two years after Jess' birth and the split with his ex, he'd dated a few women, but it hadn't felt right. He had a new life with a young daughter. He'd needed more of a time-out to focus on Jess and figure out what he really wanted in a committed relationship.

After all, any relationship he formed now wouldn't just affect him.

He finally felt ready to meet the right person, something he'd admitted to Mark and Paige a few months ago. They'd offered plenty of help and encouragement, including babysitting, thank God. Never once had they offered to set him up with their friends, and for that he was grateful.

Jess had been supportive too. Just look at how she'd talked to Sadie for him last night. He kissed her forehead because he couldn't help himself.

"Mmm...Daddy," she murmured and nestled into his arms.

"Mornin', princess," he whispered, smiling.

He took the stairs slowly, careful to let her sleep. The weather was hot and muggy when he opened the back door and crossed his driveway to the Bradshaws' back door. Monday through Friday, he brought a still-sleeping Jess over to their house so he and Mark could take a long run. He was right on time this morning, already dressed in his running outfit. If he got to drawing early, he sometimes lost track of time.

Mark promptly opened the door in response to his light rap. His friend gave him the proverbial man nod, and Riley took the back stairs and walked quietly to Haley's bedroom down the hall. His daughter's best friend had a foot thrust out from under the blanket, her purple Disney princess nightgown visible. Man, did that girl love purple. Her room was a temple to all things purple, and as an artist, Riley could analyze the different shades—aubergine, lavender, grape, and violet. He pulled out the already-made trundle bed and laid his daughter on the mattress.

He heard the shower running as he left the room. Paige was already up, like usual, and she'd have the girls fed by the time he and Mark returned. All Riley would need to do was help his daughter get dressed. Not that he'd have to do much. She had strong opinions about what she wanted to wear, and he always let her choose. Now that she was seven, she was more than capable of handling buttons, zippers, and tying her shoes. His little girl was growing up, and damn if he hadn't cried after he'd dropped her off the first day of school.

That was one of his jobs. Paige fed the girls in the morning. He dropped them off, picked them up, and watched them until his friends got home. In return, they would sometimes babysit in the evenings or on the weekends so he could get some overtime work done. He wasn't sure what he would have done without them these last five years. When he first moved in next door, he'd been struggling to get back on his feet after taking on full responsibility for Jess, a decision he'd never regretted.

When he strolled into the kitchen, Mark was stretching his hamstrings. "Thank God our daughters love each other." The girls had taken one look at each other as toddlers and, without any prompting, hugged. It was like it was meant to be.

"You're telling me," Mark said, glancing up. "Did you drink enough water this morning?"

"Yes, Mom, I'm good," he teased. "You need to stop worrying about me getting dehydrated."

"It's hot out. Okay, let's roll."

Once outside, they hit the pavement with a good stride, easing into the run. They both liked to warm up before increasing their pace.

"I'm feeling pretty spry this morning," Riley announced as they made a left off their street, following their normal route.

"Work going well?"

"Yes," Riley said, feeling a bit like a rooster as he stuck out his chest. "And I have a date Friday night."

"Hey! Way to go, man. Who is she?" Mark slapped him on the back as they jogged, causing him to laugh.

The image of Sadie in her yellow sundress came to mind again. Man, she was beautiful—and artistic too. Plus, his daughter had all but set them up.

Online dating might be practical, but he'd heard stories

about people lying about everything from their age to their relationship status. After the mistakes he'd made with his ex...well, now he was an old-fashioned guy with trust issues.

Until last night. He'd wanted to ask Sadie out from the minute he'd set eyes on her.

"Sadie, the woman from last night," Riley said. "Jess outed that I liked her, and I asked for her number on the spot. We talked a little last night, and she agreed to go out with me on Friday. By the way, did Paige decide to join her quilting class? I don't know if she leans toward that kind of hobby, but Sadie's work is stunning. Jess was on me all night to order a princess quilt from her, but I don't want to muddy the waters until we get to know each other better." His daughter hadn't liked the thought of waiting, and Riley knew she was going to be back on him like a duck on a June bug.

Mark didn't respond right away, and Riley turned his head to study his friend. Mark noticed and flashed him a quick smile. Too quick.

"Something wrong? You didn't see something in her that I missed, did you? She's not some kind of closet psychopath?"

Mark was a proverbial wizard when it came to reading people.

"No, I think Sadie is a lovely woman," Mark responded, patting him on the back more casually this time. "And Paige did agree to attend her quilting class."

"I can hear the 'but' a mile away," he said, running a little faster from his jitters. "Tell me what you really think."

Mark went silent again for a few more long moments, and Riley resisted the urge to press the man. When his friend was like this, he wouldn't be rushed.

"Let's head back to the house," Mark said. "I need to talk to Paige before I can respond, and I don't want to keep you on the line." Pivoting his head to meet Riley's eyes, he added, "It involves a confidence. Otherwise, I would tell you. You know that."

Yes, he did. He and Mark didn't make hearts out of construction paper and write 'BFF's on them like their daughters did, but he knew they were as close as brothers. Heck, they spent the holidays together. Whatever this involved, it was serious. What in the world was going on?

Mark turned around and picked up the pace, which Riley was happy to match. When they reached the Bradshaws' driveway, Mark said, "Better wait here. If the girls see you, we won't have another moment alone."

Riley nodded as Mark took off toward the house. His mind spinning out a dozen different scenarios, he crouched down and pulled a few of the never-ending weeds that always shot up back between the cracks in the sidewalk in front of his house.

"Hey!" Mark called, making his head shoot up. "Let's take a walk. We've got enough time."

Walk, not run. "Sure." Riley threw the weeds aside and brushed his dirty hands on his shorts.

Mark took off at a stroll, his arms locked behind his back. Dread rolled through Riley. Something was definitely off.

"There's no easy way to say this, but I think you should know... Sadie is Paige's half-sister."

He stopped short. "You're kidding! Why didn't she say so?"

Paige had told him about her messed-up mom and absentee dad, which had made her more than sympathetic to his situation with Mandy, his ex. But she'd never told him the full story. This was the first he'd heard about any half-siblings.

"They'd never met until last night."

"Oh. Wow. That's like... I'll just shut up now and let you talk."

Mark looked him in the eye, and they started walking again. "Paige's mom became pregnant when she was in high school. The father was much older and married with four young children. They met at church, and though it's unclear from Paige's mom who seduced whom, she wasn't old enough to properly consent."

It was statutory rape. A crime. Riley stopped walking again, the injustice rolling over him. "That's...that's... utterly despicable. What kind of a man does that?"

"Well, knowing Paige's mom, she wasn't totally a victim, but that doesn't make it right. Suffice it to say, from what Paige and I managed to piece together after we got married—her mom's not one for truth—it affected Sadie's family very seriously. The man in question disappeared, and his ex-wife ended up remarrying and becoming a minister. After meeting Sadie last night, it appears the family turned around a tragedy and did just fine."

"So has Paige, if you ask me," Riley said. "I mean, she's one of the best people I know, and you guys are like the rock of Gibraltar as a couple."

Mark smiled. "Yeah, we're really lucky to have each other. I hope you find someone you feel that way about too."

"Can I do anything for you guys about this?" Riley asked. "I mean, I should probably cancel my date with Sadie, right? I don't want to get in the middle of anything." It gave him a sinking feeling to even say it, but Mark and his family were his support system. He owed them so much more than that.

"No, Paige and I talked about this. We don't want you to cancel anything. It's only one date. Go out. See how you feel. See how she feels. We know this is rare for you. Like I said, Paige is going to go to the quilting circle and keep an open mind and heart. Sadie was so earnest—and brave— to show up like she did. The quilt she gave to Haley..."

"The one with the moon and starts?" Riley asked. "Her artistry is incredible."

Mark nodded. "You know better than anyone how

much a person's art is a reflection of them. It takes a special person to make a quilt like that for a sickly baby in the hospital."

"Yes, it does," Riley said, remembering the phrase stitched in the corner of the quilt. "Precious One" took on an even greater meaning.

"Of course, you spend most of your time drawing comics about maiming and killing people," Mark drawled, "so clearly you have more inner demons than you like to let on."

"Comic books always tell the tale of the fight between good and evil," he said, one corner of his mouth tilting into a smirk. "When it comes to channeling anger, I just have to think about my ex. Gives me all the fuel I need."

Mark glanced over at him.

"I'm kidding!" He held up his hands. "Mostly. I only have those thoughts at holidays and on Jess' birthday when I can't explain why her mom's not around. Why she doesn't even send cards."

"It's only natural to be angry," Mark said. "Paige used to get angry around birthdays and holidays too, waiting to see if her mom would call her or send anything. Then she decided she was sick of all the lies and the drama. She realized family doesn't need to be determined by blood. Now, Skylar has no power over her."

"She's not wrong," he said, looking up at the hazy sky. "I just hope I can help Jess feel that way too. I...worry... about her. You know?"

Mark put his hand on his shoulder. "I know. You guys are going to be fine, and we're here to help in any way we can."

"Ditto. And I'm serious about not going out with Sadie. This might be too complicated." He felt he had to say it again, after everything they'd discussed.

"No, you should give it a try," Mark said. "It's not going to be a problem for us."

Riley thought Mark was being more than optimistic. Complications were what had landed him where he was today, raising his daughter by himself.

Chapter 3

The new baby Crenshaw stretched his little arms in his sleep, wiggling under the quilt in his bassinet—a quilt Sadie had made just for him. The first time she saw Boone in the hospital nursery, she'd gotten of vision of his quilt. Sometimes it worked that way. A path of golden stars of various sizes shot right through the middle against a navy background. The phrase "Future Rockstar" had seemed like a fitting addition to the corner because even if he didn't follow in Rye's footsteps as a famous country singer, Boone Crenshaw was going to be a force of nature.

Now, looking down at him, Sadie felt her heart gush with warmth as she reverently touched his dark curls, impressive for a newborn. "Oh, he's the most beautiful baby in the world."

Tory reached out and touched his little fingers. "Boone makes me feel like I'm witnessing a miracle every day. I tear up. Rye tears up. Heck, if we weren't so happy I'd wonder about our emotional state."

Sadie was hoping the baby would give a natural boost to everyone's mood before she shared the news about Paige. That was why, with Rye and Tory's permission, she'd invited her siblings and their extended family for a meeting at Rye and Tory's house the Thursday after her visit to Paige.

"I imagine having a baby is a pretty emotional experience," she said, unable to take her eyes off Boone.

"I was worried Rye might be a caged tiger when he announced he was taking a self-appointed paternity leave, but he's surprised me. He pretty much sings to him all the time, and don't tell him I told you, but I've caught him standing outside the nursery like a little kid, waiting for Boone to wake up from his nap."

Sadie smiled. "Rye's come a long way in a short time. It's hard to believe it's only been a couple years since he met you and reconciled with his family. I remember when he used to claim his life aspiration was to grow older like Tom Jones—still famous, still a ladies' man." And now Rye, who'd always been as good as a brother, wasn't just a family man—he was truly family. His beautiful sister had married her brother, J.P., making it official.

"The good old days," Tory said dryly, laughing.

"What days are you referring to, sugar?" Sadie heard a familiar, and completely unmistakable, voice ask.

Rye stretched his arms out in the doorway.

"Never mind," Tory replied.

"Fine," he said, coming into the family room and crossing to where Sadie and Tory were sitting, waiting for the rest of the McGuiness siblings and the others. "Hey, little guy. Daddy's back from his phone call. Now we can have some fun."

Boone only stretched his little arms in response, continuing to sleep.

"This sleeping all the time is getting old," Rye muttered. "I don't care if his pediatrician says it's normal. I want to play with him. Hello, Sadie."

She bit her lip. "Hello, Rye."

"You nervous, honey?" Rye asked, peering down at her. "What do you have going on? I told Tory it was a little weird for you to suggest we all get together on such short notice without any of the parents. I mean, heck, we're all having Sunday dinner like usual."

Suddenly all her nerves were back.

"*Rye*," Tory said.

He held up his hands. "I'm just making observations. Can't a man make those in the privacy of his own home? I'll make myself useful and get the door."

Tory shot him one of her patented looks and patted Sadie's arm. "Don't worry. Whatever it is, we're here for you."

Sadie knew that. She'd prepared for this meeting almost as much as she'd prepared for her visit to Paige. Her speech was memorized, and she'd prayed extra hard for strength. Things usually worked out when she did that.

Her sisters appeared first, flanked by their spouses. Susannah and Jake looked radiant, and Shelby had pretty much taken to glowing after her engagement to Vander.

Sadie made sure not to meet his eyes. Vander was a private investigator, and part of her suspected he might guess what she was up to simply by looking at her. She also hoped he wouldn't be upset that she hadn't asked for his help finding their half-sister. After all, he was the one who'd help them track down their real daddy, Preston.

Rye's sister, Amelia Ann, gave Sadie a saucy wink. Her husband, Clayton, also Rye's manager, did the same. They weren't blood family to Sadie, but they were family all the same.

"*Sadie*," she heard her brother, John Parker, call out. Everyone referred to him as J.P. except for his beautiful wife, Tammy, Rye's sister.

Sadie met her older brother's gaze and instantly gulped. He knew! Somehow he knew.

"Darn it, Sadie," Shelby said, coming over and kneeling in front of her. "You went and found our half-sister, didn't you? Did you think we wouldn't guess?"

Tears popped into her eyes. Somehow it was a relief they'd sussed it out on their own, no speech necessary. "I suppose it makes sense since you were the one to come up with the plan to find Daddy."

No one else said a word, but Shelby reached for her hand.

"I couldn't help myself!" she cried out, feeling her eyes well with tears. "She's our sister. I...just couldn't stop thinking about it."

"Oh, don't cry," Shelby said. "I had Vander find her already too. I just didn't know what to do about it."

"You did?" she asked.

"Of course," Shelby said, putting her hand on her heart. "If I weren't so focused on being with Vander, I probably would have come up with a plan by now. What did you do?"

"I invited her to join my quilting class," Sadie said. "When I saw Boone in the nursery, I walked by the NICU too, and it broke my heart to see those preemies and sickly newborns. I told the rest of the ladies in my class about it, and we agreed to make quilts for babies in the NICU. I told Paige it was for a good cause. But she already knew about us." Sadie still hadn't gotten over that shock.

"Wait a sec," her sister Susannah said, darting over and kneeling beside Shelby, whose mouth parted like a trout. "*She knew about us?*"

"Sounds like we'd all better sit down," J.P. said, ever the practical one. "And start at the beginning."

When everyone had found a perch, she told them how easy it had been to find Paige and how nice she seemed on Facebook.

"Yeah, I found her in less than five minutes," Vander said. "She wasn't concealing anything. I took it from her Facebook photos that she isn't in touch with her mother or her grandparents. I agree she looked pleasant. And her husband is a middle school guidance counselor."

"Well, that's a noble profession," Rye said. "Young people with problems are terrifying."

Tory shot Rye another look. "Keep going, Sadie. Tell us what she said."

"Well, I was so nervous when I arrived, but her next-door neighbor was looking after Haley—that's Paige and Mark's daughter—and his own. They're both seven and they reminded me of Annabelle. Know their own minds. I wasn't as nervous for a while. I showed them the baby quilt I'd brought as a sample, and then they saw my picture of Annabelle's princess quilt."

"Okay, that's great, but get to the point," Shelby said, tapping her knee. "What did she say when she saw you?"

Sadie still wouldn't forget that first moment. "Her husband had just introduced himself, and I said my first name, but before I could get to my last name, Paige said it for me. I've never been so...shell-shocked. Okay, I have, but this was up there."

"Sadie!" Shelby cried out. "Get to the point."

"Fine, in sum, her mother sounds like a horrible person who told her all sorts of lies about our daddy and us. Paige doesn't talk to her now. She's made her own family with Mark—who is the sweetest guy—and their daughter. She just figured we were part of a closed storybook."

"How did she take you coming to her home?" J.P. asked.

"She's coming to my quilting class!" Even now, the very idea of it made her want to cry tears of joy. "She said it took a lot of courage for me to find her."

"Oh, good Lord, I'm going to start bawling," Shelby said. "Sadie McGuiness, don't you just beat all."

Sadie wiped away her tears. "Susannah, what do you think?" Of all her siblings, she was the hardest to read in these moments. She had also been dead set against finding their daddy in the beginning, so Sadie was especially nervous about her opinion.

"I'm...hopeful," her sister said in a raspy voice. "I've thought about her too, you know. She didn't deserve to be born into a situation like that, and we've all been hurt by the same man. Even if she's never met our daddy."

The mere thought of him still hurt Sadie, and she wondered if she'd ever give up the hope that her daddy might up and change and reconcile with them. That he'd repent for all the bad things he'd done. Despite the way he'd run away from Vander over a month ago, his tail between his legs, she couldn't help hoping. How did a daughter completely close her heart to the man who was her daddy?

Jake put his arm around his wife, and she snuggled close. "You were pretty brave, Sadie."

She shrugged. "I figured being invited to a quilting class was low pressure. You know?"

"Does she even like to quilt?" Shelby asked.

She found herself laughing. "I don't know. But she'll be there Monday night."

"Do you think we could come too?" Shelby asked.

"But you don't like to quilt."

"I still want to meet her," Shelby said.

"Me too," Susannah reiterated with a nod.

Sadie had hoped for this possibility. Prayed for it. All her sisters together, united by an activity she loved. Still...

"I feel like I'd better ask her," she said. "I mean, one McGuiness might be enough of a shock at first. Let me find out how she feels."

Like she probably should have done before agreeing to a date with Paige's next-door neighbor. Heavens, she hadn't expected he'd call her that same night. Men always said they were going to call, but some waited three days because that's what all of the dating articles said about not looking too eager. But Riley had not only called, he'd sounded eager about it too, and in her surprise and excitement she'd agreed to a Friday night date. They'd hung up before she could properly think it through, and she'd paced a little that night, wondering if she was doing the right thing.

Except something told her it *was* right. Riley wasn't just handsome. He'd appreciated her talent, and he was sweet. The way he had with those two girls was a clear indication of that. It had been a long time since she'd met a man with those attributes. Was she crazy for not wanting to pass this up? And what was she going to tell him about her and Paige?

Oh, stop it, Sadie, this is not the time to be worrying over that.

"That sounds like a reasonable approach," J.P. said. "Of course, I'd like to meet her too, though not at your quilting class."

"I can just see you sewing together those squares, J.P.," Rye drawled. "No offense, honey."

"None taken," Sadie told him.

"Have you thought about what to tell Mama?" J.P. asked.

The million-dollar question had arrived. "Of course. I figured I'd tell y'all first. After all, she's our half-sister—no relation to Mama per se. I don't want to hurt Mama, but after everything we put her through…"

Everyone's faces seemed to fall. The pain they'd felt from that particular revelation had nearly decimated them, and they were all healing in their own time.

"I figure Mama always chooses love," Sadie said softly, "even when it's hard—and she'd be happy for us if it turns out Paige and all of us become friends somehow."

She didn't use the word *family*. She'd made sure to keep her expectations low this time.

"Let's see how your first quilting class goes with her before we decide anything. It might be a good idea for you to go alone this time, Sadie," J.P. said.

"Whew!" Shelby said. "I would have gone to your class, but quilting is so not my thing."

Sadie couldn't help but smile a little at that. Her sister had never had the patience to sit and sew.

"When and if the time comes," J.P. said, "I'll mention something to Mama. I have a feeling she's expecting it."

Susannah and Tammy nodded their heads in agreement.

"She has to know," Shelby said. "I mean, after we tried to find Daddy..."

"Maybe she thought you'd be so disappointed by his actions you wouldn't want to look for your half-sister?" Vander said.

"I can see how you might think that," Shelby said, "but Mama would know we wouldn't let a disappointment like that put us on our backsides forever."

"I wouldn't expect anything less," Vander said, looking at her in that special way that showed his regard. "I have to say, after doing a thorough workup on Paige and her husband, I'm hopeful too."

"That means a lot, coming from you," J.P. said. "Okay, so Sadie will continue to be the McGuiness ambassador and see how things go with Paige. Should you feel like it's okay to share, please tell her that all of us hope to meet her someday."

"Oh, I kinda hate it that you got the jump on me," Shelby said, "but I'm also so darn proud of you. This took guts."

"It sure did," Jake said. "Way to go, Sadie."

Sadie felt her cheeks heat. She hadn't done it to be brave, but it meant a lot to her to hear them say so. She'd always felt like the little mouse of the McGuinesses—smaller and softer than their larger-than-life personalities. The rest of them had seemed driven from the get-go, but it had taken her a while to find her purpose. College hadn't helped her, and for a time, she'd struggled to match her love of quilting with a job she loved. Now she was leading the quilting circle at work and making big decisions and speaking up inside her family. Progress…

"Anyone want to see her pictures on Facebook?" Shelby asked, reaching for her phone.

As her family clustered around her, Sadie hoped she had enough bravery in her to mention her date to her half-sister before things got too serious.

Chapter 4

"Dad, I think you should wear this for your date tonight. Haley agrees with me."

Riley gave his drawing one last look. If the girls were on a tear about fashion, he wasn't going to get any more work done today. The colors he'd chosen for his new female superhero, Lady Justice, still didn't feel right. Should she wear red? Was it too cliché?

"*Dad!* I'm talking to you."

Swiveling around in his white ergonomic office chair, he gave his daughter his full attention. And winced when he saw her holding up his navy sport coat. "Oh, come on, Jess. It's only a first date. I want to keep things casual. Plus it's hot out. I'll sweat."

Haley simply shook her head, silently telling him that he didn't have a clue. The two of them had impressive skills when it came to ganging up on him.

"Ladies, I know you have strong feelings about this, but I can dress myself for a date," he told them, shifting his feet on the floor to make his chair rock back and forth. If they would just go back to playing princess like usual, he might figure out his color scheme.

"Dad!" Jess said, marching forward with the sport coat. Her face was scrunched with determination. "You can still wear a T-shirt under it, but we need to find one that's clean and doesn't have any holes."

Riley took the coat from her little hand. Jess looked like a princess on a tear in her yellow gown and sparkly green tiara. Darn, she was so cute he wanted to pluck her up. So he did. She screeched in his ears.

"I don't see why I can't wear a T-shirt with holes," he joked, nuzzling her under the chin while she kicked at him. "No one could see them under the jacket."

"Stop it, *Dad*! This is serious. Put me down. This minute."

He kissed her on her chin and set her down. Fighting a smile, he watched her brows narrow and her hands anchor onto her little hips.

"That is not how you treat a princess," she informed him. "Right, Haley?"

"Right," her best friend said, keeping strategically close to the doorway, ready to run if he tried to tickle her.

"All right, I'll wear this," he said, picking up the sport coat that was now lying on the floor after the melee. "But I get to pick my own T-shirt."

Jess' eyebrows rose. "We'll see."

Sure enough, by the time he was ready to escort Jess to the Bradshaws, he was wearing everything his daughter had picked out. Looking in the mirror, he had to admit the kid had taste.

"See, I told you," Jess said, opening the front door. "You have fun tonight."

He shook his head as he picked up his car keys.

"Hey, Sadie!" he heard Jess call out. "Dad, Sadie is here."

He frowned. He was supposed to pick her up. Following his daughter out, he felt his breath catch in his throat at the sight of her. She was standing in a soft ray of sunshine in the waning evening light. Her brown hair was up in some twist. The line of her neck was going to drive him wild. He'd told himself not to expect a goodnight kiss, but now he was pretty much certain it was all he was going to think about.

Her dress was a deep pink, the hue of a beach sky right before sunset. Her arms were bare, and she was clutching a gold purse that matched her sandals. In that moment, he knew exactly what color he was going to use for his female superhero.

Gold was a power color, and sexy as hell.

He realized Jess was talking to Sadie, but he'd been so captivated he hadn't heard a word. Shaking himself, he strode forward.

"Hi," Sadie said brightly. "I know you were going to pick me up, but I need to…ah…talk to Paige first. Hope that's okay. I'll just be a sec."

She took off toward the Bradshaws', and given the story he'd heard from Mark, he had to wonder what she intended to do and say.

Jess turned around and faced him. "Well, that was weird. I'll go see what that was all about. Be right back, Dad."

"Jess, come back here."

He watched as his daughter hurried toward the Bradshaws' front door, ignoring him. He thought about going in after her, but that would add another layer of awkwardness to the situation. The smart thing was to wait for her.

Sweat was already popping up under his sport coat, courtesy of the weather. Crap. Just his luck the weather was still in the low nineties and muggy as hell. Should he stand in his front yard like a moron or go back inside and wait? Sadie had said she'd be back in a sec, but for all he knew, the two women could get to talking. He checked his watch. They still had an hour until their reservation at the restaurant.

"Hey!" he heard Mark call out.

"Hey!"

His friend headed over. "Seems Sadie was nervous about your date given the situation with Paige. She wanted to make sure it was okay. Paige is reassuring her. You know, the more I see Sadie, the more I like her."

"Good," Riley said. "I didn't plan on bringing up the sister thing, but should I?"

Mark shrugged. "Maybe you should mention it in passing, tell her that you made sure there weren't any concerns either. You're both acting like responsible people."

"Thanks, Dad," he said dryly.

Mark laughed. "You look pretty good. Did Jess dress you?"

"Stuff it," he responded, kicking at the bicycle tracks Jess and Haley had left on the lawn. He'd tried to tell them to stay on the sidewalk, but Jess insisted princesses biked wherever the urge took them. He was starting to wonder about her new teacher. What seven-year-old said that kind of thing unprompted?

The Bradshaws' front door burst open. "Dad! Sadie is coming."

He struggled not to roll his eyes. By now all of the neighbors were going to know he was going on a date, as if his sport coat wasn't indication enough. "Thanks, honey."

"You bet!" Jess said. "Haley, let's get out our batons and wave at Dad and Sadie as they leave."

"Oh, I can't wait to see this," Mark said, shoulders shaking. "It's like you're being presented at court as a couple."

"Shut up, man," Riley said under his breath.

"I should grab my phone and video this," Mark said.

"I'm going to kill you."

He didn't mean it, of course, but he was getting embarrassed. A few of his neighbors had trailed out onto their front porches, likely at the commotion.

"Hey!" their neighbor across the street called, jogging

down his steps. "You guys having a party?"

Mark glanced over at him, biting his tongue. Riley felt his jaw clench.

"Nope," he replied, "just going out with a friend."

"Here she comes," Jess announced, acting like an announcer at a pageant or reality TV show, and she and Haley ran down to the edge of the steps, batons in hand, as Sadie emerged.

"That's some friend," his neighbor commented. "I didn't know you had a friend like that, Riley."

He was sure his cheeks were red as he started toward Sadie, who was smiling at the girls as they twirled the batons through the air, ribbons flapping everywhere.

"Have fun, you two," Jess said. "Dad, don't worry about being home early. I promise to go to bed on time. I can always stay at Haley's."

Sadie's cheeks were now as red as his were. Man, he hoped she wasn't thinking he'd put his daughter up to giving him the house all to himself.

"I'm so sorry," he said softly when he reached her. "Here I thought picking you up at your house was the gentlemanly thing to do. Now I realize it was the sanest course of action."

"It's okay," she said, meeting his eyes. "It was my fault. I changed the game plan."

"And I know why," he said, nodding to the Bradshaws' house. "When Mark told me about your connection to Paige, I made sure they were okay with us going out. I didn't want things to be awkward for anyone."

"Me either!" She gave a nervous laugh. "Paige assured me she's totally cool with it, and I feel better knowing you know. I'm not fond of secrets."

He shifted on his feet. "Who is?" Then he thought about his ex, who'd seemed to thrive on secrets.

Don't go there. This is about you moving on.

"Shall we go?" she asked. "I can follow you to the restaurant if you'd like."

He didn't hesitate. "No, I'd rather pick up my gentlemanly duties, if that's okay with you."

"I'd love that," she said, tucking her head to the side in the most adorable fashion.

"You look beautiful, by the way."

"You do too," she said, her eyes casting down almost coquettish-like. "Jess mentioned helping you."

Her lips twitched, and he found his own mirroring hers. "That's great. Now you realize I'm a lost cause when it comes to all this stuff."

She gave him a studied look. "Oh, I think you're wrong there. So far you're doing pretty good."

"I can do better," he murmured in a low voice. To his shock, he realized he was flirting. *Flirting!* So he wasn't dead in the dating department, after all.

"Are y'all going to leave? My hand is getting tired from waving!"

Leave it to his daughter to insist on the final word. He hadn't even realized she and Haley were still sending them off princess-style. Paige was on the front porch, he noted, a soft smile on her face. That reduced some of the pressure in his chest.

He extended his arm to Sadie. "Shall we go, my lady?"

Her smile turned from radiant to luminous in a heartbeat. She fitted her hand through his arm, the warmth of her body beckoning.

He felt a sharp ping in his chest, like something was breaking free. He felt himself smiling back at her, not caring that nearly all of his neighbors were watching. Not caring that they'd become a spectacle. He was in awe of the way the waning light captured the gold in her brown eyes.

Gold.

The color held new meaning. It was the color of Sadie.

He was a goner.

Chapter 5

By the time Riley parked the car at Nashville's famous Printer's Alley, she knew a few more things about him.

He liked to hum, and it was downright pleasant to the ear. He'd kept up a delightful rumble as he'd maneuvered the car through the downtown traffic.

He also didn't feel the need to talk for the sake of talking. She rather liked that. She figured Jess was probably the talker in the family. That little girl and Haley sure as shooting had warmed her heart with their enthusiasm over their date.

Paige had been shocked to see her at the door, but her surprise had melted into kindness as soon as Sadie awkwardly explained her concerns. Her half-sister had put a hand on her arm, insisted that she not worry about it, and told her that Riley had already brought up the same thing.

Her reassurances had given Sadie a happy burst in her veins, so much so that she'd felt like she was walking on air when she'd gone outside to meet Riley. The kids' sendoff had been oh-so-sweet, and even if they never had another date, she would always remember the beginning fondly.

"Skull's Rainbow Room was highly rated as a great

first date spot, and it has live music," he told her when he came around to open her door. "I hope you like it. We're a little early for our reservation, but we can see if they'll seat us."

Printer's Alley was chock full of places suited to every palate. She'd never been to this particular restaurant before, but she was eager to see the place where Tim McGraw had gotten his big break. Rye had also played there a few times back in the day.

"I've always wanted to check it out," she said. "I haven't been down here since the Fiddle and Steel Guitar Bar closed its doors. That's where Rascal Flatts was discovered, you know."

"No, I didn't," he said, putting his hand under her elbow as they walked through the crowd on the brick-lined street. "I know it's heresy in this part of the world, but I'm not a country music lover."

She stopped suddenly. Okay, so this might be a problem. Not only were there two Grammy-winning country music stars in her family circle—Rye and Susannah's husband, Jake—but her big brother represented singers and wrote songs. The McGuinesses had country music running through their veins.

"You're kidding! How could you not love country music? It's got passion and soul, and most of the songs simply break your heart before putting the pieces back together again."

He tucked her close as people walked around them. "Personally, I think it's a lot of guys running around in tight jeans, trying to prove their masculinity by singing about how much they love apple pie, the American flag, and their hunting dogs. And the women are mostly fake. Half of their songs are about how much they love hearth and home, and the other half are about doing tequila shots."

There was some angst in his voice she didn't understand. Truth be told, she had to work to keep her mouth from falling open. How totally rude of him to say that! But she was too much of a lady to point it out. "What kind of music do you listen to, then?" she asked instead.

"I love New Wave bands like Echo and the Bunnymen. 'Under the Milky Way' is a classic! 'Bed Bugs and Ballyhoo' is one of my faves."

Bed bugs? Well, Brad Paisley had made her laugh with his song about ticks. "I've never heard of those bands. What do they sound like?"

"They have a unique sound." He shrugged. "I like people who have integrity about what they put out. It's the artist in me."

Part of her agreed, but how could he assume nobody in country music had integrity? Why, the country singers she knew were some of the best people there were. "I see."

"I also like The Church," he said, his brows creeping closer together as he studied her.

Whew! Relief coursed through her. She'd wondered about that. "I like church too. My mama's a preacher."

"Ah...not that kind of church." He shifted on his feet as though uncomfortable.

What other kind could he mean? she refrained from asking. This conversation was going nowhere fast.

"Anyone else you like?" she asked, hoping for a silver lining.

"Public Image Ltd. is awesome! If I had to pick a favorite song, I'd have to say..." He paused and guided her to the side of the building out of the way of the crowd. "'This Is Not A Love Song.'"

So he wasn't a romantic, after all? She was becoming confused.

"Who is *your* favorite country singer?" he asked, clearly trying to salvage the conversation.

"Well, I'm partial to Rye Crenshaw and Jake Lassiter," she said, going strictly with family for reasons of loyalty.

"I don't know them," he said. "But I only like—"

"Wait! You don't know Rye Crenshaw or Jake Lassiter?" Her voice rose, causing people to turn their heads to look at them. Even passersby had trouble believing it was true.

"Have you been living under a rock?" a tall bearded man asked, stopping next to them. "Sorry, I overhead your conversation."

Riley shrugged, seeming uncomfortable.

The bystander looked Sadie up and down. "Honey, you need to dump this guy and cut a rug with me tonight. It's un-American not to like country music, and we don't need our women hanging out with—"

"All right, that's enough," Riley said, holding out his hands. "I'm not trying to slam your jam. Everyone deserves to have their own taste in music."

"Not in Nashville, they don't," the tall man said, getting into his face. "You need to move along, mister, before I show you what's up."

"I understand your loyalty, sir, but my friend is right," Sadie said, putting her hand on the tall man's arm to settle him down. Up close, the man looked like a lumberjack. If he was violent, he might take a swing at Riley. While Riley was tall too, he was leanly muscular. One punch would level him, given the difference in their sizes.

"If you change your mind, I'll be having a beer at the bar over there." Lumberjack Arms gave her a saucy wink. "You'd better treat this little lady right, son, or you'll answer to me."

"If I didn't treat her right, she wouldn't be out with me, man," Riley said, clearly not backing down.

Was he crazy? Lumberjack Arms had over a hundred pounds on him. She wasn't sure she wanted to be out with a man who seemed to have so little sense, especially when it came to potential violence.

"Thank you again, mister," she said, hoping to smooth things over. "Honey, we need to get along. Bye, now." She gave a partial wave to the tall man and pulled Riley toward Skull's Rainbow Room before a fight could break out.

"Oh, what a beautiful atmosphere," she said, pretending to be distracted by the beautiful dark wood interior.

Riley gave their name to the hostess, who didn't blink that they were early, and soon they were shown to a table in front of the black-and-white checkered stage with a long L-shaped wood and marble extension. The server gave them cocktail menus, and she decided on a drink with passion fruit, lime cordial, and rum. Couldn't go wrong with something island-like in her opinion. Perhaps it would jazz up her mood. Oh heck, she might as well find out if they weren't going to suit. She should be used to that kind of disappointment by now. Only Riley was so different from the men she normally dated, so much more outspoken and opinionated.

"If you don't like country music, isn't this place a strange choice?" she asked Riley. "I mean, it's not like you knew I loved country music."

He settled both elbows on the table, having left the cocktail menu where it sat. "This isn't a country place anymore according to my buddy. He said the entertainment was unique."

"And you figured you liked *unique*," she said, the picture forming.

"Did I mention it's been voted one of the best first-date nights in town?" he asked, leaning back in his chair and then popping forward again.

"Yes," she said. Of course, an interesting place alone couldn't make a first date turn out well. "What cocktail are you going to have?"

"I'll probably just have a beer," he said. "I might not like country music, but I like beer. Have I been somewhat redeemed in your eyes?"

Was beer somehow redeeming? Goodness, he confused her. "No redemption is necessary," she said to be polite.

The server appeared and took their drink order, giving them the chance to pivot the conversation. She was just thinking of what she should say when Riley turned to her and asked, "What's it like being a preacher's daughter?"

Of all the questions she thought he'd lead with, that wasn't one of them. "It's great. My mama is a wonderful woman and a powerful motivator. She touches a lot of people. I'm proud to be her daughter."

He took a moment to think on that, humming softly under his breath. Sadie wondered if he realized he was doing it. There was something endearing about it, and yet it seemed like another sign he wasn't comfortable with her.

"You don't find there's any extra pressure on you to... ah..."

"Live up to a certain standard?" she asked, visions of past dates with guys from church playing in her mind. "Many people think so, but mostly I just do what I think is right. When I don't know, I pray about it. Usually the answer comes. I mean, I'm not a saint..."

"But you go to church every week, huh?" he asked, keeping his hands around his water glass like he expected it to take off on a vacation.

The way he said it implied that was a problem for him.

"Don't you?" she asked.

"No, actually," he said, fiddling with the menu. "I don't really like established religion myself. Too many rules and thoughts created by other people. My parents raised me and my brother to think for ourselves and do the right thing. I want the same for Jess."

The waiter arrived with their drinks just then, giving her a moment to think on his answer.

"Are you against church itself?" she asked, needing to have a better handle on this.

He cleared his throat. "Religion and politics really

aren't first-date topics, are they? See. I told you I was really out of touch."

Perhaps they should be, she thought. They certainly cut to the chase.

"Tell me about your family," she asked. "Do they live around here?"

"My parents live in Florida now, and my brother, Tyler, lives in San Francisco," he said, grinning. This was obviously something he felt more comfortable talking about. "He's got a great wife, two of the best kids on the planet, and the most incredible job ever. He works for DreamWorks."

Goodness, it was as obvious as the nose on his face how much Riley loved his brother. That was something she could work with.

"You don't miss him?" she asked. "I couldn't stand being so far away from my siblings. I count my blessings every day we all live in Dare River."

"We see each other as often as we can," Riley said. "Since I freelance, I can work anywhere, so Jess and I go as often as we can. She's mad about her cousins, and my parents visit from time to time, although they have this new dog they treat like a kid."

"Do you like dogs?" she asked, thinking of how many they had in their extended family.

"They're okay," he said, his mouth turning up. "I'd rather have something exotic. Like an iguana."

Sadie grimaced. The server reappeared and asked if they were ready to order, saving her from replying. She had no words.

"We got to talking," she told the server. "Just give us a few minutes." Determined to focus, she opened her menu.

"The food is supposed to be really good," Riley said, checking out the menu as well. "Would you be interested in sharing the veal sweetbreads with me?"

Her stomach curdled at the thought.

"I'm just crazy about the thymus gland of a baby cow," Riley said, looking at her over the top of his menu. "Of course, it might be the little sucker's pancreas, and that would be totally wicked."

She was going to barf right there. "No, I think I'll pass, but you go on ahead."

He started laughing. "Oh, you should see your face. I was teasing!"

She blinked. He was teasing? Had he been teasing about any of the other things? His admiration of reptiles, maybe? Being on a date with him was like playing in a ping-pong match.

"I mean, who eats that crap? I probably shouldn't say it too loud. I'm all about exploring what's out there, but please. Putting a baby cow's innards on a dinner menu is too much."

"Whew," she said, trying to join in the laughter, "you had me going there for a moment. You like to make jokes, don't you?"

His shoulder lifted. "I suppose. I've never thought about it that way. Some things just strike me as funny. I mention them in conversation, and sometimes I write them into comic book storylines."

"You write too?" she asked, eager for them to find some surer footing. "Well, aren't you talented? I've never been great at writing or telling jokes. I pretty much fall for anything. As you could tell from the sweetbread thing."

"I think it's cute," Riley said, taking her hand. "Did I tell you how pretty you look tonight?"

She was conscious of her sharp intake of breath at his touch. His hand felt like a warm fire. Goodness! "I...ah...don't recall just now. But thank you. I hope I told you how nice you look."

As she gazed at him, she felt that pull again, the feeling that had encouraged her to accept a date with him. All the little ways their conversation had stumbled receded to the back of her mind.

"You did," Riley said, running his thumb over the back of her hand in sexy circles. "And you smell good too."

"It's just a little perfume."

"Just a little perfume," Riley repeated. "I love the way you say that too. Like it's not a big deal. Heck, putting on this sport coat and some cologne was about as epic as Batman saving Gotham again."

She fought a smile. He was serious, and she didn't want to hurt his feelings. When a man went to extra effort for a woman... Well, it did things to her insides. "Do you often speak in superhero metaphors?" she asked.

"Sometimes," he said. "Being a single dad is like being its own brand of superhero, I suppose. And Jess likes me to make up stories. Of course, she thinks she's a princess, so I figure our family has an active imagination."

"You're a great dad," she said, shocked to find herself twining her hand more around his own.

He leaned closer to her, and she caught a whiff of his cologne. It had notes of balsam pine and a touch of musk. Totally hot. Her pulse started to race as he used his other hand to caress her cheek.

Whoa! What was happening? The push-pull she felt was going to give her whiplash.

"I can't stop looking at you," he said. "I already want to draw your cheekbones and your...lips. I know I'm supposed to have some idea of what I want to eat tonight, but I honestly don't care. I just want to sit here and hold your hand. Is that okay?"

She wasn't sure how to respond. "Our server might object," she said, withdrawing her hand. "I mean, this is a restaurant, and people in the service industry live on tips."

"I'll order the prime rib, but I'll have to ask the server to cut my meat so I can keep holding your hand. I'll promise to tip him more."

She started laughing. "You're incorrigible."

"No, just focused," Riley said, caressing the back of her exposed neck.

Part of her wanted to tell him to stop. The idea to put her hair up had been mostly practical. The weather was still hot and muggy. But she found herself wishing he'd tug on the baby curls at her neck, which was totally shocking. She might not be a saint, but she didn't let a man touch her like this on a first date. Sometimes she didn't even want to kiss the guy at the end.

"Yes, I can see that," she said, looking into his eyes. The blue was so magnetic. She needed to find a fabric that resembled it. Maybe there was something to all those theories about pheromones.

"You really are gorgeous," he said in a low voice. "Even if you like country music."

That popped her out of the pull of attraction. "I suppose we'd better be ready to order."

He gave her a look and then settled back into his chair while she scooted back as well. Some people were staring at them, she realized, blushing. Well, what did she expect, putting on a show like that?

"You shouldn't be worried about expressing yourself like that," he said softly. "Being a woman is what makes you beautiful."

Now that confused her even more. Was he saying she wasn't acting like a woman? Afraid to express herself? Piano music began to stream down from the stage, and she realized the live music had started. He was right. It wasn't country. She took some deep breaths to center herself, trying not to be obvious about it. Their server finally came over, and she selected the scallops because the portions were usually small, and she suddenly wasn't hungry.

"Okay, tell me something else about you," Riley said, reaching for his water.

He drained the whole glass in one fell swoop and had the audacity to wink at her. Wink!

She ran him through the basics as if by rote, from being a native of Nashville to working at the craft store. When their meal finally arrived, she picked at her food while he asked her questions about quilting. Finally, something she always loved to talk about.

"I haven't seen many quilts, mind you," he said, "but I always had the sense they were two-dimensional. Yours are three, and that's totally cool. I mean, do you see the pattern before you start or do you work in pieces to create it? When I draw, it goes both ways."

No one had ever asked her that before, and it made her focus more clearly on him. He was watching her like he was truly listening, but even more, like he was trying to figure her out. Maybe she was as foreign to him in some ways as he was to her. Maybe it was time for her to start over with him in her mind and see where things went.

Didn't her mama always tell them not to judge people too hastily?

"I usually see it. Most quilters use pattern books and that's how I started, but one night a few years ago, I realized I was bored with what I was seeing. I didn't want to make the same kind of quilt as everyone else anymore—does that sound boastful?—so I started to sketch, and suddenly I had this new pattern of an ocean swirling on a beach with a sun. I kinda left the regimented square pattern behind after that. Mostly."

Funny how Riley's eyes reminded her of one of the blues she'd used.

"That was my breakout quilt, you could say. The ones I sell are in my new style."

"Your quilts are works of art," Riley said.

"That means a lot, coming from a professional artist such as yourself," she said, feeling a new kind of warmth in her chest, the kind that came from someone appreciating her talents. Sure, her family encouraged her, but she figured they had to. They were family. They'd thought her first rug quilt was precious, and it had been riddled with so many mistakes no one with a lick of sense would have bought it.

But most of the men she'd gone out with had treated her quilting as a hobby. No one had realized how important it was to her. Could Riley be the first?

"The show doesn't start until eleven," Riley said after the server removed their dinner plates. "How about another drink and dessert?"

She nodded, and they shared the pecan pie. Riley reached for her hand after they finished dessert, and she found herself becoming more and more comfortable as they listened to the piano player over the roar of the crowd.

When the show finally began, Sadie was delighted to see the band members were wearing tuxedos. A woman in a vintage sequined dress à la Joan Crawford appeared on stage to introduce the performers.

"I hope you like burlesque," Riley said, scooting closer to be heard over the band. "I was assured it's tasteful."

She certainly hoped so. She'd never seen a burlesque show before, but from what she'd heard, it was risqué. The first performer sang like she was straight out of old Hollywood. The next woman tap-danced in a costume best described as a loose-fitting ballerina outfit. But when the woman after that came out in an outfit made of balloons, she held her breath.

"Oh, boy," she heard Riley mutter. "I feel like I need to apologize in advance for what I think is about to happen. You've given me the impression you might not be comfortable—"

She jumped in her seat when the woman burst the first balloon, then watched in both fascination and shock as she proceeded to playfully lean over and start popping the ones flanking her bottom. *Goodness...* He'd brought her to a show like this for their first date? Who did he think she was? This felt like the opposite of the church men assuming she was saintly, and she wasn't sure what to make of it.

"Would you like to leave?" Riley said. "Don't feel like you need to stay for me."

She thought about it for a moment. The woman had clothes on underneath the balloons. Sort of. Plus, she doubted they could pin down their server during the show.

"It's...fine." If she got uncomfortable, she could look away. She didn't like to think of herself as a prude, but it was kind of true.

"Note to self," Riley said. "Never bring a preacher's daughter to a burlesque show. No matter how tasteful."

Okay, that had her stewing again. The show was over quickly, and she sat back in her chair, feeling a lingering warmth in her cheeks from blushing.

"That wasn't too bad, was it?" Riley asked, like he was unable to read her. "I didn't realize the act was so short. Likely for the best, right? Are you ready to go?"

She had her arms gripped tightly around herself. "That would be great."

It took Riley a while to catch their server's eye, but soon they were heading down Printer's Alley. The night crowd was a little rowdy and music and laughter spilled out of the other establishments. He tucked her close, which she didn't find comfortable, but he didn't try and hold her when she pulled away. Silence stretched as they walked back to the car.

Inside, he didn't turn the engine on. "Are you sure you're okay? I would hate to think I made you uncomfortable. I mean...you're Paige's sister and all."

Yes, she was, and it was good to be reminded. Their date might not have been what she'd hoped, but she would see him again socially should she and Paige continue to be friends. She turned in her seat to see him anxiously tapping the gearshift. Something about his lack of ease made her feel better.

"Let's just say you managed to broaden my horizons tonight."

"That's nice of you," he said, "but if we still know each other for your birthday, I probably won't buy you any balloons. In case it reminds you of tonight."

That made her laugh. He had an odd sense of humor sometimes, but it was unique.

"Or maybe I'm wrong..." he amended, smiling devilishly. "I suppose if we still know each other then, depending on how things are going, I might just buy you balloons after all."

Shock rolled through her, but she bit her lip and said, "I think you'd look great with those attached to your bottom."

"Touché." His chuckle was dark.

When they arrived back at his house, he walked her to her car door, but didn't make a move to kiss her. He must have gotten the memo. She'd pulled her keys out as he'd pulled up.

"Goodnight, Sadie," he said, his mouth turned up at the corners in a smile. "Thank you for coming out with me tonight."

She didn't tell him that she'd had a good time because she wasn't altogether sure it was true. It had been interesting and confusing and downright uncomfortable. But somehow in the quiet night beside him on the street, what she remembered most was the intensity with which he'd listened to her talk about her quilts, her passion. And how he'd called them works of art. Then there was how he'd touched her with those warm hands. And even though she hadn't liked everything he'd said to her, he was honest, brutally so, and there was something to be said for that, wasn't there?

"Goodnight, Riley," she said, opening her door and climbing into her car.

He stepped back, and she took off. By the time she arrived home, she still wasn't sure she wanted to see him again.

He was different from anyone she'd been attracted to, and somehow that scared her.

Chapter 6

As Paige parked her car in front of Oodles of Spools, the sun was a golden ball over the horizon. The parking lot in the strip mall was hopping with a Marshalls and Home Goods down the way. Somehow she hadn't expected this much traffic on a Monday night.

She took a deep breath, trying to keep in mind a couple of pertinent facts.

Going to Sadie's quilting class was the right thing for her to do—despite the pond frogs jumping in her stomach.

Riley might not have hit it out of the park with her half-sister, but he liked her despite their differences—enough for him to have blushed while saying so—which served as its own character reference.

When her sister had appeared in her life out of the blue, Paige had feared her whole sordid past was being dredged up again. But something about Sadie, who'd approached her so bravely, had moved her. She'd found the strength to listen to what she had to say, and they'd managed to connect in their shared vulnerability. Then her sister had pulled out that beautiful quilt, which could almost have been made with her in mind. The heartbreaking phrase, "Precious One," in the corner had seemed to ping Paige's bones.

Her original decision to put the past behind her had been the best thing for her. But now...

Her sister had extended a hand to her, and Paige had known it was the right thing to take it.

She glanced over to the front door and noted Sadie waiting for her just inside. The door opened a crack and then closed, as if in indecision. Then it opened again, and this time her sister—it was easier to refer to her that way, she realized—hustled out and stopped short, throwing a hand up in an apparent wave.

Sadie was wearing a hot pink sundress with pink pumps and looked like she was hosting a tea party instead of teaching a quilting class. Paige looked down at her navy capri pants and simple white T-shirt. She hadn't thought to wear anything dressy.

"Just be yourself," Mark had whispered in her ear after kissing her goodbye by the car. "When you do that, everything always works out."

She had been glad for the reminder. Part of her was anxious for her sister to like her, and Paige knew Sadie was probably feeling the same way. It was the human thing to feel. But in his sweet, caring way, Mark had told her to expect to feel vulnerable, and so she did. But as she grabbed her purse and left the car, she realized she felt hopeful too.

Sadie's heels slapped against the concrete as she ran to meet her halfway, and from the momentum her sister was gaining, Paige could tell Sadie wanted to hug her. So she leaned in, and they hugged in the middle of the hot parking lot.

Her sister's arms were gentle, and when Sadie nestled her face into her neck like a long-lost friend might after an eternity apart, she gripped her closer and softened into her embrace. Tears started to fall from her eyes, but she didn't want to break the moment by apologizing for getting that pretty pink dress a little wet. Then she felt a similar wetness on her neck, and she knew Sadie was crying too.

"I'm so happy you came," her sister whispered.

"Me too," she said hoarsely, sniffing.

They broke apart and spent the next minute staring at each other. She noted Sadie's earlobes were unattached like her own, and their jaws curved the same way. Mark's love had healed Paige of the wounds of her childhood, and now she realized her sister's love had the power to heal a few other parts that hadn't seen the light of day. Gratitude circled her heart.

"I'm so glad you invited me to this, Sadie."

The woman gave a serious sniff and laughed. "Me too. Goodness, we're already blubbering, but it feels so perfect, doesn't it? I mean, every time I see you, I catch another glimpse of one of my mannerisms or the way your ears are shaped like mine, and I just want to bawl my eyes out. We've lost so much time together, but we're here now, and it's going to be wonderful."

"Even if I don't like to quilt?" Paige joked, because after going online and researching it, she worried there were too many techniques to master. She wasn't sure how that would go. Of course Mark had claimed it would help that she was a web designer. Like they were the same thing, God bless him.

"Of course," Sadie said with a huge smile. "I have to tell you, when you're ready, all of my siblings would love to meet you. Either one on one like this or together. They...they're..."

Paige's heart seemed to cheer. *They want to meet me! They want to meet me!* Her hands tightened around Sadie's. "I would love to meet them too," she said, and then gave into the urge to hug her sister again. "I didn't know I was going to feel like this right away."

"I did," Sadie said, hugging her hard. "Before I even met you, I just knew I was going to love you. How could I not? You're my sister."

The way she said "sister"—so confident and full of ownership—sent a tidal wave of warm water through Paige's heart. Her eyes leaked out the excess, and she found herself confessing, "I wasn't as sure as you. I mean, I don't really love my own mother or her family."

She was grateful Haley would never hear the words "bastard child" or be slapped for asking for more milk because she'd already drunk more than her share.

Sadie eased back. "I'm not sure I could love our daddy, after everything he's done, so I understand. It's like I'm conflicted. I pray about forgiving him and loving him like I would any child of God, but I just can't feel that way yet. And I pray he changes and…"

"Becomes the parent he was supposed to be, the loving and kind one." Paige nodded. "I had to let that go, but it took me a long time. I've mostly managed to forgive my mother, and Mark says I do love her, but he always sees the best in me. She thinks I ruined her life, but now that I have Haley, it's impossible for me to imagine how any mother could hate her child like mine seems to hate me."

Sadie rubbed her arm in comfort. "I'm not a mother, but I understand that feeling in my own way. I can't completely understand how a daddy could abandon his kids. The Christian part of me wants to say he must have been hurt somehow, somewhere, but really, that's about character."

Character, Paige thought. Yes, that was exactly right. It was either something you did or didn't have, and she'd always strived to be unlike her mother in that essential way.

"Sadie!" someone called suddenly. "Is everything all right?"

They both looked over. An older woman with tightly permed white hair had the door propped open with an ample hip.

"Goodness," Sadie exclaimed. "In all of the excitement, I plumb forgot about the class. Everyone is waiting inside." Turning back, she raised her voice and said, "Coming, Leanne. I got caught up."

Paige noted a few other women were watching them through the glass windows of the store. "If it's all right with you, I'd prefer to just say we're long-lost relations on your father's side for now."

She and Mark had talked about this. Neither she nor Sadie needed any extra pressure from other people. Besides, she didn't willingly share the details of her birth with anyone. When asked, she simply said her father had left when she was young.

"Oh! I was planning on telling them we were new friends connected through a family member. But I like your idea better. It has more of the truth to it, and I really am terrible at keeping anything under wraps. My face gives everything away. Are you ready to go inside?"

"Yes," Paige said, feeling oddly better after the emotional release. "Haley and Jess have the odd notion that I'm going to come home with a princess quilt. They don't seem to understand you can't make a quilt during a ninety-minute class. Certainly not a beginner like me."

"You might surprise yourself," Sadie said, linking their arms together and leading her to the store.

"I love the name, by the way. Oodles. It's kinda funny."

The woman named Leanne was watching them approach as though she were presiding over an exclusive bridge club. Paige had a feeling this woman wasn't at all convinced she belonged in their class. She made an attempt to smile at her as the air-conditioned store enveloped her. The scent of pecan pie tickled her nose, and she caught sight of a brown candle flickering.

Spools of fabric filled the store, organized by color and type, the display so magical she felt she'd wandered into a fairy land. The tulle was closest to Paige, making her think of the tutus Haley and Jess loved to put on when they were playing princess. The yarn display, again a shower of color, stood against the wall closest to the door.

"Everyone," Sadie announced, putting her arm around Paige's waist. "I want you to give a warm welcome to our new class member. This is Paige, and we've just gotten connected. She's a relation on my daddy's side, but we never knew each other until recently."

"Oh, now I understand why you're all dressed up, Sadie," Leanne commented. "I was wondering what y'all were doing, crying in the parking lot. That seemed rather odd."

"We were..." Paige said, trailing off at the realization that Sadie must have gussied herself up for *her*. Somehow she'd never imagined another woman wanting to impress her like that.

Sadie gave her a look and a sweet squeeze. "Happy to see each other, I guess."

"That's so nice," a grandmotherly woman next to Leanne said. "I'm Ada, and I've been quilting for nearly fifty years. My man passed last year, and Sadie invited me to come and quilt with her group since my nights get lonely. Welcome, Paige."

"Ada does more volunteering than God intended," Leanne informed her, "but we love her all the same. Welcome to our group. I'm Leanne."

Paige already had her name down, thankfully. She made sure to take a mental snapshot of Ada's face so she would remember too.

"I'm Whitney," said a young blond woman who looked to be in her mid-twenties. "I joined the class a few months ago when I found out I was pregnant. I want to make a quilt for our baby."

"It's your first?" Paige asked, feeling a soft smile spread on her lips.

Oh, how she wished... She and Mark had been trying

to have a second baby for five years, but she hadn't gotten pregnant yet. Mark wasn't concerned. He said their family would be perfect no matter what happened. Paige mostly agreed, but she really wanted to have another child or two. Growing up, she hadn't wanted anyone else to share in her hell, but Haley's situation was different. There was so much love and joy in their family, she thought it would be sad if there weren't more children to enjoy it.

"Yes," Whitney said, putting her hand on her tummy. "Do you have children?"

"A daughter," Paige said. "She's in second grade already."

"They grow up in a blink, don't they?" the woman next to Whitney said. "I'm Mae, by the way. Welcome to the class, Paige. I expect your little girl will want you to make her a quilt."

Of all the women, Mae exuded a special warmth. Perhaps it was her similarity to a plain-clothes Mrs. Claus, what with her radiant smile and soft white hair.

"A princess one," Paige said, laughing. "I have a feeling she's going to have to wait a while."

"Not at all," Mae said. "You sit by me sometime when you're more comfortable, and I'll show you a few of my tricks. I cut corners, you see." Her wink was downright charming.

"Your quilts stay together and are beautiful, Mae," Sadie said. "I don't see that as cutting corners. You're just efficient."

"Is that what we're calling it?" the last woman in the group said.

Her dark red hair could only come from a bottle, and she had an edge for someone who looked to be in her forties.

"I'm Imogene. Nice to meet you, Paige. Welcome. I'm newly divorced—my worthless husband of twenty-two years hooked up with a skank ho right out of college. My kids are grown, and my oldest thought I might release some of my pent-up anger through quilting."

"How's that been working for you, Imogene?" Leanne asked with a flat drawl.

"Every time I stick a pin into a square for piecing I just imagine it's his dick."

Sadie gasped along with Paige. *"Ladies.* That's—"

"Awesome," Whitney said. "I hope his dick falls off for cheating on you. I hate cheaters."

Leanne looked to be smiling despite herself. "Amen!" she said loudly.

Imogene held up her hands at Sadie's look. "Okay, no man bashing. Sorry, Sadie. Paige, I brought the snacks tonight. I can't cook much, but I can manage to make a box cake and frost it. Hope you like carrot."

Cake and women with strong opinions. This was already sounding fun. "Thank you, Imogene. I'm particularly fond of the cream cheese frosting."

"Me too," the woman said, slapping her curvy hip. "I like to think the carrots make it the healthiest cake you can eat."

"Thank heavens you like cake," Leanne interjected. "We had a girl a few months back who brought kale chips when it was her turn. Imagine that! She was always complaining about all of the sugar we were eating."

"At least she didn't last too long," Ada said. "She wasn't much for quilting, turned out."

"I hope I'm going to like it," Paige decided to admit. "I mean, I've always thought quilts were beautiful. My great-grandmother used to wrap me in one when I was little. I don't remember the pattern much—only that every patch was from an old flannel nightgown."

"Those are the best," Ada said. "I kept my girls' nightgowns for just that purpose."

Sadie glanced over at her, and Paige forced a smile. She'd love her great-grandparents, but her great-grandmother had died of a heart attack when she was younger than Haley. Her great-grandfather had taken it into his head that headstrong Skylar was to blame, and he'd up and kicked them out. The flannel quilt had been left behind in the madness of their departure, and she'd thought of it many times since, wishing she'd insisted on stuffing it into the one suitcase they'd left with.

"So your great-grandmother quilted?" Mae asked.

"I believe so, but I never saw her do it," Paige admitted. "By the time I came along, she had arthritis so bad she could barely peel and cut a potato." Of course, her mother had never helped much around the house, preferring to run off at night with a string of men she kept around. No wonder her great-grandfather had held a grudge.

Leanne nodded. "I feel her pain. I like to think quilting keeps my joints loose. Well, I suppose we'd better get back to it. Half the class is gone by now probably."

"Oh, don't be so dramatic, Leanne," Ada told her, using a firm hand to steer her toward the circle of folding chairs. "We have plenty of time. Whenever a new member joins the group, it's important to make them feel welcome. Otherwise, we could all quilt at home."

"Amen," Imogene said.

"Oh, don't starch up your girdle any more than usual, Ada," Leanne replied. "You won't be able to walk out of here later, what with it being so stiff."

"Like I would wear a girdle in this heat," Ada said. "At my age, I've earned the privilege of letting everything God gave me hang out."

"Gravity's a bitch," Leanne said, pointing to her own sagging breasts. "These used to be perky. Just you younger ones wait."

"Leanne," Sadie said in a stern voice.

"Sadie doesn't like me to say 'bitch,' but sometimes it's the only word to get the job done."

"Shall we sit and resume?" Sadie asked. "Paige, we have some water and sweet tea set out by the cake. Just over there." She pointed to the folding table in front of the upholstery fabric. "I see everyone has already helped themselves."

"You were out there forever," Leanne drawled.

"Enough, Leanne. Paige, the bathroom is to the back right of the store," Ada said. "That's usually my first question when I go somewhere."

"When you reach a certain age," Leanne said, "that's the only question besides when your Social Security check is coming that matters."

Paige had to purse her lips not to laugh at these two women and their tall tales of aging. She felt more confident about her decision to join this group. She hadn't been so sure about the whole thing on her way over.

"You can sit between me and Mae," Sadie told her. "We're all working on baby quilts right now for the hospital. Except Whitney, who is working on her own baby quilt. You're welcome to make one for your family, of course."

Haley had been somewhat pacified by the beautiful baby quilt Sadie had given her. Even though it was much too small, she slept with it most nights.

"No, I'm happy to make a few quilts for the hospital," she said. "That way I can figure out what to do for Haley's big princess quilt."

"That's a sound plan," Sadie said. "Since you're a newbie, what I'd like to suggest is that you think about the colors that make you the happiest. Usually that's the easiest place to start. Then we can talk about a pattern."

"Most new quilters get a little intimidated by the millions of patterns out there," Mae told her. "Best keep it simple in the beginning, honey, and Sadie is a pro at guiding you while helping you make something fun and pretty all your own. You can work on your confidence and your quilting techniques as you go along. The two go hand in hand."

"Like bread and jam," Ada said, reaching into a cloth bag and pulling out the beginnings of a patchwork quilt.

Each woman seemed to have a special bag beside her chair. She'd missed that memo.

"I didn't know about tools," Paige leaned in to tell Sadie as soon as they were seated. "And I don't have a bag."

"Don't worry none," Sadie said. "I have extra tools for new students. I figure everyone needs to find out if they love quilting before they invest in the tools. You'll need a medium rotary cutter, a cutting mat, a special ruler I'll show you later, and a few other things."

"I don't have a sewing machine either," she whispered. "And I don't really know how to use one either. I mean, I haven't done any sewing since Home-Ec in high school."

"The sewing machine part is a piece of cake," Leanne said. "A few of us still like to hand stitch, but it's only because we have more time on our hands than you young people."

"You look too young for a Home-Ec class," Ada said. "Where did you go to high school?"

Sadie looked eager to hear her answer. "In a small town outside of Knoxville," she said. After their hasty departure from Texas, she and her mother had moved in with her grandparents, who'd relocated due to the scandal. While they'd ended up kicking them out after a few months due to her mother's wild stunts, they'd remained in the same town. Her grandparents would give them money from time to time since her mother couldn't hold down a job. She'd heard them say more than once that the only reason they hadn't cut all ties to her mom was because of Christian charity. Of course, her mother hadn't wanted a job or any responsibilities—her only ambition was to jump from man to man. Her grandparents had pitied Paige, but pity wasn't the same thing as love.

And that pity had, more often than not, been soured by flat-out unkindness. There were times they'd called her a devil's seed and told her she was predisposed to follow in her mother's path, something that had terrified her until she'd grown older and realized there wasn't some bad-seed gene in her DNA. She could make her own choices to be a good person. Her mother's choices might affect her, but they didn't predispose her to self-destruction.

"You'll catch on real quick, honey," Imogene said. "When I started six months ago, I didn't know how to sew a button. Now I can piece a pattern together and sew it right up. Lickety split."

Somehow Paige didn't think it was that easy, but she smiled back at the women who were sending encouraging smiles her way. She was moved by how quickly they'd integrated her into their group.

"We have a sewing machine here for students to use," Sadie said. "Let me show you the squares we have available for students. Most of the long-time quilters love to hunt for the right fabric. Some even cut up squares from old clothing like those flannel nightgowns you mentioned. Ada made the most beautiful quilts out of Perry's clothes and gave them to her children this past Christmas."

Ada gave a quick nod. "My sister hemmed and hawed about it being maudlin. She thought it would be more fitting to give his clothes to the Salvation Army. Like she knows better. I mean, I volunteer there four times a week. It's a great place to buy clothes for fabric, Paige."

"Your sister is a busybody," Leanne said, shaking her head as she pulled a quilt in progress out of her bag, "and you were right to go with your heart. Those quilts are going to be passed down for generations. You mark my words."

Whitney took out what looked like a bunch of colorful squares held together by stickpins. "Whitney, look at how much you accomplished since last week," Sadie said, rising and crossing to the young woman.

"I spent most of the weekend working on it. I'm so glad you had me practice on a few other quilts first though. I needed to get the basics."

"Whitney is an artist," Sadie said, turning toward Paige to include her in the conversation, "and she had a vision of what she wanted her baby's quilt to look like. She drew it for me, and together we created a simple design."

"Of course, I might change my mind next week when we find out whether we're having a boy or girl," Whitney said. "Sadie can tell you. It's taken me a while to settle on something. I want it to be perfect."

"That's right," Mae said. "You have your ultrasound next week. I can't wait to hear what y'all are having. Paige, Sadie is really good at bringing someone's vision down to their skill level."

Paige felt the first whisper of panic. She didn't have a vision.

"It's only natural to want to come in here and make a quilt like you've seen at an art bazaar," Ada added. "Best to keep an open mind in the beginning."

Paige had never noticed quilts before at art shows. She and Mark didn't really go to art shows. When Riley watched Haley, they liked to go out to dinner and a movie or hang out with their other friends.

"Or on Pinterest," Leanne said, ripping some cloth up at the seam like she was pulling weeds out of the garden.

Paige could never imagine ripping anything up so confidently. How did she avoid tearing the fabric? Oh, this was going to be so much harder than she'd thought... Then she reminded herself she was here for Sadie and a good cause. It didn't matter if she became a master quilter overnight.

"I end up looking at pin after pin on Pinterest," Leanne said, "instead of quilting on my own some nights."

"That's because your Horace doesn't keep you guessing anymore," Ada teased.

The woman barked out a laugh. "My goodness, Ada, we've been married for almost forty years. If he kept me guessing at my age, I'd probably have a heart attack. Paige, I picked up quilting when he retired. I had to get out of the house, and it gave me the chance to create a sewing room. He has his new reading room, and I have my getaway. Keeps a marriage going, let me tell you."

Sadie was laughing softly. "Come on, Paige. Let me show you the squares."

Paige felt her nerves intensify as she followed her. She knew it was only natural when a person started something new, but there was still a part of her that wanted to know what to do right off the mark. The same part that wanted to impress her sister.

"I don't normally start off showing new students how to cut their own squares unless they're like Whitney and have something specific in mind. She looked at tons of fabric all over Nashville, let me tell you."

"I'm not that ambitious," Paige murmured.

Sadie had led her to a cluster of shelves in the back of the store. "Beginners typically find it easier to deal with pre-cut larger squares. These are five-inch," she said, pointing to a stack of squares, "but we have some that are a little smaller or larger. A nine-patch quilt is very simple and traditional. Less to piece together and easier to sew."

It couldn't be too hard, right? It was just a machine, a needle, and a thread.

"You can also make a quilt out of strips of cloth, what we call a strip quilt. Also a lovely option. When I mentioned it to Rye—who's one of our brother's best friends—he said I couldn't make him one of those since he's a family man now."

Sadie laughed, but Paige was still reeling from the stripper reference. Did that mean their brother was crude too? Somehow, just from spending time with Sadie, she doubted it.

"You'd have to know Rye. Anyway, you select the strips and piece them together. Again, less to piece since you're starting with a baby quilt. Those only run somewhere around thirty-five to forty-five inches, although it depends on your vision."

That vision thing again. She felt her hands form fists by her side.

"We can also make a nice border around your squares if you want," Sadie said. "This first one is about having fun, keeping it simple, and making something you'll be proud of. I'm pretty much here to help you with anything." She took down a stack of squares and then an equally large pile of strips.

"We've already ironed the squares and strips, FYI, so if you'd be mindful as you comb through them, I'd appreciate it. Of course, you're going to have to iron your seams once you sew them together, but it's easier to piece the squares if they aren't wrinkled."

"That makes sense," Paige said, taking in the myriad of squares. It was a veritable treasure trove.

"As you can see, there's a mixture of solid colors and patterns. You might want to mix and match—use some of the single color squares in, say, pink and yellow, with some of these polka dot squares. Do a ruffle border. Keeps things interesting. The colors are complementary, and it creates a different effect." She paused. "You look overwhelmed, Paige."

"I'm okay," she said, breathing shallowly as she eyed the squares. There were so many of them... "It's all new, you know?"

"You'll be fine," Sadie said, patting her arm. "But promise to tell me if you don't take a shine to quilting. It won't hurt my feelings. I mean, *none* of my sisters quilt. That's probably why I cried a little when they all volunteered to take my class so they could meet you."

Oh, if that didn't pull her heartstrings... "That's... really sweet of them."

Sadie nodded. "Why don't I leave you to look at squares for a bit while I check on everyone else? Oh, and I need to mention this before I forget. We've already pre-washed the fabric for these swatches. Personally I always do that because you don't want to spend all that time quilting only to discover some of your squares have shrunk in the dryer." She made a face.

"I hadn't thought of that," Paige said. Goodness, there was so much to remember. She should have brought a notebook. Next time.

"That's why you're taking a class," Sadie said, smiling. "It's always easier to learn something when someone shows you, I've found."

"Who taught you?" she asked.

"My sixth grade teacher, Mrs. Polski, used to quilt while we were taking tests," she told her. "I took an interest, and she ended up showing me during recess and after school a few times a week. She was a dear woman. She gave me her all of her quilting materials—fabrics, old pattern books, you name it—when she learned she had stage 4 liver cancer. She died a few years ago, but I feel her around me sometimes when I'm quilting. She was a member of our church, which was how we kept in touch as I grew older."

"She sounds like a lovely woman," Paige said. Then, because it was important to be honest, she blurted out, "Sadie, I don't have a vision. For the quilt."

"That's okay," she said. "That's part of the fun. Sometimes I toddle around for days, trying to come up with what I want to say in a quilt. Just let your imagination go. Or put your hand on your heart and listen for the first word that comes to mind."

Paige didn't have to put a hand on her heart. Suddenly she heard the word, and it was so loud, she pressed her hand to her mouth, fighting emotion.

"Sadie, I have my word."

Her sister put her arm around her shoulder, as if sensing her emotion. "That's great. What is it?"

"Safe," she whispered. "I want the baby who receives this quilt to feel safe."

She never had felt that way as a child, she realized again sadly. Until she got away from her mom to go to college, she'd been on pins and needles her whole life.

"That's a beautiful intention," Sadie said, her eyes filling with tears. "I know you'll put it into the quilt. Every quilter I know talks about sewing love and other intentions into their work. In some cases, I've even written down a short prayer on a piece of thin cloth and sewn it between the batting and the backing. But don't tell anyone. That's one of my secrets."

Paige had never heard of anything sweeter. She didn't pray much on her own, although she went to church with Mark from time to time for Haley. But she really loved the idea of writing down a prayer and putting it into a quilt. Of everything she'd heard tonight, that made her warm to quilting the most. Mark had always said prayer was like the wishes you wanted for yourself and those you love, which felt like a rather profound way to describe it.

"All right, let your heart show you what patches or strips confer the beauty of safety to a newborn baby," Sadie said. "You can even take a whole bunch home and play with them. You know, arrange them into different patterns. I like to do that sometimes. It's like Play-Doh for adults, making different shapes and then starting over again."

Paige had never played with Play-Doh. She'd never even colored as a child because her mother had said coloring was for sissies. *People are mean, Paige, and life will kick you in the teeth if you let it. You have to learn to be mean right back.* She hadn't really believed her mother, but no one at home had given her Play-Doh or coloring books, no matter how much she'd asked. In fact, one time her mother had found a coloring book a friend had given her and thrown it away.

Mark said it was why she'd chosen website design. There were no tangible materials for anyone to take from her. That realization had kinda broken her heart.

"Thank you, Sadie," she said, hoping her sister understood she was grateful for more than this little tutorial.

"You're going to come up with something beautiful, Paige, again and again. I just know it. I'll be right back."

Her sister turned to leave, and Paige knew she couldn't wait a moment longer to share what she'd been thinking this last half hour. "*Sadie?*"

"Yes, Paige?" her sister said, spinning around, her dress flaring out at the edges. She seemed to sense something in her tone because her smile dimmed.

"I'd like to meet the rest of your...I mean...ah...our siblings. Maybe y'all could come over this Saturday? I'd like it to be just us five at first, but I'd feel better if Mark was with me. Riley can watch Haley."

"Oh, of course," Sadie said, her lip starting to tremble. "We can host you too. You don't need to go to any trouble. I mean, there are more of us and—"

"It's no trouble," Paige said, trying to keep it together. "I'd...like to do something."

"We'd love that! We'd just... Since you mentioned him, I feel I should share that I'm still not sure Riley and I hit it off. I mean...there were times when I felt this pull and then others...we have totally different views on important things like...but he texted me afterward. Oh, crap. I shouldn't go into details. He's your friend, and I'm sorry."

Paige gave her an assuring smile. "You'll both find your way. I'm staying out of it."

She blew out a breath. "Whew! That's good to hear. I mean, I don't want this to be weird. We have enough going on without any complications. I mean he—" She slapped a hand over her mouth.

"It's okay, Sadie," Paige told her, fighting the urge to grin. Her sister was clearly conflicted. Again, not her business.

Sadie was blushing too, just like Riley had, which only made the situation more endearing.

"I'm going to make some quilt magic to get my mind off this little talk," Sadie said, laughing and leaving the storage shelves.

Paige had no trouble seeing the magic around her. *Sadie* was the magic.

Who else could have made her fall in love with her long-lost sister in the scope of a couple of days, join a quilting class, and agree to meet her long-lost family?

Chapter 7

"Sadie!"

She'd barely cut her engine after parking on Paige's street when she looked over and saw Jess running down her front porch and across her yard in a green princess dress. Since Sadie had worked a morning shift at Oodles, she'd driven over alone for the meeting with Paige and the rest of her siblings. Saturday traffic had been nonexistent, so she was early. Staying in her car and waiting for her siblings no longer looked like an option.

"Hi, Jess," she said when she exited her car.

The little girl waved her princess wand and kept running, her hemline dragging in the freshly mowed grass.

"Jess!" she heard Riley call out from his porch.

Her gaze locked onto him, and everything seemed to still around her. He had on a black T-shirt and faded jeans, and he looked good. Somewhere she heard, *Yum,* and shook herself. The attraction was still there, darn it.

Sadie had the sudden compulsion to dart back into her car. The one text Riley had sent had been to thank her for dinner, and she'd responded with equal manners, but their exchange had ended there. She wasn't sure how she felt about that, especially since she'd found herself thinking about Riley more than expected, but she'd decided to let it alone.

Oh, please don't let this be awkward. She had enough on her hands with the epic McGuiness meeting with Paige.

"Hello, Sadie," he called as he ran after his daughter. "Jess, we talked about this. Come back here. Sorry about this. I know it's a big day. *Jess!* I mean it."

"Hi, Sadie!" the little girl said when she reached her. "Dad said Haley and I were supposed to leave you alone, but I just had to say hi. Sadie! I didn't know you were Paige's long-lost half-sister. That's so neat! It's like when Rapunzel realizes she's the lost princess and reunites with her parents."

Riley scooped her up in his arms. "Excuse my daughter. She only speaks Disney and clearly needs to learn a lesson in listening to her father." He nuzzled her neck, and she let out a giggle.

Okay, *this* was the man she was attracted to. The attractive guy who was so sweet with his daughter. The funny guy who made her laugh. "That's okay. I'm early."

"Dad, you *had* to say hello to Sadie," Jess said. "I mean, you really like her."

He made a face. "Again, I'm sorry for this. I'll just take this one back to the house..."

Jess pushed against his chest, and he lowered her to the ground. "I'll leave y'all to chat. But don't worry, I'll be back."

"God, she sounds like a mini-Terminator when she says that," Riley said, rubbing the back of his neck. "You know... Arnold—"

"Schwarzenegger," she said. "I understand the reference."

He rocked back on his heels. "So, how have you been?"

"Good," she said, nodding her head. "Busy this week, what with Paige's first class and now today..."

"Yeah, it's incredible," Riley said, pinning her with that intense blue gaze. "I don't think I've ever seen a display of so much courage. It really inspired me this week with my new female superhero."

That took Sadie by surprise. To her knowledge, she'd never inspired anything before. People and events typically inspired her, not the other way around. "That's wonderful to hear. How did it…inspire you?"

He gestured to her. Not in a rude way, mind you. The way his hands moved was oddly inviting, like he was framing her in his mind somehow, seeing the individual pieces that made her up. She saw her quilt designs that way, and she suspected he drew like that too.

"I thought I was on the right path for my superhero, but after meeting you, she seemed cliché somehow. You know, like some sort of stock character. Even the name I'd come up with didn't fit anymore. I…you don't want to hear this."

Oh, yes, she did. "Please. I really do."

"Well…even though I know we had some ups and down on our date, there were moments where…it was like time slowed down."

She almost gulped. That was how she'd felt only moments ago.

"Or simply stopped altogether," he continued, his gaze searching her. "It's like you had the power to alter time. My time. Our time together. Ah…I'm not making any sense."

"No, I…think I understand what you mean. At those moments, it was like all our differences—"

"Didn't matter," he said, finishing her thought.

"I was going to say that," she said, fighting the urge to put her hand on his chest. She wanted to be closer to him, to confirm that his heart was beating as fast as her own.

He looked down, and she took a breath. "Sadie, I don't normally explain myself, but I want to with you."

The way he shifted on his feet told her just how hard this was for him. She waited for him to continue.

"I don't like country music because Jess' mom had big dreams of being a star, and she was a really destructive force in my life and Jess', so I associate the music with her. It's not fair perhaps..."

"But understandable," she said quietly. "Thank you for telling me that, Riley. I might have been a bit of a prude about the burlesque show, and I'm sorry."

Suddenly his hand was covering her forearm, and he was gazing into her eyes. "No, I shouldn't have taken you there for a first date. The balloon act...even I was a bit shocked, although..."

Was that a twinkle in his eye now? She found herself smiling.

"Although you can dig it," she said, making him laugh.

"Dig it?" he asked. "I love that. Really, I love the way you talk."

She decided to put it all out there. "Even when I talk about going to church?"

"Ah," he said, nodding. "Best to pull off a Band-Aid all at once, right? I didn't mean to offend you. I'm not against church per se. I...don't like people who talk out of both sides of their mouth. Since I was...a young kid, I've... drawn what I see, and some so-called 'religious' people told me I was bad for drawing what I did."

She tried to imagine someone saying that about one of her quilts. "Oh, Riley, that's terrible."

"I want to live in a world where..." He gestured to the sky. "Where people do the right thing because they believe it's right. Not because someone or some institution tells them so. Does that make sense?"

His hand was still cupping her forearm, and she laid her hand over his. His eyes locked with hers. "That's how I feel too," she responded.

"Good," he said, nodding and taking a breath. "Sadie, I really like you. I even...this is going to sound weird, but I admire you. Coming to Paige's front door like you did... like I said, you're an inspiration. Plus, you're really beautiful, and I...can't stop thinking about you."

She found herself gripping his hand to keep herself anchored. "I haven't stopped thinking about you either, Riley."

"Would you...go out with me again? Forget about our first date? Because I'd...really like that. A lot."

Her chest felt tight, and she had all sorts of emotion rolling through her, but she didn't want the moment to end. "I'd like that too. A lot."

His exhale seemed wrenched from deep inside him. "Good. Ah...how about...heck...I'll just ask...tonight? Seven? I mean, you have church tomorrow, right? And quilting class Monday? I don't think I can wait until Tuesday. Plus it's a school night, and I try—"

"Tonight would be fine, Riley," she said, fitting her hand around his finally. She had a good feeling about today's family meeting with Paige, and she didn't want to wait any longer to see him.

Their hands lowered, and he gave hers a healthy squeeze. "Ah...I should confess something though."

She held her breath.

"My thoughts on iguanas remain the same," he said, his mouth curving.

She felt the corners of her mouth curve too. "I can deal with that. But no more balloons. Deal?"

He turned her hand and shook it. "Deal."

She heard an approaching car and looked over to see J.P.'s SUV coming down the street. "My family is here."

Letting go of her hand, he stood in front of her with an easy smile. "I'll see you later then."

"Yes," she said.

"I'll pick you up at seven." He started jogging back to the house. "I'd better corral Jess before she escapes again."

By the time she turned back around, J.P. had parked his SUV in front of the Bradshaws' house. Her siblings were filing out, and everyone was fussing with their clothing. Each of them had worn their Sunday best. Even J.P.

"I'm so nervous I could throw up," Shelby said, linking arms with her when she reached her.

"I was thinking the same thing," Susannah said. "How is it you look so calm, Sadie?"

Because she'd made another date with Riley, she realized. No, it was more than that. His presence affected her in a good way. She rubbed her arms, his touch lingering somehow. "I had a few moments to settle."

J.P. rubbed Susannah's back. "It's only natural to feel a little off. Let's remember Paige is probably feeling the same. We're all going to take it easy."

"*Easy?*" Shelby muttered. "When I'm about to meet our half-sister for the first time? Ask me anything else, J.P."

Susannah reached for her other hand and gripped it tight. "I'm ready."

"All right," J.P. said. "Let's go."

They walked down the sidewalk to the front porch. Their lawn was also freshly mowed, and even the bushes in the front looked as though they'd been trimmed. Unlike the first time Sadie had stepped onto the porch, there was no purple bicycle. In fact, there were no toys at all and the floor looked freshly swept.

"She bought a Welcome mat," Sadie said, noticing the new item in front of the door as she rang the bell.

"She did?" Shelby asked. "Oh, my God, I'm already tearing up."

"Keep it together," Susannah said. "We don't need to show up crying."

The front door opened, and there stood Paige. Somehow she looked tiny, rocking on her heels, her hands fisted around her waist like she was trying to hold it together. She had on a blue cotton dress paired with cream-colored heels. Her hair looked like she'd blow dried it out in waves. Apparently, they'd all decided to wear their Sunday best, and suddenly all thoughts of Riley were gone.

This was their moment—as a family.

Susannah crushed the bones in her hand, and Shelby gave an audible sniff.

The corners of Paige's mouth lifted in a smile. Then fell. Then lifted again.

"Welcome." She laughed nervously. "I'm Paige."

J.P. moved through the door first and enfolded her in a gentle hug. "I'm J.P. and it's a blessing to meet you."

Sadie felt tears track down her cheeks, and Paige was dashing at tears too when J.P. finally let her go. She seemed embarrassed to realize it. "Oh, I didn't mean to cry."

"Me either," Shelby said, rushing forward and wrapping their sister up in a fierce embrace. "But I can't seem to stop it. I'm Shelby, by the way. And goodness, you look so much like me. I wasn't expecting that. Sadie, why didn't you tell me?"

"I think she looks more like Susannah," Sadie said.

"Don't squeeze her to pieces or freak her out," Susannah chided softly. "Give the woman some room. I mean, the three of us are new to her."

"She can handle it," Mark said, appearing in the hallway. His eyes were wet as well, Sadie noticed.

He crossed to J.P. and shook his hand. "I'm Mark, Paige's husband."

Shelby let go of Paige with an exclamation and then hugged Mark enthusiastically, making him laugh.

Susannah stood before Paige for a moment, as if not quite sure of what to do, before putting her hands on the woman's shoulders. "It's a real joy to meet you, Paige."

"Oh, for heaven's sake, Susannah," Shelby said. "Go ahead and hug her. You know you want to."

Paige laughed and opened her arms awkwardly. Susannah was a little rigid at first, but then she folded into their sister. Sadie knew she was trying to hold it together, but how in the world could anyone expect them to do that?

Mark seemed to realize how delicate Susannah's emotional state was because he simply put his hand on her arm gently and introduced himself.

Paige shuffled forward to Sadie. "Hi."

"Hi," she said, wiping at the corners of her eyes. "It's... it's—"

"I know," Paige said, hugging her tightly. "It's a big day. *Thank you*, Sadie."

"You made this happen as much as I did," Sadie said, rocking them both in place. "You could have sent me on my way when I showed up here unannounced."

"All right now, Sadie," Shelby said, tapping her foot. "Give the rest of us a chance to get to know Paige."

Paige wiped her nose when they broke apart. "We made a few snacks."

"I don't think I can eat yet," Susannah said.

"Neither can I," Paige admitted, crossing to Mark and taking his hand. "Let's go into the family room."

They shuffled in and found seats on the navy-colored sofa while Paige and Mark took the matching loveseat. Sadie hadn't been in this room before, but it was painted a soft yellow. She found herself smiling at the photos lining the wall to her right. They told the story of Paige and Mark as a couple. The two of them racing down the aisle, an expecting Paige with Mark's hand on her rounded belly, and them holding hands while looking down at a newborn Haley.

"I wasn't sure what you might want to drink," Paige said, "so I went with sweet tea and water. We can make hot tea or coffee if anyone has a hankering."

"This is more than enough," J.P. said, gesturing to the coffee table where everything was arranged, including a vegetable and cheese tray and a platter decked out with apple slices, oranges, and a few nuts drizzled in honey.

"Yes, thank you," Shelby said. "We didn't want you to go to any trouble."

"It was no trouble," Paige said, her hand firmly in Mark's.

Sadie could feel everyone's mood shift and decided to call it out there. "We're all falling back on our manners. I mean...it's totally fine. I don't think there's some sort of right or wrong way to do this."

"Sadie!" Susannah exclaimed.

"Well, I'm only trying to break the ice a little," Sadie said, giving her a look. "We all want to feel comfortable, but no one knows how to begin. So I'll refrain from saying, 'Paige, this is a lovely room.' Susannah is an interior decorator, you see, so she knows far more about that sort of thing than I do."

Paige nodded. "I know that. I mean I...went online and looked y'all up when Sadie showed up."

"At your front door," Sadie couldn't help but add. "Golly, I was nervous."

"I imagine we all are," J.P. said, patting her knee to settle her down. "I know you and Sadie have had some time to talk, but I was wondering how you and Mark met."

Leave it to J.P. to ask that one. The way Paige looked at Mark for a moment confirmed what an easy answer this was going to be.

"In college," Paige said. "I took one look at him in psych class and knew I wanted to go out with him. I was trying to straighten myself out, so I didn't think I wanted to fall into anything serious, but..."

"Lucky for me I was both good-looking and a good talker," he joked, rubbing her back.

"We didn't expect to get married so young," Paige said, still looking at him, "but we just couldn't seem to stop ourselves."

"We knew what we'd found with each other," Mark said softly. "I understand a few of you are married or soon-to-be."

Sadie nearly came out of her skin, thinking for a moment he meant her, but she realized he was talking about Shelby.

She listened as her siblings ran them through their own love stories in brief. When Shelby mentioned that she and Vander had met because they'd hired him to find their daddy, Paige's eyes darkened. But she soon rallied and asked more about everyone's lives before filling them in on her own story—how she'd put herself through college to become a website designer.

"And Sadie tells us you're a middle school guidance counselor," Shelby said, engaging Mark.

"Yes," he said, "and I love it. As far as I'm concerned, it's the best job on the planet."

"He's so great at it too," Paige added, leaning in and pressing her cheek against his, "but mostly, he's the best man I've ever met."

"What a blessing y'all found each other," J.P. said. "I think there's a guiding hand that leads us to our mates. It's wonderful to see you so happy. Tell us about Haley. Sadie said she's a sweetheart."

"Well, she's a little shy, here and there," Paige said. "She...ah...knows about y'all now."

"I'd also like to tell my children, Annabelle and Rory," J.P. said. "I hope you don't mind me asking, but what were you comfortable sharing with your daughter?"

Mark shot a look at Paige, who nodded, and then answered, "We told Haley that Paige has learned that she has some siblings who are really nice people. She understands that we don't see Paige's mom or dad or grandparents because they're mean. We both know Haley will have more questions as she gets older, but for now we try and be honest—and brief—and describe things in a way she can relate to."

"I totally understand that," J.P. said. "My wife was abused by her ex-husband, and her oldest boy knew about it toward the end. We've told them he's a bad man who will never be allowed near them again, and for now, it seems to be the right way to handle things."

"It's important to protect children from the harsh reality of things," Paige said, her tone hardening. "My mother didn't do that for me."

J.P. sighed and leaned forward. "I know it's an ugly thing to talk about, and we don't need to talk about it in any detail, but Paige, I want you to know we are appalled by what our daddy did. We're very sorry he hurt you and your mother."

"He didn't do right by y'all either," Paige said, "but we've all overcome that, thank God. We are not responsible for our parents' choices. That's something I realized a long time ago. My mother made some very bad decisions, and she continued to do so throughout my childhood. I'm not going to be around that kind of destructive energy again, and neither is anyone in this family."

"We completely agree," J.P. said. "I only wanted you to know that had we known about you, we would have reached out years ago. Okay?"

Sadie felt her eyes fill with tears, and she wasn't the only one.

Paige nodded. "I appreciate you saying that. After meeting Sadie, I can't say I'm surprised. I need to tell you that I didn't reach out to y'all because my mother said a lot of conflicting things about y'all, and frankly, I didn't want to open that door. I was...making peace with the way things were with my mom and how I...was conceived..."

Mark put his arm around his wife, and they all waited for her to pull herself together.

"Doing that was pretty much the hardest thing I've ever done," she said hoarsely. "She's a liar and a user, and while I have some compassion for the fact that my conception and the events around it were part of what messed her up, she continued to repeat the same destructive patterns with me along for the ride. I decided to stop speaking to her when I was a sophomore in college. The last straw was when she came after Mark for money to support her drug habit."

Sadie nearly gasped. She hadn't known that. "Oh, honey."

"I also didn't want to open a door I thought y'all might want to keep closed," Paige said. "I wasn't sure you'd want anything to do with me."

"You tell us how you'd like to proceed, Paige," J.P. said in a gentle tone. "You should know that we don't plan on having to anything to do with our father after the events of the past few months. Frankly, after what he said to Shelby's fiancé, I wouldn't want to hear him out even if he wanted to talk to us."

Sadie wanted to agree, but there was still a part of her that couldn't let go of the hope that her daddy would change. Hadn't she seen it happen to other people? Call her fanciful, but he was her *daddy*.

"I don't *ever* want to talk to him," Paige said. "That's unequivocal."

J.P. nodded. "You should know that in our search for him we ended up meeting his mother, Lenore, a grandmother we never knew. She's actually a lovely woman. Had a hard life and is ashamed of her son. We're in the process of building our relationship with her. We'd hoped to move her from Memphis to an assisted living facility here in Nashville, but none of them would take her bulldog, who is both her protector and friend. That made Me-Mother—that's what she likes us to call her—shut down all talk of moving. We try and visit her from time to time... and that's something you're more than welcome to be a part of if you'd like."

"I'll have to think about it," Paige said, looking pale. "I don't know..."

"Who can blame you for taking your time? I mean,

you only met us. We actually might be crazy people or downright mean." Shelby made a dramatic show of rolling her eyes and sticking her tongue out. "I mean, thank heavens for Facebook. Right, Sadie? Because if you hadn't looked so nice, what with you and Mark and your Haley, I don't think Sadie would have shown up at your door like she did."

"Facebook, huh?" Paige said, shaking her head. "Well, I knew y'all weren't crazy or mean—at least it didn't appear that way when I looked you up years ago. I just didn't feel I had the right to reach out..."

She made a gesture with her hands like the words wouldn't come, and Sadie eased herself up from the couch and came forward to sit by her feet.

"It's okay, Paige," she told her softly. "We understand."

The woman inhaled like she was fighting a serious cry. Sadie took her hand and squeezed it. "Like I said to you before, we...all of us...only want to get to know you better."

"And love on you like a sister," Shelby said, dashing tears off her cheeks, "if you'll let us."

"I honestly don't know what that feels like *for me* even though I've watched Haley and Jess—her best friend—be together that way," Paige said, laughing and crying. "It's like I have an idea about what it's supposed to look like, but it isn't grounded in me somehow. Does that make sense?"

Sadie nodded. "I feel that way about having a daddy love on me even though I see other daddies do it with their daughters. Whenever I hear the phrase 'daddy's little girl,' it's as foreign to me as something scientific...like a superconductor."

"Oh, Sadie," Shelby said. "I hadn't really thought about it that way, but I feel the same about the whole daddy stuff."

J.P. and Susannah nodded as well, and Paige gave a watery laugh.

"The family I grew up in was pretty much a freak show. But I've already fallen for your sister here, and I don't think it will take me long to fall for y'all too."

"I'm writing it down that someone fell for Sadie first and not J.P.," Shelby said, winking tearfully at their older brother. "J.P. has been our rock since Daddy left, and like you said about Mark, he's one of the best men we know. Other than our mama, we wouldn't be as 'normal' if it weren't for him looking out for us."

"They're not trying to suggest you need me to look out for you," J.P. told Paige. "Beyond the fact that you're obviously a strong woman, it's clear as glass Mark here has your back like a husband should. But I'm here for you—we all are—should you need us. Beyond the getting to know you and all, which I hope will continue."

"I'd like that very much," Paige said, wiping more tears. "I need to ask though. How does your mother feel about all of this?"

Everyone looked at J.P. "We agreed I would talk to Mama once we met with you, and that's something I'm planning on doing after church tomorrow. I don't know whether your mother said anything about our mother—and honestly I don't need to. I only want to tell you she's a good woman who overcame a horrible situation. What's more, she helps a lot of people as a preacher. She's got one of the most open hearts imaginable, and she would never hold any bad feelings toward you. Like you said, none of us are responsible for our daddy's choices."

"All J.P. is saying is that you don't need to worry that our mama would ever hurt you," Sadie said, feeling the sweat in Paige's hand. "You've already been so hurt—like we were when our daddy left...and then a few months ago when we learned why. None of us want any more hurt to come to this family."

On that they all agreed. Sadie wouldn't have asked Paige to join her quilting class otherwise.

"It must have taken even more courage than I originally thought for you to come to our front door, Sadie," Mark said, gazing steadily at her face. "Thank you."

Sadie remembered what Riley had said about her courage inspiring him, and she found herself breaking into a huge smile. She'd done that. And all by herself.

"Yes, thank you," Paige said, leaning down and giving her a half hug.

"Well, it surprised the heck out of me," Shelby said. "I was planning to reach out to you too, only I hadn't gotten to it yet. I'm newly engaged, you see."

"Meaning she has her mind on other matters," Susannah said, elbowing Shelby in the side.

"I'd like to meet your partners," Paige said. "I appreciate you allowing Mark to be here."

Shelby waved a hand. "We didn't want you to feel ganged up on. I mean, this is a lot for anyone to take in."

"It hasn't been that bad and I chose my home turf to be more comfortable," Paige said. "Honestly though, I took one look at that baby blanket Sadie brought over, and that was it. I knew she was someone I wanted to know."

"She's always worn her heart on her sleeve," J.P. said. "To my mind, it's her best trait."

"Are you trying to say Susannah and I don't, J.P.?" Shelby asked, giving him a determined look.

"All of the women in this family have big hearts," he said with a slow smile. "They each have their own unique way of expressing it."

"J.P. appears to be a diplomat," Paige said, smiling.

"He's had to be, having three younger sisters," Sadie told her, feeling her heart glow. "Now he has four."

Paige's eyes grew wider as she took in the fact that she'd been included in that number.

"I hope that's okay to say," she immediately said. "I mean—"

"She knows what you mean, Sadie," J.P. said in that steady tone of his. "It's going to take a while for us to build up our relationships, but from where I'm standing, they look to have a strong foundation."

"I couldn't agree more," Mark said, standing. "Now, why don't we break out something stronger to celebrate? I took the liberty of buying some champagne."

Paige's head swung in his direction. "You did? I didn't see it."

"It's in Riley's fridge," Mark said, ruffling her hair softly. "He's our next-door neighbor and close friend. His daughter Jess is our daughter's best friend."

Sadie was grateful Mark hadn't mentioned anything about her personal connection to Riley. If their second date went well, she'd tell the rest of her siblings about him.

"You know me, honey. I believe in celebrating. I had high hopes for this meeting. Be right back."

Paige watched as Mark left and then turned and looked at all of them. "He brought back a bottle of champagne from his parents' house to open after our first date. With their permission, of course. He said he wanted to celebrate being with the most beautiful woman in the world."

"I love him!" Shelby said. "I can see why you married him young. He's a keeper."

Paige stood slowly, keeping a hold of Sadie's hand. "I'd like you to meet Haley...if that's okay."

Sadie felt a smile spread across her face.

"We'd love that," J.P. said. "My kids are going to want to meet her too, I expect. We'd love to have her over for a play date when you feel comfortable."

"Thank you," Paige said. "I'll let you know. Umm...let me go get her."

As she left the room, Shelby lurched out of her chair and flung her hands into the air. "Oh, she's so wonderful. Thank you, God!"

Then she launched herself at Sadie, hugging the starch out of her.

"You did good, Sadie," J.P. said, rising from the sofa.

When he knelt on the floor and wrapped his arms around them, Shelby pressed her face into his neck. Their family was starting to feel complete. Funny how she hadn't known something was missing before learning about Paige.

"Get in here, Susannah," Shelby drawled.

Soon they were all hugging each other, and Sadie felt her heart explode with joy like the champagne coming their way.

Chapter 8

According to Riley's late-afternoon debrief with the Bradshaws, the sibling reunion had gone swimmingly, and his friends had been delighted to hear he and Sadie were going out again. Sadie was bound to be in a good mood too, and despite the epic thunderstorm that had rolled into Nashville, the violent bolts of lightning and percussive thunder sounding like the very sky was being ripped open against its will by a super-villain, Riley found he was eager to see her.

Jess had screamed at various intervals while insisting he wear the only other sport coat in his closet, a tan one this time. Riley was still tugging on his ear, hoping she hadn't made him deaf for life.

"Dad," Jess said from the doorway as he slapped cologne on his freshly shaven cheeks, "tonight you need to pick up some flowers for Sadie. And this time you'd better kiss her goodnight."

His daughter had strong opinions about courtship, it turned out, most of them springing directly from Disney movies. She'd embarrassed the hell out of him, asking in front of the Bradshaws if he'd kissed Sadie goodnight after their last date. He'd told her a true prince never told, and she'd simply responded, "Well, that's really silly. *Everyone* knows a prince kisses a princess goodnight."

Chastised by a second grader on romance. It had felt like a low moment. Especially since he hadn't had a kiss to speak of.

"Flowers," he simply replied to her latest request. "Check."

"What *kind* of flowers, Dad?" she asked him, edging closer and adjusting his jacket like she was a Parisian fashion designer.

He knew a trick question when he heard one. "What kind of flowers would you recommend, Jess?"

She gave a dramatic sigh, cute as a button in her *Beauty and the Beast* nightgown. He'd already seen to her bath and gotten her in her nightgown. Knowing her, she'd probably have a snack at the Bradshaws' before she went to bed.

"Well...I think you should give her daisies."

He'd been expecting roses. "Daisies?"

"Yes. You see, Flynn Ryder gives Rapunzel daisies for her hair. Sort of. It's not important. Focus, Dad."

How did she know he was starting to sweat?

"I mean, Snow White had roses, but we figured that's an older Disney movie. And Haley's grandpa gives her grandma roses for their anniversary, and they're like really old."

The logic employed by his daughter sometimes mystified him so much he thought NASA should study her brain to predict the future of the human race on Earth.

"Where am I supposed to get daisies, Jess?"

"At the store, Dad," she informed him in her take-no-prisoners tone.

"The grocery store?" he asked, checking his watch. If he left right now...

"Yes, Haley and I checked it out in the grocery store after your first date with Ms. Sadie. They're by the produce aisle."

He shook his head, marveling at their strategy. He hadn't even expected another date with Sadie, and here they'd been preparing for it. "Okay, if I'm going to get flowers for tonight, I need to hustle."

"Cool!" She jumped in the air. "Let's get you on the road."

He scooped her up, making her laugh.

"Oh, you smell so good, Daddy."

He didn't hear that term of endearment often anymore. She was getting older and apparently saying 'Daddy' just wasn't as cool.

"Do you know how much I love you?" he asked, stopping in the hallway.

"So much," she cried, throwing out her hands and grinning.

"You're my whole world," he said, giving her angel kisses with his nose against hers.

"Dad, that's so sweet," she said, "but it's time for you to broaden your world. I won't always be here, and I want you to be happy."

Crap. She was going to make him cry. He'd had that thought as well, but for some reason it struck him differently hearing it from her.

"Oh, Jessiekins, you're growing up way too fast," he whispered, kissing her cheek. "Okay, enough mushy stuff. Let's get you over to Haley's house." When he and his daughter arrived at the Bradshaws' back door, he was running a little late. But he'd just text Sadie. He figured flowers would be a good reason for some slight tardiness.

"Hey, good-looking," Paige said, smiling when she opened the door. "Ready for your date?"

"Yes, he is," Jess said, hugging his leg and then running inside. "Have fun, Dad!"

"Yes, have fun, Riley," Paige said.

"Don't rush home," Mark called, jogging over to the door after closing the dishwasher he was loading. "Jess is staying the night like usual."

"Tell Sadie hi for me," Paige said.

Riley nearly took a step back.

"Is that weird?" she asked. "I'm just so happy things turned out like they did today. They're all so wonderful."

"It's good to see you on cloud nine. I'll tell her you said 'hey.' Okay, I'm outta here. The girls have insisted I pick up some daisies for her."

The grocery store was a zoo and people were cranky from the torrential rain no umbrella in the world could protect you against, but he found the daisies, except they were potted and not wrapped in a bouquet like he'd expected. The mixed bouquets had a couple of daisies, but it didn't seem like enough.

He texted Paige, refraining from asking, *Where are the f-ing daisies?* Instead he said, *Daisies are in a pot. Help.*

She gave him a LOL and a smiley face before typing, *The girls said they imagined you giving her the plant and plucking one of the stems and putting it in her hair.*

Holding the pot in the middle of the crowded produce section, his first thought was, "You've got to be kidding me."

Then he picked it up and headed to the express checkout, texting Paige back a smiley face when he got to the parking lot. Soaked, of course.

When he pulled up in front of Sadie's townhouse, he took a moment to smooth back his wet hair in the mirror. The rain was going to make it curl up like the Oxford comma, no doubt. Sometimes he hated the humidity of Nashville. But it was home. His parents might have moved to Florida, and his ex might have made him hate the country music scene, but there was still something about the town he loved. The artiness. The creativity that seemed to blow through the air.

But rain should be outlawed on dates, he decided as his umbrella blew upward off its spikes the minute he emerged from the car. Here he was trying to make a good impression, and Mother Nature was messing with him. He fought a growl, focusing on holding the broken umbrella and the pot of daisies.

Then he heard someone call his name through the storm, and he looked up and caught her curvy silhouette outlined in the doorway. *Oh, the lines...* The daises almost slipped out of his hands. He ran toward her, stopping short on her blue and white Welcome mat to dry his feet.

By God, she was a vision.

Her dress was one of those little black varieties men lit candles to in pure male gratitude. It ended a respectful inch above her knees, but he found himself thinking about the mist from the rain landing on them and how he wished he could turn himself into that mist like a shape shifter.

"It's raining cats and dogs outside," she said. "Come in. You're soaked."

He held out his umbrella. "The storm broke it," he responded like a total moron.

Then she gave him a soft, luminous smile, and he accepted he was going to be a moron for the rest of the night.

"You're so beautiful," he said, feeling like he was in a trance.

She took the broken umbrella from his outstretched hand and laid it on the floor outside her front door. "Come inside, Riley."

He followed her in, her perfume wrapping around him like the fog rising from the sidewalk outside her porch. Where had the fog come from?

"Are these for me?" she asked, gesturing to the pot of pink daisies in his hand.

His movements felt like he was underwater. He slowly snapped a stem from out of the pot and tucked it behind her right ear.

Even over the thunder of the rain, he could hear her sharp intake of breath. The girls hadn't steered him wrong. Sadie was feeling what he was feeling all right.

"I couldn't find an iguana at the grocery store, so these will have to do."

She surprised him by punching him playfully. "These are better. Do you need a towel?"

He lifted a shoulder. "No, I wear rain all the time. I've found it makes my complexion better. Don't you?" *What in the hell was he saying?*

Then she started laughing, and he felt himself return his body. Was his attraction to her making him levitate or something?

"Riley, you're too funny." She picked up her purse, and he noted it was gold. "Shall we go?"

He nodded and couldn't help but notice what an incredible ass she had when she bent down to pick up a perfectly dry golf umbrella resting in the corner. After they exited her house, he unfurled the umbrella to shield them from the rain as she locked the door.

"Care to share where we're going?" she asked when they were inside the car.

The rain sounded like a million nails raining down, and he felt time slow again. Outside, there was no world. In this moment, there was only him and Sadie, with her perfume curling around him like the fog had, albeit even more inviting.

"I gave some serious thought to this after the first-date mess up," he admitted. "How do you feel about pimento cheese beignets and pork belly pop tarts?"

She made a sexy humming sound. Oh, his brain was going to turn to mush tonight.

"Sounds delicious."

He started the car and took off, the windshield wipers on high. Even still, he drove slowly, both for safety and because he wasn't so sure he wanted this moment to end.

"Good. I thought we'd go with a normal restaurant like The Farm House. Sounds pretty wholesome, right?"

There was a pause, and he reached for the radio.

"Do you think we need to do wholesome because of me? Riley, I'm no farm girl."

The rain was coming down in sheets, and this was clearly an important issue for her. He pulled over to the shoulder so they could talk and give the weather some time to settle. "I figure we worked our way through some of my hang-ups this morning. Do you want to let me know why this bothers you?"

"I don't mean to make a big deal of it, but we went from a burlesque venue to a farm restaurant. It's like we swung in the opposite direction. Do you see what I mean?"

"Not really," he answered. "Sadie, it's a farm-to-table restaurant. I loved the story I read online about one of their farmers bringing in fresh trout. They used his name and everything. For me, it was like they were honoring the man's art. Trust me, if you've ever gone fishing—my dad used to drag my brother and me out—you'd know there's a lot more art than science to catching a fish. And the food and venue look great...but that doesn't seem to be what's upsetting you."

When she didn't say anything, he turned in his seat. She was looking straight ahead with her hands fisted in her lap.

"Sadie, talk to me."

"Some people think...I'm a goody two-shoes because I'm a preacher's daughter, and they have this idea in their mind of the kind of woman I'm supposed to be."

Suddenly it all clicked. "Ah...so you thought I'd reverted to seeing a cardboard cutout of you and not the real you."

"Yes," she said quietly.

Then she looked up and met his gaze, and her brown eyes looked so vulnerable he wanted to reach across the center console and hold her. Funny how he'd been told he was too "out there" while she'd been penned in for being the daughter of a preacher.

"Sadie, I might not know you well, but I still *see* you. It's the artist in me. When I look at something, I can't help but see. You're radiant when you talk about quilting, and when you showed up on Paige's doorstep, you were brave and sweet and kind and so beautiful you took my breath away."

Her chest rose with a deep breath, and he pressed on, "I want to know you if you're willing to share more of yourself with me. I promise to be honest with you about who I am too, although it might take me some time to share some of the tougher stories, ones about Jess' mom. I don't just want to have fun with you, Sadie McGuiness. I want to know you. All of you. Okay?"

"Okay," she whispered. "Then I guess The Farm House sounds great."

He fought a smile, wanting to be sensitive. "Hopefully it won't have floated away in this storm. I mean, I won't eat soggy beignets or pop tarts. I have my standards."

Her mouth curved. "I'm glad you have such exacting standards. We should get a move on then."

And so they did. The meal was excellent, and they both relaxed with each other this time. Riley was delighted to learn that besides their different taste in music and his stance on church-going, they had a lot in common. She loved Andy Warhol, which surprised him, but the more she talked about it, the better he understood her. Sadie admired artists who depicted essential truths about their subjects in their work.

Her love of family was like a hot toddy to him. She told him stories about growing up with the best brother in the world looking out for her and the adventures she'd had with her sister Shelby, who'd always urged her to spread her wings—and sometimes talked her into trouble.

She thought everyone was too busy, running around like chickens with their heads cut off, which was why she didn't spend much time on social media and didn't pick up her phone during dinnertime. When he'd explained he felt the same, but had to check his phone now and then to make sure everything was okay with Jess, she waved a hand and said, "That's as it should be."

He ordered coffee and dessert even though he was crazy full just to spend more time with her. The gold in her brown eyes was shining brighter than ever, and her laugh caught him in the heart every time. When he coaxed her into trying the white chocolate bread pudding, the humming sound she made had him shifting in his chair.

"I think we need to go soon," she said, eyeing the empty restaurant. "We've closed the place down."

And yet he didn't want to leave. He wanted time to slow like it had earlier so they could stay there forever. "Yes, but I'm not ready for tonight to end. Would you like to take a walk with me?"

She blinked. "In this storm?"

Rain wasn't going to send him home tonight. "You have a pretty big umbrella. Besides, it doesn't look like it's raining hard anymore."

"I'd love to," she said softly.

After taking care of the bill, they left the restaurant to discover the storm had faded.

"There's something special about the world after the rain," he commented as they walked to the car.

"It's like everything has been washed clean," she said, putting words to his thought.

Looking at her under the streetlight, he gave in to the temptation he'd been fighting all night and touched her cheek. "You're so beautiful."

Her body was close to his under the umbrella, something they really didn't need anymore. But it kept her close, and he liked that. Wanted that.

"Come on, I have the perfect place in mind."

He drove her to the riverfront and then navigated them down to the spot that had come to mind during dinner. "There's a lot of art to love in Nashville," he told her, "but The Ghost Ballet sculpture is one of my favorites."

The giant curving metal seemed to reach for the sky without ever quite reaching it.

Sadie studied it next to him. "From the name, I expect it's supposed to have something to do with ballet and movement, but to me it's like a dream."

He turned toward her. "Tell me more."

"Sometimes the parts of a dream never quite meet, and that's how I see those metal staircases. It's like they can't connect."

"Maybe they're already connected," he said, pointing to the base of the sculpture and the metal pins anchored into the two pieces. "It's like each part needs to be free to move in its own way even though they're together."

He wondered if that might be how they were if they continued to see each other.

"I like that," Sadie said, craning her neck to look up at the piece.

Her hand brushed his, and he took that as a sign to take it. "Sadie, I'd..."

She angled her body to face him. "Yes?"

She was going to make him ask. "I'd like to kiss you."

"Go ahead," she said, her voice the definition of invitation.

When his lips finally settled over hers, her mouth opened slightly, and he felt the world tilt like the sculpture before them. He closed his eyes, awash in the sensation of his mouth moving over hers. There was no sound but their commingled breath, and somehow that drove him wild. When he kissed the side of her mouth and leaned back to look into her eyes, she followed him. He gave her another slow kiss before breaking away again.

"Wow," he said softly. "You give new meaning to one of my favorite songs, 'Lips Like Sugar.' I'm going to want to do that again."

"I'm going to want you to do that again too," she confessed.

Oh, her voice…so lush and inviting in the dark night.

"Glad to know we're on the same page finally."

And with that, he kissed her for what seemed like an eternity in the new time they seemed to create together.

Chapter 9

Staying out with Riley until almost four in the morning on their second date hadn't seemed so late until she'd looked at an actual clock. And over the course of the next couple weeks, they continued to close down restaurants and stay out late.

Then there was the texting... She'd never imagined texting a man could be so fun. Or so hot. Not that it was sexting or anything even close. That wasn't her. This was classic flirting, and it was magnetic and fun and it fired her up. The texting would start after he put Jess to bed at around eight. She was usually quilting around that time, but she'd set her materials down as soon as her text alert went off. They'd carry on texting back and forth for the next hour or so.

She liked the way he expressed himself, everything from the words and colloquial phrases he used to the emoticons he chose. He'd texted her a camel—a symbol of endurance, or so he said—to make her laugh after a particularly strenuous day at work, and once he'd insisted they carry on a whole conversation in emoticons to see which of them would crack first. Some experts said the biggest sex organ was the brain, and for Sadie, that certainly seemed to fit the bill. Riley made her think about things differently, see them differently, and she liked that.

One night, after warning her that he was about to say something corny, he told her that she seemed to stop time for him. She'd immediately understood. He did the same for her.

And he didn't just take her to the typical dinner and a movie type dates. He took her to see sculptures and art galleries and street art like the Wings mural in the Gulch, which had inspired her to add angel wings to her baby quilts, while she showed him a few magical coffee shops she'd discovered who featured local artists. Their taste in music might be different, but there were so many new places for them to explore together, even in a place called Music City.

When he arrived to pick her up for their date on a Friday evening, a month and worlds away from their first date, she noted his new sport coat with a smile. He'd confessed Jess insisted on dressing him for their dates, and she thought that was adorable. Having grown up without a father, she treasured the way he loved his daughter and she looked forward to the stories he told her about their adventures together.

"I like the green," she said, fingering the sport coat. "It's a good color on you."

"I like the gold dress," he said. "Honestly, it's like I've hit a wall and I just can't go on until I've kissed you. Like right now."

She laughed as he closed her front door and fitted her body against his. "Aren't you impetuous?"

"Starved is more like it," he murmured against her lips. "God, Sadie, you drive me wild, what with the browns and golds and... You're a goddess made flesh, and I want to devour you sometimes."

She knew that and was trying to balance things physical between them. They'd done some serious kissing and caressing, but nothing more, and while she was itchy, she was struggling with the "more" parts. She might want him, but she didn't feel ready for the next step. He seemed to know that.

She felt his chest rise. "Then kiss me," she fired back.

He pressed his mouth to hers without any more discussion. The kiss was hot and luscious, and she felt as swept away as driftwood down a river.

"Oh, Riley," she whispered, breaking their connection. Maybe he was starving, but her body heat had surely topped out the Fahrenheit scale.

"I can't get enough of you," he said, running his hands down her curves, ones she'd never truly celebrated before meeting him. "I've been thinking about this all day."

"I know," she said, "but this is really fast for me." She looked straight into his eyes. Maybe it was time to stop dancing around it.

Those cerulean blue eyes were feverish, like she imagined hers were, but also a little tight at the corners.

"I did the fast thing with Jess' mom, and it was a disaster. We're in no hurry."

He still hadn't told her the full story about Mandy, his ex, but she knew he would when he was ready.

"I don't want to make the same mistake with you," he said. He stepped back from her, but took her hand and brought it to his lips, kissing it softly. "Apparently, some of Jess's movie-watching habits are rubbing off on me."

"I like old romance," she said, touching his cheek.

"I know," he said, kissing her hand again. "Why do you think I do it?"

Her whole body seemed to sigh, and as he went to release her hand, she moved in and wrapped her arms around him. The embrace was more of a thank-you, and he stroked her back in response like he understood.

"Riley, I've dated off and on over the years, but I've

only *been with* one other guy, and that was after two years of serious dating. We both thought we'd end up getting married."

Now she wondered how she ever could have thought of marrying Kevin. They'd both been so young and so eager. All she'd focused on was him being a "good Christian man." For her, that had meant he went to church, prayed with her, helped old ladies across the street, and didn't kick dogs. Okay, the last part was a joke, but it was also kind of true. Their connection hadn't gone much deeper than companionship, mutual kindness, and a connection to the church. They had never pushed each other. He'd thought her quilting was a hobby and hadn't really understood the driving passion behind it, one that had led her to happily spend hours alone—without him.

"Keep talking," he said, stroking her hair.

"It's just…I don't think I could be intimate with someone I wasn't involved with…ah…long term." She looked up at him. "But you tempt me to test that theory."

"I understand," he said instead. "I'm not a player, Sadie, but I can't hide that I want you like crazy. We'll just take it slow. Okay?"

A smile tugged at her mouth. Some men might try and make her feel guilty. She'd known he wasn't one of those.

"I want you to feel comfortable with me, Sadie. Safe."

"You really are one of the good guys," she said. "I knew that the first time I met you. In spite of your interest in iguanas."

"I can't believe you told me to stop texting you the lizard emoji," he said. "That seemed like a violation of my First Amendment rights."

She snorted. "Call a lawyer."

He slapped his forehead and released her. "That's brilliant. That's exactly what I need. Wait. I need to write this down. My female superhero still isn't right, but this…"

She only smiled. She was used to this by now—him

pulling out his phone in a fit of excitement, writing down notes for his comic strip. He was inspiring her as much as she was inspiring him.

"Yes, that works," he muttered, totally focused on his phone.

She loved to watch him when he was awash in the grip of a creative vision. Time seemed to slow again, and she suddenly wanted him to be by her side for...

Well, forever, she realized. She could see it. Her hand settled over her heart. *Too fast, Sadie? Yeah, now you know why.* She could see him as a lifelong partner.

"Thank you for that," he said, pocketing his phone and kissing the corner of her mouth. "You inspire me like none other."

"I feel the same way." She wrapped her arms around him. "It makes me a little scared," she admitted.

"Of what?" he asked.

"Of how much I already feel for you." She paused, looking into his eyes. "You make me feel like my life is so much bigger than I ever realized. Like there are more textures and colors than I ever imagined possible."

He took a breath before saying, "I feel the same way. Jess made me feel that way too...when she was born. With you, it's a little different, but in some ways it's the same. You know?"

She thought she did. "Yes."

"To exploring more textures and colors," Riley said.

And as he leaned in to kiss Sadie, she knew there would come a time very soon when she would want them to explore each other in a new way.

Chapter 10

Sunday mornings were usually quiet around the Thomson house. Riley and Mark didn't go for a run. Sometimes the Bradshaws were at church, leaving Jess a little rambunctious without her usual partner in crime.

This morning was a bit too quiet though as he set aside his new sketches for his superhero on the kitchen table next to his steaming cup of coffee. Sadie had sparked another idea for him the other night, and he'd decided his superhero's love interest would be a male lawyer. He liked the idea of the two of them helping people find justice, working together but separately like the stairways in the sculpture he'd brought Sadie to see. He'd shared his early thoughts with his brother, his brainstorming partner since childhood, and Tyler had been excited about it too.

Sadie had unlocked something else for him. He couldn't stop thinking about the whole "time stopping" thing he felt whenever they were together. He wanted his superhero's special skills to be related to time, but he wasn't sure what form that would take yet. Well, he'd figure it out. Of course, he couldn't ignore that his superhero was starting to resemble Sadie. The same brown-gold eyes, the same angle to her chin... Man, he was falling for her. Like off-the-tallest-building falling. It was probably a good thing they were taking things slow. If and when they made love, he was sure it was going to be powerful.

As Riley wandered through the house, he wondered where in the heck his daughter had gone. He called her name again, but it went unanswered. Not normal.

They'd just finished breakfast and laughed over his superhero-shaped buttermilk pancakes. Then he'd gotten to drawing and lost track of time. *Time again*, he thought. *What a powerful concept.*

When he reached the doorway of his office, a hurried scraping sounded before everything went still. He cocked his ear.

"Jess?"

He walked into the room and paused. He strained to hear, and that's when he caught the faint sound of breathing. *What in the hell?*

Rounding his desk, he stopped short. His daughter was pressed against his desk on the floor in her nightgown.

"Why are you hiding, young lady?" *And in my office,* he wanted to add.

"I'm...not hiding," she said, arranging her nightgown so Rapunzel from *Tangled* wasn't marred by wrinkles. His kid hated wrinkles.

"Then what are you doing in here? Jess, I called your name a couple of times and you didn't answer."

"I was...ah...trying to help you with your new superhero," she finished, putting a finger to her face like she was making this up on the spot.

He crouched down onto one knee. "Funny, I was just working on this downstairs. Tell me more." She'd already told him how much she loved the gold he was using in the superhero's outfit. *Thank you, Sadie.*

Her lips moved back and forth, her mind clearly preparing to serve up the biggest fib on the planet. Jess was often imaginative, but this felt different somehow.

"Well, Dad, your super woman is going to need a few more powers if she's going to...break into houses and find evidence, right?"

"Keep going."

"I thought one of her powers might be that she could muffle sound," she said, her green eyes brightening like a light bulb had turned on behind them. "That way no one can hear her."

He stroked his chin. It wasn't a bad idea. "How would she do that?"

"Well...she could put a force field around herself," Jess said, smoothing her nightgown out over her little legs. "That way the sound is contained. Like she's in her own bubble and nothing can get in or out."

For a moment he simply stared at his daughter. *Is that what you do, baby?* Sometimes it seemed like she was always on, but there were other times when she was downright contained. She'd sit in the corner of the couch with her legs tucked under her, a couple of comic books or coloring books at her side, and just stay that way for hours. It made him nervous when she got quiet like that.

"That's a great idea, Jess," he said, reaching to pluck her up.

She scooted back and stood her ground in front of him. "I'm going to get dressed."

He watched as she ran out of the room. Something was wrong. She never stepped away from him. Scanning the space where she'd been hiding, he looked for clues. When he noticed the bottom drawer of his desk wasn't completely flush against the main desk, his heart clutched in his chest.

No, she couldn't have.

Opening the drawer was like opening a ticking bomb, but he did it. He had to know if anything was out of place. Sure enough, the one picture of Mandy he'd kept was lying at an odd angle, not straight like he'd placed it. He'd burned plenty of them in a fit of anger, but this one... this one captured the woman he'd fallen in love with his first year out of college. He'd been excited about having a "real" job as a comic book artist, and Mandy had been equally filled with passion for music. They'd loved bandying song ideas and lyrics back and forth, and she'd made him laugh by improvising lines while playing her guitar. Occasionally, he'd return to his desk to find she'd written fake dialogue for one of his comic book panels, and the two of them would bust up laughing. He picked up the framed picture, studying that woman. How had he not recognized it when the partying and recreational drug use they'd indulged in over the next two years of their relationship had led her down a dark path of chemical abuse? If only he'd seen it early enough to put a stop to it...

But then there would be no Jess, and she was everything.

He fell onto his butt and had the odd compulsion to cry. His baby girl had snuck into his office and somehow found the picture he'd kept of Mandy, the one he'd hoped to share with her when she was older, old enough to better understand why her mother wasn't in her life. He'd shown it to her when she'd asked upon entering kindergarten, when it had become more confusing why everyone else had a mom and not her, but he hadn't kept the photo out. The experts had said it was a fine balance, keeping the reality around without encouraging hope the missing parent would return.

Anxiety squeezed his diaphragm. How had she found the photo in there? Jess knew his office was off limits. Worse, why was she sneaking around and lying to him about looking at a picture of her mother?

Man oh man, he needed to talk to Mark. His friend was the one who'd helped him figure out what to tell Jess about her mother—truthful and kind but short on details.

Bottom line: how could he tell his daughter her mother hadn't wanted her? That she'd tried to OD on oxycodone upon learning she'd gotten pregnant despite using birth control. He'd begged her to have the baby, and when begging hadn't worked, he'd told her he would pay her for the time. She'd insisted on having an abortion, but he'd upped the ante by taking out a loan, and like a surrogate, she'd had the baby and left without once holding her daughter.

Left as if their time together had meant nothing, and the child they'd made together meant even less.

If someone had told him that as an adult, it would have cut him to pieces. How was a little kid supposed to handle that news? She wasn't. He wanted to wait until she was in junior high or high school. Then he could sit her down and they could discuss the whole thing in a truthful yet kind way.

In the meantime, he was doing the best he could to love her and be everything she needed in a parent. But today...

Today he would grieve for his daughter.

Shaking himself, he rose and left the office to find his daughter. She was in her room, fingering her collection of bows and barrettes.

"You're dressed!" he said, forcing a smile. "What's the hair accessory of choice today?"

When she didn't say anything in response, only extended a yellow bow, he had to force back tears. She was hurting, and he didn't know what to do about it.

"Can I put it in your hair?" he asked, crouching down next to her. "I know I don't do it as good as you do, but—"

"Okay," she whispered, ducking her chin.

He picked up her brush and was trying to get a hold of himself when she edged back and settled against him in that perfect gesture of trust, something he never failed to be grateful for. This little person trusted him. She knew he would slay any dragon for her. She knew he would help her climb to great heights and make sure she didn't fall.

Trust.

It was a superpower second only to love if you asked him.

He began to brush her hair softly. The fine, curly brown hair was so much like his, but her eyes were all Mandy. He didn't reach for the bow she held, focusing on showing his love for his little girl by brushing her hair.

"Daddy?" she whispered softly, letting the hand holding the bow fall to her side.

"Yes, honey," he said, his heart filled with both love and hurt.

"I love you," she said in that same soft voice. "Thanks for being my dad."

He had to swallow the lump in his throat. What had brought his on? "Thanks for being my daughter. We do a pretty good job, don't we? Me being your dad and you being my kid. I mean, it's like a special bond between Batman and Robin or something."

"Or Elsa and Anna," she said, a half smile on her face.

Like most parents who had watched *Frozen* or sung "Let It Go" a thousand times with their kids, he had the odd urge to stab himself with a fork. Man, he was so glad that craze had (mostly) passed. He'd gotten really good at the troll voices though.

"I thought you and Haley were like Elsa and Anna," he said, running his hand over her hair.

She lifted her shoulder and handed him the bow. He did his best to position it evenly on her crown like she liked. When he was finished, she turned and threw her arms around him. He rocked her, trying to assure her everything was okay.

"How about we go to the park today?" he asked. "I don't know what the Bradshaws have planned, but maybe we can take Haley with us. What do you think?"

"Can Sadie come with us?" Jess asked.

He lost his balance at that and ended up falling on his butt, Jess cushioned in his arms. "Ah...I think she has plans. I mean...on Sundays she goes to church and then has dinner with her family."

"Dad, why don't we go to church?" she asked, looking him straight in the eye.

Had there been some meteor shower directed at parents today? "Well, not everyone goes to church, and we don't because... I feel it's more important to decide what's right on your own rather than to have someone else tell you what is. It's called being spiritual."

"Is that what we are?" she asked. "Because I need to tell some of the other kids at school. They keep asking, and I know we're not Baptist or Methodist or Church of Christ."

"Exactly!" he exclaimed, grabbing onto that thread. "You see, everyone believes in their own way. It's like seeing life through...ah...their own superhero goggles."

"You mean like Batman seeing in the dark?" she asked.

Crap, how had this turned into an existential discussion about superheroes? "Sorta. You see, Batman believes he can only do good when it's dark whereas Superman believes he can do it any time." That was simplistic, but it worked.

"But they both have to keep their identities secret," she added, fully versed in all things superhero thanks to him.

"Yes," he said, "but you see, what they're trying to learn is that they can do good things anytime, even as Bruce Wayne or Clark Kent. They don't need a mask or a false identity. They don't even need to use their superpowers."

"Because you don't have to have superpowers to do good things," Jess said, smiling a little now. "Everyone can do something good if they decide to. Like Han Solo."

Oh, Lord, they were moving from superheroes to *Star Wars*. Someday, some guy was going to thank him. "Exactly."

"Princess Leia could have been a Disney princess," Jess said, moving her hands to readjust her bow.

Riley refrained from going into all the reasons why Princess Leia really was a Disney princess since George Lucas had sold the franchise to that company.

"She certainly is brave," Riley said.

"Yes, and all princesses are brave," his daughter informed him. "Daddy, let me up. I need to see if my bow is straight."

She looked in the mirror and cocked her head. He held his breath. Getting her bow straight was up there with tying her shoelaces evenly.

"Okay, we're good," she said. "Dad, do you know how happy Mrs. Bradshaw is to have her brothers and sisters in her life? She talks about how happy she is all the time and how she never imagined them ever being this nice. It's really great to see her that way. Haley is so happy too. I mean, she's got all these aunts and uncles now."

Dread was rolling through his belly. "Mrs. Bradshaw deserves to be happy."

"Haley even has cousins! Did you know that, Dad? One is in kindergarten and another might be our age. Mrs. Bradshaw said they've finally invited Haley over for a play date. Isn't that great, Dad?"

"It's great," he replied, trying to decide whether he should say anything more—like *Paige is really lucky because her mother was even more of a bitch than yours*.

He really needed to talk to Mark. There was something stirring here.

"Dad, I know you said Sadie had plans, but maybe she can come over for dinner tonight?" She turned around and hugged him. "It would be so much fun!"

"It's a school night," he told her. "And please call her Ms. Sadie."

Was it too early to have her hang out with him and his daughter? The way he was feeling about her... He probably needed to talk to Mark about that too. He was going to owe him a case of beer for all the psych support.

"I'll go to bed on time, Dad, I promise," she said, gripping his T-shirt to get his attention.

"Honey, Sadie has plans all day. She'll be tired. Let's shoot for another time, okay? I mean...I'm just getting to know her."

"Well, I want to get to know her too," Jess said, her lip firming up. "Haley really likes her and so does—"

"This is how dating works, Jess," he told her. "I get to know her first, and if I decide that I like her enough, I'll introduce her to you."

"But I've already met her, Dad!" Jess said. "And she's Haley's aunt."

His stomach felt like it had a rock in it. "The Bradshaws are just getting to know Sadie and her family. Didn't they just have another sibling outing for coffee last week? They need to take things slow—like I do with Sadie."

"But when you know someone is good and special, you don't take things slow," Jess said. "You just know."

What Disney movie did she pick that up from?

"This isn't a fairy tale, Jess," he said, kicking himself. He was about to tell her this was real life and some people sucked so you had to be careful out there. He'd promised himself he wasn't going to say things like that. He liked to encourage her imagination, her belief in magic.

"Fine."

"I'm sorry I said that." He lifted her chin when she looked down at her feet. "I just want you to understand that it takes time to get to know people sometimes. Like in dating. That's all."

"But I can't get to know Sadie if I don't spend time

with her," Jess said.

"Ms. Sadie." He was going to be disarmed by a kid's logic. "I know it seems a little unfair, what with Mrs. Bradshaw and me getting to know Sadie better right off the mark. But you need to trust me on this. I want to make sure—"

"That she's going to be around for a while," Jess said in an aggrieved voice. "I know how it works, Dad."

"Oh, you do, do you?"

"Yes, other kids at school talk about it. You date a woman to see if you want her to be your girlfriend, and when you do, then I get to meet her. But I'm just saying that we don't have to wait that long because she's Haley's aunt. I mean, even if she doesn't last as your girlfriend, I'll still know her because of Haley. I mean, Dad. You know she's my BFF."

The awkwardness was amping up, and soon it would be on par with things like the chicken pox or measles. "I don't want you to get hurt, Jess, if Sadie and I end up not..." He trailed off, not knowing how to phrase it.

She socked him in the chest. "I'm tougher than I look, Dad. It's not like I'm starting to wish she might become my mother someday. I mean, I already have one of those."

That made his head reel. "Jess—"

"Dad, you are making this *way* too complicated. I'm going to go play princess in my castle."

He sat back on his heels as she left the room.

Chapter 11

Teaching people about quilting had been a learn-as-you-go process for Sadie.

In the beginning, she'd focused too much on techniques and mastery. She'd quickly learned it was the fastest way for people to lose their enthusiasm. Their whole bodies would lock up from stress and frustration. She'd taken an entire Saturday over a year ago to reflect on what she'd first loved about quilting. For her it had been the colors of the fabric and the piecing of the squares into some form of a pattern. *Her* pattern...

That had cinched her beginners' curriculum, and it had been more successful. Students' enthusiasm stayed high once they got over their fear about creating their own patterns. To help make it easier, she'd made the precut squares of fun fabric colors and patterns. The students found it easier to tackle using the rotary cutter and a cutting mat once they had some confidence and a feel for how a quilt came together.

Any kind of knowledge came piece by piece, she'd found, just like the process of making a quilt.

As she looked up from her current baby quilt to see Paige walking into Oodles of Spools with a bright smile on her face, she couldn't help but grin in return. Putting aside her project, she gave a knowing wink to Ada, who was unwrapping the cookies she'd brought, and went to her sister.

"Hi, there," she said, pulling her into a hug.

"Hey." Paige squeezed her tightly in return. "I have to tell you. I pretty much floated on a cloud after our last outing."

Sadie and her siblings felt the same way. J.P. had spoken to their mother privately, and it had gone well. She'd told him she was happy for them, that she wasn't surprised they'd sought Paige out.

"That sounds like how we felt," Sadie said. "A few people are eager to invite you over to meet the rest of the group and your niece and nephew now that we're more... comfortable with each other. You think about it and let us know. There's no rush. If you'd like to have another smaller group meeting, we can arrange for you to meet J.P.'s family on your own with Haley. We don't want to overwhelm you."

Paige waved to Whitney as she came in, and Sadie did the same.

"I finally have ultrasound pictures," the woman said, holding them up and bouncing in place. "We're having a girl! We found out today! Thank God. I wanted to kill them when they moved my appointment."

Everyone cheered, and the photos were passed around the room.

"We didn't have this kind of technology in my day," Mae said, lowering her glasses a touch on her nose. "For nine months, you wondered whether your baby was a boy or a girl. That was some nice dreaming."

"But hard on the clothes-making or buying," Leanne commented. "And picking out a paint scheme for the nursery."

"I smoked my way through three pregnancies," Ada said with a dark laugh, "and they all turned out healthy as horses. Now everyone watches what a woman does during her pregnancy. It's like someone dosed the women and their babies with a fragile pill or something. I feel for the younger generations. They're more scared than I was."

Whitney blinked for a moment and then laughed. "They really do put the fear of God in you. I've even tried tempering my sneezes. It's like I'm afraid the baby will fall out or something."

"They can't fall out," Leanne said. "God made a good plug to keep everything in."

"Leanne!" Mae chided.

"Well, it's true," the woman said. "I mean, your water isn't going to break until it's good and ready to. Mind me on this one. And you aren't going to really dilate until that baby is ready to pop."

Mae touched Leanne on the arm and gave her a pointed look.

"All I'm saying, Whitney," the woman continued, "is that you have nothing to worry about. I hate how much young people seem to worry these days."

Sadie had heard this proclamation before, so she took Paige's hand and led her to the circle. "Congratulations, Whitney! We're all so happy for you."

"Yes, we are," Paige added softly. "Congratulations."

"Are you going to change anything for your baby quilt now that you know it's a girl?" Sadie asked.

Whitney shook her head. "No, I thought about it for a sec, but I still like my original idea and I think my skills are strong enough to pull it off. There's going to be a highway of gold squares, flanked by the soft green ones on either side. It represents our baby having a golden path for life. Sadie helped me design it once I told her what we wanted to convey."

"I just tried to pick out squares that I liked, ones that seemed to match," Paige said. "And then I got nervous and felt like I needed to watch y'all the past couple weeks, but I think I'm ready to show you what I have."

"That's what you're supposed to do, Paige," Ada said. "Sadie is giving you access to your own charm pack, so to speak. She's letting you pick out what you like and then she'll help you put it together in a design that works for you."

"A charm pack?" Paige asked.

"Think of it like one of those pre-packaged meals you can buy where all the ingredients arrive. You only need to follow the instructions."

"Ah…" Paige said, her brow wrinkling.

"Sadie, you take Paige on back and see what she has, and I'll work with Whitney if she has any questions," Ada said.

It was a relief to have long-time quilters like Ada and Mae in the class. Beginners came and went, she'd found, but a few of the more experienced ladies had become anchors even though they still paid the class fee like everyone else. Plus, her quilters had formed a kind of community, something she hadn't envisioned at first. Quilting circles were becoming increasingly rare, she'd discovered. Sadie liked to think she was preserving her own form of that treasured tradition. Not that she was going to ask Paige to pay the class fee. After all, Sadie had invited her.

Just today Karen had suggested Sadie start a day quilting class, thinking there might be some stay-at-home moms or retired women who would prefer an earlier start time. Karen's two knitting classes, both held during the day, had waiting lists now. She'd thought about adding another class, but fabric cost more than yarn. Another quilting class would bring in more money beyond the class tuition. Sadie didn't see a downside.

"Everyone sure they're okay?" Sadie asked, looking around at the group.

They all nodded, so she took Paige to the table and asked her to bring out the squares. Her sister now had a workbag, a navy one with the phrase "Art Is Love" emblazoned on one side.

"I think I'm finally happy with a pattern," Paige told her. "Haley helped with the squares. Of course, she still wants a quilt for herself, but I told her this first one is for a little baby in the hospital who needs it more. Plus, she has your quilt, which she loves. She sleeps with it almost every night."

"Oh, that's so sweet," Sadie said. "I'm glad she loves it. We'll have to come up with a special princess design for her once you're more comfortable."

Of course, she had ideas, not only for Haley but for Jess too. Even though she hadn't spent much time with the little girl, she felt like she knew her through Riley. Maybe he needed a quilt too. Would that be weird? She'd never even seen his bedroom. Oh, goodness, talk about putting the cart before the horse. This was so not the slow program they'd agreed to.

"That will be fun," Paige said. "Mark said he'd never imagined anyone would get so nervous over a few squares of cloth. I told him to butt out."

Sadie couldn't help laughing. "Okay, show me. I'm dying to see."

Paige laid out the squares she'd chosen. Her sister had gone mostly with shades of dark blue with a couple patterned squares resembling the night sky for the top part. In the topmost left corner, the first square she'd selected depicted a happy-faced crescent moon. Midway through the pattern, her squares turned into shades of yellows and gold, ending with the square depicting a happy sun grinning from ear to ear in the bottom right corner.

"Oh, Paige!" Sadie exclaimed, putting her hand to her heart. "This is stunning."

"You think?" her sister asked, straightening one of

the squares to form a perfect line with the others. "Haley was emphatic about the night turning into day, and that seemed to fit my theme. No matter what time of day, a baby should always feel safe. Be safe. Especially at night."

Sadie wondered how many nights Paige hadn't felt safe. Her heart ached when she thought about it. Even though their daddy had abandoned her, she didn't remember feeling unsafe with the rest of her family around her.

"Haley was fearless with the squares, moving them around and around. I re-ironed all of them. Don't worry. I brought the ones I didn't pick in a separate container."

"Sounds like Haley is a good partner in crime," Sadie said. "You're lucky. None of my sisters ever wanted to play with the squares with me. But that was all right because I kinda liked doing it all by myself. I mean, as the youngest, I felt like I was following in everyone's shoes in school, but quilting was always my thing."

"Of course, Haley asked if you have a quilting class for kids, but I told her she could just help me. I'm really excited about it actually. I can see it better in my mind, kinda like when I design a website. You have to choose a theme that fits the information you want to convey, and then find a clean and crisp way to share it."

"Look at you! You've found your groove."

"And it's precious…finding something special to do with your daughter. My mom and I never…"

She trailed off, and Sadie put an arm around her. "Well, you have me and Haley, and any time you want to come over to my place and quilt, you let me know. We… ah…don't have to stick only to class."

Paige's watery smile gave Sadie the courage to be fully vulnerable.

"I really love spending time with you, Paige. Getting to know you better is…well, it's one of the greatest blessings ever."

"I feel that way too," she said, dabbing at her eyes.

"About all of y'all."

"Are you two crying again?" Leanne asked.

She and Paige looked at the doorway. Leanne wasn't alone. Imogene stood next to her, crunching on a chocolate chip cookie.

"Oh, you have your pattern," Imogene said. "Goodness, that's wonderful. Everyone! Come see Paige's design."

The whole class bustled into the workroom, exclaiming their delight.

"You could add a ruffle around it to give it a little more whimsy," Leanne suggested.

"Or a strip border," Ada added, fingering the squares. "Way to go, honey. The baby who receives this quilt is going to treasure it as they grow up."

"Nothing says love like a quilt," Mae said. "It's beautiful, Paige."

Sadie studied the pattern, feeling an idea niggle at the edge of her brain. Then she envisioned the fabric she needed to make it happen. "Oh, I have an idea! Give me a second." She darted out into the main part of the store and zipped through a couple of aisles until she found the fabric she wanted. She picked it up and brought it back to the women, laying it beside Paige's pattern on the worktable.

"How about a border with this fabric?" she asked Paige. "I think it will add to the feeling of safety you want to convey. This fabric looks like starlight, so it's rather like saying the heavens are watching over this new baby."

Paige got choked up, and oddly so did Sadie and the rest of the women. Even Leanne gave an audible sniff.

"Didn't I tell you Sadie has some great ideas?" Mae said, patting Paige on the back gently. "Oh, honey, what an incredible first quilt. You're a natural."

"I haven't done any sewing yet and it's my fourth class," Paige said with a laugh.

"Goodness, you should have seen my first quilt," Ada said, wiping her nose with her sleeve. "It was a strip quilt and probably one of the ugliest things this side of the grave. But I loved that quilt. Made my daddy take a picture of me holding it on the front steps of our house."

"Mine was a rag quilt," Mae said, "and probably uglier than yours, Leanne. But I loved it too. Honey, you never forget your first quilt."

Sadie thought back to her first quilt, also a rag quilt made from scraps of cloth she'd begged her mom to cut from the old clothes she wanted to donate to the church clothing drive.

"No, you really don't," she said softly. "Be sure to take a picture. Every quilt you create deserves to be remembered. I wish I'd known that when I started out, but now I take a picture of each one."

"All right, everyone," Imogene said, "let's get back to it. There are more cookies to eat and more babies who need quilts."

The women returned to the circle, leaving the sisters alone together.

"I also know what I want to sew inside," Paige whispered. "'May you always be safe.'"

Sadie fingered the squares, feeling her heart clench. "That's beautiful. Every baby should be safe."

"Yes, they should," Paige said in a hoarse voice.

"Let me show you how to piece it," Sadie said, patting her on the arm. "It's like sharing your life story with a new friend. One page at a time."

Paige's smile widened. "Is that a pun?"

Page. Paige. Oh, goodness, her brain had hijacked her and she was becoming a total mushball. "Not intentionally. Forget I said it. Now, we're going to need to measure some batting and some backing for your quilt, but let's get you to piecing it."

Paige stopped her with a hand. "I'd like to meet up

sometime this week to quilt—or have a glass of wine."

Just like sisters, Sadie thought with a little shiver of pleasure. "How does Thursday sound?"

"It sounds great."

And together, they assembled the top face of her quilt, piece by piece, just like they were doing with their relationship.

Chapter 12

Paige was dancing on her way to the car to see Sadie and her sisters when she heard Riley shout her name. Between Monday night and Wednesday, somehow her one-on-one quilting date had turned into a full-on girls' night at Sadie's. Tonight she'd not only see her sisters but the other women in their extended family. They were bringing her into the fold slowly, but she was gathering momentum. She wanted to meet everyone! She'd been so excited she'd even painted her toenails—a rich orange—after getting home from work tonight.

Riley ran across the yard with something in his hand. "Hey there!"

"Hey back," he said, dancing in place, but his dancing was completely different than hers. While she had Pitbull's "Greenlight" playing in her head, it looked like his internal soundtrack was spinning something like Gavin James' "Nervous."

"Something on your mind, Riley?" she asked.

"Well...you're seeing Sadie tonight, and I thought..." He thrust out the object he was holding. "Can you give her this card for me? I couldn't...pass up the chance to give her something. I mean...something tangible is more romantic."

Oh, could he be any sweeter? "You know, Riley... You could ask Sadie out more than twice a week." They were on the Wednesday and Saturday plan right now.

He kicked at a pebble on the driveway, and it ricocheted off the rim of her wheel. "I know, Paige, but we both agreed to take things slow."

Slow? When he was acting like an eager puppy? "Why do you need to take things slow?"

He stopped moving. Ran a hand through his thick hair, a puzzled look on his face. "Well...it's early and—"

"Since when have you followed the rules?" she asked. "Riley, if there's one thing I admire about you it's your independent thinking. You always listen to all sides of an argument and then decide for yourself. If you like Sadie so much, why in the world aren't you going out more?"

"I'd like to see her more than two days a week," he said, punching the air. "But I'm a dad, and I..."

He trailed off at her look.

"Fine, I even had a weird thought about joining her quilting class to spend more time with her, but that was a low moment. Can you imagine me quilting? Not that it isn't okay for men too, but seriously, I would hate the sewing and—"

"Riley, you still haven't told me why you're taking things slow. I mean, I know it's different, but I fell for Sadie pretty much the night we met, and I already love her. Does that sound like slow to you?"

He shook his head, turning the card end over end. "No, and it's really unlike you, which is why I know she's so great, so right for you."

This wasn't the normally decisive Riley she knew at all. "You aren't sure if she's right for *you*?"

"I told you. It's early."

"I knew I wanted to be with Mark the rest of my life on our first date," she told him. Of course, he knew the story. Haley and Jess had made her tell it at bedtime more than once with Riley in the room.

"Yeah, but you guys are special. Like an alien couple or something. I mean, do you know the odds of finding a bond like that? It's like one in a trillion."

She scanned the sunset cresting over the roofline of her house and thought for a moment. "Riley, I know things with Mandy were terrible, but you can't tell me you don't believe in true love. I know you. I've read a few of your comics. There's always a love interest. Besides, you've watched too many Disney movies with the girls for it not to affect you."

"Please don't extrapolate anything about my character based on my knowledge of Disney. I watch those movies with Jess and Haley because it makes them happy. It's what a good dad does."

She knew he was downplaying things...a lot. Riley had created a special fairy castle in the playroom out of cardboard and old curtains. He'd hunted for special princess costumes for the girls, saying they needed to celebrate their own identities as Princesses Jess and Haley. Disney princesses like Belle or Ariel were their friends; they didn't impersonate them.

"How many times have you played the heroic prince and told the girls to hold out for true love?"

"I don't want them to end up effed up like me," he said, rocking back on his heels. "Excuse my language, but you know what happened with Mandy."

"Sadie isn't Mandy," she said straight out. "And you know it."

"But Jess is...young and...I don't want her to form an attachment to someone who might not be in my life later. Despite the fact that she's clearly going to be in yours."

Mark had told her about Riley's worries about Mandy, how Jess had been looking at pictures of her mother in his office. She and Riley hadn't explicitly discussed it because her men—like she thought of them—took care of each other.

"I'm not saying we aren't going to have to..." She searched for the right words. "To heck with it. I'm just going to tell you straight out. Jess is a smart girl. And she's resilient. If you and Sadie don't end up becoming a thing or break up after being a thing for a while, she isn't going to be destroyed by it. Not like I might have been when I was a kid. And do you know why?"

He worried his lips before responding, "Why?"

She put her hand on his T-shirt. "Because, Riley Thomson, Jess knows you love her like crazy. And she knows I love her and Mark loves her. Haley is her sister for life. And Sadie and Shelby and Susannah are mine now, thank God. She'll find a way to still love Sadie and adjust to the change. In fact, I expect she'll love Sadie for Sadie, whether she's your girlfriend or my sister or Haley's aunt, and Sadie will love her right back. No one can have too much love in this world, Riley."

He tapped the card on his thigh for a moment. "I know you're right, but you didn't see how vulnerable she was the other day, Paige. Mark must have told you what happened. She never sneaks around like that usually, and she was so quiet."

"That wasn't about Sadie, Riley," she said gently. "That was about her mother."

He looked to the house, and she rubbed his back.

"I hate this," he whispered. "I want to protect Jess from the truth, but I know someday she's going to ask me straight out...and I don't want to lie. When I think about what the truth will do to her, I want to cut off my own arm to prevent it."

Paige thought about Sadie's mom again, a woman she'd been thinking about a lot lately. Mrs. McGuiness had kept Paige and her mother a secret because she'd wanted to protect her children.

"You know...Sadie's mom protected her children from the truth about their dad and my mother—and me,

I suppose. She did it for decades. Like you, she wanted to prevent them from feeling more pain, something any loving parent would want for their child. Will it hurt when you finally tell Jess? Yes, but when the time comes, you will be there, and so will Mark and me and Haley."

She paused, looking him in the eye, then added, "Riley, Sadie told me she was glad her mother had finally told them all the sordid details about my mom and their dad because that was what brought them to me. You can't keep thinking of the worst-case scenarios."

"I know, but it's hard not to when all the evidence seems to point to it. Mandy's still a junkie based on the update I had that private investigator do last year, and she could try and use Jess. Seek her out at school and ask her for money. Kidnap her. Dammit, Paige. You know how Mandy showed up that one time when Jess was little. I had to call the cops."

She did, and she also knew how paralyzing the fear could be that a drug-addict parent could come back again. Still she said, "You need to trust yourself…and Jess."

When she reached out and hugged Riley, she felt his arms come around her.

"Whenever you get overwhelmed by something like this, you call Mark or me. Sadie and the rest of her siblings are new additions to my family, but you and Jess…you've been family for years."

"Shit," he said, the muscles in his back bunching as he fought emotion. "I'm glad you're my family too."

"Look, all I'm saying is don't go slow with Sadie because of rules or because you're trying to regulate how much Jess might come to love her," she told him. "If there's one thing I've realized it's that only a silly person or someone truly afraid of life tries to regulate love like it's out of something like a gas pump. I mean, if I'd let my old experiences with my mother and her men influence how I felt about Mark, we would have never made it past the first couple of dates."

Riley gave a hoarse laugh and let her go. "You're underestimating Mark."

"Maybe," she said, "but you can't make anyone love you. I had to step over the fears I had from my past and take his hand."

"Are you saying I need to take Sadie's hand?" he asked, taking a deep breath.

"If you want to," she said, gesturing to the card he still held, "and from where I'm standing, Riley, you definitely look like a man who wants to."

"Shit," he said again. "Paige, I drew her."

"You what?"

"I drew her likeness and put it in this 'Thinking of You' card. I mean my female superhero has been looking more and more like her, but I've never…" He waved the envelope. "I'm either a moron or a—"

"Man falling pretty hard for a really wonderful woman," she finished, cutting him off from putting himself down. "Riley, she'll love the card. Now, give it to me so I can run. I'm going to be late for my first girls' night with the McGuinesses."

He handed her the card. "So let me sum things up. I'm supposed to make up my own mind. Keep the course with Jess. And take Sadie's hand."

"Yep," she said, rising on her tiptoes to kiss his cheek. "I'll be your love messenger."

"Oh, please don't say things like that," he said with a grimace. "It sounds so—"

"Lovey dovey?" she quipped, dancing her way back toward her car. "Trust me, you're a certified love dove right now, Riley."

He groaned.

She cocked her hip and gave him a smile. "Honestly, it looks really great on you. But you need a haircut."

When she reached the stoplight on the main road that would take her to Sadie's, she checked the mirror to make sure she looked her best.

Honestly, Sadie and her new family looked really good on her too.

Chapter 13

Sadie lurched off the sofa and ran toward the door when the doorbell sounded. It could only be Paige.

Everyone had arrived early to give her a warm welcome. Of course, Shelby had insisted on helping her set up, fussing uncharacteristically with the placement of the napkins next to the snacks. Susannah had rearranged the flowers she'd brought while the other women chatted nervously.

Throwing open the door, Sadie held out her arms. "Welcome!"

Paige moved in for a hug, and Sadie felt her heart soar like it did every time she saw her little sister.

"Everyone is so excited to meet you. I mean...see you again. You know. I mean Tory baked a cake, and she has a newborn."

After giving her one last squeeze, Paige released her. "Good heavens, a newborn! When Haley was that little, I barely had time to go to the bathroom. Ah... before I forget. I have something for you. From Riley." She handed over an envelope that immediately sent Sadie's pulse into overdrive. "I'll just take in the champagne I brought."

"Hi, Paige," Shelby said, rushing in to hug her. "I brought champagne too. Great minds. Oh, honey, it's so good to see you."

Sadie watched as Shelby ushered her into the family room. Then she turned to the card and slit the envelope with her finger.

The card was blue and emblazoned with the message "Thinking of You" in swirly letters, what Rye would call a girly card. Inside was a folded up piece of thick paper. When she opened it, she gasped.

Riley had drawn her. Oh goodness, that man. He'd only captured her face, but heavens...she'd never felt more beautiful. In the drawing she was smiling, and her chin was ducked down just a touch. But it was the look he'd captured in her eyes that captivated her the most. They were filled with love and laughter. And strength...

"My goodness, Sadie McGuiness, that's you!" Shelby declared. "I was coming to see why you were still by the door, but wowza, I get it. Your man drew this?"

Of course, after their magical second date, she'd totally blabbed about Riley. Her excitement had spilled out of her like sunbeams and she'd needed to tell them. Before she knew it, Shelby had snatched the drawing from her fingers.

"Look what Sadie's man drew! It's her. Our Sadie!"

Amelia Ann cuddled close to Shelby and oohed and aahed. "It's stunning. He captured you perfectly, Sadie."

"Did he?" she said, fingering the pearls she'd worn. She'd always thought God had done his best to make her pretty, giving her nice hair and decent features, but beautiful had never entered her vocabulary.

"Oh, he's a goner," Tory said. "No guy draws a woman like this unless he's totally fallen. It's like Rye writing me a song."

"A song?" Paige said, smiling. "How lovely! What's it like to have someone write you a song?"

"Pretty sweet," Tory said. "I'm Tory Crenshaw, by the way. The one with the newborn baby."

"Oh, congratulations!" Paige said. "You shouldn't have gone to the trouble. Wait, do you mean Rye...Crenshaw?"

"Yep, that's my man," she said. "He's eager to meet you once you've met our 'gaggle of girls.' That's his name for it. He might be a little old-fashioned and sometimes annoyingly sexist, but I love the heck out of him. And now we have Boone."

"Somehow my sisters failed to mention...ah...you'll have to show me some pictures of Boone," Paige said with a smile. "Babies are the best."

Tammy introduced herself as J.P.'s wife and extended her hand, as gracious and collected as always. "You've made a lot of people I love very happy, and for that I thank you. I...welcome to the family."

Paige coughed out a laugh and clasped her hand. "Oh, I didn't expect to start crying. Sorry. It's been...the most wonderful emotional roller coaster. Sadie...ah...you might text Riley about your drawing. He was a little nervous when he gave it to me."

Sadie pressed her hand to her chest, feeling her heart glow inside. Amelia Ann was introducing herself, so Sadie hustled into the kitchen where she'd left her phone. Paige would be fine.

I love my drawing. You're so sweet I want to kiss you.

His reply came seconds later. *Save it for Saturday. I have some of my own kisses stored up for you. And whew! Glad you liked the drawing. I hoped it wouldn't weird you out.*

That puzzled her. *Why would it?*

Because it would imply I've been thinking about your body. Totally true FYI. I thought a head pose would be classy.

She barked out a laugh. *Full body is next, huh?*

Gulp. Don't you have company?

"Okay, enough with the texting," Shelby said, snatching her phone from her and typing.

This is Sadie's sister, Shelby. I'm taking her back to the party. Love your drawing. Be nice to my sister or answer to me. Haha.

"Shelby!" Sadie exclaimed after grabbing her hand to see what she'd texted.

Don't worry, I'm one of the good guys. Okay, that was lame. Have fun, ladies.

"One of the good guys," Shelby drawled. "I like him even more. When are you inviting him to Sunday dinner?"

The other women appeared in the doorway, surrounding Paige as if parading her through the center of town.

"We were going to open the champagne," Tammy said, "but we can come back."

Shelby marched forward with her phone. "Look what this man texted back. Isn't he adorable?"

Amelia Ann winked at her. "I like the way he said he was one of the good guys."

This wasn't how Sadie had envisioned at all. She watched helplessly as they passed her phone from one woman to the next, wanting to grab it away.

Tammy burst out laughing. "Oh, Paige, are you totally put off by us?"

"Not at all," Paige said, laughing as well. "I'm so happy to be here with y'all."

Sadie reached for Paige's hand. "Let's pop the champagne and toast to your first girls' night with us." She was eager to change the subject, and she didn't care who knew it.

"Paige..." Shelby drawled, ignoring her signals. "You know Riley. What do you think of him?"

"Shelby McGuiness!" Susannah exclaimed. "That is none of your business. Let Paige enjoy herself."

"He really is one of the good guys," Paige said, motioning with her hand. "I love him to pieces."

"And I expect he's pretty good with his hands if his drawing is any indication," Shelby said, fanning herself.

"Enough!" Sadie exclaimed, reclaiming her phone from Shelby again, who had lingered over the texts. "Do something useful and pop the champagne before I pop you for being a busybody."

"I still say you need to bring him to Sunday dinner," Shelby said, opening the refrigerator door and grabbing the champagne she'd brought. "The men folk are going to want to get a good look at him, and honestly, so do I. Sadie, you're totally gaga for the man."

"We're not talking about this another second, Shelby," Sadie said, taking the bottle from her and opening it.

"Shelby, why don't you cut the cake out there? I'll serve it," Tammy said, taking her arm and steering her out of the kitchen. Thank goodness someone in the family listened to cues.

"Sadie, if you pour, I'll take in the glasses," Susannah said.

"What can I do?" Paige asked, looking around.

"Come sit with me in the living room and tell me more about your beautiful daughter," Amelia Ann said, ever the smooth one. "I understand she's in second grade."

And so it went. They drank champagne and told stories, stories that seemed minor and insignificant unless you looked below the surface, Sadie thought, rather like the backside of a quilt.

When they opened the second bottle of champagne, Tory called it a night, noting Boone was going to need to nurse in a while. Tammy took the opportunity to say goodnight then as well. When Amelia Ann rose to her feet with them, sighing about an early conference call, Sadie finally caught on.

They were leaving Paige alone with her sisters.

She settled back onto the couch and took a mental snapshot of Shelby pouring Paige more champagne and teasing her about what a *fine* man Mark was. The sultry way she said it caused Susannah to start giggling. Her sisters were in high spirits, and it was wonderful to see. It was wonderful that the family fold had expanded in such an unexpected way.

Paige tucked her feet under her body and fingered the quilt hanging over the sofa she was sitting on. "This is beautiful. I was hoping to see more of your work."

"Sadie gives most of her quilts away," Shelby said, kicking back and putting her feet on the coffee table.

Susannah wisely moved the empty champagne bottle so she wouldn't knock it over.

"Everyone at church is always asking her if she can make them one," Shelby continued. "Some people have even exaggerated being seriously ill to play on her sympathy. When Mama figured that out, she was outraged."

"I'd like to meet your mother sometime, I've decided," Paige said softly, "if it wouldn't make her too uncomfortable."

All the spit dried up in Sadie's mouth.

"I mean...I've been thinking about it since our last coffee date, and I talked it over with Mark. I don't want her to feel uncomfortable with me around...I...want to tell her I would never do anything to hurt any of you."

Sadie's eyes welled up with tears, and she felt Susannah reach for her hand.

"Part of me wants to apologize for my mom," Paige said, her voice strained, "but Mark reminded me for the millionth time that it wasn't my fault. But still...I want to tell your mom I'm really grateful to her for raising such a wonderful family. Oh, heck..."

She put her hand over her mouth.

Shelby wrapped an arm around her.

"I got to wondering how much better my life would

have been when I was a kid if I'd had y'all, but I know that's not useful thinking."

"I wish we could have known you when we were young too," Susannah said. "But we can't undo what happened. We can only be grateful we have one another now."

"And have fun together," Shelby said with an audible sniff. "We'll talk to J.P. about you meeting our mama. She seems to have taken the news pretty well."

"That's Mama," Susannah said. "I didn't say anything to anybody, but Jake went to her office at church after J.P. told her. He said they had a downright nice talk."

"I can't wait to meet him," Paige said. "First Rye and then Jake Lassiter. I'll try not to geek out."

"Just be yourself," Sadie told her. "They're normal people too. Well, Jake is—I'm not sure you can call Rye 'normal.' If it makes you feel better, we were total fan girls over Jake in the beginning, but we've...progressed."

"Progressed," Shelby said with a laugh. "I like that."

"We'd like to invite you and Mark over to our house to meet everybody," Susannah said, laughing, "but J.P. thought it might be more fun for the kids if we all met at his and Tammy's place. They have the tree house, you see, and the chocolate garden."

"A chocolate garden?" Paige asked, breathless. "That sounds magical."

"Wait until you see it," Sadie said, taking her hand. "Someone will tell you and Haley the story."

"Likely Annabelle," Shelby said. "That girl loves to embellish these days, and my is she good at it. If you listen to her long enough, you'll start believing the flowers themselves are made out of chocolate, and you might eat every last one of them before figuring it out."

"I can't wait," Paige said, looking at each of them.

"Is this Saturday too soon for y'all?" Susannah asked. "Everyone is—"

"Crazy eager to meet you," Shelby finished for her.

"I'll talk to Mark, but I think we're good to go," she said. "Wait! Sadie, don't you and Riley have a date Saturday?"

"We do," she said, feeling torn.

"Oh, you two should just change it to tomorrow night. Riley was going to watch Haley for Mark and me, so I know he's free. Sadie, are you?"

She felt like a strong wind was blowing over her. "Ah... yes. I'll text Riley later."

"Then it's settled," Paige said with a nod, making Shelby snort. "Can I bring something on Saturday?"

"Champagne seems to work," Shelby said, draining the last of her glass. "I love girls' night, but I have to say I'm partial to how eager Vander is when I come home after one of these nights. He's on me like a duck on a June bug the minute I walk through the door."

"I hope Mark reacts that way," Paige said, laughing. "I haven't really had a girls' night before."

"Well, you have a girls' night with us," Shelby declared. "Now, I need to go home to my man and make some sweet music."

"Shelby McGuiness, you are terrible!" Sadie said.

"You mean 'insatiable,'" Susannah said, laughing. "I'm going to head home too. Jake gets a little worried about the dark back roads."

"If you'd like to see my current quilting project, Paige..." Sadie gestured with her hands, hoping she would stay a little longer.

She was eager to text Riley, but she wanted more time with her sister.

"I can stay a little longer," Paige said.

Susannah and Shelby hugged her warmly, and Sadie got a little teary-eyed at the sight of all of her sisters together at last. Paige looked so much like them.

"See you Saturday, honey," Shelby said. "And don't be a stranger in between. You text me anytime."

"I don't have your number," Paige said. "How is that?"

"We've been letting Sadie be the messenger," Shelby said. "Well, we're going to change that right now. If you give me your phone, I'll put everyone in your contact list."

Paige retrieved her phone from her purse, and soon she had everyone's cell phone, including Rye's.

"Are you serious?" she exclaimed, eyes wide as saucers. "Rye Crenshaw's number is in my phone."

"He's not the first man I would call," Shelby said, honest as ever.

"I don't know what to say...this is so weird," Paige said, staring at the screen before shaking herself. "Mark won't believe it. I mean it's crazy enough that you're *married* to Jake, Susannah, but Rye Crenshaw..."

"Yes, he's a country god, lowercase G, just ask him," Shelby said dryly. "All right, I am now officially out of here. Unless you need me to stay and clean up. Although I did come early and help you set up, Sadie."

She almost gave her sister a look for that comment. Like it would hurt Shelby to clean up more than once in a night.

"I can help her," Paige said. "Y'all go on. And thanks. For tonight. For...being so nice and welcoming."

"Oh, this is just the beginning," Susannah said, kissing her on the cheek. "Bye, Sadie. Thanks for arranging this."

Yes, everything had come off nicely. When she was alone, she might just pat herself on the back. For the youngest in the family, she was showing strong signs of leadership. She thought of the strength exuded by Riley's drawing of her and shivered. It moved her something fierce that he thought of her that way.

After their sisters left, Sadie and Paige sat side by side on the couch. "Are you okay?" Sadie asked, taking her hand.

"I think I'm overwhelmed," she whispered, squeezing

her eyes shut. "It's not the whole Rye thing."

"I know it's not."

"It's...this...oh, dear." She launched herself at Sadie and hugged her. "Everyone is so wonderful. I never imagined. I'm going to start crying, and it may not be pretty. I can leave."

Sadie wrapped her arms around her sister. "I can handle it. I might cry some myself."

Paige completely let go, and Sadie sure as shooting did some crying too. The emotion of these last weeks seemed to have built up like a bathtub with the water left running.

"Goodness, I don't think I've cried this much since I was pregnant," Paige said after blowing her nose.

"But it's good crying," Sadie said, thinking about the horrible hot mess she'd been after discovering the truth about their daddy.

Sometimes she still cried over him, although she didn't say anything to anyone.

Paige wiped her eyes. "Yes, it is. Mark says the same thing. I've never seen a man more comfortable with tears, but heck, at least one kid cries in his office on a daily basis. Growing up, I never did cry. My mama didn't allow it. Said it made you weak."

"J.P. is comfortable with tears too," Sadie said. "He was always a good shoulder to cry on growing up. Still is."

"Can I see your quilting stuff?" Paige asked. "I've been thinking about it all day. Then I should get on home."

"Come on," she said, standing. "I use the spare room for my supplies, but I mostly quilt here on the sofa or in my bedroom."

They climbed the short stretch of stairs to the second level. She'd tidied up in the spare bedroom earlier, so she had no compunction about showing it off.

"Oh, my goodness," Paige exclaimed when she turned on the light. "*That's* a quilt?"

Sadie watched as her sister ran forward to the bed

where her newest project was laid out. "Yes, I've been working on the baby quilts and a made-for-order quilt from the store, but this one is my ongoing large-scale project. It's called The Promised Land, and it's in the Japanese quilting style. I've been teaching myself some of their techniques by trial and error." She refrained from launching into the differences. Even Ada's eyes had glazed over when she'd tried to describe it in depth.

"Japanese?" Paige asked, her eyes glued to the quilt in progress. "There are so many small pieces, and the way you use them... Sadie, this is like a painting."

"That's what I thought when I saw my first Japanese quilt," she said, coming forward to stand next to her sister. "There's a lot of emphasis on geometric shapes like the sun I designed, and the way they use stitching...it's like they create threads of magic throughout the quilt. The hand piecing and sewing takes a lot of time, but I find it relaxing."

"The stitching makes it look like a gentle breeze is flowing across the land," Paige said.

Sadie studied the half-finished quilt. For this quilt, she was piecing the design as it came to her. So far, she had the sun and the blue sky, and yes, she'd used the classic sashiko stitch to make it seem like the wind was gently blowing.

"I'm still playing with how I want to design the land, but I know there's going to be a waterfall leading into a small river. Lush trees. Maybe a field of flowers in the right corner."

Her mind started to spin new ideas, and she shook herself.

"Sadie," Paige said, grabbing both of her arms and staring at her with big eyes. "You have to submit this to a show or a museum when you're finished."

She ducked her chin, flushing. "I don't know. It's my first large-scale Japanese quilt. I've been making smaller ones, working on my stitching. Every stitch has to be evenly spaced and perfect, and while that appeals to my OCD nature when it comes to quilting, I don't think I'm on that level yet."

"I think you are," Paige said, shaking her gently. "Sadie, you aren't just a quilting teacher in a craft store or even someone who sells her quilts for money. You're an artist."

An artist? That seemed like too big of a word for her. "I'm creative, I'll give you that."

Paige narrowed her eyes. "You don't see it... All right, I'm going to have Riley work on you. If there's one thing he knows, it's art. Maybe between the two of us, you'll start to believe this about yourself."

Sadie remembered Riley saying something about her being an artist, but at the time she'd thought he was just being nice—and flirting. After all, he'd only seen a few of her projects on her phone. "I know God gave me a gift."

"But you don't see how completely incredible it is," Paige said. "Can I take a picture of this? I'd like to show Mark and Haley. It's...exquisite."

Oh, the nerves bubbling up made her want to rush forward and cover up her work in progress. "But it's not finished. I mean—"

"Please," Paige said. "I promise I won't show anyone else. Well, Jess will likely insist on seeing it once Haley tells her about it. I mean, those two share everything. I'll probably end up showing Riley too...except *you* could, of course...when you invite him over."

Her sister's wink made her face turn from merely warm to middle-of-the-summer hot. "We're taking things slow."

Paige rested her weight on one leg and studied her. "You too? I thought it was only Riley holding back given his past with Jess' mom."

The woman who'd liked secrets, didn't want Jess, and

had made Riley hate country music. She didn't have a full picture yet, but the image she'd formed was dark. "No."

"But I see…no wait, I *don't* see. You're head over heels about him. I can tell. Why are you so set on being slow? Because you think he needs you to be?"

"I think I need to sit down," she said, moving toward the rocking chair she kept by the window.

"What are you afraid of? I don't mean to be so personal, but I love you, and I love Riley to pieces. Why in the world aren't you two going for each other like crazy?"

She pressed her hands to her hot face. "Well, I can't just jump into bed with him. I mean, it's not like we're even committed, and he hasn't told me he loves me." Of course, she hadn't told him either because it *was* early, and truth be told, she wasn't sure it was the big L love. The little l love was pretty clear though.

"Are you a virgin?" Paige asked.

Her eyes flew to her sister's. "What?"

"Sorry, that was really personal," Paige said, sinking down onto the floor in front of her. "But I'm diving into the sisterhood deep end here. I hadn't thought about it, but you're the daughter of a preacher and you go to church. It's totally okay with me if you are. Mark and I were each other's firsts. We're both really glad about that actually."

Oh, goodness, she thought, rocking in her chair. "There was someone in college, someone I thought I'd marry…"

"I see," Paige said, putting her hand on her knee. "And Riley?"

"He wants to, I think," she said, rocking forward. "I mean, *yes*, he wants to. And I do too, but it's not that simple. He's not ready for something serious. He wants to take this one step at a time. Have fun together and see what happens."

"Yes, I imagine that's what he's told himself," Paige

said, "but here's the thing about Riley. Underneath all the jokes and the entertainment, he's really sensitive. He has this huge heart, and sure he's a guy like all the rest...but he's also not. I have to tell you, Riley wants someone he can have fun with *and* be serious about. He doesn't want to play around."

"I didn't think he did," Sadie said, "but we've only just met and—"

"Hogwash," Paige said. "Time doesn't factor into love. I mean, look at us."

Sadie waggled her eyebrow suggestively at Paige, laughing. " *Us.*"

"You know what I'm talking about," her sister said. "Okay, one last sister thing. Sex between two people who care about each other is beautiful, and I figure you and Riley will know when the time is right. Mark and I waited a little longer than I would now because it's just so awesome between us, but in retrospect, the time we chose was perfect."

The mere thought about having sex with Riley was making Sadie lightheaded. "It's a huge step."

"It is," Paige said. "As someone who was born to two people who made a terrible choice, no one knows that better than I do. But Mark also helped me learn how to trust my heart, and I know you can trust yours. I mean, Sadie, look at your heart!"

She gestured to the half-made quilt on the bed, and Sadie felt her throat close. She took a deep breath and then another.

"We're going out Saturday, no, tomorrow," Sadie said. "I'll see how things go. But I hear you. Love shouldn't be bound by a timetable."

But should something like lovemaking be bound by commitment? She was going to have to be true to herself because it very much did for her.

Chapter 14

"*Well, over-fast dates never turned me on,*'" Riley sang on the way over to pick Sadie up.

He was listening to Prince's "Raspberry Beret," and he had a moment of confusion. Was that really the lyric? Had Prince said such a thing? He paused the song and called up the handy little helper on his phone. He'd named her Xena, after *his* favorite princess. Jess might love Rapunzel, but he liked his princesses with a little less clothing and a lot more edge. "Look up lyrics for 'Raspberry Beret.'"

He listened as Xena recited the words, and when they reached the line of the song he'd been unsure about, he had to laugh. Boy, had he been off. Prince had sung about overcast days. Not over-fast dates.

He was clearly trying to talk himself down about tonight. His subconscious had tried to use one of his music idols to confirm that he shouldn't rush anything. After his talk with Paige, he'd wavered back and forth between going faster and keeping it slow. A long-term relationship took time to cultivate, didn't it? He'd even made a list of what he could do to cultivate their connection, but it hadn't helped.

The minute he saw her, he knew what was going to happen. His mouth would dry up, his remaining brain cells would disappear, and he wouldn't be able to form a decent sentence. And his dick? Well, it would want to take over, and that wasn't a good idea. Sadie was a lady. He respected her. There was no way he was going to ruin this by scaring her off.

He checked his image in the rearview mirror. He was presentable if not over-groomed. Jess had insisted on brushing his hair, and when he hadn't been looking, she'd swooped in one of her hands and slicked on some hair product. The surprise of it had jolted a girly shriek from him. The product was Mark's, apparently, and he'd had no choice but to allow his daughter to shape and reshape his hair to her crazy specifications.

As he left the car, he tugged on his new sport jacket, the one he'd bought online with Jess in his lap. It was a brown suede—perfect for fall, his little girl had said.

She was growing up so fast.

It seemed like he was duty-bound to keep something in his life from going too fast. *No over-fast dates*, he told himself as he rang the doorbell.

He imagined himself cloaked in armor, impenetrable to female wiles, impervious to beauty and sexiness.

"Holy shit," he uttered when she opened the door. Framed in the soft light of the hallway, Sadie wore a stretchy gold dress that seemed glued to her curves, curves he'd only guessed at before. These curves were surely capable of melting a superhero's special armor as if it were plastic. And she'd knocked it out of the park by wearing gold again. *Hubba, hubba.*

"Hi," she said, smiling, her lips lush and wet in a delectable soft pink.

"Hi," he said, gathering himself.

His nose twitched when her scent reached him—something lush and musky, like a rare flower that grows after a volcano explosion—and it felt like hot lava had landed on his skin.

"I wasn't going to kiss you right away, but hell…"

He grabbed her to him, his intensity lifting her off her feet. She wrapped her arms around him as he held her in mid-air and kissed her senseless. He threw off his stupid immunity cloak and pressed her body into him, her curves warm and lush under his hands.

"Oh, Riley," she said, breaking for air before diving into his mouth again. Her bottom lip, so perfect and plump, insisted he suck it softly. She moaned low and deep, and he felt the vibration all the way to his toes.

"We should probably leave," he murmured, kissing her softly in bites now.

"No," she whispered back, her breath hot against his mouth.

He tightened his hands, trying to commit the feel of her to memory, when her answer registered. "No?"

"No," she said, pulling him inside by the lapels of his jacket.

In that moment, he decided he needed a sport jacket for every day of the week because the feel of her yanking on it in urgency and desire was one of the best freaking feelings in the world. Like finishing his first comic book or seeing Jess take her first steps.

He let her lead him inside, but his foot reached out and kicked the door closed behind them. His feet shuffled against hers as they continued to kiss. Lips. The line of cheek. The underside of jaw. The neck.

"I'm wild about this part of your body," he murmured, breathing in her fragrance.

She shook her beautiful brown hair, hair exactly like his new superhero, and he touched it with his fingertips. He wanted to touch her everywhere. That little misheard jingle about over-fast dates played in his mind…

"Sadie."

Her hands found their way inside his jacket, so curious and so hot.

"Okay, this time we really need to stop." He was close to begging.

"Just a little more," she whispered against his mouth like a siren.

They fell into a deep kiss, and together they shuffled forward as though they were doing a slow, sensuous two-step.

"Okay, seriously," he said, close to declaring the medical certainty that all of the blood in his body had pooled to one place, a place they weren't ready to talk about on the slow program.

"Riley, I've been thinking," she said, tugging on his lapels again.

"You drive me out of mind when you do that."

She tugged on them again, this time with a Cheshire cat smile on her beautiful face.

"Good," she said with a note of glee in her voice. "Part of me wants to drive you wild. Riley, maybe we don't need to go as slow as we thought. I'm not saying we need to have sex yet because I really do need to feel like we're committed to each other, but perhaps we can enjoy...more than kisses. Oh crap, I'm getting embarrassed."

Her hands left his lapels, and she turned her back on him. He leaned in and tucked her against him, his cheek seeking hers as a way to reassure her.

"No need to be embarrassed," he said softly. "Some people go from kissing straight to sex, but there are no rules we need to follow."

Her body settled back against him. "Riley, I really, really like you."

When she spun around and faced him, he rocked back on his heels. Her brown eyes were luminous, the gold flecks shining, but the set of her jaw reminded him of Xena when she was on a mission.

"I mean...I might be falling in love with you," she said, her voice full of the strength of conviction.

He searched inside himself, wanting to be equally as honest with her. In that moment, he felt like every superhero faced with a decision. He could tell her the truth or he could fade back into the darkness, hoping his prophesy that she would be better and happier without him was true. But the truth was as loud as thunder, as unavoidable as lightning marking the sky in angry fire.

"I might be falling in love with you too," he said, touching her cheek.

"Time doesn't seem to matter," she said, putting her hand over his fast-beating heart.

There was that word again, and it raised the hairs on his arms.

"Paige was right. I don't believe time has anything to do with love. Love just happens, and while I don't know every little detail about you, I know what I feel for you, Riley Thomson."

"Sadie." She was making him believe in every storybook ending in the comic books.

"I have enough faith in the divine plan to believe you just might be the answer to my prayers...only they're prayers I didn't know I was making." She framed his face with her hands. "I mean, I prayed for a godly man, one who would respect me, go to church with me, and pray with me before we made love. But I've met men like that, and they didn't—"

"I can't do any of that," he said, his heart dropping to the floor. If that was what she wanted, he couldn't give it to her. He didn't think he could change who he was even for the woman who was stealing his heart.

"I know," she whispered, "and it doesn't matter. Do you know why?"

Oh, he was scared to hear the answer. He thought about turning away for a nanosecond, but he wouldn't let fear hold him back. He wouldn't let him separate it from her.

"Riley...you're so much better than what I imagined." She wrapped her arms around him. "You make me laugh. You listen to me. And most of all, you see me! *Me!* The drawing you gave me... Riley, no one outside my family has ever seen me like that."

"You're so easy to see," he told her, holding her close. "You're like the richest golden color palette. Your heart is in everything you do, and it's beautiful to behold."

"So is yours," she said, looking up at him. "You're a wonderful father and a great friend to Paige and Mark. Riley, I...I don't know all the reasons you want to take it slow. I don't know fully what happened with Jess' mom. But I want you to let me in. I want..."

His heart was pounding in loud beats. "What do you want?"

"I want us to make a go of this and be...committed... like boyfriend/girlfriend," she said in a fierce voice. "I've felt like a coward most of my life, and then my sister, Shelby, talked me into finding our daddy. I was scared, but I couldn't let her do it alone. And in doing it, in facing it, I found a courage I'd never expected to see in myself. I found I wouldn't break into a million pieces or blow away in tough times. I was so much stronger than I'd ever realized."

She looked like a goddess come to life. She awed him.

"When I decided to choose love and find Paige, I cinched it. I'm brave. I'm bold. Then there's you...you've helped me see that too."

And beautiful, he thought. "Yes, you are."

"Riley, I'm not going to let my old ways of doing things shape how this thing between us progresses. I know Jess is the most important thing in your life, and I think that's wonderful, but I want to be more to you than bedtime texts and Friday nights. I also don't plan on coming between you and Jess. If anything, I'd like to celebrate her place in your life."

He pressed his forehead to hers, unbearably moved.

"I just want to be with you," she said.

"Me too," he replied, tightening his hold on her. "I want us to be committed to each other too. Be a...thing. Sadie, I've been struggling with this, but in this moment, I can't seem to remember why. Would you come over and spend time with me and my daughter? She's been wanting that, and it could include a picnic or flying a kite...or playing princess. She likes to keep her options open. "

She put her fingers to his lips. "It doesn't matter what we do, Riley. I'll be happy for it. Grateful for it."

"I do need to tell you all about Jess' mother sometime," he whispered. "But I can't do it right now. It's a sad, dark tale, and I'm still ashamed of it."

"Oh, honey," she said, wrapping him in the most beautiful benediction. "Whatever it is, I'm here."

He kissed her cheek. "Oh, Sadie, I know we haven't gone out tonight yet, but what are your plans for Sunday? I know you go to church and hang out with your family..."

She was quiet for a moment. "No, I can make that."

"We're no longer on the slow program," he said, allowing his fingers to caress her hip. "We've progressed to the committed program."

"Indeed," she said, "and that was my plan."

He laughed. "If you knew what my plan was tonight... Let's just say yours was so much better. Now, I need to see this Japanese quilt Paige told me about. I have strict instructions to help you believe you're an artist."

"Really, Riley..." she said, ducking from his gaze.

"No 'really, Riley,'" he answered, lifting her chin until she met his eyes. "I mean it. Show me the quilt, Sadie."

"Fine," she said, taking his hand and leading him upstairs, "but this is really personal for me. Your opinion means so much."

When they reached the room, he stopped in the doorway. "Is that it?" he asked, pointing to the half-made quilt on the bed, a quilt unlike any he'd ever seen. It was more like a painting. From this angle he couldn't see how she'd made the sky look like it was a windy day—he only knew that it did. Whatever her technique, it showed a magic and an artistry that awed him.

"Yes, that's it," she said, clearing her throat.

"My God," he managed to say. "Sadie, it's...it's...I need to compose myself. Can I touch it?"

When he ran his fingers over the precise stitching, he shook his head. "I can feel the wind blowing. Sadie...this is...one of the most beautiful pieces of art I've ever seen. The blue and gray hues you used for the sky, the stitching...it feels alive to me. My God, I never knew. Sadie, this tops anything I've ever created."

"Oh, don't say that," she said, her face stricken. "I didn't mean for your feelings to be hurt."

He looked over and smiled at her. "Oh, they aren't. I'm great at what I do, and I love it. But some people's artistic vision and ability is out in a...different stratosphere...like Beethoven or Warhol or Chagall. Your work is going to go in a museum someday. Mark my words."

"Huh?" she spurted out.

He almost laughed. "Sadie, you shouldn't be selling your quilts in the craft store anymore. You need a bigger audience. Heck, you should be charging a buttload for something like this."

Her chest rose with a huge breath, and she looked like she was going to have a panic attack at that thought.

"Okay, let's leave those last points for another chat," he said, holding out his hand. "Come here and take a deep breath."

She clasped it and stood next to him, calming herself. "I called it 'The Promised Land.' It's where all things are possible."

"I like that," he said, aware of the biblical reference. It wasn't heavy-handed though. She was conveying an idea he could relate to—a place full of purity and warmth and comfort. He wanted to live in a land like that.

"I'm glad you like it," she said.

"I more than like it," he responded, facing her. "I want to take a picture and text my brother because his mind is going to explode, and then you'll have one more person telling you the truth. Sadie, you're an artist."

She ducked her chin. "I just do what I love."

Okay, he was going to have to be a little tougher. "Yes, but I want you to do something for me."

Her smile was immediate when she met his gaze. God, she was beautiful. "Every morning and every time you start quilting, I want you to say, 'I'm an artist.' Will you do that for me?"

Because if she needed to start there until she could do it for herself, that was totally fine in his book.

"I'll try," she said, "but—"

"Remember what Yoda says," he interrupted. "'There is no try.'"

She leveled him a look. "Seriously, did you have to bring a Yoda reference into this moment?"

"It's who I am," he said with a shrug.

"I think you need to kiss me," she said, her lips twitching. "To help convince me I'm an artist."

"I can do that," he answered, kissing her softly on the lips. "How long do you think it's going to take for you to believe it?"

"A pretty long time," she whispered.

Oddly, he was more than okay with that.

Chapter 15

"Here we go," Paige heard Mark say beside her as she scanned the row of people waiting to welcome her on the simple front porch.

"I didn't expect this..." she said, gesturing to the welcoming committee.

Her sisters were standing next to their men, save Sadie, who was holding a newborn, likely Tory and Rye Crenshaw's. When her eyes found Rye, she wanted to shiver. My goodness, he was compelling in person. *Pull it together, Paige.*

Two kids broke away from J.P. and ran toward their car. Paige knew they had to be Rory and Annabelle, and she couldn't help but smile. Both of them were adorable, the little boy dressed in a white dress shirt with a red bow tie and the little girl in a yellow dress dotted with hearts. In her hand was a princess crown, and somehow Paige knew it was for her daughter. How sweet!

Haley jumped out of her booster seat. "Oh, they look so nice. Can we get out of the car yet?"

Mark chuckled and patted her knee before opening his car door. Haley didn't need an invitation to burst out after him. When Paige opened her own door, she realized her seat belt was still on.

Her husband gave her a knowing look and waited until she was standing next to him. Taking her hand, he squeezed it once before turning his attention to the children.

"Hi there!" the little girl fairly shouted as she ran up to Haley. "I'm Annabelle and this is my brother, Rory. We're your cousins, and we're so happy to meet you. This is your crown. Sadie told us you like to be a princess. Me too!"

Haley gave the younger girl an inquiring look as she took the crown. "Are you going to wear one?"

"Yep," Annabelle said, putting her hands on her little hips. "Mama said we can wear princess outfits later, but she made me put on this dress first because you're company. Do you want to see our tree house? Aunt Susannah painted the inside, and there's a prince and a princess."

"Welcome to our home," J.P said, coming down the sidewalk at an easy pace.

He shook hands with Mark and then gently kissed Paige on the cheek.

"It's good to see y'all. I see you've already met Rory and Annabelle. They've been eager to meet you."

"Do you like dogs?" Annabelle asked her daughter.

"I like small ones," Haley said.

"You need to meet Barbie," Annabelle told her. "She's my dog. Uncle Rye gave her to me when we moved here."

"Annabelle, give her some space," Rory said. "There's plenty of time for her to meet the dogs. Haley, if you need anything, you just let me know. Dad asked me to watch out for you today."

Although Sadie had told her about the awful man who was Rory's biological father, it was wonderful to see the affection between the boy and J.P. Clearly J.P. had become his father in every way that mattered.

J.P. sent Haley a wink. "There's a lot of people, and Rory knows where everything is. Haley, do you want to put your princess crown on?"

She lifted her shoulder. "I'll wait until Annabelle does, thank you."

"Annabelle, run along and get your crown," he told her. Turning back to Paige and Mark, he said, "I think you've met almost everyone."

"They haven't met me." Paige watched as Rye Crenshaw ambled forward. "Hi, I'm Rye." He shook hands with Mark, patted Haley on the head, and then pulled Paige in for a hug. "Everyone else seems to be observing some crazy welcome wagon rules. I might not be your blood kin, but this brother of yours is my brother just the same. I hope you're prepared to share him because I can't do without him."

His big hit, "Cracks in the Glass House," had gotten her through some tough times. Maybe she could tell him someday. "You're in my phone." Wait. Had she really just said that?

Rye barked out a laugh. "I heard that flustered you a touch. You're welcome to holler at me anytime if you need something. Despite what some people might say around here, I'm pretty responsible."

"No you aren't, Uncle Rye," Annabelle said. "You let the dogs out all of the time and—"

"Hush." Rye plucked her off the ground. "You've been listening to your Aunt Tory. Well, come on, y'all. There are more people to meet. Vander! You're the newest member of this here family. Come on forward and meet our new kin."

Paige felt her nerves tighten when she heard Vander's name. He was the one who'd helped her siblings find their father. He'd talked to him. And being a private investigator, she imagined he knew every sordid detail there was to know about her mother. She felt Mark lean in, sensing she needed extra support.

Shelby marched forward, hand in hand with a striking man. Vander.

"Rye, only you would upset the apple cart," Shelby said, giving him a little shove. "We talked about the introductions."

"Y'all are over-complicating things," he said, "and making these nice people more nervous."

Her nerves had to be fairly obvious, Paige realized with some chagrin. She'd barely said two words since leaving the car.

"Hi, Shelby," she muttered, coughing to clear her throat.

"Don't mind Rye," Shelby said, giving him a look. "This is my Vander, and trust me, he's always responsible."

"Nice to meet you," Shelby's fiancé said in a flat Yankee cadence, his eyes steady on her. "I'm really happy this has turned out to be such a happy reconciliation."

She had to cough again. No doubt he'd seen some unpleasant reunions in his line of work. Thank God her daddy had cut and run from them. She never wanted to meet him.

"Hey, y'all," Susannah said, coming up behind the couple. "This is my husband, Jake."

The handsome man gave them a kind smile. He was quietly magnetic—the complete opposite to Rye's larger-than-life persona. "Good to meet you. Welcome. You let me know if you need anything too."

"We've listened to you on the radio," Haley said to him, tapping her crown against her leg. "You too, Mr. Crenshaw."

"It's plain ol', Rye, sugar," he insisted. "Clayton, get on over here. Now, you've already met my sister, Amelia Ann. Her husband, Clayton, is my manager."

"And then some," a tall man in a white cowboy hat said. "Nice to meet y'all. We're happy the McGuiness clan found you. Sadie surprised us some with her gumption."

"I always knew she had more than she was letting on," Rye said. "Come and meet my baby boy, Boone. He's the light of my life."

Along the way, they stopped to hug Tammy, who was on her way into the house. Tory came forward and welcomed them warmly.

"I see you have the best seat in the house," Paige said to Sadie, her eyes zooming in on the little miracle swaddled in a white blanket. "Oh, he's so beautiful."

"Hi, Paige," Sadie said, that baby-glow on her face. "Hi, Mark. Hi, Haley."

"Mama, can I see him?" Haley asked, rising on her tippy toes.

Mark picked her up, and she reached out a hand to touch him.

"Gently now," Mark told her. "Y'all have a beautiful boy there."

He gave her a look. When she'd gotten her period again yesterday, he'd told her they'd just keep trying and wrapped her up in his arms. Her heart pinched with worry. Would they ever have another baby?

"We think he's the most beautiful baby in the world," Tory said, "but we're partial."

"Takes after me," Rye drawled, rocking forward on his cowboy boots and touching the baby's soft cheek.

"In some areas," Tory said, elbowing him in the gut. "You'd think Rye had invented babies from the way he goes on sometimes."

"Well, sugar, I did invent this one," he said with a slow smile. "With your help, of course."

She shook her head. "Tammy probably has the whole meal laid out by now. Let's find you some drinks."

"Amelia Ann went in to help her," Rye said. "What can we get y'all? A bourbon?"

Rye Crenshaw was offering them bourbon?

"I'll have one," Paige found herself saying.

Mark swung his head to look at her, but he was smart enough not to say anything. "Will you now? I'll have some tea."

"Can I have a lemonade?" Haley asked.

"We always have that stuff around here," Rye told her. "Sometimes with rosemary, although for the life of me I can't imagine why. It grows like a weed at our house."

"It's an herb," Tory told him in a flat voice. "Like you'd know."

Mark started to laugh before he cut it off. Clearly they both found Rye entertaining.

When the country music legend took her elbow and steered her inside the house, she nearly jumped out of her skin. "Let's get you that bourbon, Paige. I like a woman who drinks during the day. I mean, my mama named me after a smooth rye whiskey, after all."

"That is so not true," Tammy told her brother.

Rye sent Paige a devilish smile. "Caught me. It's such a good story though. It's a shame to let it go."

When Rye poured himself a drink so he could toast her, she had to take a deep breath to keep from feeling lightheaded.

"To family, new and old," he said, clinking their glasses together. "I heard you had a difficult spell with your own, and well, so did I. Happy to say it's all behind us now. We're all glad you're here, Paige. These here McGuinesses are pretty wonderful people."

"Yes they are."

"Let's shoot it, shall we?"

"Shoot it?" she repeated, noting he'd given her a healthy pour.

"Down the hatch," he said, and then he tipped his glass to his mouth and drank the bourbon in one fell swoop.

She bit her lip and thought, *Oh, what the hell*, and tossed her bourbon back the way he had. Fire shot down her throat. It took effort not to break into a fit of coughing.

"That was a nice toast," she rasped out.

"I thought so," Rye declared. "Now, I'm going to take

my son back from Sadie. I never get to hold him at a family gathering. I swear, it's like the women in this family become wolves, passing my kid on from one hungry woman to the next."

He left the room, and this time she touched her throat and coughed out the last of the fire coating it.

"You actually drank the bourbon!" Susannah exclaimed from the doorway of her brother's study. "I mean, I know Rye has a powerful effect on people. He's like a tidal wave."

"Were y'all standing outside the study, watching?" Paige asked, finally seeing the group of people gathered in the doorway.

"You think we'd miss the show?" Shelby told her. "You get points. Personally, I loved seeing the look on Mark's face," she added, coming into the room. "I thought he was going to lose it."

Paige looked down at the empty glass in her hand. "Where should I put this?"

Clayton came forward. "I'll take this off your hands and get it to the kitchen. Good job there. You need to call Rye's bluff every once in a while."

She stared at his back as he left the room. "Does he mean Rye was joking about the bourbon?"

"Who knows?" Susannah said. "But probably. None of us women drink it."

"Why don't we get you something a little smoother?" Shelby said.

"Nothing smoother than bourbon," Vander said, his lips twitching.

"I can't believe you drank bourbon with Rye!" Sadie said, coming inside and grabbing her by the arms. "You aren't drunk or anything, are you?"

"My wife handles her liquor pretty well," Mark said, resting against the doorframe and smirking at her.

"I haven't done shots since we were in college." That

hadn't gone so well for Mark. She'd drunk him under the table, so much so she'd needed to then take care of him. He'd been so embarrassed the next day.

"Tequila," Mark said in a deep voice. "Not my finest moment."

"Tequila is the devil," Shelby said, shuddering.

"So is Southern Comfort." Susannah grimaced.

Jake pulled her close and wrapped his arms around her. "You did shots of SoCo, honey?"

"I know," she said with a sputtered laugh. "It was at a tailgate party. What was I thinking?"

Everyone was laughing, and Paige crossed to Mark. She leaned against him and looked at her new family. Everyone was smiling at her like she'd hung the moon.

"They're pretty great," Mark whispered in her ear. "Way to go, tiger."

She was still beaming when J.P. offered to show her the chocolate garden and sweet-talked Tammy into turning the last preparations for dinner over to Susannah and Shelby so she could join them. Holding Mark's hand as they strolled though the gardens under a sunny sky, she was conscious of how happy she felt—and what a precious feeling it was.

"With fall coming in, the garden isn't quite as it was a few months ago," Tammy told her. "But it's still beautiful."

Tall grasses the color of chocolate blew in the breeze next to a plant Tammy identified as Chocolate Drop sedums. Rory ran over and joined them, and J.P. encouraged the boy to tell them the story of the chocolate fairies. According to Rory, the fairies looked out for the families who planted chocolate gardens and made them chocolate each night as a thank-you. Her lips twitched when he pulled her aside and whispered that he knew the chocolate fairies weren't the ones who put chocolate under their pillows every morning. Annabelle didn't know yet, so she and Mark had to keep the confidence.

Both she and Mark promised the little boy, and when she caught J.P.'s loving smile, her heart seemed to soak in all of the magic around them. This family—her new family—was becoming almost as vital to her as Mark and Haley, and Riley and Jess for that matter, something she'd never imagined happening.

"Are y'all finished with the garden tour?" Rye shouted from the back porch. "Some of us are starving!"

"There are appetizers in the kitchen," Tammy yelled back. "I swear that man eats more than a teenage boy."

"I hope I can eat as much as Uncle Rye when I grow up," Rory said, racing toward his uncle.

Paige caught sight of Haley and Annabelle running across the back of the house with what looked like rainbow streamers flying behind them. Rory might have been asked to watch out for Haley, but Annabelle had made it her mission to make her feel at home. She was so glad her daughter had found another friend.

Once the tour was over, she caught Vander watching her from the back porch. She decided she needed to firm up her courage and speak to him. If she couldn't face him, how in the world was she going to face Louisa McGuiness?

She squeezed Mark's hand, and he must have understood what she needed because he kissed her cheek and headed off after the others to find the appetizers.

"Would you take a walk with me?" she asked Vander.

He nodded and came down the porch steps. The chocolate garden called to her, and she sought out its beautiful warmth again.

"I know you were the one who helped everyone find Preston McGuiness," she said, not wanting to refer to him as her father.

"Yes, I was," he replied, tucking his hands in his pockets as they stopped near a cluster of maroon flowers with chocolate leaves.

"I've never even seen a picture of him," she told him, looking down at her feet, waves of vulnerability washing over her like the low tide in Dare River. "In all honesty, I'm not sure if I even want to."

He was silent, as if waiting for her to continue.

"I looked you up online," she said, feeling it was only fair to meet his eyes as she said so. "I know you're a well-respected private investigator."

He nodded.

"I...what I'm trying to say is..." She felt her throat burn with heat. "You would be thorough. You would know... everything there is to know about my mother, Skylar Watkins."

His face didn't give anything away, and she rocked back and forth on her feet.

"I want you to know I'm nothing like her," she said, clenching her hands. "She's...made her choices, and I don't condone them or even pretend to understand them."

"I know you're nothing like the woman I read about, Paige," he told her, reaching out to hold her forearm. "You don't need to worry that I'll think less of you because of what your mama did. You've clearly risen above your background, and I admire that."

She blew out a breath. "Mark and I had to cease all contact with her. She was coming around for money for drugs, and it..."

His touch was oddly comforting. "I know all that, and you did right. You chose your family. Sometimes people who are troubled never stop trying to take."

"Is Preston McGuiness like that?" she asked, old fears circling like creeping jenny on her insides. This was why she understood Riley's lingering fears about his ex. "I... need to know. I mean, it's a fear I can't completely shake... that the two of them are the same and I won't be able to avoid one or both of them coming around. I haven't told Mark it still sneaks up on me. That fear."

Vander waved to someone, and she looked over her shoulder to see it was Shelby, standing on the edge of the porch with J.P., watching them with concerned looks.

"Let's walk a bit," Vander said, guiding her to the river path.

The quiet of the trees seemed to embrace her, and she took a moment to gather herself.

"What I'm about to say, I say as both a member of this family and a private investigator. I figure you need to hear both perspectives. When Preston McGuiness ran on me from the little town he'd been holed up in for about a year, I knew he was a coward."

Her belly clutched. Only a coward could have done what he'd done.

"Later, when I met him at his mother's house—Lenore is a wonderful woman, by the way, although she's had a hard life—I found him to be a worthless excuse for a man. Selfish. Destructive. A total victim. He looks like J.P. in some ways, but he's nothing like anyone in this family. Louisa has done her job as a mother, and every one of the McGuiness children has done the rest to become who they are today."

His confidence in Lenore McGuiness, her grandmother, made her wrap her arms around herself. Hadn't the McGuiness children told her the same thing?

"Would Lenore want to meet with me? I mean...I'm... Some people might call me—"

"You're her granddaughter," Vander said, cutting her off. "We haven't told her we've found you yet or how wonderful you are. Shelby said you didn't want to talk about the past."

She'd thought that at first, but learning there might be an opening with the grandmother she'd never known... She'd lain awake at night thinking about it.

"But to answer your original question, you don't need to worry about Preston McGuiness ever taking anything from you." He kicked at a rock on the ground, using an angry, punishing force. "I'll be blunt, even though it's hard to say this to you. He said he'd never wanted to find you."

Her heart, one she'd thought healed by love, felt stabbed by a million stickpins. She stopped and turned her back on him.

"He blames me for being alive then?" she asked.

"He blames everyone," Vander said, coming closer to her. "Paige, he's... I've seen a lot of men like him in my time, but because I love this family, I hate him for the selfish, mean-spirited coward he is. Frankly, every one of you is better off without him. I mean, you've dealt with plenty of misery from your mother from what I can tell."

"And I didn't need another deadbeat parent, right?" She gave a tortured laugh. "Sometimes I don't understand life."

He kicked at another rock. "Me either. You may know this already, but my daddy was murdered in a Nashville alley twenty-five years ago. The killer was never found and brought to justice, and I've had to live with that."

This time she put her hand on his arm in comfort. "I'm so sorry."

"This year something amazing happened," he said, a half smile crossing his lips. "Boone was born on the day my father died, and even though that little boy doesn't know it, he's changed that date forever for me. It'll always be the day I lost my daddy, but now I'll spend it with this new family of mine, celebrating one of us."

Tears gathered in her eyes.

"I can't say I understand life either, and perhaps Louisa has been impacting my way of seeing things, but there seems to be something greater at work. While I don't claim to understand it, I respect it. And I'm grateful for it too."

She gave a nod and dashed at the tears in her eyes.

"I watched this family learn about something so dark, so painful...something that hurt every one of them down to their bones. Then I watched them come together and love each other through it. And then Sadie, who is supposedly the baby in the family that everyone looks out for, went out and found you. All on her own. She didn't come to me. She didn't go to anyone. She just...up and found you. And you and Mark and Haley seem to be terrific. Again, I don't understand how life works most days, but I find I'm grateful to see you here among the McGuinesses."

"Oh, goodness, I'm totally going to cry," she said. "I'm sorry. You should just leave me here for a minute."

He pulled her into his arms. "That's not what a future brother-in-law would do."

She'd never imagined him being this kind, but she found herself pressing her face into his chest, tears streaming down. "I'm so grateful for y'all too."

After she collected herself, they walked down the dirt road. When the house came into view, all of her siblings were waiting for them. She could feel their concern radiating toward her.

"Vander, there's only one last thing I want to ask," she said, stopping in her tracks. He did the same. "If there's any health issues I need to be aware of on Preston's side."

"I have that information," he said, rubbing her arm. "The family wanted it too. I'll give it to you at the next get-together."

"Thank you," she said with a soft smile.

"If you ever need any help or want to know anything, you just tell me. I'm here for you too, Paige."

"Again, thank you."

"We should probably head back. Everyone looks a touch concerned. But there's something I wanted to tell you first. You don't need to be afraid to meet with Louisa. She's one of the most loving women I've ever met, and this will help both of you, I believe."

While she believed all of the warm fuzzies about Louisa, she was the daughter of the woman who had ultimately ruined her marriage and home life. Surely even a pastor couldn't shake that kind of ugliness.

"I'm happy to go with you if you need," Vander said. "I've been part of a lot of difficult conversations surrounding Preston."

"That means a lot," she said. "Other than Mark and Riley, our neighbor...and Sadie's beau, as you probably know...I haven't had a lot of men stand up for me."

"Well, you have a whole bunch of people who will now," he said, putting his hand to her back and leading her forward. "And I'm glad to hear that about Riley. Sadie means a lot to us."

Her siblings reached out to her a little extra when she and Vander reached the porch. Sadie and Shelby hugged her. Susannah offered to get her a lemonade. But it was J.P. who stopped her and looked directly into her eyes.

"Everything okay?"

As she studied him, she thought of what Vander had said, how J.P. favored Preston. She realized this was the closest she would ever have to a firm picture of her father in her mind. Then she discarded that because she didn't want to search for similarities between her deadbeat father and her siblings. Her siblings were so much more than he could ever be.

"It is now," she told him, and surprised them both by leaning in and kissing him on the cheek.

He flashed a smile at her, and when she turned away, Mark was waiting to enfold her in his arms.

"You're the bravest woman I know," he whispered in her ear. "I'm so glad you're mine."

She should have known he would sense the upshot of her discussion with Vander.

"Back at you," she said, squeezing him tight.

When they all went inside and gathered around the large dining room table for dinner, the children's table tucked at the end, Paige was moved when J.P. asked everyone to join hands.

She was sitting between Mark and Sadie, the man of her heart and the first of her sisters to make her feel loved and wanted.

"Dear God, I want to thank you for the food we are about to eat and for all of the lovely hands that prepared it. But most of all, I want to thank you for bringing our sister, Paige, to us. For looking out for her while we were apart. For the wonderful man you blessed her with in Mark. And for the beautiful daughter they have in Haley. This family has always been in your hands, and despite tough times and heartache, we're grateful for the love you've continued to give to us. And we look forward to sharing more family dinners and get-togethers with Paige, Mark, and Haley. Amen."

"Amen," everyone echoed.

"That was a really good prayer, Dad," Annabelle said, leaning forward and looking at Haley. "When you make someone cry, it's a *really* good prayer. Who needs a tissue?"

Eyes awash in said tears, Paige started to laugh and then put her hand over her mouth to cover it, not wanting to hurt the little girl's feelings.

"I do!" Shelby said, dabbing at the corner of her eyes.

Annabelle leapt up and ran out of the room, returning with a box of tissues. Most of the women took one when she came around the table offering them. Rye grabbed three and blew his nose loudly, causing Paige to giggle.

"That prayer got to me right here," he said, pointing to his heart. "Preacher boy there knows how to say it. Paige, you should see the music he writes for me and Jake and a whole host of other singers. He's got a gift."

It struck her that she'd been listening to her brother's heart through Rye and Jake's music for as long as she could remember. She'd gotten to know J.P. long before meeting him. No wonder she loved the singers' songs.

"How about another bourbon after dinner, Paige?" Rye asked, waggling his brows.

"Why not switch to tequila?" she countered.

Everyone looked around at one another, waiting to see how he'd respond. Tory shook her head and tucked Boone closer to her chest, rocking him softly back and forth.

Rye sat back in his chair and nodded. "Gold or silver?"

So, he wasn't a man to fold. In that moment, she decided she wouldn't give in either.

"We could start with silver and go to gold, if you like. I can do either or both."

There was an audible pause before his lips twitched. "Whatever you say, sugar."

She nearly bounced in her seat, hearing him call her that. And while they never did end up having bourbon or tequila, which she'd suspected might be the case, it didn't matter in the end.

She'd become one of them.

Chapter 16

"Jess, you look beautiful," Riley told her for umpteenth time.

"Dad," his daughter said in that tone of hers, "I have to look really spectacular for my first outing with Sadie."

His heart continued to spasm with pain as she reached for a third outfit to try on. This was why he'd been worried about them meeting. His daughter was making a huge deal out of it. And, of course, it was. He and Sadie were committed to each other now. That meant something to both of them.

"Sweetheart, you're the most beautiful girl in the world. All of the outfits you've tried on look spectacular." He refrained from repeating that Sadie wouldn't care what Jess wore. That hadn't gone over well.

"This is important, Dad," she said, tugging on the blue dress Paige had bought her last Christmas. The bodice was covered in little red hearts, which only served to remind him that his little girl was wearing her heart out in the open today.

She was nervous.

Then again, so was he. He wanted to know that he'd made the right decision. In the moment, it had seemed like the perfect suggestion, but that dark voice every superhero wages war with had whispered in his ear all night. He'd countered by calling those whispers bullshit. After all, the Bradshaws' time with Sadie's family had gone incredibly well. They'd even popped by last night to tell him and Haley about it. There was no reason to think their outing would be any different. Sadie was Sadie, after all, and he was as wild about her as she was him. And she adored Jess.

It's all going to be fine, he silently repeated again, rubbing the tense muscles in his stomach.

"Do you want me to get Paige and Haley to help you choose?" he finally asked. Maybe it was time to call in the troops.

"That would be great," she said, looking at herself in the mirror over her small girl's dresser.

He thought about texting Paige, but he could use a break from the tension in the room. "I'll be right back."

Dashing down the stairs, he jogged across the short divide between their properties and rapped on the door.

Mark yelled, "Come in," and he opened it to find the Bradshaws seated at the kitchen table having lunch.

"I need some help," he said without preamble. "Jess can't decide what to wear."

Haley jumped up and ran toward him. "I'm on it."

He glanced at the clock in the kitchen. Sadie would arrive in about twenty minutes. Surely that would be enough time.

Paige crossed the room to give him a hug. "Breathe. It's going to be fine. She only wants to make a good impression."

"But Sadie already knows her and likes her," he said, hugging her back. "It breaks my heart to see her trying so hard."

Paige patted him on the cheek. "I know it does. Don't worry. We've got her. Why don't you hang out here with Mark until she's ready?"

He nodded, and she ushered him into the room before leaving and closing the back door behind her.

"I'd offer you a drink," Mark said, "but..."

"Yeah, but," Riley responded. "Sorry to interrupt lunch."

His friend came over and slapped him on the back. "You didn't. Paige and Haley were practically jumping out of their seats. They were both hoping to see Sadie before y'all headed out. In fact, Haley might have asked us if she could go with you. We had to explain this was separate time."

Riley put his hands on the kitchen counter and bent over at the waist. "I won't deny I'm a little jumpy right now, but I'm still really glad things went so well for y'all yesterday."

"Me too," Mark said, "and today is going to be great too. Y'all need to relax a bit."

"No kidding," he said, rocking back and forth with his hands on the counter.

"Jess is going to be fine," Mark said, "and Sadie will be careful with her. I expect even more careful than she is with her quilts."

Riley shook his head. "And that's saying something." Her Japanese quilt had blown his mind.

"I think we have a winner," Paige announced from the doorway.

He turned around, not having heard the back door open. "Oh, Jess. You look so beautiful, sweetheart."

"See, I told you I needed another outfit. This is so much better, right?"

She spun around, showcasing the dress she'd worn most of the summer—a stretchy cotton dress accented with some white see-through fabric at the sleeves and skirt. The dress was a little formal for an outing in the park, but she'd topped it with the jean jacket she'd talked him into. Besides, he knew she felt like a princess in it.

He walked toward her and scooped her up. He often had moments where he felt he could see her growing up right before his eyes. This was one of them.

"I'm glad you feel better," he said, tucking her freshly combed hair behind her ears. "We're going to have fun today."

"Yes, we are," she announced, wrapping her arms around him.

"I love you, sweetheart," he whispered, nuzzling her neck, knowing it always made her giggle.

"I love you too, Daddy," she whispered, tucking her little fingers into his hair like she had when he used to rock her to sleep.

"Jess!" Haley cried. "Let's go wait for Sadie."

His daughter started squirming, so he set her down. The little girls grabbed each other's hands and ran out of the kitchen.

Paige had tears in her eyes. "Oh, Riley."

He coughed. "Let's not get overly emotional here. It's not like the day we sent them off to kindergarten."

"That was a day," Mark said, opening the refrigerator. "Come on and have some iced tea. We can all wait for Sadie together."

They didn't have to wait long. She was ten minutes early, as if she was equally eager for their outing. The girls ran out immediately, and Riley strode onto the porch, loving the way Sadie was fussing with her hair as she left the car. Almost like she hadn't had time to give herself one last inspection.

"We're over at the Bradshaws, Sadie," Jess informed her when the girls met her in the middle of the sidewalk leading to the house. "We were waiting for you."

Sadie bent over and gave his little girl a hug and then did the same with Haley.

"Didn't I say she was going to be careful?" Mark said, slapping him on the back again.

He shot his friend a look and then headed off the porch to greet Sadie.

"I'm really excited to go to the park with you today," Jess was telling her. "We're going to have a great time."

Riley took a deep breath. This was going to be fine. Jess' voice had regained its confidence, which meant she was going to relax. They were all going to relax.

"Hey," he called out to Sadie, making her straighten.

She pulled her gaze away from the girls, and her brown eyes locked with his. He felt the usual pull toward her, accompanied by a deep sense of rightness. Leaning in, he kissed her cheek.

She nestled close for a moment before stepping back again. "Hey there. Sounds like everyone is ready to have some fun. Haley, if it's okay with your mom, I'll pop over and see y'all before I head home."

"Yes, please," Haley said, hugging her waist. "Please tell Annabelle and Rory how much fun I had yesterday. We have to make a play date soon."

"We will," Sadie said, chucking her under the chin. "Hey, Paige and Mark. Everyone wanted me to say how great it was yesterday. We can't wait to do it again."

Paige and Mark finally came off the porch to hug her, and Riley knew they were trying to give them space. He was grateful his friends understood.

"Do you want to come inside for a while or head straight to the park?" he asked Sadie.

He had to fight the urge to wrap his arm around her waist and bring her close. The pressure of everyone watching was checking his natural tendencies.

"Let's head on over to the park," she said. "I've been inside most of the morning."

"Right," Haley said. "You were at church. We didn't go today. How was it?"

"My mama gave a really nice sermon," she told the little girl.

"When am I going to meet her?" Haley asked. "Is she like my grandma since she's your mom and my mom is your sister?"

Paige immediately put her hands on her daughter's shoulders and turned her around. "No, honey, she's not your grandma. Remember? Sadie and I have different mamas."

Sadie seemed to have stopped breathing, and he moved closer and rubbed her back.

"Haley, why don't you say goodbye to everyone for a bit and come inside with me? I have the urge to make you two young ladies a new princess tent."

"You do?" Haley asked.

"Cool!" Jess said, hugging Mark's leg. "Maybe we can play in it later after we get home from the park."

Riley knew Mark was creating something special for Jess and Haley on the off chance that things didn't go smoothly today. His buddy had his back, and it made him feel less pressure about the outing.

"Okay, let's go," he said. "We'll see y'all later."

"Count on it," Haley said in a voice much like Mark's, making Paige muffle her laughter as the Bradshaws walked back to their house.

He, Jess, and Sadie headed to his car, and he opened the passenger door.

"Oops, I need to get my purse," Jess said, running off to their house.

He and Sadie stood silently by the car, looking at each other. His eyes skimmed down her scoop-neck navy tee and tan Capri pants. Her flat-heeled sandals were gold, a color he would forever link with both her and the character she'd inspired for him. She looked good enough to eat, and he'd bet the farm this wasn't what she'd worn to church.

"She insisted on having a purse," he found himself telling Sadie.

"I had one when I was her age," Sadie said, smiling at him. "It's going to be fine, Riley."

His fingers grazed her cheek. "I know it. She just...it took her a few times to decide what to wear."

Her hand rested on his chest. "I know the feeling."

"I just threw this on," he said, his heart starting to beat faster. "It's only a day in the park."

"Exactly," she said, rubbing the tension over his heart away.

"But it's not," he said softly after a long moment.

"No, it's not," she replied in an equally quiet tone.

Chapter 17

"I so want to kiss you right now," Riley told her, putting a hand on her hip.

His deep voice sent waves of heat straight to Sadie's tummy, burning up all her nerves. "Me too."

Jess came flying out of the house. "I've got it. I've got my purse."

"Well, that's a relief," Riley said, opening her car door for her so she could hop in. "Maybe I need one. Can you name a superhero who has a man purse?"

"Tony Stark probably does," Jess said, buckling into her car seat. "Right, Dad?"

Thinking it might be better to play along, Sadie slowly nodded.

"You don't know who Tony Stark is," he said slowly.

"No way!" Jess cried out from the backseat. "He's like the coolest."

"Iron Man," he explained, though that didn't really help. She'd heard the name, but that was it.

Her face flushed, and she couldn't help but shrug defensively. "You don't like country music and I don't know superheroes besides the main ones."

"Sadie, you should watch it with us sometime. Dad knows all the lines. He loves *Iron Man*."

Watching a movie all snuggled up against Riley sounded good...no, better than good. But she wasn't really a superhero movie kind of girl.

"Let me guess," he said. "You like movies like *Steel Magnolias*."

"My sister, Shelby, was named after the character Julia Roberts played." She played with her seatbelt. "I saw *Wonder Woman*."

"Of course you did," he teased her.

"It was the best movie ever." Jess bounced in her booster seat.

Sadie glanced his way before she spoke. Maybe it marked her as a softie, but... "I don't like it that the man she loved died."

"Yeah, that was kinda sad," Jess said from the back. "But he died a hero and that's all that mattered. Right, Dad?"

"Ah...that's how we see it with our superhero perspective," Riley explained to her. "Dying is a natural part of life, and when you do it for the greater good—"

"You're a hero," Jess interrupted. "And we love heroes at our house. Dad actually told me you're a hero for finding Mrs. Bradshaw like you did, Sadie. That's why he's using you as the model for his new superhero, although she's not quite right yet."

Oh goodness. "That might be the nicest compliment I've ever received."

"Maybe you need a cape, Sadie," Jess said. "Dad could design it for you. He designs outfits for Haley and me all the time. Right, Dad?"

"Yep. That's me. Superhero outfit designer."

It surprised her how much she loved hearing him called Dad. This man she was getting to know, the one who made her blood boil, was also gentle and kind with children. He was a wonderful father to his daughter.

"You're smiling," he said in a soft tone, his hand stroking the steering wheel.

It looked like he wanted to reach out and touch her like he did on one of their date nights. Usually he would hold her hand or run his hand down her arm while he was driving.

"I am," she said, leaning back in her chair and taking in the blue sky and sunshine. "It's a good day for the park."

"I ordered it up," Riley said.

"With his special weather powers," Jess said. "Right, Dad?"

He was smiling too. "Yeah, Jess. We speak two main languages in our house, by the way. Disney and superhero."

"I'll get the hang of it," Sadie murmured, turning in her seat to look at Jess. "So, what's your favorite Disney movie of all time?"

"Old school or recent?" Jess fired back, her green eyes flashing with excitement.

There were different tiers? She could do this. Annabelle loved Disney too. "Both."

"Old school is *Cinderella*," Jess told her, "and recent is *Tangled*. Now you."

The little girl was pointing at her with all the effusive energy of a seven-year-old. "Well, I like *Sleeping Beauty*... I'm not sure about a recent movie. Does *Beauty and the Beast* count?"

The little girl nodded. "Who's your favorite Disney hero of all time?"

Oh, goodness, she'd hadn't counted on a quiz. "The beast. Because he overcomes his selfishness by choosing love."

"You're a romantic," Jess said. "Right, Dad?"

Riley was chuckling under his breath. "I already knew that. Okay, Jess, favorite Disney villain of all time?"

"That's easy!" Jess said. "Rapunzel's pretend mother in *Tangled*."

"What?" Riley said, shifting in his seat. "I thought it was the witch in *Snow White*. When did you change your mind?"

She shrugged. "Haley and I have been discussing this, Dad. It's Rapunzel's *pretend* mother because nobody should ever lie about being someone's real mother."

Sadie caught the frown on Riley's face. He was upset by this answer, and she wanted to reach for his hand to comfort him. She thought about asking Jess a question to change the subject, but this topic was deeply personal and not one she felt she had the right to delve into.

"But the witch in *Snow White* was her stepmother—"

"It's totally different, Dad," Jess told him. "She wasn't pretending, and she didn't steal any babies. Snow White's dad married her. He was so stupid."

Riley's frown was thunderous. Sadie sneaked another peek back at Jess. The little girl wasn't smiling anymore either. There was an undercurrent of battle in the car, and she wondered again about the story with Jess' mom.

"You know I don't like you to use the word *stupid*, Jess," he said in a gentle voice, a voice that was still filled with love.

She'd heard Tammy and J.P. correct Rory and Annabelle in such a voice.

"But you're right," he said, gripping the steering wheel now. "Snow White's dad made a bad choice when he married the queen."

"He was taken in by her beauty," Jess said. "Sometimes men are so stupid."

"Jess! Who told you that?"

"One of the girls at school," Jess fired back. "But she's right. Only someone stupid gets taken in by a bad woman. Beauty isn't a good enough reason."

"Maybe she was nice to him," Riley said. "Maybe..."

Sadie's heart hurt when he stopped and took a deep breath.

"Dad you always said maybes don't get the job done," Jess replied.

He took another breath. "I know I do, but it's not always black and white when people make bad choices, Jess."

"Dad, you always tell me that good people don't make excuses. They take responsibility."

Sadie felt the urge to sink deeper in her seat, hoping to look less visible. This conversation wasn't one she felt comfortable joining.

"You're right, but sometimes good people make bad choices because they don't have all the information. Like Star Lord in *Guardians of the Galaxy 2*. He didn't know why his dad left him or that his dad wanted to use him for bad purposes."

"Star Lord didn't make the bad choice," Jess replied in a voice ringing with certainty. "His dad was the bad guy."

"I'm not saying this right," Riley said. "Jess—"

"Dad, you just drove past the park."

Sadie looked out the window, and sure enough, they were coming to the next cross street.

"Ah...I'm... Oh, forget it. I'm turning around." He checked both sides before making a U-turn and driving them back to the park.

After he pulled into a parking space, he gripped the wheel for a moment before getting out of the car and walking around to help Jess out first. She had her door open before he could reach for it.

"Can I go swing?" Jess asked. "You'll be able to see me. Then maybe you can push me."

He ran his hand down her hair, and she pushed at it.

"Dad! Don't touch my hair. I made it perfect."

"Fine," he said with the hint of testiness in his voice. "Go on and swing. Sadie and I will watch you, and in a little while, I'll push you."

"You'd better," she said, sprinting off.

He sagged against the frame of the car. "I feel like I should apologize. That must have been awkward for you. Hell, it felt like sinking in quicksand for me."

With Jess at a distance, she could reach out and rub his chest. "Hey, you're okay. She's a kid, and kids like to ask questions. I've heard my niece and nephew ask some humdingers, and my brother and his wife did the best they could like you did."

"I want to beat my head against this car," he said, "but that won't change the past. Dammit!" He turned around. "Can you see her? I need a minute."

"I can see her," she said softly. "Take your time."

"It's like she's putting the pieces of the past together subconsciously," Riley said softly, "and she's just a kid. I keep hoping it's going to take her longer to figure things out." He paused for a long minute, and finally said, "Sadie, I should probably tell you about her mother."

"You don't have to do it now," she said, putting her hand on his back, her eyes on Jess kicking her feet and starting to swing.

"This isn't how I thought today would go, but maybe a brief snapshot would be helpful after what you heard in the car," he told her, turning back to face her. "Mandy, Jess' mom, got pregnant while we were dating. She was on birth control, and I still don't know what happened except Jess was supposed to be born somehow. She was like this special creature who came into existence out of sheer will or something. Like the Thing in *Fantastic 4* or Magneto in *X-Men*. Please tell me you know X-Men. Never mind."

He would use a superhero allusion, she thought.

"I didn't realize it at the time, but somewhere down the line the partying Mandy and I were doing as stupid young twenty-somethings had taken a turn. Oh, shit this is hard. I don't want you to think less of me."

When he gripped the top of the car, she rubbed his back. "I won't. I promise."

He took a breath like he was gathering courage and then said, "We were deep into drinking and some recreational drugs. We told ourselves it helped our art. But Mandy got tripped up in it, and I didn't..."

She didn't know how to help him suddenly. "It's okay."

"No, it's not," he whispered, his head turned away. "I didn't see it, so when she got pregnant with Jess, she ODed. I found her, and somehow they managed to save both of them."

"Oh, honey, I can't imagine," she whispered, her heart shattering in the face of so much hurt. "You must have been so scared."

"Only problem was Mandy didn't want to be saved," he said, coughing briefly. "She told me since the ODing hadn't worked, she wanted to have an abortion. Told me it was her choice since she would have to carry the baby to term. They don't hire a lot of up and coming singers who are pregnant, turns out. She didn't want to be saddled with a kid."

Sadie wanted to run to Jess and wrap her arms around her. Someone hadn't wanted this little girl?

"Her not wanting the baby," he whispered, "and overdosing on purpose...I couldn't believe it. I mean, she was our *baby*. I'd never thought much about kids, but once I heard about Jess, I couldn't... She's my..."

"Child," Sadie said, watching as the little girl kicked her feet to swing higher. "I would have felt the same way even though I know people need to make their own choices."

"Yeah, except the dad's choices aren't always factored in," he said, "and Mandy wouldn't listen to me. I finally came up with a plan. I told her I would pay her to have Jess, almost like a surrogate, the same amount she felt she would have made for the nine months of her pregnancy. I told her I would raise Jess alone. Ask nothing from her ever. My only conditions were that she couldn't use during the pregnancy and she'd sign over custody once Jess was born."

Relief washed over her. "You did right," she said, hugging him.

"Mandy high-balled the amount she thought she could make, but I got a loan. Paid her. Got her signature on the agreement. As part of the deal, I insisted she have regular drug tests. I...I worried about what the effects on our baby would be. It was hard on her, but Mandy did it."

He paused, looking down at the ground. "I'll be honest...I thought she might change her mind when she saw Jess. That she'd at least want to hold her for a few hours. That maybe the old Mandy would come back. But no... She handed her over without any fucking human emotion and then asked the nurse for some painkillers."

He swiped at his eyes, and she had to blink back her own tears.

"I still can't understand how she could do that. I don't think I ever will. I mean, I know chemical abuse messes people up, but she was so...bright and wonderful when I first met her. My love for her...kept me blind to what was going on, and that's on me."

Now the earlier conversation between Riley and Jess made more sense. "You aren't to blame for her choices."

"Yes, I am, because they put Jess in danger." He wiped his nose. "I cried like a baby when the doctors told me she was healthy. Earlier tests had been inconclusive."

Hearing that only reaffirmed Sadie's belief in miracles. Angels had protected that little girl.

"The worst of it is that Mandy came back on Jess' first birthday, wanting money," he said. "Her drug problem was much worse, but she was still trying to make her career work. She blamed me, and she blamed Jess. And my parents and my brother's family were there to see the whole sorry scene unfold. I had to call the cops. Oh, Sadie."

The story kept getting worse and worse, and Sadie had to fight to control her own emotions in the face of his. "You kept her safe."

"I have a P.I. do a yearly update on Mandy," he said. "She's still in Nashville, but she's never tried to contact me again. I...calling the cops wasn't easy, but it made her leave. She took off before they could arrive. My parents took it hard when I told them everything. They hadn't realized how bad things had gotten for her, for us. I'd tried to keep the full story from them because I knew they'd be upset, hell, disappointed, but I ended up telling them, and they...it's like they stepped back. I think they moved to Florida so they could pick and choose when to...step in. I don't blame them."

What a horrible first birthday for Jess and the father who had gone to tremendous lengths to bring her into the world. She couldn't comment on his parents, so she only said, "But six years have passed without any contact from her, and that's a good thing."

He ran a hand through his hair, making a mess of it, before meeting her eyes again. "Jess seems to have questions about her mother now that you and Paige have connected, and I just don't know how to handle them. I can't tell her the truth right now, and I wonder if I ever can."

Part of her felt guilty suddenly. "Oh, Riley, I'm so sorry. I never imagined me coming to find Paige would—"

"No, it's fine," he said, taking her hands and looking into her eyes. "Sadie, I'm so glad you found Paige. I mean, if you knew how much it's meant to her and Mark and Haley. She had a hell of a time growing up, and she deserved a lucky break."

Sadie had trouble considering herself a lucky break, but she supposed they were fortunate to have found each other.

"I've got to figure out...hell, I don't know." He paced in place. "I have one last thing to ask you, and I want you to be completely honest with me."

The seriousness of his tone had her shaking her head.

"Do you think less of me for telling you I did drugs now and then? Sadie, I swear to you that I haven't once touched them since learning about Jess, and I never will again. They...were a part of that life, and they're something I'm not proud of."

She touched his cheek so he would look at her. "Riley, I don't judge you for any of that. After hearing the whole story, I think you're even more wonderful than I ever knew."

He swiped at a few tears that leaked out. "Thank God. I was so scared..."

"Let that go," she said, framing his face. "I see you too, Riley Thomson, and you're a good man and an amazing father, perhaps one of the best fathers I know. And this comes from someone who didn't have one and did a lot of wishing for one." Still did, come to think about it.

"We should go. I know we can see her, but..."

This outing was supposed to be about them having a good time. She took his hand, and together they headed off toward the swings.

"Riley, your vast knowledge of superheroes and Disney movies gives you an edge with kids, but you also have something else going for you."

"What's that?" he asked, running his thumb over the back of her hand.

"You're well versed in loving Jess. That's the best language any kid can hear from a parent. I mean, I only had one of them too, and I mostly turned out okay, didn't I?"

"More than." He blew out a breath. "I'm totally in love with you, Sadie McGuiness, and after today, I hope you haven't gotten scared off. Because I'm going to be really honest with you. I want to make this work."

With the happy shadow of Jess swinging on the swings washing over them, she took his hand and placed it right below her heart. "I love you too, Riley. And I'm not scared. We'll find a way to make it work."

"I don't care if there are a million kids around, including mine. I'm going to kiss you." His mouth turned up. "On the cheek."

She gave a watery laugh as he gave her a quick peck. "Maybe when we get to your house, we can watch *Iron Man*. I need to become better versed in your language."

"Sadie, you already are in all the ways that count," he said. "Now, I'm going to push my daughter and...settle down."

She watched him approach the swings and take his place behind his daughter. In a moment, she'd join them, but right now, she wanted to settle her own emotions and savor the sweetness of the scene.

He had been there for Jess from the moment she'd come into being, Sadie now knew, and that made him one of the greatest heroes she'd ever met. How funny that he didn't need to be a superhero to achieve it. Love was his superpower.

She'd have to tell him later because like her not seeing herself as an artist, she wasn't sure he realized that about himself.

Chapter 18

Riley's so-called Plan Sadie was about to commence. Their first outing with Jess had been so momentous, he'd come home and immediately started planning something...a surprise...a thank-you. A declaration.

He loved her. She loved him. She hadn't run after hearing the news about Jess' mother. She hadn't judged him, and he'd realized later how much he'd secretly feared she would. There was still a dark, tortured part of him that judged himself for what had happened with Mandy. Clearly he needed to let that go, and the old hurts and self-judgments had started to fade away when she took his hand and placed it over her heart.

Any comic book fan understood on some level that love healed the dark places. It wasn't all about good fighting evil and winning. No, every superhero went through a transformation when he fell in love.

He'd researched like a madman, looking for something romantic and finding fault with other people's suggestions. He didn't want to two-step with her at Wildhorse Saloon or head out to Belle Meade Plantation. She might like it, but it wasn't him, and if he wasn't comfortable too, he'd totally be off his game.

Brainstorming with Mark over their morning runs

had helped. Mark had reminded him that he was good at creating magic with the girls. Why not with Sadie?

Finally he'd come up with what he hoped was a respectable plan. Paige assured him her sister would find it charming. He sure as hell hoped so.

He'd asked her to come over Wednesday night. The Bradshaws would take care of Jess, although his daughter had insisted on greeting Sadie at some point. She was as excited about the surprise as Riley was and had even helped set it up. So had Haley since the girls were joined at the hip. Paige had weighed in here and there.

When the doorbell rang, he checked his preparations one last time before heading to the door.

"Hey," she said, standing in the fading light in another pink dress, this one the shade of bubble gum.

If there was one thing he knew for sure, Sadie loved pink and seemed to wear it when she wanted to...exude love, he thought, although it might be corny of him. He'd seen at least five shades of the color so far, from dresses to accessories. Gold, he'd realized, she reserved for moments when she needed extra confidence.

He knew the favorite colors of all the women in his life, he realized. Jess loved raspberry. His mom loved apricot. Haley loved purple. Paige loved blue. Hell, he was embarrassed to realize he even knew Mark's favorite color: green. But he wouldn't admit that under torture.

"Hey," he said, his voice growing husky. "How is it you become more beautiful every time I see you?"

"Oh, Riley," she said softly, the gold in her eyes captivating.

"I didn't get a chance to properly kiss you on Sunday and after everything... I really need to make up for that. Like right now."

"Let me come in first," she said, stepping inside. "I was expecting my usual welcoming committee."

He pulled her against him and took her purse and set

it on the table in the foyer. "I made a deal with the girls. You'll see them in a little while."

Her body fit perfectly against him, and he leaned down and took her mouth in a slow, drugging kiss. He'd always loved kissing, and kissing Sadie had quickly become one of his new favorite occupations. Her lower lip was lush and enticing, so he sucked on it gently. When she moaned, he felt something inside him snap. Pulling her closer, he increased the pressure of his mouth on hers, their kisses growing more urgent. He was breathing harder. Needed air. And he didn't give a damn.

She moaned and wiggled in his arms, and he put both of his hands on her hips. He'd found himself sketching those lush curves during the day, adding them to his female superhero, and the feel of them made him groan. He had visions of dragging her onto any available surface and fitting their bodies together at last.

But that wasn't part of the plan, so he reached for control and gentled the kiss. She moaned again like she didn't want him to stop, but the timing wasn't right. He kissed her neck and cheek softly and pulled away.

"We need to stop," he whispered. "Besides, I have a surprise for you."

"You do?" she asked, pressing back.

"Yes. Come with me."

He took her hand and led her toward the opening to the dining room.

"I'm going to put my hands over your eyes and lead you in," he said. "Unless you want me to blindfold you. But that seemed a little *Fifty Shades* to me."

Her mouth was twitching. "I suppose that depends on my surprise."

"You didn't just say that." He blinked. "Sadie, I want you like crazy, but I'm really trying to honor your feelings about sex. Please, for the love of God, don't put those kind of images in my mind. I'm trying to hold it together as it is."

Her brown eyes darkened. "Maybe you should stop trying so hard."

"Whoa. What?"

"You heard me," she said, a flush settling over her cheeks. "I've done a lot of thinking since last weekend. We've already come a long way, but it feels like something changed on Sunday. You sharing the full story about your past with Jess' mom... It was brave, and it made me love you more...and so...I'd...like to take the next step with you."

Baring his soul like that had made her decide this? He blinked a few times more times. "Are you sure?"

"Yes."

"Completely sure?" he added, wanting—no, needing—her to assure him again.

"Yes."

When she took his hand and placed it over her breast, his breath caught. Her heart was beating fast, likely as fast as his was now.

"Riley, I love you—all of you—and I want you," she said in an almost whisper. "I feel really at peace about it. And that's how I know it's the right thing."

That same peace seemed to settle over him. "I love you too, and I want you like crazy. Wait, I can do better than that."

He took a deep breath and ran his thumb over the back of her hand.

"I want you more than I've ever wanted anyone, and I love you more than I imagined I could love a woman. Sadie, time doesn't seem to matter with you. It's like a truly great drawing. When it's right, it just flows out of me. It's when I don't trust myself or my vision for the drawing that it takes forever."

"Oh, Riley. I love the way you talk."

His free hand stroked her cheek. "Guess what? You're going to love the way I make love to you too."

Her chest rose with a rapid intake of breath, and he could feel her arousal.

"I plan to do it quite thoroughly," he uttered, his voice husky. "With relish. Sadie, I want to learn every part of you. Every sigh. Every dip of your figure. Every inch of your beautiful body."

Her cheeks were bright red. "I want that too, although I'm a little embarrassed. I'm not very good at this. I... don't want to disappoint you or anything. I mean, I've only been with one man, and I was so young. Sometimes I didn't know what I was doing. He was a virgin too, and..."

"Are you finished selling yourself short?" he asked.

She took a deep breath. "Was I?"

His brow cocked. "Yep. Sadie, you're going to do great. Know why I know this?"

"Part of me can't wait to hear," she said with a small smile. "I think you're about to compliment me."

Ah, she was a smart woman. "Sadie, you like texture and beauty and movement, and you pay attention to details. That's all making love is, although to be honest, I don't think I've really made love. I'm..." All right, time to be more vulnerable. "I'm excited to explore it with you."

"Me too," she said, leaning up and kissing him on the cheek. "Oh, Riley. I never imagined something could feel so right."

"Me either," he said, "but it's perfect. Now, before we get carried away, let me show you the surprise."

He turned her around and placed his hands over her eyes. "No peeking," he said, leading her into the dining room. The candles flickered, and he took inventory. Everything was as it was supposed to be.

Removing his hands, he said, "Okay, open."

"You made dinner?" she asked. "How sweet! Wait... what in the world is this?"

She walked forward to the chest resting at the end of the table, wrapped in a bright pink bow.

"It's your treasure chest," he told her, praying he wasn't going to turn beet-red from embarrassment. "I felt like you needed this."

Her eyes blinked, but she made no move toward it.

"Open it," he said, coming to stand beside her. "It's not like any fake snakes are going to spring out."

"I never even thought of that." She gave him a look. "What did you do?"

He was so used to Jess diving into gifts, he had to tamp down the urge to open it for her. "Well, look inside and see."

She was tentative, he realized, and then he wondered if she was unaccustomed to having people give her surprise gifts. She was the one who was always giving. He'd have to change that up.

Her hand opened the chest slowly, and then she looked at him, her eyes crinkling at the corners. "Clothes?"

"Vintage clothing," he told her. "Antique fabrics. For your quilts."

"Oh!"

"I didn't know how you'd want them cut, and I didn't feel right about doing it, so I just...bought you fabric I thought you might like to use for quilting."

When she didn't move, only stood there staring into the chest, fear jolted through him. Had he done something wrong? He put his hand to her back.

"Are you okay? I thought—"

"Oh, Riley, it's wonderful! Simply wonderful. I'm... overwhelmed. Where did you find them?"

"I visited every vintage clothing shop in Nashville," he told her. "It was an adventure, let me tell you. I figured you work at a craft store and have access to plenty of fabric, but...well...I read how Japanese quilters use old clothing and it struck me that I could give you a treasure chest filled with old fabric for you to use however you want."

"I don't know what to say." She reached slowly for the

red and pink Japanese kimono and drew it out. Under it was a black and gold textured dress from the 1960s, followed by a couple of cloth purses in colorful prints.

That gold dress had been a no-brainer.

"I went with my gut on what colors and fabric you might like," he told her. "I hope it's okay."

She laid the pieces he'd bought one by one on the dining room table, fingering the material. "Oh, yes. You did great! I love the colors. And the textures you chose…I can do a lot with this."

When she drew out the gold lamé dress from the 1970s, he said, "I know how much you love pink, but gold is your second favorite color. Well, I think so."

"Is it?" she asked, beaming at him as she ran her fingers over the dress lying in her arms.

"You like to use it mostly as an accent," he told her. "Maybe you're not ready to show the world you're that powerful yet, but I can see it. When I think of you, I see gold."

The right side of her mouth turned up. This one was another one of those things he could see about her that she could not. "You do?"

"I do," he said, stepping closer and laying his hand over hers. "Your heart is pink, but your body is all gold to me."

She set aside the dress, her eyes lush and inviting. "Oh, Riley, if I hadn't already decided to make love with you, this would have cinched it. You…no one has given me a better present than this. No one."

Emotion flooded through him. "Whew! I was a little worried you might think it was weird."

"No," she said, hugging him. "It was the most thoughtful idea ever."

Then she pressed back and put her hand on his chest. He felt the power of her touch down to his toes.

"Riley, you see me. And you understand me. I…there

are no words for how precious a gift that is. I… Well, I just love you. Please make love to me."

His hands settled on her hips. "I will. Don't you worry about that. But I promised Jess and Haley that they could come over after you opened your present. Of course, I was hoping we might eat first but—"

"If we have them over now, we can move along to other things, right?" She gave a slow smile. "I can eat fast."

He laughed. "My kind of woman. But we don't need to rush. We have all night. That is, if you're okay with doing this on a weeknight. Otherwise, we can wait for Saturday. I…didn't expect this. But I'm good either way."

I'm good either way? He was a moron.

"I'll shut up now."

She lifted onto her tiptoes and kissed him softly on the cheek. "I…ah…bought condoms. I…ah…wasn't sure what kind to get, so I got a few. Oh, goodness, this is embarrassing. I had no idea there were so many varieties. I mean, it was like trying to buy nail polish."

He bit his lip. "Nail polish."

"Only a woman would understand," she said, her eyes narrowing. "Wait until Jess and Haley start doing their nails."

"You think they haven't tried to talk me into that already? I have eight kinds upstairs." He shuddered. "Trust me, I get the reference. Quick dry. Glitter. Topcoat. Sadie, I…ah…bought some too. To be prepared. It wasn't assuming. Only…ah…hoping."

He felt it was important to add that last part.

"Go call over the girls then," she said. "I'm going to look at my fabric."

Would it be too obvious if he ran out of the house at full speed to fetch them? Mark would laugh for sure. Paige too, likely. Although maybe it would be kind of weird for her, him having sex with her sister? He wasn't going to think about that. Everyone was an adult, after all.

"Riley?"

He turned around from the doorway.

In her arms was the silk kimono he'd fantasized about her wearing after they made love. He might ask her to keep that one. And the textured gold dress...

"Thank you."

She hugged the fabric to her as if it were the most precious treasure in the world, exactly as he'd intended. He walked out of his house at a measured pace to fetch the girls, smiling.

When everything was this perfect, there was no reason to hurry.

Chapter 19

The girls were adorable as they sat on the dining room table flanking the treasure chest, telling Sadie how beautiful her quilts were going to be with the fabric Riley had bought. They peppered her with questions about the kinds of designs she imagined. Was she going to make a baby blanket? A princess quilt? Their voices were honeyed with hope when they asked her that.

Jess had strong opinions about the silk kimono being perfect for a princess quilt. Hadn't they made a Disney movie about Mulan, who'd saved China by dressing up as a boy to serve as a soldier?

Riley finally called it quits, telling Haley and Jess it was time to go back to the Bradshaws. Paige had sent her hellos but hadn't come by, likely sensing they'd want to be alone with the girls. Sadie kissed each girl on the cheek and hugged them tight.

When Riley returned, he held out his hands. "Whew! Those two. They get riled up so easily. I kinda felt bad, leaving Paige and Mark to deal with it."

He shifted on his feet, and she realized he was nervous. How sweet! She felt a wave of nerves roll through her own tummy as the silence in the room grew more pronounced.

"Are you hungry?" she asked.

"Are you?" he asked right back.

She wasn't sure she could eat much. Her stomach wasn't giving her the best indication of anything right now other than anxiety. "I could eat something. You made it, and you're probably hungry."

"Okay," he said, shifting from right to left again. "It's...I need to turn on the grill. I made kebobs."

She found herself smiling. "You did?"

"It's a trick I learned with Jess," he said, shrugging. "If you make food pretty and colorful she's more likely to eat it. Also, she likes to build things, and with kebobs, she can help."

She was struck anew by the thoughtfulness that went into so many of his everyday choices. Was every parent conscious of such things? Tammy and J.P. were, but she'd thought they were unique.

"You really are a great dad," she told him.

"Flatterer," he said, lurching forward like he needed to unseal himself from his spot. "You haven't seen me on my bad dad days. We flew to my brother's place for the holidays when Jess was about a year old, and we got stranded in Chicago. I had to carry her on my shoulders through the airport, our luggage and her carrier seat in my hands, because she started to cry every time I sat down. I ended up barking at a man who ran into me, and it got a little contentious when he got in my face. I might have called him a few prize names, ones I was grateful my daughter couldn't pronounce at the time."

She kept smiling.

"I'm babbling," he said, holding out his hands. "Are you nervous too? It's kinda caught up with me."

"Me too," she said, inching closer to him. "Maybe you should hold me. That always makes me feel good." *Calm*, she almost added, but didn't know how he'd feel about that, especially right before they made love for the first time.

He pulled her against his chest. "Like I said, it doesn't have to be tonight."

She'd stayed awake all night and been a total flake at work thinking about nothing else. "I don't want to wait any longer."

"When you make up your mind, you're... I'm the same way." His fingers brushed her cheek. "Would you come upstairs with me then?"

She suddenly found it difficult to breathe. "Yes. Should I bring the—"

"I've got that covered," he said, fighting a smile.

"Are you laughing at me?" she asked.

"No," he replied immediately. "I'm only...I can almost see you in the store. Worse than nail polish. That's pretty funny."

When he started laughing, she socked him. "You shouldn't laugh. I was trying so hard to figure out what to buy. I almost called Shelby, but I was too embarrassed. Plus, then she'd pepper me with questions about you and when she was going to officially meet you."

His brows drew closer together.

"You don't have to meet them until you're ready," she added. "I mean, it's totally cool." What was she saying? Totally cool?

"Do you want me to meet everyone?"

"Of course." She didn't even have to think about it. "But I know this is a big step."

So was telling her about Mandy. He nuzzled her neck. "Making love is pretty big. Let's focus on one thing at a time. Ready to go up?"

She fought the urge to gulp. "Yes, of course."

When he took her hand, she curled her fingers around his. He looked down at her, his blue eyes filled with love. "It's going to be great, Sadie. Trust me."

"I do," she whispered.

He kissed her, ever so slowly at first, until they both

seemed to flow into each other again. Her rapid heartbeat smoothed out as he ran his hand up and down her back, settling them both down, getting her used to his touch.

She broke the kiss. "Let's go upstairs." Love was flooding her heart, and the nerves had retreated to the edges of her consciousness now.

The stairs creaked here and there as he led her up. She'd never been upstairs, and her gaze eagerly took in the colorful artwork on the hallway walls. One was a landscape done in what looked like black pencil while another boasted a superhero cloaked in a black cape, only his eyes showing.

"Are these yours?" she asked, unable to see a signature in the low light.

"Yes," he said, kissing her hand. "Jess' artwork is in her bedroom and a few other places. She loves to see it when she wakes up every morning."

"I love that you encourage her talent."

He stopped in a doorway and flicked on a light. "This is me. Let me turn the lamp on. Candles?"

She felt a little lonely when he let go of her hand, so she wrapped her arms around herself. His room was decorated with a combination of black and white with a few splashes of red. Somehow he'd brought color and panache to the minimalistic décor.

"I like it," she told him.

He looked up from smoothing out the wrinkles on the bed, something she might have normally found amusing. "I'm awash in girly colors mostly, and that's okay. But I needed something a little more..."

"Manly?"

His perfunctory nod was endearing. "Let me grab the candles from the dining room. I totally forgot... Be right back."

He left the room at a quick pace, and she measured his progress by the squeaks on the stairs. When he blew back in, he was using the bottom half of his black T-shirt to hold the candles.

"Glass got hot," he explained.

She caught a flash of his flat abs, and a ribbon of heat twirled through her. They were about to get naked. More heat danced through her senses, and she had the urge to fan herself.

The candles clattered when he set them down, and she heard him swear under his breath.

"Did you burn yourself?" she asked, crossing to him.

"Third degree," he said with a dramatic eye roll. "We need to find a doctor immediately."

She felt her mouth twitch. "Let me see."

He held out his hands, and the size of them struck her anew. They were large and strong. And pretty soon they were going to touch her. Maybe he needed encouragement.

"Riley," she said in a husky voice.

"Yes, Sadie?" His voice was equally affected.

"Put your hands on me."

Was that too bold, she wondered? But then his blue eyes flashed dark, and his hands covered her breasts. She inhaled sharply. Well, he didn't mess around. That was probably best. The way they were dancing around making love, someone needed to move them in the right direction.

His fingers stroked her through her thin bra. She'd gone with her most romantic bra and panty set made of lace the color of ripe apricots. When he tugged down the bodice of her dress, he hummed in that way he had, telling her he liked what she'd chosen.

"You are so beautiful," he said. "Let me show you how much."

His fingers tugged her dress down, and she stepped out of it and the strapless heels she'd specifically chosen for tonight. He ran his hands down her sides and then rested them on her hips. Under his intense study, she felt lush and a little vulnerable.

"My God, Sadie," he said, his hands tightening on her waist. "Your curves are going to drive me wild."

She felt a part of her soar, the one who was all woman, the one who wanted to feel sexy in the arms of her man. "I'm glad, but are you planning on getting undressed anytime soon?"

His eyes locked with hers. "You think you're ready for that?"

He'd meant it to be a joke, but she surprised herself by lifting up his shirt and running her fingers along that flash of abs she'd seen earlier.

"Okay, yeah, you're ready," he murmured, lifting his shirt up and off.

Her face started to heat when he unzipped his cargo pants and slid them down his legs. She wasn't surprised to see him wearing boxers, but she tried to fight a grin in response to the design. Superheroes, of course.

He gestured to them, shaking his head. "I didn't know about your plan. Otherwise, I would have worn something different."

The Batman symbol covered his erection, and the word *POW!* was illuminated with a yellow spotlight over his left leg.

"When I'm having trouble drawing, which I struggled with today because I couldn't stop thinking about seeing you tonight, I put these on," he explained. "They're my favorite boxers. You can laugh. Clearly you win the underwear contest."

"Do you have more superhero boxers?" she asked.

He waggled his brows. "I'll save that answer for another time. A man has to have some secrets. Are you sure you still want to make love with me? I mean...this is major geek stuff."

Her shoulders shook from repressed laughter. "Ah...

are you planning on saying, 'Pow,' or quoting any other superhero while we're making love?"

He pressed his fingers to his brow. "God, no! I swear. I know I drop into Disney and superhero quotes sometimes, but I promise that ends in the bedroom."

Clearly he'd taken her seriously. Way too seriously. "Riley, I was kidding," she said through giggles, "but thanks for reassuring me."

"I'm glad you're finding this so amusing," he said. "Well, there's only one thing to do."

He shucked his boxers down and threw them across the room into the corner. "I figure this has to be better, right?"

Her breath stopped at the sight of him. She'd only seen one other man completely naked, and she didn't remember much in all honesty. The sight of Riley standing there, so firm and hard, made her gulp. He was so big. She knew she was staring, but she couldn't help herself.

"Did I shock you?" he asked. "I can put something on if it's—"

"Don't be silly," she said, forcing her gaze off him. "I'm...you're..."

"Yes?"

"Big," she blurted out.

His lips twitched. "Only big men can wear superhero boxers."

She didn't believe that for a minute, but she found herself smiling. "Is that so?"

He leaned in, his body not touching her. "Yes, in fact, there's one other rule. Only men with herculean stamina in bed can wear them too. Care for a demonstration?"

Lord, she was going to overheat. "You'd better before I explode."

He picked her up, and her muscles froze in surprise. Walking to the edge of the bed, he laid her down and settled himself on her side. He lowered himself to her and took her mouth in a hot, drugging kiss.

She opened to him, and his tongue slid inside to dance with hers. The kiss held more power than the ones they'd shared before, and she knew it was because he wasn't holding back. When his hands ran down the sides of her waist, she wiggled closer, fitting herself to his front. The heat and hardness of him had her squirming. Then he rolled onto his back and pulled her on top of him, his hands grabbing her butt. She lurched. He seemed to undulate against her, which sent more heat flashing through her belly.

"Oh, Riley," she whispered, "I want your hands all over me."

His hands opened the back of her bra, and together they took it off. He shifted them again, flipping her onto her back this time. His fingers caressed her softly, first up her arms and then settling on her breasts. Soon they were tingling with desire. She wanted to open her legs, she realized. Wanted his hands there too. She wasn't sure how to tell him, but then his mouth lowered to one of her nipples, and she forgot everything except his lips on her flesh. When he started to suck, she was sure she was going to lose all sense of decorum.

Her fingers slid into his hair, and as he tugged on her breast, she tugged on his curls. He switched to her other breast, and her back arched off the bed, trying to get closer to his mouth. Feeling an urgent need between her legs, she squirmed under him.

As if he could read her mind, or her body, he slid his fingers under the edge of her panties and touched the wet heat of her.

She moaned. "Take them off."

He slid them down her legs, and even the slow caress of the fabric sent a frisson of heat through her. She was burning from the inside out. He ran his hands up her legs slowly, and even though her eyes were closed, she knew he was looking at her. She had a moment of embarrassment, and then his fingers started to stroke her where she was burning.

"Yes, please," she heard herself utter, her voice husky.

She felt warmth fill her insides as he stroked. Her legs started to shake, and the edge beckoned to her. This time it felt higher, and there was a brief moment where she wanted to draw back.

"It's okay, Sadie," he said, continuing to touch her softly. "You can trust it. Just let go, love."

Sinking into the bed, she seemed to fall backward. Her body clenched around his fingers, and she moaned low and deep in her throat. Her legs shook as he continued to caress her through her release, and it felt so luscious, so powerful, tears filled her eyes.

"Oh, God," she cried out.

"That's right, babe," he said, shifting away from her.

She opened her eyes and watched as he rolled a condom on. He took her hand and placed it over him. He was hard and beautiful, and she felt the words rise within her.

"I love you. So much."

He placed himself between her legs, and as he slid gently inside her, he said, "I love you too. Come with me again."

His hand drew her leg up, and he inched inside deeper, making her body tighten again. She gasped as he filled her. Her hands grabbed his shoulders as he started to move.

"That's right," he whispered. "Move with me."

She closed her eyes and surrendered to a rhythm her body seemed to know. He thrust. She rose. He retreated. She followed. Love and heat created a special beat inside her.

He started to thrust faster, deeper, and both of them were making love sounds. She came again, and he froze over her. For a moment, their bodies seemed to beat with the same pulse, and their groans mixed with the same fervor as their sweat.

"Holy crap," Riley said, falling over her, his elbows preventing him from crushing her.

"Oh, Riley," she whispered. "It's never been like this."

"Me either," he said, kissing her neck. "My God, Sadie. You..."

He didn't finish his sentence, and he didn't need to. "I know."

After he rolled off her and disposed of the condom, he brought her back to his chest. She felt sweaty and realized she didn't mind a bit. The feel of it against her body made her feel sexy, like she was maybe the sexiest woman in the world.

"That was like poetry," she whispered, searching for words to make sense of what had been such a monumental moment for her.

"Yes," he said, kissing the top of her head and then running his hands through her hair in the sexiest way possible.

"I'm going to want to do that again," she said, kissing his chest. In fact, she wanted to shut herself away with him for three days and do nothing else.

"Me too," he said, turning on his side so they faced each other. "Sadie, I love you. I think I should meet your family."

His intense regard caused another wave of pleasure to roll through her, and this time she had no problem putting words to what it meant.

He was taking his place next to her.

Chapter 20

Paige knocked on the Thomsons' back door and entered to find Riley whistling as he stirred spaghetti sauce. He had on the apron she'd gotten him for his birthday two years ago—plain black with the white, bold-face words Super Chef across the chest. Mark had seen him this morning for their usual run, but she'd given him some space in case he felt a little weird about Sadie spending the night. She'd heard her sister's car pull away around dawn. Truth was she felt awkward about it too, but she couldn't have been happier for them both.

"Hey!" she finally called out.

"Oh, hey, I didn't hear you."

He banged the wooden spoon on the edge of the pot in a sharp staccato and then laid it on the spoon rest.

"Smells good," she said, sniffing the air. "You use the fresh rosemary from my garden?"

There were giggles from the family room, and she smiled. Whatever the girls were doing was keeping them amused. She loved the fact that her daughter was so happy here with Riley and Jess that she didn't always want to come home. Paige had never had a safe haven like that when she was a kid.

He nodded. "Yeah. So are we going to be a little weird

with each other? Because I'd really love to avoid that."

"I don't see any reason for it," she said. "I'm happy for y'all. I love you both. You know?"

She and Mark had talked about how important it was for them to be supportive but not pushy.

"I love her," Riley said softly.

She wanted to do a jig, hearing that. She worried about Riley sometimes. He worked hard, and he was completely devoted to Jess. Other than her and Mark, he didn't have too many close friends. Riley might joke about being a loner, but she knew what loneliness looked like, and there were times he was lonely. She hadn't known what to do to help other than invite him over and become his family.

Mark had assured her Riley would find his way, but some hurts sink down to the bone, and it was hard for someone who'd never been hurt that way to understand the lingering sting of it.

"I'm so glad," she responded as softly.

"And she loves me too," he said, picking up the wooden spoon and stirring. "I feel...really great about that. Ah... also I told her I think I should meet her family. I mean, we're dating, and she's important to me, and her family is everything. You know?"

"I know," Paige said. "Like I said, I'm beyond happy for you both. So, she loved the treasure chest? I mean, there was no way she wasn't going to. It was the perfect surprise."

Riley's thoughtfulness was one of the traits she most loved about him. He was always giving little gifts to the girls and even to her and Mark. Last month, he'd come across an old autographed photo of Justin Timberlake from the year she'd graduated high school and bought it for her, knowing about her high school crush on the singer. And he'd gotten Mark a special T-shirt for Father's Day, thanking him for being Jess' second father.

When they'd agreed to take care of each other's kids

should something happen to any of them, Riley had gotten pretty emotional, saying that while he'd known his brother would take care of Jess, it meant the world to him to think she and Haley wouldn't have to be split up. She'd cried too that night, and they'd had a whiskey to seal the deal.

"She's coming over for dinner tonight to spend some time with Jess. I got an earful today about sending her back to your house so soon last night."

She bit her lip. "Do you need Jess to spend the night again?" she asked. The first few weeks after she and Mark had become intimate were still a happy blur.

He tilted his head to the side. "I've been struggling with it. I want to spend more time with Sadie, but I don't feel right about throwing off my routine with Jess. You know? What kind of dad would I be if I let my daughter sleep over at her best friend's house for the next couple of weeks?"

"I get it," she replied, coming over to stand next to him by the stove. "You'll figure it out."

"But I don't feel comfortable having her stay over with Jess here," he said. "Is that weird?"

Paige had grown up with a non-stop carousel of men sleeping over, and it had scared her to wake up and find strange men in the house. Things were different with Sadie, but she understood Riley's concern and respected it.

"You need to do what you feel is best," she told him, rubbing his tense back. "I imagine Sadie is traditional in that area too."

"Yeah," Riley said. "That's why she left before Jess got up. We didn't want her to ask questions about why Sadie had slept over. It's one thing to share that we stayed up really late, but…"

"Yeah, we have plenty of time before the serious questions."

"Just remember our deal about bra shopping and tampons," he said, putting out his fist for a bump.

She answered the gesture. "You got it."

"Thank God," he said, slapping his forehead. "Either one of those scenarios might have actually killed me."

There was a knock on the front door, and then it opened and Sadie called out, "Is anyone home?"

"We're in here," Riley said, a smile dancing across his face. "Excuse me."

"I should get Haley," she murmured.

He put his hands on her shoulders. "Chill. She is your sister, after all."

Sadie appeared in the doorway, and Paige made a show of stirring the spaghetti sauce to give them a moment alone.

"Hey, Paige," Sadie said.

Her sister's cheeks were flushed when she finally looked over. "Hi. I just came over to get Haley."

But Sadie was clearly embarrassed, and Paige didn't want her to be. Setting down the spoon, she hurried over to hug her. "I'm so happy for you. Relax. Breathe."

Riley made his way to the stove and started messing with the spoon, stealing Paige's diversion tactic.

"Thanks," Sadie said, hugging Paige back. "I needed that, I guess. I didn't want it to be weird."

"It's not," she told her, drawing away. "I'm happy for y'all."

"Me too."

"Why don't you stay for a glass of wine?" Riley asked. "Tell Mark to come over. Better yet, why not make it a family dinner?" He looked at Sadie as he said it, and she nodded slightly and said, "Yes, I'd like that."

Paige felt an unexpected lump in her throat. Riley and Sadie were family, and it meant the world to her that they'd include them.

"I'll run home and get him." He might have started

dinner already since it was his night, but she couldn't imagine he'd done much yet since they'd only just gotten home.

Mark was chopping zucchini when she walked back in. "We've been invited for family dinner."

He looked up, his hand stilling on the cutting board. "I'll put the steaks back in the fridge for tomorrow night," he said without hesitating. "Think we could bring the zucchini?"

"Pack it up," she said. "I'm going to grab a bottle of champagne."

"Good idea," Mark said. Grinning at her, he added, "He's so happy. It's great to see."

"Yes, it is," she replied and pulled out a bottle from the wine chiller.

They went across the yard again and let themselves in through the back door. Jess and Haley were talking to Sadie about their day at school. Riley was leaning against the counter next to her, his whole face awash in love.

Paige took a mental snapshot of the scene. Despite what she and Mark had discussed—that they shouldn't put the cart before the horse—she loved the thought of where this might lead. She imagined what it might be like if Sadie moved in one day. It would be wonderful to stop over and find Riley and Sadie cooking in the kitchen together, or working companionably on their art.

"Mama," Haley shouted, running over and hugging her. "Hi, Dad."

"Hey, pumpkin," Mark said, kissing the top of her head. "How was your day?"

"Great! Isn't it cool that we're all having dinner together? Jess and I are so happy Sadie is here. She's so great. Right, Mom?"

Sadie glanced over, and Paige had the silly urge to blow her a kiss. "Yeah, she sure is."

"You brought champagne?" Riley said. "Cool. I've

never had champagne with spaghetti."

"I brought zucchini too," Mark said, holding up the plastic container. "It's fresh cut. Figured we could sauté it and serve it as a side."

"Beats the bagged salad I had in mind," Riley said. "You know how much Jess and I love salad."

"Yuck," Jess cried out, putting her hands around her throat. "Superheroes don't eat vegetables."

"What about Popeye?" Sadie asked.

Paige saw Riley bite his lip. Even Mark and Haley stopped what they were doing, knowing what was coming.

Jess put her hands on her hips and stared up at Sadie. "Popeye *isn't* a superhero."

"He's not?" Sadie asked.

"Of course not," Jess exclaimed. "He's a cartoon character. All the difference in the world."

Sadie pursed her lips like she was fighting a smile. "You don't think Disney princesses eat vegetables?"

Jess and Haley both shook their heads, and Mark barked out a laugh.

"No, they don't," Jess said. "We've seen every Disney movie at least five times. We're experts."

"There's no arguing with them on this one, Sadie," Riley told her. "But we're going to eat zucchini tonight because Mr. Bradshaw brought it. Aren't we, Jess?"

"It's the polite thing, I guess," the little girl said with a sigh.

"I brought cake for dessert," Sadie said, tapping Jess on the nose. "Is that permitted?"

Jess twirled in her princess outfit, and Haley followed suit.

"Princesses *love* cake," Jess said.

Riley snatched her up and gave her belly a zorbert, making her scream with laughter.

"I'm going to pop the champagne," Paige said, crossing to the cupboard that held the glasses.

Riley didn't have champagne glasses, so she chose the red wine glasses and poured each of the adults a portion.

"To family," Mark said, lifting his glass.

Everyone echoed the toast, and Paige watched as Sadie and Riley shared another special look. She had to hold back an excited squeal. For a woman who'd never imagined wanting a family, she'd found herself a pretty great one.

They sat around the table and feasted on the spaghetti, the girls giggling as they made the noodles dance on their forks. Tomato sauce stained their faces, and Paige volunteered to clean them up after dinner. Jess had to be coaxed repeatedly to eat the handful of zucchini on her plate.

But Paige's attention kept returning to Sadie, to the notion that her sister seemed to belong with them all. She would have to tell Mark later, but from the way he was smiling at the couple, she imagined he'd concluded the same thing.

The Italian cream cake Sadie had brought was delicious, and Riley's shock at learning it was homemade made them all laugh.

"When did you have the time?" he asked.

She flushed to her roots at the allusion to the activities that had kept her otherwise occupied last night.

The girls drew shapes in the frosting with forks before Mark called it, announcing it was bath time. Their groans were long-suffering and totally expected. They never liked to be separated.

"Dad, can I spend the night at Haley's house since Sadie's here again?" Jess asked out of the blue.

Riley froze in spooning the leftover spaghetti into the Tupperware he'd brought to the table for cleanup. "Ah..."

Sadie's eyes widened. "That's so sweet, Jess, but—"

"No problem," Jess said, waving a hand like a mini-adult. "It's what friends are for."

"Jess Thomson, where do you learn these things?" Riley asked with a sigh.

"School, Dad," she told him, "and movies, of course. Boyfriends and girlfriends have sleepovers when they're dating."

School? Who would have imagined Jess would be up-to-date in the dating game? Even Mark cleared his throat, and Paige almost reached for Sadie's hand. Her face was beet-red now, and Riley wasn't faring much better.

"Jess, Haley, come and help me load the dishwasher," Paige said, hoping to break the tension. She herded the girls into the kitchen and helped them wash off their plates and load them.

"Did I shock Dad?" Jess asked her, shutting the door to the dishwasher. "Betty at school says boyfriends and girlfriends can't get serious unless they spend the night with each other."

Paige had to control her eyebrows from rising at this revelation. "How does she know that?"

"She has an older brother and sister," Haley said, leaning her head against her leg. "And her dad got married again this summer. Betty knows everything."

"I doubt that," Paige said, but she imagined Betty knew more than she should at that age. She'd been the same way, what with her mom's lifestyle.

"Boyfriends and girlfriends have to have sleepovers to have sex," Jess told her.

Okay, *now* her eyes were wide open. Where in the world was Mark? She could use some backup.

"Do you know what sex is?" She decided to ask straight out because if they did, they'd have to have a talk.

"Yes, it's all the kissing and touching you see on TV and in the movies," Jess said. "That's what boyfriends and girlfriends do."

Paige blew out a breath in relief. Okay, she could handle this. "Yes, that's one of the ways you show someone you care about them."

"Mommies and daddies hug their kids and boyfriends and girlfriends kiss and touch each other," Haley told her with a serious nod. "Like you and Dad even though you're married."

She sank down to one knee in front of them. It struck her that she didn't have to sink down quite so far as she used to. They were growing up so fast. "Your dad and I wanted to be boyfriend and girlfriend forever so that's why we got married."

Jess nodded. "That's how it's supposed to be. Do you think my dad and Sadie will get married?"

Shaky ground, Paige knew. She glanced at the door, but no adults were coming to relieve her or back her up.

"I don't know," she said honestly. "It's a big decision. You have to be completely sure—like down-to-your-toes sure that you love that person enough to spend every day with them. The person has to be extra special."

"I know," Jess said, shaking her head. "It's like me and Haley. We're BFFs, and no one else is that special. I mean, Betty wanted to be my BFF, but I don't like her as much as Haley, although I didn't tell her that. I didn't want to hurt her feelings."

"That's good," Paige said. "We should always try to be kind to other people."

"Exactly," she said, cuddling close. "I told her I can only have one BFF. That's what it means. I think she understood."

Paige smoothed the little girl's fine hair back over her shoulder. "You did good."

"Do you think Sadie understands that she can't be my mom?" Jess asked.

She fought a gasp. "What do you mean, honey?"

"Well, I already have a mom, and even though she's

not here right now, that doesn't mean she's not my mom." Jess put a finger to the side of her mouth. "I mean, no one can take her place."

Paige had to fight tears at that. What could she tell this little girl? She stroked her hair until she had an answer she was sure of. "You know what, Jess? I only have one mom too, like you, but I would have given anything to have a woman like Sadie come into my life and love me."

"But she's still not my mom," Jess said, pulling away and staring at her with troubled eyes.

This was becoming too complicated, Paige thought. She would need to share this conversation with Riley. Jess was his daughter, and she didn't feel right about continuing on this way.

"Okay, let's get everybody ready for their baths," she said, rising.

"She's not my mom," Jess told her again.

Haley closed the distance between them and put her arm around her friend. They looked like a little unit of solidarity.

She still wasn't sure how to respond, so she kept it factual. "No, she's not."

Jess finally nodded and took Haley's hand. "Let's go do our baths at your house."

They dashed out of the kitchen before she could call them back. At moments like these, she questioned whether the keyless locks she and Mark and Riley had installed in their doors were such a good idea. They didn't have to wait for an adult to let them inside. Part of that was about letting them grow up, something they seemed to be doing pretty fast these days. She sunk against the counter. It wouldn't hurt anything if she took a moment before following them. She needed it.

"Where are the girls?" Mark asked, walking into the kitchen with the Tupperware in his hands.

"At our house, taking baths," she said, cracking her

neck. "Where are Riley and Sadie?"

"They stepped into Riley's office to chat in privacy," he said, putting the leftovers in the refrigerator. "Are you okay?"

She shook her head, still troubled about Jess' insistence that Sadie wasn't her mom. "I'll tell you later. Why don't you head home and oversee the girls? I need to wait for Riley."

He spanned the distance between them and cupped her face in his hands. His gaze was seeking, and she let him see everything she was feeling, the sadness and the worry. When he kissed her lightly on the lips, she folded into him.

"It's going to be okay," he told her.

She rubbed her face against his chest, fighting the urge to cry. Jess was so tough sometimes. Had she been that tough at that age? That worldly? For some reason, her sadness deepened, realizing she'd been even more so. She'd started locking herself in her room, and away from her mom's visitors, starting in kindergarten. Sometimes she'd even slept under her bed, her favored hiding place lest one of those men should break into her room.

"Hey," Mark said, wrapping his arms around her. "What is it?"

"Later," she whispered. "I really need to talk to Riley. You go on."

He kissed her sweetly on the lips one last time and then rubbed her back. "Say goodbye for me."

After he left, she found the disposable wipes for the counters and scrubbed them until they sparkled. She was washing the pans when Riley and Sadie entered the kitchen.

"Where is everyone?" Riley asked.

"Mark went over to make sure the girls were getting their baths done. Jess seems to have decided she's spending the night. Riley, I need to tell you what she said.

There's this girl at school..."

His face grew even more shuttered as she shared their conversation. For a moment she wondered if she should have told him alone, but she trusted Sadie. Besides, Sadie was involved in this family now, and this impacted her too.

When Riley turned his back to compose himself, Sadie glanced her way, her face stricken.

"I should leave," Sadie said.

"No," Paige said abruptly. "I might be out of line, but...Riley, I did the best I could, and you'll need to talk to her. But as someone whose mom is a lot like Mandy, I can tell you the one way you can really help her. You just have to be patient with her. To keep loving her. No, Sadie isn't her mom, but you're a good woman who cares about her, and that's so important. I wish...I wish I'd had someone like that."

Riley blew out a breath. "She's been acting so weird lately. Mark says it's only natural, but I don't like this. Not one bit."

"I should go," Sadie said, rubbing his back. "You should talk to Jess, Riley. I feel like I should apologize."

He pulled her into his arms. "There's nothing to be sorry for. She's... I'll talk to her. Don't worry."

"Okay," Sadie said, forcing what Paige knew was a fake smile. "Thank you for dinner. Please tell everyone goodbye for me."

"I'll walk you out," Riley said.

"No need," Sadie said. "Go to Jess. I'll walk out with Paige after we clean up."

He kissed her cheek, but his eyes were already on the back door. "Don't clean up. I'll call you later."

They ignored him and silently fell into a pattern together, Paige washing the pans while Sadie dried them. When they finished, Paige looked at her sister. There were lines of worry around her mouth.

"When your mama started to date the man she ended up marrying, how did you feel?"

Sadie neatly folded the dishtowel and then leaned back against the sink. "I was older than Jess when Mama and Dale got together, but I remember J.P. gathering all of us girls together and telling us that he'd always look out for us as our older brother. That Dale didn't change anything."

"So you had a sibling reassure you everything was going to be all right?" Paige asked, realizing maybe Jess needed to be told the same thing.

"Yes, but then Dale took J.P. on a long walk after church one day and told him how much he loved our mama and how much he admired J.P. for being the man in the family for so long after Daddy left. Dale asked if J.P. might be willing to share some of those duties with him, things like taking out the garbage and mowing the lawn."

What a smart man, Paige thought. Rather than force his way into the family fold, he'd inquired how he could be of service.

"Dale is the most even keel man you'll meet, and he's always content to stay in the background. J.P. told us that while he'd agreed to let Dale help with some of the stuff around the house, he was still the one we could come to if we needed something. And that's how it's always been even though we all love Dale."

"I hope I have a chance to meet him," Paige said. She was still feeling her way through the right time to meet Mrs. McGuiness, but everything she'd heard about the woman and the way she ran her family made her less anxious.

"Riley was supposed to meet everyone this Sunday, but now I wonder if we should cancel things." She pressed her hand over her eyes. "I was so excited ..."

Paige enfolded the woman in her arms. "Hey, you keep on being excited because tonight over dinner I felt the bond strengthening between you and Riley and Jess. Even with my family. These are just growing pains. Okay?"

She hoped that was true, but sometimes looking at Jess was like looking in the mirror to her past, at the young girl who was so hurt and troubled and defiant.

"I hope so," Sadie said. "I don't want anyone to get hurt, especially that little girl. I know what it feels like to grow up without one parent. It...sucks."

For Sadie, that sounded like a curse word. "Let's get you into your car. Riley will talk to Jess, and if Mark and I can do anything to help, we will. We love her like our own."

Sadie grabbed her hands. "I know that, and I'm so grateful y'all have each other. When he told me about Jess' mom, I went home and had a good cry. I never..."

"She's a bitch," Paige said straight out. "Jess is lucky to have Riley. No one could have protected her or loved her better."

"That's why she has to be comfortable with me coming into Riley's life," Sadie said, her eyes dark with worry, "because I'm coming into hers too."

"It's going to be okay," Paige said, hugging her again.

She prayed that was the truth.

Chapter 21

Riley had agreed to meet Sadie's brother—and Paige's, he added when the thought struck him—out of pure desperation.

His daughter had never shut him out like this before. She refused to tell him about her conversation with Paige even though he'd gone to the extreme measure of sketching a picture of them talking to each other. He sometimes drew them together to show her what he felt in his heart, and she'd liked it before.

Not this time.

She'd set aside the drawing. The worst part was the way she'd completely closed down on him, and Haley, ever the loyal friend, wouldn't tell him anything either.

Jess was happy about Sadie. He knew that, but this was stirring up other things inside her, ones she didn't fully understand.

When Sadie had first suggested he talk to her brother, his knee-jerk reaction had been to refuse as graciously as possible. But hearing about J.P. and Tammy's situation had helped him feel less alone. Other people had ushered their children through difficult times and made it work. Besides, he wanted Sadie to feel better. A tangled ball of guilt and worry, she'd asked him more than once if he felt they should stop seeing each other for a while until Jess was easier with her feelings about her real mother.

Riley knew that wasn't the answer. He just had no idea what was. All of his normal tools with Jess had struck out. Perhaps Sadie's brother could give a helpful take on things.

When the doorbell rang at the agreed-upon time, Riley set aside the drawing he'd been fussing with the whole morning and headed downstairs.

Opening the door, he had a moment of surprise. J.P. looked so much like Paige in the eyes and mouth, more so than Sadie did.

"Hello, I'm Sadie's brother, J.P.," the tall and composed man said, holding out his hand.

"I'm Riley," he said, shaking it. "Wish we were meeting under different circumstances, but I appreciate you coming to talk with me all the same."

J.P. nodded and came inside. "If I can be of any help, it will be a blessing. I know how hard it can be when your child is struggling. It's the sort of thing that weighs on you unless you have someone to talk to."

"I have plenty of people to talk to," Riley said, "but the one person I really want to talk to isn't talking back. My daughter, Jess, can be… Oh, she's wonderful and sweet and curious, but in rare moments like these she can be incredibly stubborn."

"And it scares you spitless," J.P. finished for him. "Makes you a good father. I felt honored you'd want to talk to me, especially since we hadn't met yet."

Riley rubbed the tension in his diaphragm. "Same goes. It's not how I hoped to meet you either. Sadie and I wanted to…I hoped to become acquainted with you at your Sunday dinner."

J.P.'s mouth turned up. "She told me. You mean a lot to her, and that's important to all of us because *she's* important. No one shares her heart quite like Sadie does."

"Do you want a drink? I know it's early for a beer, but I have iced tea, water, soda. I could make coffee."

"Is it sweet tea?" J.P. asked.

"Yes," Riley answered. "I use honey." Man, he sounded like such a moron.

"That's fine then." J.P. followed him into the kitchen. "I like your art on the walls. Sadie says you work on comics, the writing and the drawing."

"Yes, it's the only thing I ever wanted to do really. My brother and I used to devour every comic book and TV show we could find. We made up our own superheroes, and we were both good at drawing. Our parents took us to the art store whenever we needed something. It was…a happy childhood." It was true regardless of the distance he now felt with his parents.

"It's important for parents to support their kids," J.P. said. "You can tell a lot about a man by how he does that. From what Sadie tells me, you're doing just fine. I hope you don't mind me saying so. It's not a presumption. I only…it's easy to doubt all the good things you're doing in moments like this."

Riley rocked back on his feet, taken off guard. "That means a lot."

Grabbing the glasses, he filled them with ice and tea and suggested they head out to the back porch. His patio set had an umbrella, after all, and it wasn't crazy humid outside for once. Plus, he'd been caged up most of the day, unable to draw much of anything. Bringing out all of his gold hues hadn't even helped him turn the tide.

"I can see why Sadie speaks about you like she does," Riley said as they sipped their iced tea. "You remind me a little of Paige's husband, Mark. No nonsense. Calm. It might be weird to say, but you're nice too."

J.P. gave an easy smile at that. "I've heard 'nice' all my life. Some teased me about it, but it's never taken. I figure being nice to people is the right thing to do. If someone wants to make an issue out of it, that's their decision."

Riley couldn't agree more. Tom Hanks was one of his nice-guy heroes.

"And I'm happy you said that about Mark," J.P. continued, kicking out his feet. "Paige deserves to have good men in her camp. I'm still working on letting go of the fact that I wasn't there to help her growing up."

"That means a lot to Paige," Riley said. "She's one of the most amazing women I've ever met, and I admire the hell out her. What she's overcome... It's beautiful. It... okay, I'm going to be weird again, but it gives me hope that Jess will be okay."

"Jess has a leg up over Paige," J.P. said, looking his way. "She has you. Having one loving parent doesn't make up for the other one being gone, but it does buffer things, I believe. When our dad left, our mama could always be counted on. I never questioned that once. It... helps. You know?"

"That's the thing," Riley said. "I don't know. I mean, I grew up with two parents who loved me and my brother. I don't know what Jess is going through, honestly. I mean...I feel like shit—oops, sorry about that—for what happened with her mom."

"But that's not your fault," J.P. said right away. "Sadie said she'd leave it to you to tell me what you wanted to about that. All I know is that Jess' mother didn't want her, that she thought her career was more important."

Riley looked down at his feet. The sun was touching his toes, but parts of his feet were basked in shadow. He rather felt like that in this moment. Should he tell J.P. the whole story?

"I won't judge you," J.P. said, "if that's what's weighing on you. But sometimes it helps to talk about it."

This man had the composure of a teacher of superheroes, someone like Dr. Charles Xavier in *X-Men*.

"Thank you for saying that," Riley said. "Let me tell

you the highlights."

He didn't share the story often, but when he did, he found himself seeing it in comic book form. He was the sappy hero who hadn't realized the woman he was falling for was actually a tortured villain in disguise. In the nick of time, he'd saved his daughter and taken her away. He'd tried to love and cherish her, hoping she could heal from the events surrounding her birth.

Usually the final strip was one of him and Jess holding hands, the sun shining in the distance, knowing they were both invincible because they had each other. Today, the final strip showed dark clouds and him trying to reach Jess, who had her back turned, her shoulders set in a hard line.

When he was finished, he wanted to put his face in his hands. "I don't know how to help her. I can't tell her the whole truth yet. Every expert says that. And I can't up and cut Sadie out of our lives just because it's stirring Jess up. She's...your sister is one of the best things that's ever happened to me, and I know Jess adores her. Jess is just—"

"Scared her mother is never coming back," J.P. said in a gentle voice.

Riley sat back in his chair. The way J.P. put it made it seem so much clearer.

"I remember when Annabelle said something like that to me. I'd finally talked Tammy into marrying me not long before that. You know their daddy abused her, right?"

Riley nodded. He had the odd urge to reach out to the man. There was no question it still weighed on him, and who could blame him? He'd punch any guy who hurt a woman.

"Rory had told Annabelle again and again that their old daddy would never come back because I was going to be their daddy now. She seemed to be happy about that, but she seemed awful down one day, and when I asked her how it made her feel to think about her mamma and me getting married, she said it made her sad."

Riley leaned forward, his entire attention on the story.

"I was a bit surprised, but I rallied and asked her why she felt that way. Her answer made so much sense I couldn't believe I hadn't arrived upon it myself."

J.P. met his gaze and took a healthy sip of iced tea before continuing, as if to give Riley a moment to think on it. "She said she was sad because daddies should love their little girls, and he obviously didn't or he would have tried to visit them. She knew he was a bad man, but she was still his baby girl. How could he not love her? Was there something wrong with her? Did he not know how good she was?"

Is that what Jess believes? It hurt him to even think about it. "I've told her before her mother's decision to be away has nothing to do with her, but maybe I need to say it again."

"It's a feeling that doesn't easily go away," J.P. said. "I felt the same when my daddy left us, and it cut a pretty deep hole in me, let me tell you. What I told Annabelle seemed to help. I let her know that she was one of best children in the world, but people like her daddy didn't like to be around good people like her. Then I told her I could see her and wanted to be around her."

Riley was moved by the scene J.P.'s words were sketching in his mind. He could see it form, panel by panel.

"That little girl threw her arms around me, and I rocked her for quite a while, let me tell you. When I told her mama about it later on, I had to hold her too while she cried."

Riley imagined a lot of tears had been spent that day. "So Jess is scared that Sadie coming into my life and hers means her mama might be out of it for good?" He stood up and started to pace. "But she *is* out of it for good."

Please let that be true.

"But Jess doesn't know that," J.P. said gently. "All she knows from what you've told me is that her mama wanted to pursue her music career and couldn't take care of her at the same time."

Right. Shit. He could suddenly see the problem. "You think Jess still hopes her mom will change her mind?"

"It's natural for a child to believe their parent should want to love them and be in their lives," J.P. said. "Sadie still feels that way, I think, even though she hasn't said much after what happened a few months ago. I have a notion Shelby and Susannah might harbor a kernel of that feeling too. Loving a child is what a parent is supposed to do. Of course, there's plenty of evidence to the contrary. But kids don't want to believe that."

"It's like breaking the magic," Riley muttered, thinking kids weren't the only ones. He knew Sadie still thought about her dad. She'd told him as much.

"Yes," J.P. said. "Exactly."

"Thank you," Riley said. "I...don't quite know what I'm going to do yet, but it's...clearer. I mean, I've talked to other people, but it's good to get a fresh perspective."

"I'm glad I could shine some light on things," J.P. said, standing up. "I should let you get back to work. You give me a holler if you need to talk more. And, Riley, I hope to see you and Jess at Sunday dinner someday soon. Everyone is really eager to welcome y'all."

When they shook hands again, Riley felt the stirrings of friendship. He spent the next couple of hours pacing and drawing, trying to figure out the best approach with his daughter. After picking the kids up from school, he left her and Haley alone in the playroom. They were content to play princess in Jess' magical castle.

When Paige dropped by to pick Haley up, he kissed her cheek and whispered, "I really like your brother."

Her eyes crinkled at the corners. "Me too. We'll talk another time."

"Yes," he said and watched from the front porch as they headed across the driveway to their house.

When he went inside, he listened for Jess, but the house was completely quiet. He firmed his shoulders and called out, "Jess, I need to show you something."

She took her sweet time, but finally she appeared in his office. She looked so small in her blue dress and yellow leggings. He wondered if she'd come out of curiosity over his drawings. He often showed her the really special ones.

"Come over here," he said, staying in his office chair.

She shuffled forward, and when she reached him, he lifted her onto his desk. She sat there stiffly, not dangling her feet like normal. He reached for the bottom drawer of his desk and took out Mandy's picture. Shoving aside all of the anger he still felt toward her, he handed Jess the frame.

"I thought you might want to put this in your room," Riley told her. "I'm sorry I didn't give it to you earlier, but... Well, I know it's hard not having your mom around, and I didn't want to make you sad."

She held the frame on her little lap. "Other kids have pictures of their mom."

Oh, baby, he wanted to say, but she wasn't ready to hear it. "I get really angry when I think about your mom because I don't really understand how she could choose her career over being here with you. I know you wish she were here, and I don't always know what to tell you about her, but I want you to know that she is your mom. No one else will ever take that place. Not Paige. Not Sadie. But who we love is our choice, and that's why we have women in our lives like Paige and Sadie."

"But Sadie is your girlfriend," Jess said. "Some of the other kids at school like Betty say she'll become my mom if y'all get married."

Part of him wanted to curse those kids for telling her such things, but they were probably from broken families too. Just like Jess, they were trying to make sense out of what had happened to them.

"Every family has a different way of handling things," he said, "and it's sometimes hard to know what's right, but all I can do is love you. Jess, you're my heart, my best girl, and the best daughter in the world. I know it's only you and me. I wish your mom had made a different choice, but she didn't, and that has nothing to do with you."

"Maybe she'll change her mind," Jess said, lifting the frame to gaze at her picture.

He started to sweat. *Over my dead body.* Instead of sharing that gut reaction, he said, "I'm not sure what she'll want to do, but I'll always be your dad. Until you're old enough to be on your own, you're with me, and Jess, it's the best gig on the planet."

The right side of her mouth finally turned up. "Even better than saving the planet from evil villains?"

His heart seemed to explode into a millions pieces before settling back inside his chest. They were back. Just like that. "Even better than that. I love you, Jess."

"I love you too, Daddy," she said, resting the frame on her lap.

"Are you going to hug me, or am I going to have to wrestle you?" he quipped, feeling like they were back on solid ground.

When she set the frame aside and came into his arms, he wrapped her up tight, but she didn't voice her usual complaint that he was squeezing the life out of her. No, she grabbed a hold of his arms and squeezed back with all of her might.

"Jess, I need to tell you that I really love Sadie, but that doesn't change anything for you. You and me are still father and daughter, and nothing beats that. Okay?"

She leaned her head against his chest and looked up at him. "What if you get married?"

He chose his words carefully. "Then she and I will be

like Mark and Paige, and we'll all...ah...be a family," he finished lamely. "But we're only dating right now."

"You love each other," Jess said. "Isn't that what happens next?"

Oh, sweet Christ. Save him from these questions. "Sometimes. Only if the two people just can't stand to be without each other."

The glimmer in her eye made him want to squirm.

"Isn't that how you feel about Sadie? You bought a couple of new sport coats and shoes. You run out of the house whenever you have a date with her. It's the same way you act when you take me to the newest superhero movie at the theater."

She was way too smart. "I do love her, but I want to make sure we'll be...compatible...and that you like her. We...I'm just getting to know her better right now, and I'd like you to do the same. But only if you want to."

"I like Sadie, Daddy," Jess said. "Everybody does. Haley already thinks she's the best aunt ever, and Mrs. Bradshaw gets all teary-eyed sometimes whenever she talks about her."

"You see everything, don't you?"

She shrugged. "You always say you can't draw anything if you don't look at life. I...I think you really love Sadie. She makes you happy."

"She does, but you make me the happiest." He kissed the top of her head. "She'd like us to meet her family sometime. Would you be up for that?"

Her nod was enthusiastic. "Sure. Haley said they're all totally cool. Especially Rye Crenshaw."

He felt himself blush a little. It had embarrassed him and then some to learn the country singers whose names he hadn't recognized on his first date with Sadie were actually her relations. "The country singer, right?"

She jumped off his lap and threw out her arms. "He's like huge. I mean, everyone listens to his music. Except you. I know you don't like country music because of my mom."

His eyes narrowed. Was there nothing she didn't pick up on? "I've loved New Wave since I was a kid. It's more my groove. But have you listened to Rye's music?"

"Yep, and Jake Lassiter's too. He's Haley's uncle, after all."

It surprised him a little that she'd hidden it from him—and pretty darn well—but he'd probably have to listen to their music too if he was going to meet them.

"You listen to whatever music you want, Jess," he said. "It's part of growing up."

"Okay, that's cool. I didn't want to make you sad or mad by listening to it."

"You don't ever worry about that, honey. I can take it." He made himself give her a wink.

"Do you think they know my mom?" Jess asked, jumping off his desk with Mandy's picture in her hands. "I'll have to ask them when we meet them."

She skipped out of the room before he could form a coherent response.

Chapter 22

Sadie fingered Susannah's blue-and-white textured curtain as she watched for Riley's car to pull up.

"You're as nervous as a long-tailed cat in a room full of rocking chairs," Shelby said from behind her. "It's going to be fine. Once Jess meets everybody, everything's going to get easier. Trust me."

Her sister put her arm around her, and she leaned in. "It's been better this week, but everything still seems so fragile."

Riley had felt like Jess was mostly back to herself. Though she'd put the picture of her mom beside her bed, she'd also told her dad she wanted to meet Sadie's extended family. Over their last date, Riley had confessed his worry that they weren't out of the woods yet. She'd tried to reassure him. Heavens knew she was praying up a storm and had asked her siblings to do the same, minus Paige. She hadn't felt comfortable asking that of her new sister.

They'd had a great quilting class this week. Paige's skills and confidence were improving, and it was wonderful to see. But Sadie had gotten to know Paige enough to read her fairly well. Her sister was also worried about Riley and Jess.

"I love him so much," Sadie whispered, clutching the curtain's edge. "I want everything to be okay."

"It will be," Shelby said, giving her a loving squeeze. "Have faith."

Faith. Yes, she'd been praying for more of that too. When she caught sight of Riley's car, she smiled as she watched Annabelle and Rory run toward the driveway. She had a feeling she had J.P. to thank for the red-carpet welcome.

"See," Shelby said as they watched Jess jump out of the car and take the flowers Annabelle extended with a huge grin. "Love always wins, honey. Always."

"You sound like Mama," Sadie said, leaving the room and heading outside with her sister.

"What a nice compliment," Shelby said, hurrying down the front walkway with her. "Hey, Riley. Hey, Jess. Welcome. I'm Shelby."

Riley kissed her sister's cheek. "Thanks. I...ah... brought white wine. Heard it was a fan favorite around here."

Shelby grabbed the bottle. "It is indeed. Thank you. Come on inside. Jess, I see you've met Annabelle and Rory."

"Yes," Jess said, venturing closer to Riley and ducking her head. "Haley told me they were nice. I didn't expect flowers."

"Rory and me figured a princess should have flowers," Annabelle said.

"We should put those in a nice vase," Shelby said, giving her a smile. "Would you like to come inside and help me pick one out?"

"Aunt Susannah has tons of vases," Annabelle said, reaching for Jess' hand and leading her inside.

Shelby shot her a wink and took off with the kids, leaving Sadie alone with Riley for a moment. He caressed her face and leaned in and kissed her sweetly on the lips.

"Last night was...beautiful," he told her softly. "I missed you when I woke up this morning. We're going to have to find a way for us to wake up together after the sun comes up."

She'd gone home around three o'clock after making love with him for hours. They were slowly exploring each other, and it was downright delicious. She hadn't expected to laugh during sex, but Riley was so funny sometimes, teasing her about things like wanting to draw her naked with nothing but a jungle outfit on, à la Jane from *Tarzan*, or dressing her in nothing but a pirate hat adorned with parrot feathers. No surprise, he had quite an imagination, and beyond the sounds they made while loving each other, the laughter held a special place in her heart.

"We'll figure it out," she said, curling her hand around his. "Are you nervous?"

He kissed the back of her hand. "Me? Nah. This is going to be a walk in the park. Paige made it out alive. I figure I have a fifty-fifty shot of it going my way. Besides, your brother likes me."

"So does Shelby," she told him with a flash of a smile. "Mama is here. I mean...of course, she is. Just wanted to... Well, she and Paige haven't met yet."

"It will happen," Riley said. "We should go inside. Otherwise, your family is going to think I'm a big weenie who needed a pre-game speech before meeting them."

"You've already met Shelby," she told him as they walked to the house. "Not too many more to meet."

That was mostly true, but it didn't seem that way as she walked him through the house, introducing him to people as they went. Thankfully, someone had suggested they not all cluster in one room and pounce on the newcomer like a pack of wild dogs.

He charmed Tory by asking if he could hold Boone, and his form of entertainment—funny faces and funnier voices—had the little boy cooing in moments.

"Hey, I'm a rockstar with kids," he said in response to the compliments that came flooding his way. "We speak the same language."

Sadie looked to the doorway where she'd noticed her mama quietly observing the scene. "You can tell a lot by the way a man handles a baby," her mama said, stepping forward. "I'm Sadie's mama, Louisa."

Riley passed Boone to Susannah, who'd held out her arms for him, but kept a hold of Boone's little fist when the boy wouldn't release him. He had to extend his other hand to her mama.

"It's a pleasure to meet you, Mrs. McGuiness. You have an incredible family here, and no offense to the other ladies else in the room, but your daughter, Sadie, is one of the best women I've ever met. She's right up there with my daughter."

His wink was downright cheeky, and she heard Tory bark out a laugh and say, "This one is as fast as a hot knife through butter. Rye's going to have some competition."

"I don't know about butter, but I like chocolate," Riley said, flashing Tammy a smile. "I hear y'all have chocolate fairies at your house. How can I get some to migrate to my place? Jess and I love the idea of waking up to a piece of chocolate each morning."

"You'll need to plant some chocolate-scented flowers and the like," Tammy told him, her face cheery. "I'd be happy to give you some cuttings from my garden or make recommendations. It's a good time to plant for the spring."

"That would be great, Tammy," Riley said. "Jess likes flowers, and so does my girl here. You know, the night of my second date with Sadie..."

Sadie half-listened as Riley shared his horror at discovering the daisies Jess had suggested he buy were still in the pot. Her mama had a soft smile on her face, but her eyes were watchful. Sadie could tell she was still gauging

Riley's character. Heavens, she hoped Mama would relax a little.

"Is anyone going to introduce Sadie's beau to me?" Rye asked, standing in the doorway with his hands on his hips. "I mean, everyone trusts J.P.'s opinion, but surely mine counts for something."

Sadie found herself watching Rye closely. Oddly, his approval was important to her.

"Like I said, butter." Tory rolled her eyes. "Your opinion isn't the only one that counts. Rather like how things are at home."

"Aunt Tory just busted your chops, Uncle Rye," Rory told him with a grin. The little boy had snuck into the room without her noticing. Tory grinned and handed him a frosting-covered wooden spoon.

"She always does," Rye said, crossing and pulling her close. "She knows it makes me crazy." He kissed her hard on the mouth and then turned to Riley.

"I hear you're making friends with my boy," Rye said.

Riley stuck out his hand, and Rye took it.

"He's a cute boy. Can't seem to help myself around babies. They laugh at everything I do."

"So you crave the spotlight too, huh?" Rye asked. "Well, I expect you can hold my son when you come around for these here family dinners. Usually the women line up and pass him around. I barely get to see him."

Sadie knew what a big concession that was for Rye, and she flashed him a smile to tell him so. His wink was quick and cheeky.

"The cutest kids never want for admirers," Riley told him. "Trust me, there will be moments when you'll consider yourself lucky to have other people gushing over your kid."

Rye studied him for a long moment and then slapped him on the back. "Do you drink bourbon?"

Sadie almost cheered, knowing Rye was giving his stamp of approval.

Riley shook his head. "No, that would be Paige's department."

Nice comeback, Sadie wanted to shout.

Rye's mouth twitched. "I really like that girl, I have to tell you."

"She's the best," Riley said with a nod. "I'd better see where Jess went off to."

Tammy put a hand on his arm. "She's outside with Annabelle, and I expect J.P. is watching them."

"Still," he said, flashing her a smile. "I'd feel better…"

Sadie inclined her head to the back door. "This way."

Before they left the kitchen, Tory gave her a thumbs up, which made her laugh.

"Something funny?" Riley asked.

"You did great," she said. And he had, from his first interactions with Boone to the way he'd batted words with Rye.

"Whew," he said, swiping his hand across his brow. "I guess we're halfway there."

"Halfway?" she asked.

"Your mother is still inspecting me." He squeezed her hand. "But don't worry. I'll win her over."

She didn't doubt it. He joined J.P. in the yard, where her brother was watching the two young girls run around.

"You have rainbow ribbon wands too, Annabelle?" Riley asked, bending over at the waist to talk to her. "We *love* rainbow ribbon wands, don't we, Jess?"

"I've already told her, Dad," Jess said.

Riley clutched his heart and sat down in the grass, leaning back and closing his eyes. "I'm the prisoner of an evil sorcerer. Will you help free me?"

Annabelle stopped running and cocked her hip. "There's no evil sorcerer around here. You're okay."

He threw his arms out dramatically. "You can't see him. He's invisible, and he's tied me up. Right, Jess?"

"Right," she responded, shaking her wand due east.

"Please, we both need to free my dad. It's the only way."

Annabelle shook her head. "I still don't see anyone."

Sadie watched her brother cover his mouth like he was fighting laughter.

"It's *pretend*," Jess told her, dropping her wand. "Don't you ever use your imagination?"

"Oh, pretend!" the little girl cried out. "I get it."

Together they proceeded to shake their wands in the same direction, and then Jess trailed the ribbons over Riley, who still lay on the ground with his eyes closed.

"He's not what I expected," Sadie heard her mama say.

She looked over her shoulder to see Mama only a few steps behind her. "Dale says I'm being a tough cookie, given how close he is to Paige. As I was watching him, I realized that part of me didn't want to like him."

Sadie's mouth parted. "But why?"

Her mama caressed her face. "Because I know they're close… It seemed to me that if I liked him, I would probably like Paige too. It's a horrible thing to admit, but part of me was hoping…oh good heavens… Part of me still blames Paige's mama for what happened to our family. Even though I know that has nothing to do with Paige herself."

"It's okay to be angry, Mama," Sadie told her, hugging her tight. "No one thinks less of you for that."

"He's a good man," Mama whispered. "Your Riley. J.P. told me a bit about their conversation, and if that and your love for the man hadn't been enough to sway me, the way he played with Boone in the kitchen would have done the trick. It won't always be easy with the daughter, but I expect you know that."

Sadie nodded. "I know that, but I keep praying. I never imagined falling in love with a man who had a child already. Part of me always thought we'd both…make that journey together first. But I love him, Mama, and part of me already loves Jess. I know I'm not her mama, and I pray for guidance about how to interact with her. Then I think about Dale, and I know how."

Her mama looked her in the eye. "That man...I never expected to find anyone to love after your daddy left. I sure as heck never planned on marrying again." She laughed. "But he has a way about him. Never asks for anything. Only loves you to pieces and hangs on your every word."

Sadie imagined her stepfather was inside the house, listening to everyone like usual. He never said much, but his presence was always felt.

"I'm glad you found someone, Mama," she told her, feeling like they were speaking woman-to-woman for the first time. "The way it feels...to be loved by a man and to love him..."

"The only kind of love to equal that is the one you have with God and with your children," Mama told her. "I imagine should you and Riley continue to love each other, you'll experience that kind someday too."

Sadie wouldn't say so out loud, but her mind had gone to marriage a few times before she could rein it back in. She blamed it on the magazine aisle in the grocery store, which was surely overstocked with bridal magazines. The images of happy couples in bridal attire had seemed to jump off the shelves.

"There's..." She wasn't sure what to say. She wouldn't have made love with Riley if she hadn't believed they could have forever, and he likely knew it.

"If you two love each other, keep moving forward together," her mama told her. "He was right to bring Jess to meet us. She needs to keep moving forward too."

Riley was racing after the girls with Jess' ribbon wand now in his possession. She was laughing as he caught her and lifted her up in the air. Mama had a point.

"What should I do to help Jess with that?" she asked.

"When it comes down to it, kids only believe in actions," her mama told her. "Words are all good and dandy, but she's at an age where she starts to see the divide we all come to see as we grow up. Some people are worth their words and others aren't. Show her with your actions that she can count on you and that you care about her and her father. She wants him to be happy too."

Annabelle launched herself at Riley, and he boosted her up in his free arm. The three of them laughed in tandem as he made a zigzag through the grass, the girls' delighted shrieks cresting along with the breeze.

"You don't remember it since you were so little, but after your daddy left, J.P. got downright protective of me. If a man at church came my way, he would stand in front of me like my little knight. I imagine Jess wants to protect Riley some too, even if it's unconscious."

That made sense to Sadie. Jess was tough. She knew that, had seen evidence of it. "I'll keep that in mind."

"Now, I'm going to have a quick chat with your man," her mama told her. "I want him to feel welcome here. I imagine he was a little concerned about my feelings about Paige and the past."

"Of course, he was, Mama," she said. "We all are."

"I'm getting to it my own way," Louisa said. "I mean, Shelby has been working on me to come with y'all when you next visit Preston's mama. If I can face Lenore after all these years, surely I can speak with my children's half-sister."

So Shelby had shared their plans with Mama. "We've been putting off the visit, hoping either you or Paige might come with us. We thought… Well, it might close the circle of the past for good."

Her mama looked off in the distance. "It might at that."

Sadie watched as her mama headed off. Riley paused in his jogging for a moment, his head turning toward them. J.P. called the girls over and asked if they would come inside with him for some lemonade. Annabelle took his hand immediately. Jess looked at Riley, who nodded, before stepping forward and heading to the house.

Tough? Yeah, Jess was tough. J.P. wouldn't be put off though. Her brother would win the trust of that little girl.

"Can I meet Rye Crenshaw?" Jess asked as the group neared her. "I haven't seen him yet. I met Mr. Lassiter though, and he's nice. Real quiet like. Your sister, Susannah, was with him, and she talked most of the time as we looked for a vase. She has tons of them, just like Annabelle said."

Sadie cast one last look at Riley and her mama. They had their backs turned to the house so she couldn't get a glimmer of what was going on. She hoped Riley would tell her later. *It will be fine*, she assured herself.

"Sure thing, Jess," she said. "Let's find Rye. He's probably with his new baby son."

Her mama's words flashed through her, and she reached out to Jess before the girl could take off. Jess' green eyes lowered, and there was a stillness in the air as she decided what to do. J.P. caught her gaze and gave an encouraging smile. Sadie held her breath as the moment lengthened.

Then Jess took her hand, and they went inside together.

Chapter 23

Riley knew things were getting mega-serious with Sadie when he met her family, especially since he ended up having what he'd term a *soft interview* with her mama.

But when his brother offered to fly out with his family to meet her, their relationship seemed to take on a new meaning.

"Tyler seems to think I'm gonna marry Sadie," he told Mark during one of their morning runs.

"Is that so?" the man drawled, biting his lip to contain his smile.

He punched his friend in the shoulder. "Is everybody thinking that?"

Mark kept his eyes trained forward. "Everybody is a fairly broad term."

"Fine," Riley said, stopping on the street. "Do you and Paige think that?"

Mark circled him, continuing to jog. "The only person whose opinion matters here is yours. Well, yours and Sadie's."

"You aren't answering my question," Riley said. "Meeting people's families is a big deal."

"I expect you knew that when you agreed to meet

hers," Mark said, punching him in the bicep and encouraging him to start running again. "Why'd you do it?"

He thought about it for a moment. Mark had a way of peeling the proverbial onion of someone's motivations. "I met them because they're some of the most important people in her life."

"Like you've become," Mark added, turning around to face Riley and running backward.

Damn if Mark didn't know how to cut to the chase. "Yeah, like I've become."

Sadie lit up like a Christmas tree whenever she caught sight of him. Her expression wasn't too different than Jess', he'd come to realize. Both of his girls were always happy to see him. He probably had the same excited expression on his face whenever he caught sight of them.

"What are you most afraid of?" Mark asked, continuing to jog backward.

Riley cut his pace down so his friend wouldn't trip on something unseen and fall. "Shit. You would ask that."

Mark skidded to a halt. "It's a relevant question."

Yeah, it was. "I'm..." He rubbed the back of his neck. This wasn't the time for a pat answer. "I'm afraid something might happen to ruin everything. I'm afraid...that I'll get hurt again."

Shit, was he really such a coward underneath all his blustering and superhero talk?

"And with Jess too," he added. "I couldn't protect her last time, but this time...I can't let anything happen to her."

"You did protect her, Riley," Mark said, getting in his face as much as he ever did. "When are you going to realize that? Some people might have gone along with the abortion even if they didn't want to. Not you, Riley."

When his friend thrust a finger at his chest, he felt his eyes widen. "Are you mad at me?"

Mark blew out a loud breath. "Honestly, it seems like

I am. Riley, I have listened to you blame yourself for not protecting Jess from her mother time and time again. Every time I tell you that you *did* protect her. And you argue with me every damn time. I wish..."

Riley stood there speechless in the face of his friend's outburst.

"I wish you'd realize you have a lot to give someone like Sadie. Hell, you give to me and Paige and Haley every day. I know you think you need us more than we need you, but dammit, you're wrong. Besides Paige, you're the best friend I've ever had, my wife considers you her brother, and my daughter... Riley, you hang the moon in her eyes."

His heart was thundering in his chest. "Are we having a personal moment?"

Mark shook his head. "Don't be dense. There's nothing wrong with two friends sharing how they feel about each other."

No, there wasn't, which was why Mark was his friend in the first place. Riley had been teased at school for being sensitive, but that very quality was something the Bradshaws seemed to value about him.

"Besides my brother, you're the best friend I've ever had too," Riley said.

A car slowed down on the street as it went by, and Mark stared down the driver. "Great. Now they think we're either having a confrontation or reenacting a scene from *Brokeback Mountain*."

"You're in a pretty good mood, aren't you?" Riley asked, fighting a smile.

"I'm...pissed off about a boy's situation at school, and what's going on with you and the McGuinesses is pinging me."

"Sorry," Riley said, starting to run again. "I'll think about what you said. Okay?"

Mark caught up with him. "You'd better. Sadie is the best thing that could happen to you. And Jess. Do you really think everybody's lucky enough to find a love like that? You're old enough to know better."

"Man, when you want to put me in my place, you don't pull any punches."

Mark glared at him. "Do you believe Sadie would be a good mother to Jess if you got married?"

"Yes, but…"

"But what?" Mark pressed.

"I'm still not sure how Jess is going to handle it," Riley said, "and that's what scares me. She's been talking to this girl at school and it's giving her bad ideas."

"Betty," Mark said. "Yeah, Haley has mentioned her to me and Paige."

"She has?" Riley asked, his footing suddenly unsure.

Mark sighed. "Yes, Haley's been asking us questions about what happens when a man who has a daughter from a previous relationship marries someone new. She's not buying into Betty's stories, but…"

"But Haley is still a little scared for Jess," Riley finished, his heart thudding with pain. "Dammit, that makes me feel like shit."

"Haley is only a little scared because Jess is," he told him. "That's only natural. You're both going through a big transition. Opening yourself up to someone new is a big deal."

"I should be able to make it easier for her." Some days being human and being a dad were incompatible, if you asked him.

"You are, trust me, and you couldn't have a better back channel than Haley. She's crazy about Sadie. She keeps telling Jess that Sadie is beautiful—inside and out."

"I love that kid," Riley said, getting choked up. "How do I make Jess feel less scared? Sadie's mom told her actions are more important than words, and I agree, but how does that work in practice? Do we just keep on loving her?"

Mark cut his pace back, and Riley knew he was about to deliver a real whammy. He stopped again, and so did Mark.

His friend put his hand on his shoulder. "Jess will most likely stop being afraid when you do."

Riley hung his head. "You're always saying our kids echo our emotions when they're young."

"It was Jung who said that," Mark said, "but yeah, there's no getting around the truth."

"So how do I conquer my fear, sensei?" he quipped, his guts raw.

"You do what every superhero does," Mark said, clapping him on the back. "You reach deep inside you, find your inner strength, and do what you know what you must do."

Mark only used superhero talk when he was really desperate to get through to him. He hissed out a breath. "I love Sadie, and I want her to be in my life."

"I know you do."

He pressed his fingers to the bridge of his nose. "Like *always* in my life."

When he looked at his friend, Mark was smiling. "There you go."

"Does it matter that we haven't known each other very long?" *Or that we've made love less than a hundred times*, he thought in silence.

Time again. Whenever he sat down to work on his female superhero, that was the word he kept hearing. She did something with time. Only he still hadn't nailed down the nuances of her powers.

"What do you think? Aren't you the one always telling my daughter that time is an illusion? That we can bend it with our minds?"

Busted. And yet he believed every word. Maybe *that* was the power he needed to give his superhero. "It's...ah..."

"Make-believe? You know better, my friend."

"You know, when you get pissy, you're a pain in the ass."

Mark barked out a laugh. "That's what Paige always says. But I tend to feel better once I've spoken my piece."

"Feeling better now?"

"Much." Mark puffed out his chest. "Are we going to run or are you going to stew some more?"

Riley stood a little taller. His feet felt more anchored into the earth suddenly. His mind flashed him a picture of Sadie laughing with him, and he remembered what else superheroes did. They followed their heart.

"No, I'm done stewing."

Chapter 24

Sunshine filtered over Sadie's eyes when she rolled onto her back. She was still sleepy, so she snuggled under the covers and kept her eyes closed. Maybe she'd fall back asleep.

"Oh, no, you don't," she heard a husky male voice say beside her. "I've been waiting hours for you to wake up. We only have a few hours before I have to go home..."

Right. He had to go home. Riley had surprised her with an overnight date. Of course, he'd had help. Paige had given him Shelby's number, and her sister had packed her a bag for the night while she was at work. She couldn't wait to thank her sisters in person.

Last night...

Well, if they asked her about it, she would tell them Riley was the most romantic man ever. He'd found them a lake house for the night, saying he wanted to wake up with her as the sun rose.

"Guess I missed sunrise," she murmured, turning onto her side.

"Considering when we went to sleep, I thought you deserved a pass on the romantic sunrise I had in mind."

She snorted out a laugh. "We were like animals last

night." And darn it all if she hadn't enjoyed every single minute of it.

He nuzzled her ear. "Amazing what a difference complete privacy makes. No one to hear. My ears are still ringing from all the screaming you did."

That popped her eyes wide open. She punched him. "You're bad to say that."

"But not bad enough to have woken you up so we could recreate it," he said, trailing his finger along her collarbone. "I've been lying beside you, listening to you breathe and wanting you like crazy, and do you know what I found myself thinking about?"

"Besides all the ways you want to make me scream again?"

She wiggled next to him and smiled when he reached for her leg and drew it over his hip. He was hard, all right, and she felt her body turn warm and willing in response.

Pushing her mostly tangled hair behind her ears, he gazed into her eyes. "I thought about how nice it would be to do this every morning."

She drew back. "You did?"

"What would you think about that?" he asked, lowering his gaze. "I mean, I know we have some things to work out with Jess, but I... Mark said I needed to stop putzing around basically, and it's all I've thought about all week."

"Riley," she said, sitting up in bed, pulling the sheet over her breasts. "What are you saying here?" Because this was one moment when a woman wanted to be sure. Really sure.

"I'm not proposing this moment," he said, sitting up as well. "I can do a lot better than this, and you deserve something really special, but I guess I..."

"Riley. What?"

"I guess I'd like to know whether you'd ever consider marrying me," he said, ducking his chin. "I mean, I know I have a complicated past—"

"A complicated past?" She snorted. "Riley, this is where your superhero language isn't helping you."

He lifted his shoulder, and she caught the vulnerability he was trying to disguise. "You know what I mean. Jess is the best thing in my life, but so are you. I know she's not yours, but... I guess I wanted to see how you'd feel about her. Long term. You know? Some women...don't want to raise other people's kids."

Her heart grew sore in her chest, and she lifted his chin so she could see his eyes. "Riley, I love you, and I love Jess. No, she's not my child, but I'll always love her and take care of her and help you with her. I'm...sometimes at sea about what my role will be, but I figure loving her and cherishing her for being herself is the best approach anyone can take."

He blew out a long breath and hugged her to his chest. "Good. That's good. I was afraid I might be making it too complicated, but she's my daughter. I have to—"

"Put her first," she supplied.

He kissed her on the top of her head. "Not first anymore. It's different. I can love you both. That's easy. It's only... She's still growing up, learning how to be herself. You've got that down. I don't worry about you, Sadie."

That was so sweet, she had to kiss him. When she did, he pulled her onto his lap, and their kisses turned slow and soft. Her heart seemed to fill up with warm water in her chest, floating happily on a sea of pleasure.

"I know you worry about Jess," she said when they broke away. "I do too. But we'll love her and figure things out. Are you going to talk to her about this?"

He nodded. "Yeah. I want to know what's best to say in this situation. Some friend at school keeps telling her how everything's changed at home now that her stepmother has taken over... I hate that. It's made me wonder if that's where some of her questions about Mandy are coming from. I want to be her main influence in life, you know?"

She remembered other kids asking her questions about her dad. Some had said mean things about him. Others had told her maybe her father was dead. Bottom line was that she knew what Jess was going through.

"She's always going to value your opinion, Riley. You share it with so much love. You don't force it on anyone."

"Thanks," he said, rubbing his neck like it was stiff. "I'm going to read more parenting magazines. Sometimes they're my friend and sometimes they're total bullshit."

She laughed. "See what I mean."

"And I really want to keep Jess in the same home," he added. "I mean, Haley is her BFF and—"

"It's fine. I'll love being next to Paige and her family." She would never have dreamed of living next door to her secret sister a few months ago. God was so good.

"I'll put you on the mortgage," Riley said. "Women need to have their fair share of things."

"Riley. It's okay. We'll work it all out." She knew that. Trusted that.

He took her hands in his, turning serious. "There's something else I have to mention. I'm... Okay, straight out and straightforward. I know going to church is important to you, and I... Well, I don't believe in things the same way."

"I know that."

"Let me get this out. I'm spiritual, if you have to put a word on it. Not religious. I want to make sure you're okay with that. I know your mama is a preacher and all and your whole family goes, and I...I would be okay with our children going to church with you, but I would like them to hear my thoughts on things too. I'd never undermine you on big points, Sadie. Ever. But I'd want you and I to discuss the things we see differently before talking to them. Kids are... They need to know we have their back."

She tightened her hands around his when he looked her in the eye.

"I would want them to decide what's best for themselves," he finished. "It's important they know what's true for them. Not just what other people tell them."

Her mama said as much from the pulpit on Sundays, but Riley didn't know that. "I'm grateful you brought this up. It's important for us to talk about these things. Shelby has talked about it with Vander some, and he feels much like you do, but he's open to their children going to church."

He kissed her hands. "I'll give this whole praying together thing a shot for you so long as you promise you won't make fun of me. You said that—"

She pressed her mouth to his and kissed him until he settled down. "You'd do that for me?" Somehow this offer struck her more than anything else he'd said, likely because he was stepping out of his comfort zone for her.

"I don't have a clue what to say to God or the Universe or whatever," he admitted, his cheeks flushing, "and I'll probably talk superhero from time to time, but I figure I can give thanks for everything I'm grateful for every night. I'll thank the Universe of God or whatever for you... and Jess...and any children we have together."

Her hand caressed his face. "I give thanks for you and Jess every night before I go to sleep."

The look he gave her would have made her knees melt had she been standing. "That makes me... Man, that gets me. Right here." He slapped his chest. "Sadie McGuiness, I love you to pieces. Thank you for coming into my life."

She snuggled closer, awash in her love for him. "Thank you, Riley."

And they sealed their future with another kiss.

Chapter 25

When Paige arrived at Oodles of Spools for her quilting class, Sadie met her at the door with her eyes dancing.

"I have the best idea," she announced, closing the door behind Paige. "Would you like to help me finish the lap blanket I made for Me-Mother? The idea struck me last night. I mean, what with us visiting her together, I thought it would be a lovely gift."

Paige couldn't help clutching her workbag in response. Every time she thought of meeting her grandmother, she got a little queasy. But she trusted her new siblings and had decided she needed to accompany them on their visit, especially since Louisa had decided they should go together as siblings without her coming along.

"Of course, I'd be happy to help," she said, and then promptly cleared her throat.

Sadie wrapped her up in a tight hug. "I know you're worried. Heaven knows I was so scared the first time, I could have peed my pants."

"I don't think I'm that bad off."

When her sister started laughing, she felt her mouth turn up into a smile.

"That's a relief," Sadie said, squeezing her one last

time before releasing her. "Come on. Let me show you the design I struck upon. I want you to add a few of your own touches. It will be great. We've never collaborated before."

"Have you ever?" Paige asked, daunted by the prospect. "Collaborated?"

Her sister looked off to the right, thinking. "No, actually. This will be the first time."

Paige felt oddly honored. "I hope I can add something. I'm still a newbie."

"You're doing great," Sadie said, ushering her into the store to where the others were starting to gather. "You've already made three baby quilts."

"And I have the sticks in my fingers to prove it," she said, holding up her fingers. "The pins and I are still making friends."

Ada laughed. "It's a badge of honor, honey. I still stick myself from time to time."

"It usually happens to me when I fall asleep while quilting. Horace starts sawing logs," Leanne said, "and I come awake and forget where I am, and prick myself in the process."

"My honey acts like me getting stuck could hurt the baby," Whitney said, putting her hands on her slightly round belly. "He's such a worry wart."

"Some men are even bigger babies than the ones we carry inside us," Mae said. "That's why I know God was right to give child birthing to us."

"Hear, hear," Leanne said, making a fist in the air.

"Let me set what I have so far down on the work table," Sadie told Paige, and together they moved to the station.

"What are y'all doing over there?" Leanne asked.

"None of your beeswax," Ada told her. "Work on your own quilt. From the looks of your seams, you need to."

Leanne held up her baby quilt, a lovely one in the

pattern of zigzag rainbows. "There's nothing wrong with my seams, you old battle axe."

"Ladies," Sadie said with a crinkled brow. *"Please."*

Paige could see that Ada was biting her lip. The women genuinely enjoyed teasing each other—even if it went further than most of them would have taken it.

When Paige turned around, she gasped. "Oh, Sadie. It's beautiful."

The lap quilt depicted a few happy puppies frolicking in the grass with a happy sun overhead. The puppies were made from a combination of light and dark brown fabric, and when Paige touched it, she thought it might be flannel. The use of different variations of browns made the puppies seem real.

"Me-Mother's greatest treasure is her bulldog, No-no. When I thought about what would make her happiest, it was puppies. I have a feeling she'd have more dogs if she could afford to take care of them."

Paige already knew about their grandma's obesity and how it had impacted her overall health. "This is wonderful, Sadie. I mean, I feel happy looking at it."

"Then we're on the right track," she said, fussing with one of the edges of cloth. "This sucker just won't lie flat. It's stubborn, but I'm more stubborn."

So far Paige had ironed and ironed, but if one of her pieces remained stubborn, she didn't fight it. Sadie, on the other hand, was a perfectionist, and her quilts showed it.

"I don't know what to add," Paige said honestly. "It's perfect the way it is."

"Oh, I bet you'll think of something." Sadie patted her hand. "I'm going to check on everyone. You stand here for a spell and think on it."

She touched the pattern, hoping that the tactile connection might jog her mind. While her siblings had shared their impressions of their grandma with her, she didn't know much of anything about Lenore. After all, she'd never met her. Maybe she needed to focus on the puppies. What did puppies like? Bones? Squeaky toys? It would be weird to depict that in a quilt, wouldn't it? Then her eyes shifted to the corner of the quilt, where Sadie had used some green fabric to convey a yard.

"I've got something," she cried out, only then realizing she'd interrupted Sadie and Imogene, who must have walked in while she was looking at the quilt.

"Be right there," Sadie said with a smile.

When her sister came over, she pointed to the corner. "How about we add a dog house and a hole where the puppies have dug in the yard? I couldn't possibly add that to the quilt, but you can."

"I love that!" Sadie unpinned the corner pieces with quick efficiency. "Come with me. Let's find some fabric."

Sure enough, Sadie managed to pull some already cut squares that would work, and then she brandished her scissors and started cutting them into puzzle-like pieces.

"You're ridiculous," Leanne said, coming up behind them. "I mean, seriously, girl. You have a gift."

"Oh, that's wonderful." Mae had joined them too as she snacked on a gingersnap. "If you add this piece..." She pointed to the one she had in mind.

"Yes," Sadie said, picking it up. "It will fit better here."

The other women clustered around, watching as Sadie worked. Soon the lap quilt had the suggestion of the doghouse and the hole in the ground Paige had come up with.

Whitney shook her head. "I'm never going to be that good. Sadie, the only word I can muster is wow."

"Puppies," Mae said, running her hand over the trio of them. "This is going to make your grandma very happy."

Paige hoped so. But mostly she hoped her grandma would be happy to meet her. Everyone had assured her she would be, but the dark seeds of self-doubt had reared their head. In some circles, she would be seen as a love child, a bastard... She knew all of the ugly words. She'd been called them frequently as a young girl, even by her grandparents.

Sadie dragged her out of her funk by asking for her help with the sewing. For a woman who liked things to be perfect, Sadie always included Paige despite the fact that she was still very new to this quilting thing and her seams were a little off here and there. Sadie handed over the ironing to Paige so she could check on the others. So far they'd donated twenty baby quilts to the NICU with the promise of more on the way. Ada and Mae and Sadie had made the most, no surprise. Whitney was starting her third one now that she'd finished the quilt for her own baby.

Paige thought again how nice it would be to make a baby quilt for a new baby, but what would be, would be. Pretty soon, she'd start Haley's princess quilt, something she'd only be able to pull off with some serious help from her sister.

Sadie came back and whipped together the back of the quilt lickety split, joking it was always the easiest. They picked out a happy yellow ruffle for the border, and once Sadie had zipped that along on the sewing machine, she held it up.

"Looks pretty good," Sadie said, turning it under the light.

"Your grandma is going to feel like the luckiest woman in the world," Leanne said, coming over. "You can feel the love in it."

"Yes, you can," Paige heard a stranger's voice say from behind them.

Sadie gasped and flew around, the quilt billowing like a ballroom dancer's skirt. "Mama. What are you doing here?"

Paige felt a punch land in her diaphragm. Sadie's mama was here? She gulped and turned around. Louisa McGuiness was smiling softly at everyone, but her blue eyes were looking directly at Paige. Could she see the imprint of her first husband's features? Paige hadn't realized how much she took after the father she'd never known before meeting her siblings. She stood rooted to the spot, waiting for...something.

"I thought I'd swing by and say hello since y'all are about ready to finish," Louisa said. "I hope y'all don't mind none."

"Of course she doesn't," Ada said, hugging the woman. "We always love to see you. Come. I'd like to show you my quilt."

Louisa headed off with the older woman, and Sadie set the quilt aside.

"I didn't know she was coming," she explained.

"It's okay," Paige said. "Riley...ah...told me it's not like she's Maleficent or anything. Oh, that's a horrible thing to say."

Sadie's mouth twitched. "I'm becoming fluent in Riley. I know what you mean. Come on, let's iron this ruffle one more time."

Normally Paige would have groaned, but she was too fixated on watching Louisa from the corner of her eye. She went from woman to woman, saying hello and exclaiming over their work. Sadie kept her busy until the other women had said their goodbyes. Sadie had told them the truth—or most of it—so they were aware of the sisters' true relationship. They covered any concern or curiosity they might have felt with kind smiles as they hugged the pair of them on their way out.

"So Mama..." Sadie fidgeted with her hands. "What brings you this way?"

Paige realized her sister was nervous, and somehow that helped. Louisa took Sadie's hands in one of her own and caressed her daughter's cheek. Seeing the love in her eyes, Paige felt like she was encroaching.

"I should leave y'all," she said, knocking into a chair when she went for her workbag.

"Actually, I was hoping you might let me buy you a cup of coffee, Paige," Louisa said. "There's a shop next door. I'll just run over before they close. Sadie, if you'd leave me the key, I can lock up for you."

Sadie's eyes shot to her hairline. "Are you serious?"

"As the pope," she said, her lips twitching. "Bad joke. Yes, honey, you go on home. Paige and I'll be fine. Paige, what kind of coffee can I get you?"

An Irish coffee? she wanted to joke. "How about a cappuccino?"

"Excellent. I'll be right back. Sadie, the key."

When she held out her hands, Sadie sprang to life. "But Mama—"

"What am I? An ogre? Come on, honey, give me the key. And then you say goodbye to Paige while I get the coffee."

Sadie stared at her for a moment before walking to her purse to produce the key. "I need to take it off my key chain."

"Then do so, honey," she said. "You can leave it with Paige. Come on and kiss me."

Sadie went over and kissed her mama on the cheek, looking dazed.

"I'll be right back with the coffee, Paige."

When Louisa left, Sadie opened her hands. "I'm so sorry. I didn't know. You don't have to stay."

She remembered how Riley had assured her about Louisa, telling her she had nothing to be nervous about. No, she would stand her ground. If Louisa wanted to talk to her like this, then she would hear her out. If she needed to defend herself, she would. But she hoped not. Everything was going so great with her siblings.

"I... It's time for me to meet your mama properly. I've been putting it off."

"I can stay," Sadie said, taking her hands.

Paige knew Sadie was partly trying to buoy up her

emotions, but it wasn't necessary. She knew her own strength. "Go on. I'll be fine." And if she needed to fall to pieces later for a spell, Mark would hold her until she felt strong again.

"All right," Sadie said, "but call me afterward and let me know you're okay."

"Go."

Sadie quickly folded up their grandma's quilt and handed it to Paige. "I want you to keep it until we make the trip to see her. Maybe it will boost your own spirits this week."

Then she was off, and Paige was left holding the gift they'd made for yet another relative she'd never expected to meet.

When the store door opened and Louisa returned, Paige turned to face her with the quilt still in her hands.

"My daughter has done me a disservice," Louisa said without preamble. "I'm only here to meet the woman everyone I love has said is so wonderful."

She extended a to-go coffee cup to Paige, who realized with some amount of alarm that she'd have to put the quilt down to take it.

"Come sit," Louisa said, gesturing to the circle of chairs now abandoned by the rest of the quilting circle.

Paige rested the quilt on her lap, feeling its warmth seep through her cold skin, and took the coffee.

"I'm sorry for the surprise visit," she said. "After meeting Riley, I didn't want to wait much longer to tell you how happy I am that my children have found you. You've...brought great love and joy into their lives."

Paige's throat thickened.

"I've prayed about what to say to you," Louisa said. "Some of my old feelings about the past have gotten stirred up, but that only showed me they needed resolution. I also want to make sure you understand that I'm genuinely glad you're in their lives. It bears repeating. I never imagined it, frankly."

"Neither did I," she said softly. "But I'm so glad it's happened. They've brought me joy too."

Louisa smiled and sipped her coffee. "I can see why everyone has fallen for you. You have an aura of kindness and a warmth about you."

Paige could feel the words rear up inside her, and the pressure of them was so great, she had to say, "I'm not my mother."

"I know that," Louisa said softly. "And I'm not Preston, your father."

Paige nodded. "Of course not. You've raised four amazing people."

"Thank you," Louisa said. "But you deserve more credit. After all, you raised yourself. From what J.P. and Vander told me, no one really looked after you."

Sadness returned as images of her childhood flashed though her mind: all of the peanut butter and jam sandwiches she'd made herself for dinner and all the times she'd had to wear a jacket over her tattered clothing to hide its neglect.

"No, no one did."

"Well, you seem to have a whole bunch of people on your side now," Louisa said. "I hear your husband and daughter are wonderful, and I already know Riley and Jess are. I hope you'll join us for Sunday dinner with your family. I…don't ever want to stand in the way of that. That's really what I wanted to say to you. I know we're not related per se, but I'd like to be your friend."

The offer made Paige's heart tighten. "I think I would like that."

"Good," Louisa said, taking a sip of her coffee.

"There's something I need to say too," Paige said, setting her coffee on the floor. "I'm not my mother, and while her actions were hers…I can't help but feel responsible sometimes."

Louisa shook her head and set her coffee aside. "Lay that to rest, child. You're not responsible. Any more than I'm responsible for Preston."

Paige felt the sorrow well up. "Still…I'm sorry you were hurt."

Louisa stood up and held out her arms. "I'm sorry you were hurt too."

Somehow she found herself standing, held spellbound by the love emanating from this woman's eyes, a love she'd never seen in the eyes of her own mother.

She walked into Louisa's arms, and they held each other.

Chapter 26

Everything seemed to be coming together in Sadie's life almost as though by design. Her whole world seemed to be expanding, and like Jess and Haley's princess playtime, she felt very much like a magical princess herself these days. Of course, it had helped her see each girl's princess quilt better in her mind. And she'd started conceiving a superhero quilt for Riley, her hero...

They were talking marriage! It sent a little thrill through her every time she thought about it. And that wasn't the only cause for celebration. Mama had up and welcomed Paige into the family, and today all of the McGuiness siblings were going to see their grandmother together.

But when they parked on the dirt road in front of Me-Mother's trailer, it was hard not to see that everything wasn't coming up roses for some. This trailer park was populated with people with broken dreams.

"It's too bad none of the assisted living facilities worked out. Maybe she'll let us buy her a place in Nashville and hire a helper," J.P. said, turning off the engine. "This place..."

Sure as shooting, it wasn't as shiny as a new penny, but Me-Mother had closed down all talk of moving after learning none of the places they'd found in Nashville would accept No-no. The rare few would only do smallish dogs, certainly not a bulldog. When J.P. had offered to take No-no, saying Me-Mother could visit him whenever she liked, she'd been adamant. *Then I'll stay here, and there'll be no more discussion.* They were still trying to find a solution that would work.

"Paige?" Shelby asked, turning around from the front seat. "Are you okay? We had a quite a shock when we arrived the first time." In fact, Paige had had a week of them, what with her meeting with Mama, but she said she felt much better after her talk with Louisa. "You can change your mind about wanting to go in. No one would think any less of you."

"No, I still want to meet her," Paige said, still holding Sadie's hand in the back seat they were sharing with Susannah. "You prepared me as well as you could."

"Nothing ever prepares me for this place," Susannah said, looking out the window. "The children need new clothes and shoes. This is the part of the South you can't tell anyone about. The poverty...I wish..."

"We do what we can," J.P. said, sitting back heavily in his seat. "Maybe we can find a local church or community group to work with to improve the conditions down here. But that's for another day."

"I'm glad we brought her the lap quilt," Sadie said. "It's sure to brighten up her place."

"Yes," Paige murmured, her gaze still fixed out the window. "I know I didn't do much, but thank you for letting me help."

"Nonsense, you did plenty." Sadie let go of Paige's hand to unbuckle her seatbelt. "We should go in. I can see No-no in the window. Me-Mother knows we're here."

"We're a little early," Shelby said, checking her watch, "but I don't think she'll mind none."

They'd made good time. The roads had been clear,

and the weather good. Sadie had felt Paige's nerves the entire three hours. Someday everyone's spouses and significant others would come with them again, like they'd done before, but for Paige's first meeting with her grandma, everyone had thought it best for it to only be the five of them. Mama had promised she'd join them someday soon.

The five of them...Sadie liked how their numbers had changed. The McGuiness family had five siblings now, and they'd shared the news with their friends at church this morning since Mama had met Paige and wanted to unseal the last secret, so to speak. This meeting with Me-Mother felt like the perfect next step. Not too bad for a Sunday.

"Ready?" Sadie asked Paige. "She's going to love you. Trust me."

They left the car with their gifts—the quilt wasn't the only one—and walked down the dirt path that had become a natural walkway. The area around the trailer was lined with weeds, and Sadie wondered if it was worth asking Tammy to pick out some flowers to plant to brighten the space. Their grandma couldn't water them, she expected, but there were plants that thrived in harsh climates.

Standing in front of Me-Mother's door, Sadie couldn't think of a harsher climate. Rusty car parts and appliances worn out from use littered the yards of other trailers. Mama had told them to always look for the beauty, but in this place, it was hard to see any under the patina of neglect and wear. Weeds flourished, and if there was one truth about weeds, it was that they overtook everything in sight rapaciously.

Well, their presence would hopefully bring some joy to the older woman. J.P. was lifting his hand to knock when the door opened. Their grandma stood there in a light yellow cotton dress with her trusted dog at her side. No-no was calm, and Me-Mother's smile was radiant.

Tears were already gathering in her eyes.

"Oh, my sweet grandbabies," she said in a hoarse voice. "It's good to see y'all. And Paige... Oh, honey, I'm so sorry for what my boy done, but seeing you... It makes my heart sing. You're beautiful. Come here, child."

Paige stepped forward and brushed at the tears streaming down her face. "Hello. I'm...happy to meet you too."

Me-Mother cupped her face. "I know I'm a sight, but you don't need fear me none. Everyone told me how lovely you are, and they're all great judges of character. They saw past this old girl's walls when we first made an acquaintance. It was quite a shock, but we managed that first time. We'll manage this time too. Come in and give me sugar. Each of you."

Paige kissed her cheek and then stepped aside for everyone to follow suit. J.P. closed the door and gave No-no a good scratching behind the ears.

"You look good, Me-Mother," he told her. "You been taking care of yourself like I asked you?"

She seemed to beam. "Yes, you sweet boy. I've been soaking my feet in those Epsom salts you brought me last time, and it helps bring down the swelling. And you brought me another honey-baked ham. How kind. Y'all shouldn't spoil me."

"We're not spoiling you," Shelby said. "The ham is from Vander. He said to tell you he'll be up for a visit soon."

Me-Mother looked at Paige. "I'm particularly fond of Shelby's man. He comes up and visits me from time to time. Although why he spends his time with an old woman like me, I'll never know."

"Me-Mother, don't talk about yourself like that," Sadie said, handing Paige the present to hold and crossing to hug her. "We visit you because we love you. Of course, if you moved to Dare River, we could all see you more often."

The older woman's eyes narrowed. "We've done talked that to death, child. I won't leave No-no here. Heck, with y'all blowing into my life like you done, I have a sight more to look forward to than I used to. I might live longer because of it. That's more than enough for me."

"Paige and I made you something, Me-Mother," Sadie said, gesturing to Paige.

Her sister extended it, and the older woman pressed the gift to her belly like it was a cherished child. "Oh, you done spoil me too much." She unwrapped it carefully and then looked at Sadie and Paige. "Y'all done made me a quilt? Oh, you precious children."

"Open it up," Sadie said, helping her with it. "The others haven't seen it yet. Only me and Paige."

"Sadie did most of it," Paige said, wringing her hands.

"Oh, land sakes," their grandma said, extending it out in full. "You made me puppies. Oh, my…" She started to cry softly. "No one has ever made me something this special before. We had homemade clothes, growing up poor, but this… Oh, you sweet girls. Thank you! Thank you!"

She pressed the quilt to her chest and came over and kissed both of them on the cheeks.

"I brought you oranges," J.P. said, holding up a burlap bag. "Does that rate a kiss?"

"Only one," she teased. "These girls are going to get kissed and often today. I mean, I just can't believe this. The stitch work is so fine, and the dogs… No-no, they're a fair bit cuter than you are, but I still love you."

She lowered the quilt to show the bulldog, and he barked, causing her to give a teary laugh. Susannah and Shelby were wiping tears from their eyes as well, and Sadie nodded when they looked at her and Paige.

Shelby mouthed, "It's beautiful."

Sadie felt a familiar pride spread through her. She and Paige had made that together. "We're a good team." She took Paige's hand and swung it like they were little girls. She wished they'd known each other then. They could have played like Haley and Jess.

"Let me put this somewhere safe. It's too precious to leave out. I made lemonade and iced tea for y'all. Would one of you girls mind helping me?"

J.P. put his hand on her arm. "You find a place for the quilt and then come sit. We'll serve. Where would you like to sit and chat? Outside?"

"Outside would be lovely," Me-Mother said. "I'm hoping those hot and humid days are behind us. I'm going to put this on my bed. It will make me happy to have it cover me while I sleep." She headed down the hall.

"Susannah? Why don't you go outside with everyone while Shelby and I prepare the drinks? Who wants iced tea?"

He counted the show of hands, and Sadie wanted to hug him for taking charge of things like he usually did.

"I can help," she offered as their grandma returned with a grin on her face.

"I can get the drinks as good as any of y'all," J.P. responded. "Me-Mother knows I'm not one of those chauvinists."

The older woman barked out a laugh. "Where were you when I needed help with laundry, boy? No man I've ever known helped out with the household chores. All right, girls, we'll let him have his way and go outside."

"Save a chair for me beside you, Me-Mother," J.P. said with a wink.

"Cheeky boy, he is," Me-Mother said with a smile. "Paige, you come and sit on the other side of me. I want to hear all about you."

Sadie took a spot in the shade and smiled as Paige told Me-Mother about Mark and Haley and showed her some pictures. The love she had for them seemed to banish the worst of her nerves, and Me-Mother's kind smile ushered them the rest of the way.

Paige didn't mention Jess or Riley, even though they were in some of the pictures, and Sadie knew it was out of respect for her new role in their life. Next time, maybe she'd tell Me-Mother all about her new man and his daughter.

Love was a miracle, and seeing Paige and Me-Mother get acquainted was a bona fide one for sure. Sadie bowed her head and gave a moment of thanks.

When she raised her head, she noticed an old car parked a couple blocks up in the back road akin to an alley. The shadow of the driver struck her. He was watching them. She didn't know how she knew, but she felt it. Goosebumps flashed over her arms. The inside of the car was dark with the noonday sun raining down on it, and she squinted to get a better look. Why was he parked so oddly and staying inside his vehicle?

After another few minutes, her pulse started to race. Hope began a drumbeat in her heart. Without thinking it through, she lurched to her feet. Her legs seemed to have a mind of their own, and they wanted to talk to the man waiting in the car.

"I'll be right back," she cried, racing down the back road.

The man's silhouette shifted, and she knew he'd looked away from her. But he didn't start up his car. A cry of joy wanted to burst from her lips, and when she was a block away, she knew why.

Her daddy was here! He'd come to see them. Had he changed his mind? God, she hoped so. She'd prayed for it for months.

This had to be a sign, didn't it?

Her feet covered the distance between them quickly, and then she was standing a few feet from his old Chevy Impala. Strength flooded into her veins, almost as if the earth under her was pumping nourishment from every root under her feet. She'd waited for this moment her whole life, and everything around her seemed to still.

He turned his head to look at her, and she felt her heart clench.

"You're my daddy," she said across the distance between them.

"Maybe I am, maybe I'm not," the man answered in an insolent drawl, leaning his hands on the tarnished steering wheel.

The comment, and the way it was delivered, siphoned every drop of hope from her.

"You're visiting Lenore. You shouldn't be. She's none of your concern. You'd best mind me on that, girl."

The arrows of his words, powered with hate, seemed to fall before they reached her. She studied him, taking in the similarities between him and J.P. He still had most of his hair, but it was gray and thin and a touch greasy, like he hadn't washed it for days. His black work shirt was tattered around the edges, and his old jeans were as faded with age as he was. Booze and stale cigarettes touched her nose, the smell adding to the bile churning in her stomach. His mouth curled in a snarl, and his hazel eyes were hard and mean.

J.P. might resemble this man, but it was the only thing they had in common.

"You're a coward," she told him, her voice resounding with inner strength.

"What did you say to me?" he asked, leaning closer to the open window between them. But he didn't open the door. He didn't come out.

Anger exploded in her veins. "If you had any courage, you'd come and meet us instead of skulking here like you are," she told him, the sun hot on her shoulders.

"Lenore tells me you wanted to move her to a nicer place to live closer to Music City," he said, and spat out the driver's window. "La- *di*-da. Maybe you should give *me* money and a new place seeing as how I'm on the run because of y'all. That asshole private investigator ruined a good job and woman for me. I deserve some compensation."

Sadie couldn't believe her ears. Then she thought about Riley and what he'd said about Mandy. Is this the way he'd felt? *"Compensation?* You have some nerve saying that after what you did. To us and to Paige."

"Paige? Who the hell is Paige?"

"She's our sister, and a better human being than you'll ever be."

"I'm Paige," Sadie heard, as her sister came and stood beside her. "I'm the child you and Skylar Watkins made."

Her father spat out his window again. "I don't recognize you as my kin. I don't claim you none. Do you hear me, girl?"

Paige flinched next to her, and Sadie took her hand. The shadows of her siblings appeared in her peripheral vision, and then they were all standing next to her and Paige in a solid line in front of their daddy.

"Y'all are just like your mama," he cried out, "causing trouble, expecting too much. Self-righteous as all get out. I don't claim any of you as mine now that I see what you've become."

"Good!" Sadie shouted back. "Because you're not our daddy. You don't deserve to be."

"Deserve?" their daddy drawled out. "You have a nerve, girl. Someone needs to teach you a lesson."

"You'd better watch your tone with my sisters, mister," Shelby said, "because I have the urge to give you a piece of my mind, and trust me when I tell you...you'll be crying by the time I'm done."

"He's not worth it," J.P. said, stepping in front of them. "You're done hurting anyone in this family, and that means Lenore too. If I ever hear you've come around again with your tail between your legs, talking about what you deserve and who you're gonna give a lesson to... Well, man, you're going to wish to God we'd never met again this side of heaven."

"And you say you're a bunch of good Christian people," he replied, starting his car. "You're just like your mama."

"Thank you," Susannah said in a hard tone. "That's the kindest thing you've said so far. Now git on out of here like my brother said."

"Trash!" Their father raked his gaze over them. "You're all nothing but trash. And that includes you too." He shifted his hateful eyes to Paige. "What's your name? Patty? You're as much a bitch as your mother before you."

"You don't talk about Paige like that!" J.P. ground out, gripping the side of his car. "She's worth a hundred of you and then some. Now, you git on out of here and never come back."

"You don't tell me what to do," he called out, putting the car in gear. "I'm your daddy, boy."

J.P. stepped back, and his shadow seemed to tower over the car. "No, you aren't."

Dirt spewed up when their father hit the gas and raced off down the back road. Sadie felt the dust settle over her face, the grime reminding her of the hateful words he'd spewed at them. She wiped it off with thorough hands.

"He's *nothing,*" she whispered, sick to her soul at the realization.

Every fairy tale she'd spun about meeting her daddy again had turned to ash around her feet now that she was face to face with his ugliness. This was the man she'd hoped to give her away at her wedding? The one she'd dreamed would love and cherish her as the daughter of his heart? The one she hadn't been able to completely give up hope on, even after the cowardly way he'd run from Vander? No wonder their mama had worked so hard to protect them all those years.

"He's not worth the toilet paper you wipe with," Shelby said, anger lacing her voice. "Sadie, you did good, telling him what for when he talked about Paige like that. Honey, are you okay?"

"He's just like my mother," Paige said, her eyes glassy with shock. "No wonder they..."

"Birds of a feather," Susannah said, holding her stomach like she was going to retch. "He's... You're right. He's nothing. The worst kind of excuse for a man. I'm glad he left us."

In that moment, Sadie was too.

Chapter 27

The fallout over Sadie and Paige's soul-crushing encounter with their father weighed heavily on Riley.

Beyond his obvious love for each of them and his hope to help them through the aftermath, he also feared Jess might encounter the same situation someday when she was older. Thank God she didn't remember her mother's disastrous "visit" on her first birthday.

He did what he could for the women he loved. For Paige, he brought out his full box of tricks. He drew comic strips about the birds in their yards carrying on irreverent commentary about the neighborhood. His favorite so far was of a husky cardinal saying to a down-on-her-luck robin, "The crazy guy in the cape must want to be a bird. But no one would adopt him."

She'd laughed and kissed his cheek, and then hugged him something fierce when he told Mark to take Paige away for the weekend while he looked after Haley. They'd both returned renewed—Mark had been worried about his wife too—even if Paige still seemed a little vulnerable around the edges.

For the woman he now referred to in his mind as his future wife, he bought more vintage fabric for her treasure chest and met her for coffee or lunch whenever she had a break from work. He also poured his heart out in one drawing after another, sometimes drawing her as herself and sometimes as his new superhero, fighting the injustice of deadbeat dads with her fellow justice-seeker, defense attorney Nathaniel Gray. The idea of time continued to ping him, though now he found himself mulling over how time healed all wounds.

Beyond the drawings, he held Sadie when she cried and he made love to her with everything he had, more concerned with comforting her than with finding pleasure. She was teaching him about the power of love every day, and he'd never been more sure of their future than he was now.

While Jess and Haley didn't know the reason for Paige and Sadie's turbulent emotions—they'd agreed to tell them there had been some sad news about a family member on the visit to their grandma—the girls had also chipped in to improve the women's spirits. Jess told him Sadie needed a feather boa because she was too big for a princess dress, and he'd bought her the pink one the girls had selected online. She'd loved it, so they'd bought one for Paige too. He'd loved watching the two girls host Sadie and Paige, both wearing their boas, in their fairytale castle in Jess' playroom, pouring them tea and giving them grapes and wheat crackers to snack on.

He told Tyler to hold off on a visit, and then told his parents the same thing when they surprised him by suggesting a visit to meet her. They were all curious about the woman who'd captured his heart.

And she had...so much so that he got up one morning and designed an engagement ring. When he felt ready, he shared it with Mark and his brother. Mark told him he was blown away and slapped him on the back. Tyler had provided a couple of comments on the movement of the design. They'd always worked well together, and his suggestions only made it better. After the next draft, Riley found a jeweler in downtown Nashville to make it.

The day the ring arrived he made homemade pizza for Jess. Haley had gone home reluctantly since she'd seen the frozen dough he'd bought rising in a bowl on the counter. Jess had been equally miffed about Haley not staying, but he'd told her he wanted to have dinner with her all by himself. That had placated her some.

When they sat down to dinner, just the two of them, he immediately took a big bite of pizza, singeing his mouth. He yelped like someone had run over his foot with a bicycle.

"Dad! You always tell me to let it cool first." Jess gestured to the slice of pepperoni she'd left untouched on her plate.

"I know." Nerves like this made you forget all the rules—even your own. "I got excited. So, I wanted to tell you something. You know I love Sadie, right? And, well, she loves me."

"You're girlfriend and boyfriend," Jess said, rising and tucking her knees under her seat. "I know that, Dad."

"That's because you're smart. So, I've kinda decided I want Sadie to be my girlfriend forever," he said, using the wording he'd heard Paige use before.

Jess blinked a few times. Riley tried to gauge if that was a good thing.

"You mean, like, *married*?"

"Yes, and while she'll be my wife, she won't ever take the place of your mother, okay? I know that kid at school, Betty, has been telling you about how things changed at home when her dad got remarried, but I promise you our lives will only get better after Sadie joins our family. I mean, you like Sadie, right? She's nice and funny, and she's like super-duper family, what with being Haley's aunt, right?"

God, he was dying here under the green-eyed stare of his daughter.

"And you'll always be my number one girl. That won't change when Sadie moves in with us. We'll still play together. She'll just...play with us. Okay?"

How many times could he say "right" and "okay" in one conversation?

"Oh, and we'll still live here. Next to the Bradshaws. You don't have to worry about that."

"Dad," Jess finally said. "It's okay if you marry Sadie."

He blew out the breath he'd been holding. "Whew! You had me on pins and needles there, kid. I thought I was going to need Batman to come in and rescue me or something."

"You're such a baby."

"Guilty."

"Dad, I knew you were thinking about this. Haley and I found the drawings of her engagement ring," Jess informed him, confirming there was nothing sacred in their house. "You must love her a lot to ask Mr. Bradshaw and Uncle Tyler for help."

"I do, Jess. Almost as much as I love you." He gave her a smile. "I love her as much as I love the Bradshaws."

"That's a lot," Jess declared, pushing her slice of pizza around. "It's a beautiful ring. Maybe you can make one for me when I get older."

Oh, his little girl. "Sounds like a plan. Do you want to see it? I found someone to make it, and it's finally arrived."

She nodded, and he went to retrieve it from his sock drawer. He'd hadn't felt right about hiding it in his underwear drawer. That had felt weird.

"Oh, it's so pretty," Jess breathed out when he returned and opened the box.

Because he felt like she would want a traditional diamond, he'd gone with a marquise cut and then had a wedding ring quilt design engraved into the platinum band. The shape of the diamond complemented the quilt pattern.

"Can I touch it?" Jess asked, reaching for it.

"Of course," he said, a bit surprised by her reluctance. "You can always touch nice things. This is a famous quilt pattern for weddings. I thought she'd like it. What do you think?"

"Oh, she'll love it for sure," Jess said, almost cooing. "Look how it sparkles."

She held it up to the light, and he got all choked up seeing his daughter hold the ring he planned to give to the other woman he loved.

"I also wrote something on the inside of the ring," he told her, fighting the last of his discomfort over the cheese factor. "'You're the fabric of my life.'"

God, he hoped no one was going to laugh at him, but the phrase had come to him, and it had simply seemed right.

"It's not too much, right? The phrase."

"No, she gets your humor, Dad. I think it's sweet." It wouldn't have surprised him if she'd patted him on the cheek like a comforting adult. "Sadie likes sweet," she added. "Like Haley. I can't wait for you to show her the ring. Can we call her over?"

"Ah...I kinda want to keep it a surprise," Riley said.

"Dad, Haley can keep a secret. She keeps mine all the time."

That alarmed him. He didn't like hearing his daughter had secrets. "Like what?"

"Oh, Dad," Jess said. "When are you going to ask her?" she said, purposefully changing the subject, he had no doubt.

"So you're completely okay with this?" he asked one last time. "If you need to talk to me—"

"It's going to be okay," Jess said. "I know she'll be my stepmom."

"But not a nasty stepmom like in a Disney movie," he felt compelled to add.

"Of course not! You'd have to be a nasty person first, and Sadie is great. Come on, Dad. Give me some credit."

All of his worries about Jess' recent emotions about her real mom started to dissipate. Maybe Mark had been right. He'd needed to stop being afraid for Jess to do the same. They had a plan now, and he knew every kid needed structure like that.

"Right. I'm being a little crazy."

Jess put the ring back in the box, but kept the lid open. "A little. Dad…are you and Sadie going to have more kids?"

He wanted to gulp. He'd hoped she wouldn't ask serious questions like that. "Yes, we'd like to. I mean, I love you to pieces, and Haley too. Sadie loves her nieces and nephew. And little Boone."

"She's crazy about Boone!" Jess said dramatically. "But I am too. He's so cute. Even when he poops his pants."

Leave it to his daughter to ground him in the realities of dirty diapers. Memories of those days with Jess could still make him shudder. The toxic waste that had come out of his kid had horrified him.

"Does this mean you'd be okay having some brothers and sisters to play with?"

"Yeah, sure," Jess said. "And Haley can play with them too. She doesn't think she's going to get any."

How did she know about that? Paige and Mark had always told her they hoped God would send them another baby. Then he stopped himself. These kids practically had telepathic powers. "Why does she think that?"

"Her mom cries when she gets her period sometime," Jess said. "Yuck, by the way. Haley and I so don't want to get our periods, Dad."

Not the period talk. He wasn't sure he could take that *and* the engagement talk in the same day. "You're a girl. It's not like you have any choice. It's like having a superpower. Except only girls have it." Thank God, if you asked him.

"Having a period is so not a superpower."

Riley couldn't help but smile as he tried to spin it around. "Sure it is. It's part of the process of a woman having a baby, which is an incredible power. But let's not get off topic. Is Haley sad she doesn't have a brother or sister? Has she talked to her mom or dad about it?"

"She talks to me," Jess said. "Sure, she wishes she had one. Mostly for her mom and dad. But she's not sad because she has me. I'm like her sister."

"Yes, you are." Someone was looking out for them for sure.

"When are you going to ask Sadie?" She picked her pizza up and took a healthy bite.

"Well, I was wondering if you wanted to ask her with me."

She shook her head and set her pizza down. "Dad, that is *so* not how you're supposed to do it. You're supposed to do something romantic and get down on one knee. Not bring your kid along. Do I have to explain everything?"

It took every effort not to start laughing. "Okay, you told me. Would you help pick out my outfit then? I want to make a good impression."

He was going to have to do some more thinking about that. Of course, he still needed to ask for J.P.'s and Louisa's permission. Okay, he didn't need to, but he felt Sadie would love that, and it might even make her cry in a good way. Those were serious points.

"Of course, I'm going to help you." She took another bite of pizza. "Aren't I your partner in crime?"

He loved it when she said that. "Yep. Always."

"Okay, now tell me *everything* you've planned so far. Then I'm going to tell you what you need to change. I mean, I've watched more romantic movies than you, Dad."

"Word."

Jess ended up making more changes to his plan than his brother had to the ring, but that's why she was his girl.

Chapter 28

"Riley, you seriously can't expect me to keep this blindfold on for the whole car trip."

"You agreed to trust me," she heard him say.

Of course she did, but she couldn't see anything under the official black blindfold he'd insisted she wear. They were going away for the weekend at his suggestion. Two whole days with him was going to be the best tonic for her still-healing heart. She was still dreaming about meeting her dad, and sometimes she woke up crying. Sometimes Riley was with her, and he'd hold her. Sometimes she had to face the hurt alone.

"I didn't expect it to take this long!" she protested. "We've been in the car for at least an hour."

"Maybe," Riley answered. "It's hard to tell when you're blindfolded. This is the only way I could think of to make sure our trip was a surprise. Settle back, Sadiekins, and get excited. You're going to love this!"

He'd taken to calling her Sadiekins in moments of teasing, alongside his other endearments of 'sweetheart' and 'my girl'. She rather liked it.

"Fine," she said. "I'll just settle back and look at nothing."

He had the gall to laugh. "I'll turn some of that infernal

country music on as a compromise."

"That would be big of you," she responded. "Please do so."

His groan filled the car, and she gave a dark chuckle. Served him right. She sang at the top of her lungs, pulling out her most honeyed Southern drawl and twang. After learning the real reason he disliked country music, she'd battled with feeling guilty about listening to it around him, but she wasn't going to let Mandy ruin it for her. Maybe someday the association would change for him too, and he'd think of her and Rye and Jake when he thought of country music, not the woman who'd hurt him and his daughter.

Riley was silent until the car stopped, breaking the music off in mid-refrain. "Remind me to never agree to that form of compromise," he said. "I'm not sure my ears will ever be the same."

"Are we here then? Show me already."

"Bossy, aren't you? The more time we spend together, the more sides of yourself you show me. And I love them all. Sadie, welcome to your magical weekend."

He undid the blindfold, and she screamed like a little kid when she spotted her creative nirvana through the windshield.

"The National Quilt Museum!" She bounced in her seat and then turned to face him. "You took me to Paducah, Kentucky! Oh, Riley, how did you know?"

"I did some research," he said, caressing her cheek. "I wanted to give you something special. It's an artist's paradise, you know."

She undid her seatbelt and slid across the console to hug him. "I know! I'd been thinking about bringing my quilting class here for a tour. You're the best."

He was grinning. "Excellent. Shall we go inside? Or do you want to head over to the cabin I rented first and come back later?"

"I want to go now!" She took another look at the museum. The brick building looked like it stretched the length of a few street blocks. "Oh, I can't believe it. And a cabin? You rented a cabin?"

"I thought it might be nice to be on the Ohio River," he said, waggling his brows, "lots of creative inspiration. I might come up with a water monster or something. You never know."

And he would too. She loved that big, beautiful imagination of his. "Riley, you are the best. Quite simply the best."

"Shall we?" he asked, and together they went inside.

She felt like a little kid, squirming with excitement and impatience, as they checked in and paid their admission. The sparkle in Riley's eyes told her he didn't mind any. They held hands as they approached the first display. "Oh, the colors. My God. They're so beautiful."

There was an assortment of quilts staged on the wall in perfect harmony with each other. They made their way to each of them. Sometimes the designs contrasted in ways that grabbed her by the throat. Other showpieces blended together, so much so that a deep sense of peace and wonder settled over her, the same kind she experienced while looking at a sunset or watching an eagle taking flight.

At one point, she had to release Riley's hand. The quilt depicting what looked like a planet in outer space surrounded by a swirling ball of fire demanded her complete attention. She wanted to touch it, and the urge was so strong, she had to fist her hands together.

"My God," she breathed. "The colors. The shape. The depth. The motion. It's…there aren't words."

"This is my favorite so far," he said. "It's like something out of *Thor*."

"I've never seen anything like this," she said. "It never dawned on me to model a quilt after something outside of our earth."

"Do I feel a birthday present coming on?" he joked. "Mine is April 23 if you recall."

"What?" She had to shake herself out of the reverie. "Oh, that's a wonderful idea."

"Sadie, I was kidding," he said. "You don't need to make me a quilt."

Little did he know she was already fussing with Jess' princess quilt and the plans for his superhero one. "I'll do what I like. Oh, Riley. This is truly...magnificent. Thank you!"

"We're not finished yet," he said, taking her hand and raising it to his lips. "Come. Let's see the rest of the collection. They have six hundred quilts, and I think we've only seen a quarter of them so far. I have a feeling you'll want to see them all."

And so they did. They passed by one masterpiece after the other. Sadie wondered if this was how a person felt in a cathedral like St. Paul's in London or Notre Dame in Paris.

She walked through the rest of the museum in bliss. Riley walked quietly next to her, a happy smile on his face. Sometimes she would become animated and start explaining technical things he didn't understand, much like he might do at a superhero museum, but he didn't seem to mind. He'd simply gaze at her while she spoke with her hands.

And when she whispered a curse about not being able to take pictures of the quilts—of course she understood artistic propriety and all—he muffled his laughter. But she'd have an easy time recalling the images and styles of quilting that had sparked her interest the most. Plus, there was a gift shop.

And what a gift shop...

She bought a stack of books about the collection and quilting books she'd never come across anywhere else. Of course, Riley insisted on buying her a Keep Calm and

Quilt T-shirt in hot pink. She jumped up and down when he presented it to her, and she didn't care who noticed. While some of their fabric pieces were tempting—like an array of silk in peacock tones—she decided to pass. She could buy any fabric at Oodles for a discount, and if they couldn't get it, she could always go online. Plus, Riley kept finding her vintage clothing for her treasure chest. She could never have enough fabric—it was like some people with shoes—but she didn't want to linger over the pieces for too long. Riley had arranged this for her, and she wanted to spend time with him.

When they reached their charming log cabin in the woods with the river view, she fell onto the couch and kicked off her shoes. "This has been one of the best days of my life." And after everything that had happened with her daddy, it felt like the biggest blessing in the world.

He stopped by the couch with the bags and leaned down to kiss her. "I'm so glad you think so. I'm going to put these in our room."

"I would get up and see it, but I'm too happy to move." *Our room.* She shivered. Oh, how she loved hearing him say that.

"You really need to see this room, Sadie," he called to her. "We have a huge fireplace, and the most amazing view of the Ohio. There are birds on it."

"Birds, huh? Imagine birds on a river. Okay, I'm coming."

She rolled off the couch and padded in the direction he'd taken. When she reached the doorway, her heart flew to her throat.

"Where did you get that?" she asked, stunned speechless by the wedding quilt arranged on the bed. No way had it simply been there—it was far too beautiful and intricate.

"I...ah...commissioned it from Mae," he said, undoing the button on his sport coat. "Come take a look."

She walked closer, the geometric interlocking rings of the wedding quilt capturing her complete attention. The quilt itself was a delicate ivory, and the rings were rendered in ocean blue, red, yellow, and sea green fabric. Then she saw the jewelry box lying open inside the center of the quilt and turned to him.

He was kneeling by her side, his face radiant with love.

"Sadie McGuiness, will you marry me?" he asked in a deep and strong voice.

She launched herself at him, and he toppled back onto the rug. "Yes. Oh, Riley. Yes! A million times yes."

He rolled her onto her back and peppered her with kisses. "Thank God, because the rest of this weekend would have been pretty awkward otherwise!" He grinned as he said it, but quickly became serious again. "We're going to be so happy. I...I never thought I'd ever feel this way about anyone. I love you, Sadie."

She locked her hands behind his neck. "Oh, I love you too, and yes, we are going to be so happy. Know why I know that? Because I'm already happy with you. Riley, you gave me a wedding quilt. And today... You see me and celebrate me like I never imagined someone would."

"Come see your ring," he said. "I... Well, I designed it, and I...okay, I'm just going to be quiet and let you look. If you don't like it—"

She pressed her fingers to his lips. "I can't imagine not loving it. Show it to me."

He rose and helped her up and then extended the ring to her. "I wanted to give you something special."

She caught the wedding quilt pattern on the ring immediately, and her heart burst in her chest. "Oh, Riley. It's...exquisite. You did this for me?"

Tears were filling her eyes, but darn it all if it wasn't normal to shed a few tears when you were agreeing to marry the man you loved.

"There's an inscription too," he said. "God, I hope you

don't think it's corny."

She turned the inside of the ring toward the light. "You're the fabric of my life." Sinking onto the bed when her knees went weak, she gazed up at him. "It's perfect, and Riley... You're the fabric of my life too."

His throat moved, and he nodded. "Shall we put it on then?"

She held out her left hand, and he took the ring and slid it down until it was nestled in the right place. The diamond sparkled, and the unique style of the ring seemed to awaken something powerful in her heart.

"It's beautiful," she whispered, letting the tears fall. "Thank you, Riley."

"Thank you," he said, sitting next to her. "I want to tell you that I talked to Jess and she's fully on board."

She put her hand to her mouth. "Oh, I should have asked. How terrible of me."

"You were overcome," he said softly. "So was I. In fact, I forgot to mention that I asked for your hand in marriage from both J.P. and your mom. I knew I didn't need their permission, but I wanted to honor you. In some ways, you're a traditionalist, and I respect that."

Once again, she felt choked up. It felt so wonderful to be *seen*, to be honored. "Oh, that makes me so happy. What did my mama and J.P. say? Anything?"

He pressed the bridge of his nose. "I'm so overcome, my brain is dead. I can't remember." Laughing, he shook his head. "But Jess chose my outfit for today, for the whole weekend really, and she approved of my plans. I asked if she wanted to be with me when I proposed, but she informed me that wasn't how it was done. Then she said a few things about chick flicks, I think. It might be her new language. She's growing up so fast."

She took his hand and pressed it to her heart. "I promise to be good with her. To love and cherish her. Like I plan to love and cherish you."

"Cherish, huh? That kinda chokes me up, but don't tell anyone, okay? Mark will give me such flak for that."

Sadie doubted it, but she understood he felt vulnerable about being an emotional man. "It will be between us."

"How about I cherish you a little now and then we go out later and hit the town? There's Robert Dafford's famous Wall to Wall murals along the river and the Bricolage Art Collective. I'm really excited about them. This place is perfect for us. It has quilts and art. It's a match made in heaven."

She linked her arms around his neck again. *"We're* a match made in heaven."

"Yes, we are," he said in a steady voice.

Then he tipped her back and made love to her sweetly and thoroughly on the wedding quilt, sealing their promise for a lifetime.

Chapter 29

After Riley and Sadie became engaged, he felt like a superhero at the end of a movie. It felt like they were being ushered from one celebration to another. Sadie's extended family had thrown them an impromptu engagement party, and the following weekend Riley's parents and his brother's family had flown in to meet Sadie and welcome her to the Thomson clan. His parents had been a little awkward at first, commenting on how much Jess had grown, but they were trying in their own way. They might never be as close as they'd once been, but he was glad the door was still open. Of course, Paige, Mark, and Haley had also thrown them a bash on a school night to celebrate her joining what Mark called their neighborhood clan.

But his daughter's celebration of Sadie had touched him the most. She'd insisted on making Sadie macaroni and cheese, one of her favorite meals, and had presented her with a homemade card decorated with a big heart. The sight of that card had put tears in his eyes.

Jess was as happy as he was, and that meant everything.

His woman had become family to his daughter, and Riley figured no single dad could ask for more.

Sadie seemed to be walking on clouds too, so much so that she'd become clumsier. He teased her about it, and she slayed him by saying, "It's this beautiful ring you made me. When the light catches it or I feel it on my finger, I just can't help but look down at it."

He stopped teasing her, and simply made more of an effort to keep his hand on her back and steer her away from things like lampposts or doorways.

They talked about a January wedding, both eager to move in together and start their lives. Of course, she'd checked to make sure Shelby was okay with that since her sister was planning a fanfare-filled wedding in May. Shelby had told her it hardly mattered who got married first—she and Vander spent every night together. Otherwise, she'd never make it to May.

Riley understood. Even though they were engaged, he still didn't feel comfortable having her sleep over, and she agreed that they should wait. Fortunately, Jess could still spend the night next door, but he didn't like to divert from their routine more than twice a week. He was her dad, after all, and dads watched over their kids at night.

His weekends became ever more filled with family events. Though he and Sadie kept their date nights sacrosanct, Jess and Haley had asked to take country line dancing, much to his chagrin, so he and the Bradshaws took turns taking them to the Saturday class. Sadie would usually come over for dinner in their neighborhood afterward. Then Sunday rolled around, and he and Jess and the Bradshaws met up with everyone for Sunday family dinner at one of the McGuinesses' homes.

But today marked a special Sunday dinner. Paige was hosting for the first time. And she was as nervous as hell.

"Of course I'm nervous," she shot back in response to his teasing. He and Mark, on her orders, were setting up the dining room. "Rye Crenshaw is going to be in my house!"

"It's not like you haven't met him," Riley said, setting another folding table next to the trio that already filled the rearranged dining room. "I mean, we've even been to his house."

That had been a day. All five of the dogs—three of Rye's and two of Annabelle and Rory's—had gone swimming in Dare River and returned a wet mess with a special gift for the kids. The dead duck had made Annabelle scream, setting off a chain of ear-piercing responses from Haley and Jess. Shelby had added her own chorus to the melody of screams before Rye had roared, "Enough," and taken the dead bird out back to dispose of it.

"That was different," she grumbled, shaking out yet another tablecloth he'd never seen her use. "This is my house. Our house. Sorry, honey."

"No skin off my back," Mark said, brushing off the dust on his shirt from the attic. "What else do you need us to help with?"

She cast a look around the room, and Riley fought a wince. She was going to change things up again. He just knew it.

Sure enough, an hour later, they were still moving the tables and chairs. Finally, she settled on her original idea of opening the French doors to the family room and arranging the tables end on end. Of course, that meant he and Mark had to follow her orders on where she wanted the family room furniture to be repositioned. When she finally said they were finished and headed to the kitchen, he and Mark man-hugged each other jokingly.

"I thought it was never going to end," Riley said.

"I heard that," Paige said. "For that, I'm going to have you peel the onions and chop the garlic."

"Great," Riley said, rolling his eyes at Mark. "I'm sure Sadie will have an extra tough time resisting me after that."

"You seem to be doing just fine," Mark said, slapping him on the back.

Nothing could be more true, so he ignored the ripe smell of fresh onions and garlic no amount of washing his hands could eradicate. He also ignored the crazy antics of Jess and Haley. They'd been running back and forth between the houses all day like crazy people.

"Okay, Madame General, I'm going to head home and shower," Riley told Paige, who was chopping the colorful trio of bell peppers into bite-sized pieces for the kebabs she'd agreed to make for everyone.

"I wish I'd never listened to you about the kebobs, Riley," she said, wiping her brow with the back of her hand. "I mean, it's going to take forever to do all of these. I should have done a casserole or—"

"But you hate casseroles, honey," Mark said, crossing to his wife. "Besides, didn't Sadie and the rest of the girls think this was a great idea? Sadie is crazy about Riley's kebobs."

"Not for Sunday family dinner!"

"Hey," Mark said, pressing his cheek to hers. "Come on, you've been working since dawn on all of this. Why don't you take a break while I spear the kebobs?"

"*Mark.*"

"*Paige.*"

Riley knew when to make himself scarce. "I'll be back in a jiffy."

Racing to his house, he let himself inside and listened for the girls. Nothing. He decided to check on them and took the stairs two at a time to the playroom. The door was closed, which wasn't unusual. Jess had informed him a couple weeks ago that they were growing up and she and Haley needed privacy. Privacy. A word to make a father tremble in terror.

He knocked. "Dad alert. Hide the silverware."

"Don't come in!" came the alarmed reply.

His patience was wearing thin after playing the part of Mr. Mover for the past couple hours. "Girls. What are you doing?"

Jess cracked open the door and gave him the stare. "Dad, we're doing some things."

He counted to three. "What things?"

"Surprise things," she said, looking over her shoulder for a moment. Sometimes he could hear his own snarkiness in her voice and didn't like it.

Haley said something Riley couldn't hear, and Jess added, "For the party. Is that okay?"

"Sure." This wasn't worth engaging over. "I'm going to shower now and get dressed. Paige is getting ready too. Haley, when are you going to head over? Your mom is going to want..."

He bit off the rest of the sentence. Paige was going to have ideas about her daughter's outfit tonight, and the little girl wasn't going to like it.

"Your mom might need your help figuring out what to wear," he said instead.

"She'll be fine," Haley yelled from behind the door.

"It would be nice if I could see Haley when I'm talking to her, Jess," he told his daughter.

"We're almost done," she said. "Then Haley is going to get dressed with me."

This was news. "What? Haley, do you have clothes?"

"Yes, Mr. Thomson, I brought them over." She appeared behind Jess. "Hi."

She looked at Jess and then back at him, and his gut stirred. What were they up to?

"Jess thought it would be fun to get dressed together since Mom is so whoo-hoo today. She started vacuuming at seven o'clock this morning. Even Dad was like, 'she's crazy.'"

Riley doubted Mark had ever said that about his wife. "Okay, you wrap whatever you've got going on and then get dressed and come over. I could use your help shucking the corn."

"Dad, seriously, corn silk will stick to our clothes."

He put his hand on the doorframe. "You can wear an apron or something."

Jess mumbled something.

"Huh?" He cocked his ear.

"Nothing," Haley said, elbowing Jess. "We'll be over soon, Mr. Thomson."

"Great. Off to get handsome."

"Good luck," Haley said sweetly as Jess shut the door in his face.

Everybody was acting a little crazy today. Except for Mark and him. Maybe Paige and the girls had drunk some special water from the local mental institution. Oh, his comic book mind liked that. He took off to the shower to let the ideas filter in for a new story. He was getting closer. At least he had his superhero's backstory. She had been institutionalized for saying she was the daughter of Clotho, one of the three fates from Greek mythology, who'd spun the threads of life. Nathaniel Gray would find her lying in the middle of the street after her escape from the asylum, and he'd take her home when she told him something about his past.

Bah! But he still didn't know her name or what she did with time. Well, it would come.

When the girls finally arrived at the Bradshaws, Riley did a double take. The sides of Jess' hair were caught up in butterfly barrettes, and she was wearing one of her best dresses with the new red cowboy boots she'd begged him to buy. Haley had on a fancy purple dress as well, paired with pink cowboy boots.

"Goodness," Mark said, drying his hands on his apron. The two of them were wrapping up the last of the kebobs in the kitchen. "Don't ya'll look fancy."

Haley twirled but Jess stayed in place and touched the edge of her navy dress.

"You think so, Mr. Bradshaw?" his daughter asked.

Riley caught the hint of vulnerability in her voice.

Was this part of his little girl growing up? Was she struggling with self-esteem?

"You look like a country rockstar," Mark told her. "Beautiful. Sophisticated. Lovely as a rose. Right, Riley?"

He came forward and sank down in front of her. "Yes, all of that. Except for the rose part. My daughter isn't just a regular rose. She's the rarest of the roses: a desert rose. The kind of rose that only comes along once in a hundred years."

Jess' mouth lifted up, but she said nothing.

"I love the way you talk, Mr. Thomson," Haley said. "Can I be a desert rose too?"

Riley touched her nose. "Sometimes sisters love each other so much they bloom together in the desert."

Haley gave Jess a squeeze. "That's like us."

"You look beautiful, Jess," Riley said, his throat thick with love. "More so than ever."

She put her arms around him and hugged him tight. "I love you, Daddy."

"Oh, my sweet girl," he said, picking her up. "I love you too. Even if I have to get sunburned to come and visit you in the desert." He kissed her on the top of her head. "Then there's all the sand I'll get in my eyes. And my underwear."

"Not your underwear!" Haley said, shielding her eyes. "That would itch."

"It would, but it would be worth it."

"You're the best dad ever," Jess said, kissing him on the cheek.

He set her down. "Glad we have that clear. Now, you two go on and help Paige pick out something to wear. Mark and I will shuck the corn since your dresses are so lovely."

When they left the kitchen, Mark tossed him an ear of corn. "Nicely done. Now shuck."

"It's like the famous Zen warrior said, 'Before enlightenment, chop wood, carry water. After enlightenment, chop wood, carry water.' Only in this case, it's kitchen duty."

Not that he minded. Even though he was shucking corn, he felt like his daughter's hero.

Sadie arrived with some of her sisters in tow, and soon he and Mark had more than enough help, so much so that they sent Sadie and Shelby on up to help Paige. Haley had emerged to tell her dad that Paige was having trouble deciding what to wear, but she'd be down promptly.

She came down about the time the rest of the crew arrived, and then things turned full-out crazy, but at least there were no dogs to add to the chaos. Riley and Mark fired up the grill while Susannah and Tammy laid out the appetizers they'd brought. And little Boone made Riley's day by extending his little arms out to him, indicating he wanted to go to him.

"I'm impressed," Rye said, coming over. "He never does that with Clayton or Vander, but that's no surprise. Both of them scare little children."

Vander tilted his head to the side, a droll expression on his face. Clayton looked like he wanted to flip Rye the bird, but his gaze landed on Rory before he could do any such thing. Riley took little Boone outside and joined Dale and Jake, who were keeping Mark company by the grill. Hampton, Rye's father, joined him by the deck, looking at his grandson.

"Isn't he amazing?" the older man asked. "I sometimes look at him and wonder how his life is going to be. I hope I get to see a good portion of it."

Riley hadn't talked to Hampton much, but he was a sucker for a man who thought like that. He often thought the same about Jess, wondering what she'd become. An astronaut? A famous artist? A banker? The world was her oyster, as far as he was concerned.

"I figure it's a gift," he told the man, "watching them become all they can be."

"Well said," Hampton said.

Boone stretched his little arms out of the swaddle, and Riley didn't have the heart to tuck them back in.

"Hates to be all trussed up like a chicken," Rye said. "I've told Tory a million times to let him be free. Don't men like to just hang?"

Riley bit the inside of his cheek. He knew exactly what Rye was suggesting. Then he caught Jess and Haley running across the driveway to their house. What were they doing? When they didn't come back out, he was perplexed. The party was at the Bradshaws', and they'd acted so excited for it... He decided to go and look for them.

"I need to check on my daughter and Haley," he announced. "Who wants little Boone here?"

"Daddy, you take him," Rye said. "I like to give everyone else a chance to hold him at Sunday dinner. Come on, bubba, let's go find the girls. Paige said you have some of your superhero drawings in your house. Maybe you can show me on the way."

Riley stumbled a little as Rye walked over with him. First, the man had called him "bubba." No one had ever done that before. Second, he really wanted to see Riley's art?

"You like superheroes?" Riley asked.

"When I was a boy, I wanted to be Batman," Rye said. "He has the best toys. Having Boone has brought all that back. I got him a Batman onesie."

Riley had to grin. "Awesome. He'll have to wear it next week. I love seeing superhero clothes on kids. I put Jess in a Wonder Woman onesie when she was a newborn. Gotta start them young."

"Exactly," Rye said. "Now where did those girls go? Sometimes I'm glad we had a boy. I mean, I grew up with two sisters. They'd always steal off to their rooms during a party."

Not Jess and Haley usually. They loved celebrations.

He let them into the house and cocked his ear. If they were inside, they were being unusually quiet.

"Let's head up to the playroom. They were there earlier."

Rye's boots sounded behind him. "Your drawings are terrific."

"Thanks," he said, but he was beginning to get anxious. When he opened the door to the playroom, he didn't see the girls.

On the worktable were loads of markers and streamers. And scotch tape.

"Did you make this castle?" Rye asked. "It's brilliant. Annabelle and Rory are going to have to see this!"

Before he could turn and respond, Riley heard a car door slam outside, followed by the sound of the girls cheering. Looking out the window, he pressed his hand against the glass.

"You've got to be fucking kidding me."

Mandy was walking toward Jess and Haley, who were standing on the sidewalk, holding what looked like a huge Welcome sign. Mandy pointed to their cowboy boots, and Jess smiled as if the sun had just risen. His daughter couldn't know how worn and brittle Mandy looked. He could see the "junkie" on her a mile away.

Anger flushed over him, sending fire from his scalp to his toes. That bitch was here! At their house. She'd broken their agreement. Again! Except this time Jess would remember.

"Who's that piece of work?" Rye asked, looking out the window next to him. "She looks totally strung out."

"My ex and Jess' mom," Riley said, running out of the room.

He yanked open the front door and flew down the stairs, only to see Mandy taking a card Jess was extending to her.

"Jess! Haley! Go inside."

Mandy looked over at him, and it sucker-punched him in the gut to see her eyes, the same green as his daughter's. Her blond hair was more dishwater now, and there were lines around her red-painted mouth. At one time, he'd thought her the sexiest woman in the world, but the last six years had turned her skeleton-thin and a touch haggard. He knew hard times when he saw it, and she was clearly at rock bottom. Well, she wasn't going to use Jess to get more money from him.

"I said, 'Go inside.' Now, girls."

Jess crossed her arms. "No. I'm meeting my mom."

"Jess. Haley. Why don't y'all come with me back to the party while Riley here talks with this lady." Rye appeared beside him and extended his hands to the girls. "Come on, now. Boone could use some holding."

"You weren't lying, Jessie," Mandy said, her mouth gaping open. "Oh, Rye, I'm your biggest fan. I came here hoping to see you today. I'm a country singer too, and I brought a demo tape for you. I just know you'll want to help me become a star once you hear it."

Riley glanced at Rye, whose jaw had clenched. "That's why you're here? But how did you know?" Everything snapped into place. "Did you contact Jess and put her up to this?"

Mandy pushed him in the chest. "You always think the worst. No, Jessie contacted me. On Facebook. Through a girl named Betty."

Betty again. He would deal with that later. "Her name is Jess," Riley ground out.

"Dad, it's okay. She can call me Jessie," his daughter said, and he tugged her to him. She'd always hated that nickname.

Mandy's eyes turned mean. "Riley, don't you dare ruin this for me. Rye, let's go somewhere and talk?"

"Lady, there ain't nowhere that I want to go with you," he said, shaking his head. "If you came here thinking that, you've been misinformed. Since I seem to be causing some trouble, I'm gonna head back to the party. Riley, I'll send Clayton along in case you need something."

"But Rye..." Mandy called. "I need to talk to you."

Riley watched Rye stride toward the Bradshaws' house without a backward glance.

"Don't go, Mr. Crenshaw!" Jess cried out. "Please! Please listen to my mom's songs."

Fists slammed into his chest, and he knew they were Mandy's. He swung his gaze back around as a boozy smell rolled over him. God, she reeked.

"You fucked this up for me. Damn you, Riley. Damn you!"

"Mom, what are you doing?" Jess asked, gripping his leg.

Mandy hit him again, and he caught her hands in his, trying to make sure she didn't hurt Jess. "Stop this. Pull yourself together. Our daughter is watching you. Don't you remember what I had to do the last time you came?" He couldn't mention calling the cops with Jess listening.

"I don't care!" She kicked at him, barely missing Jess. "You destroyed my chance for a record deal. I hate you!"

Haley was crying now, and she pulled Jess away. His daughter was staring at him and Mandy in shock.

"Jess. Haley. Go to the Bradshaws'. Right now!" He had to get Mandy out of here. "You need to get in your car and drive away, Mandy. I mean it."

"No!" She kicked at him again and connected with his knee.

"Ouch. Stop that."

"Don't hurt him!" Jess cried, launching herself at Mandy. "You leave my daddy alone."

Riley wrestled Mandy away, trying not to bruise her arms. He knew she'd find a way to press charges if he wasn't careful.

"I'm fine, Jess. Go inside. Right now! Haley, take her."

"I've got her," he heard Mark say as his buddy ran up to them. J.P. was right behind him, and together they scooped up the girls.

"Take her inside," Riley said, trying to evade Mandy's fevered kicks. "I don't want her to see this."

"Lady, you'd better calm down before I call the cops," Clayton said when he reached them. "Riley, let her go. I'll handle her."

"I had to call them last time," Riley said, looking at Mandy's feverish eyes. "Don't make me do this with our daughter around."

"I don't care," she screamed.

Vander stepped forward and grabbed Mandy and put her in a restraining hold before he could blink. "We've got this. Go to Jess."

He stopped and stared at Mandy. "If you ever come back, I'll throw everything the law has at you. I'll put you in jail if I have to." Nathaniel Gray would consider that justice.

"You're an asshole!" Mandy screamed. "You're a fucking asshole. Like I ever wanted that kid. I just want to be a star."

As he stared at her for the last time, he couldn't believe he'd ever wanted her either.

Clayton slapped him on the back. "Go on now. Go to your daughter."

His guts reared up and part of him wanted to double over. Jess! She'd seen everything. Seen what her mother was.

There was a line of people in the driveway and some of his neighbors were coming out of their homes. He ran up the steps to his house and followed the sobs from his little girl.

He found her in the playroom with Mark, on her stomach with her hands covering her face, sobbing her heart out. Haley was nowhere in sight, and he hoped to Christ she was with Paige.

"I've got her," he said softly when Mark lifted his head. "Thanks for bringing her here... Oh, God, I'm so sorry."

"Not your fault," Mark said. "I'll leave you two."

He gave Riley's shoulder a squeeze on his way out.

Riley crossed to his daughter and knelt down beside her. "Come here, sweetheart. Let Daddy hold you."

She kept on sobbing, and he leaned closer to hold her. "Please, Jess."

She rolled over and shoved him away.

"*Jess.*"

"No! No! No! It wasn't supposed to be like this. I only wanted to meet my mom. I thought she might like me if she met me. Like Paige got along with Sadie. And Betty helped..."

He reached out to her when she stood up. "You should have talked to me about it. Your mother—"

"She doesn't want me!" Jess said and kicked the chair at her workbench. "I made her a sign and learned a country song to sing to her. And she didn't want any of it."

She picked up the markers and started to throw them at the castle.

Riley sat back as she raged. "Oh, honey, she's not a good woman. That's why she's not around. It's not you, Jess. It was never you."

"All she wanted was to meet Rye," Jess said, heaving up her writing tablet and throwing it across the room. "I told her I'd introduce her to him. I thought she was a country singer like him. I was only trying to be nice, like Sadie was when she invited Paige to her quilting group."

And Mandy hadn't told her differently, of course. He rose and approached her warily. "Jess, your mother has changed a lot since you were born. She's gotten meaner. That's on her."

"She's horrible!" Jess said, shoving at the chair. "How could she be my mother? How?"

He prayed for the right words. "She didn't want to be

a mother. Some people don't have courage."

Her face was bright red. "She hit you! She made Rye hate me."

"No baby," Riley said, holding her arms. "Rye doesn't hate you. And don't worry about me. I had on my Dad super armor. She could never hurt me."

No, Mandy could only hurt him by hurting Jess, and she'd landed close to a fatal blow today.

"Why didn't you tell me she was like that?" she asked, knuckling away her tears.

He swallowed the lump in his throat. "Because I knew it would hurt you. Jess, it hurt me when she didn't want to be your mom. I was trying to protect you."

She pushed away from him. "It's all lies. All of the movies."

He couldn't stand anymore. "That's not true. You're a miracle. You and me. None of that changes."

She ran over and pulled all of her princess dresses out of her own treasure box and tried to rip them. "It's not true. None of it's true."

Riley ran forward and grabbed her hands. "Jess, honey. Stop."

She pulled away and started to kick at her castle. The cardboard turret, so lovingly painted by their hands, toppled and fell to the ground.

"No one lives happily ever after. Not princesses. Not anyone!"

She fell to her knees sobbing, and he gathered her against his chest, fighting tears himself.

He would give everything he had to return her innocence to her.

But there was no superpower on earth that would do that.

Chapter 30

By the time darkness fell, even Sadie's mama told her she was going to go home. Riley still hadn't emerged from his house next door, and Sadie wasn't sure what to do. There was only one light on in the house—in the playroom—and no one wanted to intrude.

Paige and Mark were taking turns with Haley, who'd alternated between crying uncontrollably and begging to see Jess and make sure her best friend was okay.

Sadie and her sisters had tried to feed everybody once things settled down, but no one had felt like eating. Though Tammy had pulled them away quickly, Annabelle and Rory were noticeably upset by the altercation everyone had witnessed. In response to Annabelle asking why Jess' mom could act like that, Rory had responded stiffly that "some mommies and daddies are horrible people—like their daddy was—and they were all better off without them."

Those words had driven a spike through everyone standing around.

When J.P. had clutched the little boy to his chest to comfort him, she'd seen a tear leaking out the corner of his eye. The pain in her heart had grown even keener.

Rye had been livid. Fans had used despicable ways

and means to approach him before, but he hated that a little girl's mother had used her to get to him. Telling Rye Mandy had come around before hadn't made him feel better. Clayton and Vander hadn't told anyone what they'd said to Riley's ex, but Hampton had joined them on the sidewalk in a legal capacity. The woman had been hysterical, and she'd screamed a litany of obscenities before heaving her demo tape at Clayton and driving off in her rundown car.

The men had huddled to talk, and when she'd crossed the room to join them, Jake had stepped out of the circle and told her she didn't need to hear any more ugliness. She'd almost gone off on him then, but he'd explained himself. "This isn't a guy thing, Sadie, but we've handled things like this before. Sort of. Let us take care of it."

Sadie had finally nodded, and he'd gone back to the group with a stilted gait.

"I'm glad everyone's gone," she heard Paige say. "This has to be the worst family dinner on record."

Sadie turned away from Riley's house. Her sister looked twenty years older tonight.

"It was like looking at my own mother," Paige said, leaning against the counter like she couldn't support herself. "I think Mandy was drunk and likely high."

"I can't imagine how terrible it must have been for you," she said, "growing up in a household with a woman like that."

"It was pretty bad," Paige said, pushing her hair back behind her ears.

Sadie noticed her sister's hands were shaking, but she didn't know how to help. She was feeling shaky herself. "How is Haley?"

"Mark is lying down with her, but she's... Oh, Sadie, I've never thought to see my little girl like this. I never thought she'd be touched by ugliness at this age. I...severed all ties with my old family to keep her safe. And when

I think about Riley and Jess... Riley will be okay, but Jess? How will that little girl forget what happened today?" Paige's mouth clenched as she fought tears.

Sadie was doing her best to hold it together, but she'd witnessed the scene in the front yard. Her mama had needed to hold her back to keep her from going to them, but she was sure she'd never forget the horrified look on Jess' face. "I... It was worse than us seeing our father a few weeks ago, wasn't it? We already mostly knew what he was even if I told myself that maybe some miracle could happen to change him."

"Miracles like that don't happen with people like them," Paige said. "They will always be vicious and mean, and they'll stop at nothing to make everyone feel as horrible as they do inside. Today I'm out of all forgiveness. Maybe tomorrow will be different, but I want to tear Mandy apart from limb to limb for what she did to Jess and Riley."

She couldn't agree more. "I know. I want to drop her into boiling oil or kick her until she's blue. But mostly I just want to wave a wand and undo it all."

She was going to have to pray for help letting her anger go, but she didn't have to focus on that right now. In this moment, all she wanted to do was help the two people she loved who were alone in that dark house next door.

"I don't know what to do," she finally admitted. "I want to go over and help, but I don't want to intrude either. Riley is the best person to help Jess right now."

She cast a glance over her shoulder and looked at the house again. Nothing. *Please God, help them,* she prayed for the thousandth time.

"I would say you could spend the night," Paige said, "but I'm not sure that's best. We're going to have a long one, I imagine."

Plus, Paige and Mark were hurting and needed space

with their daughter. "Of course. Is there anything I can do for you?"

Paige shook her head. "Unless you have a time machine so we can go back to this morning, I'm afraid we're all going to have to deal with this."

There was no mistaking the resignation in Paige's tone. "I feel like I owe you an apology or something. Jess' mother wouldn't have shown up if Rye and Jake hadn't been here."

"I'm too tired for this guilt party," Paige said, pushing up off the counter and standing tall. "This isn't the first time that woman showed up uninvited, so you stop thinking like that right now. Sadie McGuiness, having you come to my house with love was one of the best things that's ever happened to me. None of this was your fault. Okay?"

Then Paige crossed to her and they wrapped each other up in love.

"Okay," she whispered, but her heart felt like it was covered in boils, hot and aching pockets of unresolved pain.

Despite what her sister said, she still couldn't help but feel responsible for this. She hadn't intended for any of this to happen, no, but she'd catalyzed it. Did Riley blame her?

As she stepped outside and walked to the car, she took one last look at his house, the house she'd started to think of as hers.

She'd never felt further away from that vision.

Chapter 31

Paige reached for the phone when it buzzed on her nightstand, careful not to wake Haley, nestled between her and Mark. They'd brought her to their bed around one after she'd awakened from a nightmare about Jess' mom taking her friend away and not bringing her back. It had been a struggle to hold it together.

Seeing Riley's text didn't help.

I'm keeping Jess home for a few days. It's bad over here. How's Haley? I'm so sorry for what happened. I can't imagine how upset she is. Tell her Jess misses her and wants to see her later, okay? Not sure when.

Mark rose up on an elbow, and she handed the phone to him. He hadn't slept much either. Last night was one of the worst nights they'd faced together as a couple, as a family, and she felt more grateful for him than ever. If they could get through this, they could get through everything.

"Tell him I'll come over to give him a break," Mark whispered. "I can't imagine how exhausted he must be."

"No, I'll go," she whispered back. Who understood what it was like to have a mother like Mandy better than her?

When she texted back, Riley's response was immediate:

Thanks, but I don't want to leave her. She's too fragile to be around anyone. I'll text later about Haley coming over.

But he didn't.

She and Mark had decided Haley was too vulnerable to go to school as well, so they watched movies with her all day. She lay on the couch with the quilt Sadie had made, acting like the life had been sucked out of her, something Paige hated to see. Haley had asked about Jess a few times, but the reassurance that she was with her dad seemed to calm her down. Her response was either to nod or say, "That's good. He needs to make sure she's safe from that bad lady."

Safe.

Such a powerful feeling...and yet so difficult to restore once it had been broken. Wasn't that why she'd chosen it as her theme for her first baby quilt? Paige hoped both she and Jess could bounce back quickly, but her heart wasn't completely sure of it. She knew some traumas lasted a lifetime.

By dinner, Sadie had texted her a couple of times for updates on the situation next door, and Paige was starting to worry too. Riley had told her he needed to spend time alone with his daughter—and had asked her to tell her whole family, but most especially Rye, how sorry he was for everything. Riley often blamed himself for things, and he was clearly taking this on. Much like Sadie was. Two peas in a pod.

Haley went to sleep early after her bath, thankfully, and Paige was sipping a glass of wine staring out of the kitchen window when she saw Riley open his back door with a trash bag in hand. Mark had kept her from going over, telling her to give their friend space.

Well, she was done with that.

She set her glass on the counter. "I'll be right back."

"*Paige*," Mark said from the kitchen table.

"You stay and listen for Haley." She hurried out, not wanting to miss her small window.

When she reached him, he was opening the trash cans. He jumped and dropped the garbage bag when she said, "Hey."

"Shit," he said. "You scared me."

Glass had clinked, and she wondered what had broken. "How are y'all? Other than the obvious?"

In the low light from the streetlamp, he looked haggard and his hair was standing up in places. But it was the stooped curve of his back that depicted his struggle. He was like Atlas carrying the world on his shoulders.

"She tore apart her castle," he said, gesturing to the plastic bag. "And Mandy's picture. I don't know how to help her. She's... It's like she's been knocked out and can't get back up."

She put her arms around him. "Oh, honey. I know it seems bad right now, but she's going to heal. I did, and I lived with a woman like Jess' mom until I was eighteen."

"I don't know how you did it," he said, leaning in. "I'm so sorry Haley saw all that. That everyone did. I let myself believe she wouldn't come back. I mean, it's been six years, but Jesus, when I run it back through my mind—"

"Stop doing that," she told him. "It doesn't help. She came back because she's an addict who thought she could get a fast-track on stardom." After seeing the woman, she knew there was no way that would ever happen. Any spark she'd possessed had been doused years ago. "She's a user, Riley."

"I know," he said, his voice coated with defeat.

"Also, Mark has some ideas for therapists you and Jess can talk to about what happened when you're ready."

He pulled back and looked at the house, as if listening for Jess. "Yeah, I know we're going to need professional help to get her through this. Last time she was so little… I'll be grateful for his suggestions. I already called my lawyer and told him what happened. We're going to file for a restraining order against Mandy. God knows I should have done it last time, but she said she'd stay away, and for a while she did. I don't know. He thinks the judge will grant it. Of course, we might need Rye and Clayton and Vander to give a statement, and I hate that. God, what they must think!"

She rubbed his back. "They'd be happy to help you, Riley. Everyone wants you and Jess to be safe. For good."

"I thought I'd done enough," he said, pinching the bridge of his nose. "Before… You know. I still can't wrap my mind around this. You and Sadie meeting like you did and becoming a family must have given Jess ideas. And that Betty."

Fear curled in her heart. "Riley, this isn't Sadie's fault." She wasn't going to comment on the girl, although she'd talked to Haley about her already. It sounded like Betty had meant well, but she and Mark had told Haley some things had to be discussed with mommies and daddies first. She'd understood.

"Of course it's not Sadie's fault," he said. "I'll tell her that. It's just…Jess is…heartbroken. I can't stand to see my daughter like this. If I'd known there was even the slightest chance of her reaching out to Mandy behind my back, I would have told her the truth."

Paige understood. "Still, Sadie's worried about you. You should talk to her. "

"I will," he said, kissing her cheek. "I just don't know what to say right now… God!"

"Riley, you just need to tell her you love her and let her help."

He nodded, but he was already turning away. "I need to get back to Jess. I'm keeping her home tomorrow. If you talk to Sadie, please reiterate that it's not her fault, okay?"

Why couldn't he see that *he* needed to do that?

When he reached the back porch, she heard him mutter, "It's my fault."

As she watched the light in the kitchen turn off, she realized she'd never felt so incapable of helping someone she loved.

Chapter 32

IN THE TWO DAYS IMMEDIATELY FOLLOWING THE INCIDENT, Sadie only heard from Riley via brief texts. She quilted up a storm. She finished his superhero quilt and Jess' princess quilt, staying up well into the night, ignoring the burning in her eyes. All her love and care for them had been funneled into those quilts. She'd done some last-minute rearranging of Jess' quilt, wanting to show her a how powerful a princess could be in her own right. And Riley's...well, his had changed as well, and she hoped he understood what she was trying to say.

She knew both Haley and Jess had stayed home on Tuesday too. Sadie understood that Riley's focus was where it needed to be—on his daughter—but when she looked down at the ring on her finger, she wanted to remind him that she'd promised to be there for him *and* Jess.

Still, not wanting to rock the boat or add to his worries, she kept silent.

When the two girls went to school on Wednesday, she decided to take a half-day off from work and visit him. Besides, she told herself, maybe the gifts she'd made them would add a ray of sunshine to a cloudy day.

He opened the door after what seemed like forever, and she had to wonder if he'd been gathering himself to face her. Paige had said he blamed himself, and she understood. Despite Paige's reassurances, she felt the same way.

"Hey," she said, clutching her purse to her belly. "I hope it's okay I came by. I knew Jess was at school, and I...I wanted to see you." *Needed to see you.*

"Sure." His eyes were bloodshot, and he hadn't shaved. He didn't smile. Only leaned against the door as if exhausted. "Hi."

"I brought you and Jess something," she said, holding out the two brightly wrapped presents.

He took them and set them on the floor. "I'll have her open them later. Come in."

"One of them is for you," she said, feeling completely at sea. "The one wrapped in green."

"You didn't have to do that."

She stood there, and the distance between them seemed to grow. "I wanted to. I hoped it would...help...somehow."

When he didn't reach for her, her worry grew. Should she hug him? Did he need space? She'd grown so used to feeling comfortable with him, but she didn't feel comfortable now. Oh, she didn't know what to do.

"I'm sorry I haven't called," he said, leading her to the kitchen. "It's been...horrible."

She set her purse down on the counter. "I can't imagine. How's Jess?" She'd ask him about himself in a minute. She knew he wouldn't want to talk about that first.

He poured them both iced tea and slid a glass across to her, staying where he was, on the other side of the kitchen island. She couldn't help but think he was using it as a barrier between them.

"Hell, I want to tell myself Jess is going to heal from all of this, but it's all too raw right now. My faith is at an all-time low. Sadie...I've been thinking..."

Oh, not those words... Those words were the portent of something awful.

"Paige has been keeping me up-to-date here and there," she babbled, not wanting him to continue his train of thought. "I'm glad you're going to take her to a child psychologist for a spell. My mama also said she knows some wonderful people if you don't click with the ones Mark gives you, although I'm sure they'll be wonderful. Mark is such a great guy, and of course, he'd have great suggestions."

"*Sadie.*"

"And Vander told me he gave you a file on Mandy in case it's a help to your lawyer. I mean, I know you have your own P.I., but maybe Vander found more information. Of course, he didn't tell me anything that was in it."

"Vander did go a little deeper than my guy," Riley said, cracking his neck. "There are pieces of information I wish I'd never learned about her, ones I'll never share with Jess, no matter what some child psychologist says. Not that it wasn't good of Vander to compile it. My lawyer said we didn't need it for the restraining order, but he included it so it would be on record."

He hung his head, and she extended her hand to him across the counter. Either he didn't see it, or he didn't want to take it, and after a few moments, she fisted her hand at her side instead.

"Tell me what I can do to help," she whispered. "Riley, I hate seeing you hurting like this. And Jess... I just want to wrap you both up in a quilt and take care of you."

"That's what I've been doing with Jess," he said, rubbing the back of his neck. "She had this old baby blanket I'd bought her, and I dug it out of storage when I couldn't get her to stop crying that first night. It helped, and oh God... My girl. My baby girl. How am I ever going to make this better?"

He knuckled away tears and turned his body away from her as if ashamed.

She couldn't stand it anymore. Moving quickly, she

walked around the counter and wrapped her arms around him. "You'll love her through it. That's the best antidote in times like these." *And I'll keep praying and praying,* she thought, *and being right here.*

He fitted his face into her shoulder. "Oh, Sadie, I feel like it's never going to get better. It's so much worse than when Mandy came back before. This time Jess understood and... Oh, God."

She tightened her hold on him. He still hadn't put his arms around her. His hands were gripping the counter's edge, his knuckles white.

"And your family? I can't imagine how upset they must be. Annabelle and Rory should never have seen that. Then there's Rye... He had no idea what he was walking into when he followed me out onto the street."

She'd already talked to Rye. "He went out there because he wanted to have your back. He didn't know she'd...try and latch onto him."

He snorted and moved away, and the arms she had around him fell away. "Latch onto him? That's a nice way of putting it. How could he have guessed Mandy would come out of her hole again to see her daughter for the first time because she knew Rye would be at the party? How could anyone? Maybe I should have..."

His voice was bitter and edged with razors, and it hurt her to hear it.

"Of course, if it had been Jake on the street, she would have 'latched' onto him too. Thank God Clayton and Vander told him to stay back. What a shit show that would have been. Mandy trying to 'latch' onto not one but two famous country singers."

"Riley, stop this," Sadie said, rubbing the tension in his back. "This isn't your fault. I mean, if you're wanting to blame anyone, it's me for giving Jess this idea inadvertently. If I hadn't met Paige like I did—"

"No. I don't want you to think for one minute this is

your fault," he said, gripping her arms. "Look at me. This was a little girl's fantasy. If I'd told her more about how horrible her mother was—"

"—you would have broken her heart earlier," Sadie finished. "No, you did everything you were supposed to do, Riley."

When he didn't look into her eyes, she put her hand on his chest.

"I mean it, Riley."

"But it all still collapsed at my feet. My parents called and told me I should have known better. They think I'm at fault for not telling Jess the truth sooner. Tyler said something to them out of concern. That was...helpful. I'd thought things were finally turning around with them."

She didn't know how to respond to that. Her family always supported each other.

He downed half the contents of his iced tea. "Sadie, I'm not sure when Jess is going to be...back to herself, and that has to be my first priority."

Her heart sank to her stomach. "Of course."

"In fact, I can't be sure Mandy is going to stay away, even with the restraining order. Threatening to call the cops clearly isn't enough to keep her away anymore, what with her addiction and dreams of grandeur. I mean, she knows Rye and Jake are part of your family. I'm afraid she's never going to leave this alone. She's unbalanced and an addict, and people like that just keep coming and using and...destroying everything they touch."

She knew what was coming, and she wanted to cover her ears with her hands. "Clayton has dealt with people like her before, and so has Vander. They can make sure she never comes around again."

Riley shook his head, and when he finally looked at her, his eyes were devoid of all the light she was so used to seeing in them. "I can't take a chance. It's not fair to you or your family. I won't be used to get to the people you love. I... Dammit, I don't want to bring any more of this shit to your door."

He wasn't thinking straight. "Riley, this isn't—"

"And with Rye and Jake in your family, Mandy's not going to stay away. I can't stop her from going after Jess. I need to remove the inducement."

That stopped her short. She hadn't thought about it that way.

"I think we should call the wedding off," he interrupted. "I need to focus all of my attention on getting Jess what she needs right now. I can't..."

The walls holding all her sadness back started to crack. "Then let's just postpone it. I can give you and Jess time. This way your lawyer and Clayton and Vander can find a way to protect Jess. Riley, I love you. Don't do this."

He touched her cheek briefly before his hand fell away. "I've thought about this day and night, Sadie, and I don't see another way."

She clutched his shirt. "Riley—"

"Sadie, I can't live with this happening again," he said, covering her hand. "I can't."

This time it was she who hung her head. His resolve was unshakeable, and she knew there would be no convincing him.

How had they gone from loving each other to this place of self-blame and fear? She looked down at the beautiful ring he'd designed for her. The diamond sparkled, but it was the engraved pattern of the wedding quilt that always made her happy. Today, all she felt was grief when she looked at it. The interlocking circles of their bond hadn't been strong enough. The first trial had broken them, and right now, she didn't see a way to mend them.

Working the ring off her finger, she fought tears, and held it out to him.

"No, keep it," he said, closing her fingers over the ring. "To remember what might have been."

What might have been? She pressed the hand to her mouth, fighting the sob threatening to destroy the last of her composure.

"I'm sorry," he said, cupping the back of her neck and looking directly into her eyes. "Sadie, I'm so sorry." The longing she saw in his gaze, heard in his voice, didn't keep him there.

He left her, stumbling from the kitchen. Almost running in his haste to get away. She cried quietly with her hand over her mouth, not wanting him to hear. Reaching for the last of her strength, she set the ring on the counter and gave it one last look. That ring had embodied everything she'd ever wanted with a man, with a family.

She walked out of his house and told herself not to look back.

Chapter 33

Riley went running after he heard Sadie's car drive off. If he hadn't dragged himself out, he would have ended up crying, and he couldn't handle doing any more of that. In the last few days, he'd done more crying than in his entire life put together. Most of it had been for Jess, but he'd cried for himself too. Like the most evil of villains, Mandy had managed the ultimate revenge, and he felt forever condemned for his association with her.

Letting Sadie go had been the right thing to do.

But losing her... He wasn't sure he'd ever get over that.

His feet raced across the pavement, anger pumping hot in time with his blood. Damn Mandy. Damn her to hell. Before she came blowing back in like a hurricane, he and Sadie had been on a solid path to being happy together with Jess and any other kids they might have.

Other kids... His steps faltered, and he doubled over at the waist as pain shot through his system.

There would be no more children. Ever.

Because there was no more him and Sadie.

He hadn't checked to see if she'd left the ring. He wasn't sure he could handle it if she had. What in the hell was he supposed to do with it? He made his body start running again. He didn't have to think about that now.

Like he'd been telling himself the past couple of days, one step at a time...

But the steps seemed harder to take the more he ran. Either he was suddenly out of shape or his lungs were refusing to cooperate. He couldn't seem to draw enough breath, and when he saw stars, he cut back his pace. Walking home gave him too much time to think, but there was no avoiding it. Right now he really wished his female superhero were real so she could alter time in his favor. He'd have her zip back to all of the destructive blocks of time with Mandy in them and change them so he wouldn't be stuck in this dark place.

When he let himself in through the front door, he ignored the two presents she'd brought. The pink one was clearly for Jess, and he'd give it to her when she got home. His own present...he wasn't sure he could ever open it.

The size of the package suggested a quilt, and if she'd made it...

He couldn't think about that now. His lawyer had called and left him a message while he was out running, one he'd let go to voicemail. He'd shower and call him back and then go pick up the girls. Paige was leaving work early, he knew, wanting to be around for Haley—and likely for Jess and him too.

His hair was still wet from his shower when he called his lawyer. The man told him the judge had granted the restraining order or protective order or whatever the hell they were called. In all his life, he'd never wanted to file one, and against the mother of his child, no less. After wrapping up the call, he looked out the window of his office. The street they lived on had always seemed like such a safe place, filled with nice neighbors.

He wondered if he'd ever feel like Jess was truly safe again. Somehow a flimsy piece of paper backed by the law didn't reassure him. He'd faltered in his job to protect his daughter.

He could never let that happen again.

Hovering in his office kept him away from the kitchen, so he stayed up there drawing for as long as he could. He kept sketching various scenes, trying to figure out how his superhero could move blocks of time around to change reality.

When it came time to pick up the girls from school, he made himself walk down the steps to the kitchen. He knew he was dragging his feet, but if Sadie had left the ring on the counter, it would be better if he put it out of the way before the girls saw it.

The diamond was sparkling from the afternoon sunlight streaming through the window over the sink. Prisms danced on the walls, but Riley couldn't find the beauty or the magic in the colors like he normally would have.

Jess was right. There were no happily ever afters.

How was he ever supposed to help his daughter believe again when he didn't?

As he picked up the ring, he couldn't stop the avalanche of sadness from pressing down on him. Holding the ring to his heart, he squeezed his eyes shut. Sadie was gone. By his own command. That was something he would just have to live with.

When he thought he was more in control, Riley walked to the front door and picked up his present. Taking the stairs two at a time, he reached his bedroom. There was a top shelf in his closet, one Jess likely couldn't reach. He shoved the present in the back, and then scanned his shelves for the best place for the ring. There was a leftover watch box on his shelf. After he closed the ring inside it, he slid the box next to the present and left.

Paige was standing beside his car when he left the house.

"You broke off your engagement?" she asked, rounding on him. "Are you crazy? Riley, Sadie is the best thing that's happened to you besides Jess. I know you're upset about what happened on Sunday, but you don't throw a lifetime of happiness away because of it. Or because of a woman like Mandy."

He didn't want to hear it, so he simply walked around her to the driver's side of his car. "This is for the best," he said, opening the door. "I don't expect you to understand."

She rounded the hood of his car. "You're damn right I don't. You love her! And she loves you! You're not thinking straight. I want to tell you you're being stupid, but that seems a little harsh."

"Yes, I am stupid. I'm going to get the girls. Are you coming?"

She glared at him. "I'm going to chalk this up to temporary insanity. Riley, I know you. I know the kind of man you are. You aren't going to let Mandy destroy the rest of your life. It would be like me saying no to Mark when he asked me to marry him because my mom could come back at any time for drug money."

This kind of reasoning was like a barrage of arrows to his heart. Paige didn't understand. It wasn't just about money. Rye and Jake were powerful attractors to Mandy, which added a new angle to the situation, one he didn't think he could get around. "I'm done talking about this, Paige. It's hard enough as it is."

"Because you're not thinking right!" She covered the distance between them. "What are you going to tell Jess? That Sadie doesn't love her? Doesn't want to be her new stepmother anymore?"

His head started to hurt. "Jess has enough on her hands right now. I wasn't planning on saying anything except Sadie was giving us some time alone." He certainly didn't plan to mention she'd be away for the foreseeable future.

"Riley, this is so the wrong move. I know you're upset—"

"Stop! Please. This is killing me. Okay? I'm doing the best I can. Now, I need to leave to get there on time. Are you coming or not?"

"I'm coming," she said, and then promptly went silent.

They drove without speaking to the school, but she was all smiles and hugs when the girls ran to the car.

"I want to go home," Jess told him when she wrapped her arms around him.

"You've got it, princess," he said, and Paige met his eyes.

Haley was quiet on the way home, holding Jess' hand. When he asked about school, Haley muttered, "Okay," and Jess said, "Fine." He decided not to ask about Betty. He'd thought about calling her parents, but that might be an overreaction right now. No doubt Paige was right, and the girl hadn't intended any harm.

He could feel Paige stewing, so he turned up the music playing in the background. The Psychedelic Furs were singing "Love My Way" and Riley couldn't have thought of a better song. He was doing love his way, and that was his right. Anger started to pump through him again, hot and insistent. No one had the right to tell him how to live his life. Not even Paige.

Halfway through the song, Paige said, "Do you mind if I change the song?"

He looked over. "Sure. Whatever you want."

She dispatched his new mantra with the flick of a switch, and he focused on getting them home without engaging with her.

When they arrived home, the girls scooted out of the back seat. Riley picked Jess up.

"What do you want to do? Have a snack?"

She shook her head. "No, I'm not hungry."

Yeah, he'd made all of her favorites, including mac and cheese, but she didn't have much of an appetite. "Okay, how about we find some paints?"

He wasn't going to ask about homework right now.

That would be like giving a kid a spanking when she was already down.

She shrugged. "Haley, what do you want to do?"

Haley was holding Paige's hand, her brow knitted with worry. "How about we watch *Enchanted?* That always makes you feel better."

"I don't want to watch that," Jess said with a shake of her head.

Since destroying her princess castle in the playroom, she'd been emphatic about her new distaste for princess movies. He wondered if those carefree days of hearing the kids laugh over a Disney movie would ever come again. God, he hoped so.

"What about *Honey, I Shrunk The Kids?*" Paige asked, suggesting one of Mark's favorites to watch with the girls. "That one's funny."

With no princesses in sight , Riley thought.

Jess lifted her shoulder. "Okay."

Riley suppressed a sigh. Finding something Jess wanted to do these days was worse than pulling teeth, and he'd floundered when none of her normal happy things had sparked her interest.

"Do you want to watch it over at our house?" Paige asked. "I'll make banana and honey sandwiches."

"Okay," Jess said again in a flat voice.

"Riley, if you want, I'll watch the girls to give you some time to do…things."

Like get your head on straight . He could read between the lines. Except being alone was its own nightmare right now. He couldn't go running again. Well, he supposed he could, but his muscles were already achy from his earlier sprints.

"I'll hang out with you ladies, if that's okay." And hope to high heaven Paige would leave him alone.

She did. Mostly. Except for the angry looks she shot him when the girls weren't looking. The worst moment came when she picked up her phone and left the room for a while. He couldn't help but wonder if Sadie had called her sister again.

Was she crying her heart out? He pinched the bridge of his nose and tried not to think about it.

When Mark got home from work, he greeted the girls warmly. The look his friend gave him clearly telegraphed that he wanted to talk, but Riley couldn't handle whatever kind of open-hearted psychological babble Mark wanted to use.

He called it quits after the movie and suggested he and Jess head on home, which she did reluctantly.

"Are we going to resume our morning runs?" Mark asked him as they were leaving.

"Let's give it a few more days," he said, feeling like a chicken shit. "I'll text you when we can get back on schedule."

His friend didn't blink. Only man-hugged him. Then Paige hugged him too, even if it was a touch stiff, and Haley. It was like each of them was reassuring him that they were still his family—and reminding him that he couldn't push them away too. Of course, with them next door, that would be impossible. Besides, Jess and Haley were BFFs. He'd never mess with that.

But as he let his daughter and himself into their house, he found himself fretting about his relationship with Mark and Paige. Sadie was Paige's sister, after all, and it was possible his behavior would hurt things between them. Hadn't his behavior ultimately damaged his relationship with his parents? When he and his friends had first talked about it, back before his first date with Sadie, he'd never imagined it was actually possible. Now fear beat its dark drumbeat in his belly.

On the way up to take her bath, Jess spotted the present and sat on the floor to open it when he said it was from Sadie.

He knew it was a quilt, but he hadn't been prepared for the sheer majesty.

The princess had green eyes and the same curve of the jaw as Jess, but she was all grown up. The main quilt color was a lush rose, and the princess' dress was a complementary pink. Her hair was long and lustrous and the same shade as his daughter's, and her arms were wide open, much like her gaze and her smile. She loomed larger than life, taking up the entire quilt. In fact, she seemed to be a giant of a woman, a woman who commanded attention, a woman...

Who wasn't afraid of anything.

Much like Sadie hoped Jess would grow up to be.

Jess was staring at it.

"What do you think?" he asked, his voice raw.

Jess stood up, and he caught the similarities again between the woman Sadie had created and the woman his daughter would grow up to be. It was like looking ahead in the future twenty years. Like she'd woven her own vision of time into it...

The hair on the back of his neck stood up.

"She's the most beautiful woman I've ever seen," she whispered.

You're the most beautiful woman I've ever seen, he wanted to say to his daughter—much like he wanted to say to the woman he loved.

"I... Daddy, can we put this on my bed? I want to sleep with it tonight."

He helped her gather it up, and his hands felt the warmth in the material. He knew he was imagining it, but it felt like Sadie's loving touch. And his throat got all jammed up with emotion.

Bath time was quiet, and afterward, Jess snuggled under the covers and he spread her new quilt over her. She gave him the first smile he'd seen from her since Sunday, and when she touched the quilt, she seemed to quiet down.

He read her story after story until she drifted off to sleep.

Then he tiptoed out of the room and left the door ajar. In the low light of the hallway, he stopped and looked toward his bedroom. His heart knew where it wanted to go. This time he listened.

In the closet, he drew down the green-wrapped present and sat on the bed. Unwrapping it would affect him. Change him. He knew it.

He couldn't help himself.

The quilt's background was a rich navy, and sure enough, the superhero depicted on the quilt looked a little like him, even though all it consisted of was blocks of cloth and thread. And thread.

He thought of Clotho again, spinning her threads of fate.

The man's eyes were large and arresting while his face seemed to be in shadow. There was a quixotic touch of a smile on his mouth, like he perpetually found something amusing. His shoulders were strong, and he appeared to be levitating in outer space from the way a trail of stars lined a pathway under his red-booted feet. The letter R was emblazoned in the center of the man's turquoise-blue superhero outfit, and he held what looked like a drawing pencil in his right hand. He wondered if she'd added it to make sure he knew she was depicting him—in case he'd somehow missed the big R on his chest. It was something he would have teased her about at a different time.

Riley then glanced down and noticed the mask the man was holding in his left hand. Made out of dark brown material, it appeared sad, almost resigned.

Riley couldn't help thinking Sadie might have added the mask on Monday after he'd texted her back to say he didn't think her coming over would be a good plan. He'd made up some bullshit excuse, but she must have known...

He'd been pushing her away already, donning a dark mask, one she didn't recognize.

Of course he didn't recognize himself either right now, and that was downright scary. After all the mistakes he'd thought he could blame on youth and young love, he'd turned around his life. But that hadn't been enough. What kind of man was he really? What kind of father was he? His internal compass seemed to have disintegrated.

He wrapped the quilt around his body, his muscles tensing in anticipation. The material held the warmth he'd felt in Jess' quilt coupled with a love so strong that his broken and armored-up heart was no match for it.

He couldn't wrap himself up in her arms anymore. He knew that. Was resigned to it. And yet, he could wrap himself in this quilt, the one made from her very hands, and pretend it was her holding him.

He'd have to find a way to settle for being wrapped up in her love this way.

But even he couldn't lie to himself that well.

It wasn't the same.

Chapter 34

Shelby stayed with Sadie that first night after Riley broke off their engagement, holding her as she cried pretty much non-stop. Texts and phone calls poured in from family, offering love, support, and prayers, and their support helped keep her occupied when she called in sick the next day. Of course, Susannah had insisted on taking the day off to be with her, and then her mama had come over to hold her tight, pray with her, and tuck her in for the night like she would a little child before going off to sleep in the spare bedroom.

Paige had come over the next night with a handmade thank-you card from Jess, drawn in bright markers. Riley had sent a card too, and the spare words had only drummed up more hurt. *Thank you for the quilt. I'll treasure it always. R.*

R. Not his full name, Riley. It was like he'd donned the dark mask after all, the one she'd added to the quilt at the last minute. She'd feared this side of him, the one trying to shut her out. She hadn't known how to fight it except by reminding him of his true nature.

And yet she was torn... He was only trying to protect Jess, which made his actions heroic but didn't lessen the pain he'd caused her. And himself. He thought they were doomed somehow with Mandy being around, and she understood that in her head. Her heart was still trying to find a way to accept what had happened. It just didn't seem fair...

Her ring finger felt bare, and she missed the solidness of the promise the quilt ring had represented. That night her brother had come over with Tammy and the kids, who'd done their best to cheer her up by drawing her sweet pictures. She'd added them next to Jess' thank-you, which now hung in the center of her refrigerator.

The other men in the family supported her in their own way. Vander had offered to kidnap Riley and bring him to a log cabin in the woods if she wanted to try and beat some sense in him, only his mention of the cabin had reminded her of their time in Paducah. She'd had to hang up because she couldn't speak over the tide of grief rising up inside her. Rye grew outraged on her behalf at Sunday dinner, and she'd left early, not needing to make up the excuse of a headache, for she had a real one.

She did her best not to ask Paige about Riley and Jess, and she didn't go over to their house. She told herself she was glad Paige was looking after them since she no longer could. And she sure as shooting didn't ask what Riley had told Jess about the breakup. She only hoped the little girl still knew how much she loved her. It helped to think of Jess wrapped up in the quilt, soaking in the love and strength Sadie had poured into it.

When her quilting class rolled around on Monday night, she braced herself for another onslaught of compassion. She dreaded the necessity of telling yet more people about the broken engagement. Her boss had been shocked, but she'd clucked and clucked about how Sadie would heal one day and God would bring her another good man.

But she didn't want another man. She wanted Riley Thomson and his beautiful daughter for her own.

Before anyone noticed her missing ring, Sadie told the women in her class about the cancelled engagement.

"But you can't be serious," Imogene said. "I know assholes, and your man isn't an asshole."

"Plus, he asked Mae here to make you a wedding quilt so he could propose," Ada added. "Only a man who truly loved you would go to that effort. Paige, you know him. How could he do this?"

Her sister gave a great sigh. "I honestly don't know."

Sadie gave her a watery smile. She knew Paige had blasted Riley for his decision—heck, she'd admitted that both she and Mark still hoped to change his mind.

"Men are such idiots," Leanne said, throwing out her hand. "Oh, honey, I'm so sorry for you, but you'll find someone better when the time comes."

"All right, enough of that talk," Mae said. "Sadie is heartbroken. What can we do for you, honey? You tell us what you need."

"Yes," Whitney said, her face knitted with worry, "you've always done so much for us. What can *we* do for you?"

"Can we just quilt tonight? In quiet? My head has been aching all day—"

"Why don't you go on home if you'd like?" Mae said. "I'll look after anyone who has questions tonight."

"Yes, go on, honey," Leanne said.

The offer was tempting, but then she thought of her responsibility to the class and the quiet townhouse that awaited her. She supposed she could call one of her sisters to come over, but...

"No, this is my job." She surveyed the women sitting in the quilting circle. "Thank you for your kindness, though. I mean it."

"You're most welcome," Ada said, reaching for her hand. "Let's just quilt then. It always helps me when I'm grieving."

"Yes," Mae said, "it keeps the mind busy...and the heart—"

"Seems to settle," Ada finished for her.

They quilted on their current projects, showing their silent support. No one asked her questions, and at one point she heard Mae whispering a prayer under her breath and knew it was for her. She prayed too while her hands worked, asking for solace, praying for peace.

After they all hugged her and she locked up and walked to her car, she looked up at the sky as she waited for the others to drive off. Paige lingered in her car, so she finally waved her off. When her sister left, she let out a deep cleansing breath.

The Big Dipper was bright tonight, and the darkness seemed to be friendly, becoming. It made her think of one of Riley's favorite songs he'd shared with her, "Under The Milky Way." Then she thought of the stars she'd included in his quilt. The star he'd given to her and she'd returned to him. Instead of making her sad, the comparison heartened her. It felt like they were winking at her, sending encouragement.

She'd always believed there was something bigger guiding everything, and in this moment, she decided to trust in it once again.

With all those stars shining all above her, she asked for a miracle.

Chapter 35

Riley's decision to call off his engagement with Sadie was sticking like a thorn in the proverbial lion's paw.

After a week of telling himself he'd made the right decision, he felt like everything in his life was on shaky ground. His artistic well had dried up, and he couldn't seem to create. His female superhero—the one who resembled Sadie—wouldn't talk to him, and the one time he'd tried to redraw her to resemble someone else, he'd broken down and cried. His relationship with Paige and Mark was suffering, and if that wasn't bad enough, Jess had finally come out of her fog and asked him about Sadie. Maybe Haley had even said something to her. They were both smart kids.

He'd told Jess he'd felt they needed to spend some time alone, and Sadie had agreed. His daughter's eyes had filled with tears, and she'd run away and slammed the door to her room, something she'd never done.

The crack of that door had reverberated in his aching heart, and he'd sat on the steps and given in to his emotions again. He missed Sadie, and he didn't want this. Any of this. Only he wasn't sure what to do about it. He was doing the right thing after all...wasn't he?

It didn't help that Mark seemed to think Jess' reaction might be because she thought yet another woman had abandoned her. That made him feel like dog shit. Especially since he was only trying to keep her safe.

When he opened the door to find Rye Crenshaw standing on his doorstep at noon the Wednesday after the breakup, he almost shut the door in the man's face. Of course, he'd wondered if one of the men in Sadie's family would take him to the woodshed for hurting her. Part of him had welcomed it.

"Can I come in?" Rye asked.

"Do I have a choice?" Riley found himself asking.

Rye's mouth tipped up. "You could say no, I suppose, but then we'd have to do it the hard way."

Riley knew it wasn't wise to challenge the man, so he stepped back and allowed him inside.

"I don't have to ask whether you're upset about how things are," Rye began, shifting his weight on his hip. "It's clear as mud. That eases me some. I'm glad I didn't misjudge you. Now I'm sure I was right to come. Do you have a beer?"

"It's noon," Riley pointed out.

"I'm an artist. You're an artist."

The point wasn't worth arguing. Riley walked toward the kitchen, Rye's boots stomping on the hardwood floor behind him. Rather than offer him a choice, like he would have done for an invited guest, he pulled out two craft beers. He popped the tops, releasing a hissing sound in the room.

Rye tipped back the beer and took a drink. "Nice. Now let's talk turkey. Shelby came and visited me the other day, and the one thing you need to know about Shelby is that she is the most interfering woman in the whole family. I love her to pieces, but she is not one to rest on her laurels."

This wasn't news to Riley—Sadie had told him much

the same thing. "I can respect that to a point."

"Good," Rye said, resting his beer against his hip. "Seems Shelby feels she finally has a bead on why you called off the engagement, and if she's right, I'm afraid I'm going to have to kick your ass."

Riley narrowed his eyes at the man. "That doesn't make me feel all warm and squishy on the inside."

Rye had the audacity to bark out a laugh. "It's not meant to. Correct me if I'm wrong, but did you break things off with Sadie because you thought your ex might come back and bother me and Jake again and somehow hurt the family? And your daughter? Although let's start with our family first."

Riley stayed silent.

"Jake doesn't know I'm here, by the way. He's a much nicer guy than me, but I think he'd agree with me on this point. If you're trying to protect us from that crazy bitch, don't. It's an insult to us as men. To our families, really."

When Rye put it that way, the whole thing sounded ridiculous. "I love Sadie, and her family means everything to her. The last thing I want to do is bring more filth to your door. That's not fair to anyone, including y'all. I also can't guarantee Mandy won't break the restraining order and come back. She's an unbalanced junkie, and I can't see her staying away for good and leaving Jess alone, especially if she's quasi-related to two huge stars."

"Do you think Jake and I haven't had people try to hit us up before?" Rye asked, leaning back against the kitchen counter. "I can't say it wasn't a surprise when it happened here, but it didn't throw me none. Clayton knows what he's doing, and Vander can be downright scary. We can handle anything that comes."

Riley set his beer on the counter and pressed his fingers to the bridge of his nose. "I don't want to be responsible for any more hurt to your family."

Rye knocked him in the shoulder. "You aren't. That

woman is, and you've handled her like a man should. Now, let's talk about you doing it for your baby girl. As a new father, I've given this a lot of thought, and I have some compassion for the decision you made. I understand why you would want to remove any so-called temptation from your ex, and here be temptation apparently."

When he gestured to himself, Riley nodded. "It's a unique situation."

"Yes, it is," Rye said, "which is why I haven't kicked your ass. Yet. Jake and I don't plan on becoming less famous to stop being catnip to your ex, but let me tell you one indisputable truth. If that bitch comes back around, we'll circle the wagons again. *Together*. To protect your daughter. If you marry Sadie, Jess is our family too. Do I strike you as a man who wouldn't protect one of his kin, especially a child? I've done it before, bubba."

His resolve was backing up Riley's throat. "I never imagined you'd help me protect her." God, he was going to start crying.

Rye put his hand on his shoulder. "The protecting isn't all on you anymore. We're family now, assuming you turn this situation around and go after Sadie. Son, you don't give up on a woman and the life you want with her because of crap like this."

"I see that now," he said. "Thank you." He felt like new bonds of brotherhood were forming with this man.

"Is there anything else keeping you from marrying our girl?" Rye asked. "Shelby said you were worried your daughter might need your sole focus, and I don't want to minimize that. However, as someone who's dealt with little kids from an abusive home, I can tell you that the best antidote is to welcome in more good people to love on them."

Paige and Mark had told him the same thing, but he'd tuned them out.

"Love heals, I've come to realize, and your Jess is

going to heal a heck of a lot faster with someone like Sadie in her camp. That girl has a heart of gold, and you know it. Then there's the rest of us. We're not too bad to have around."

No, they weren't, and he'd seen it from the beginning.

"You've been invited to be part of our family, and from where I'm standing, that's a pretty good gig. And since Sadie loves you… Well, you have a lot to offer all of us. You and Jess. We need another good man like you in our camp. Think on that for me, will you?"

Riley nodded, and Rye set his beer on the countertop.

"I'll get out of your hair," Rye said, "but like I said, Sadie's ours, and that makes you and Jess ours too since she wants y'all. Besides, Clayton and Vander are more terrifying than any superhero duo imaginable when it comes to protecting our clan from bad people. Trust me on this. You just call them if ever the time comes. We're all here for you, Riley."

With a manly slap on the back, Rye walked out of the kitchen. Riley heard the front door close, and he made his way up the stairs to his daughter's bedroom. As he looked at the beautiful quilt Sadie had made for Jess, he reaffirmed his daughter was going to become this woman—the fearless, happy princess. He was going to help her and he was going to let people like Rye and the rest of their family support him, but he knew Jess already had the seeds inside her. Hadn't they been obvious these last few days? After the trauma of her meeting with her mother, she'd slowly but surely come back to herself.

She and Haley had started playing and laughing again, although not as much as usual. Still, they hadn't stopped. Their friendship was stronger than ever.

Riley had been too caught up in his own head to see the lesson his daughter was teaching him, to see how sometimes terrible moments could strengthen the bond between people if only they continued to trust and support each other. And he needed to show Jess that good men like him didn't retreat from bullies in order to protect the people they loved. They fought with the tools available to them. Nathaniel Gray used the law, like he'd done. And his superhero...she stitched together time with the thread her mother gave her. But she could also change the blocks, and as he stared at the quilt, it all came together. She might not be able to change the past, but she had the power to reorient it—to stitch it back together in a way that could free people like Riley, who felt imprisoned by their past choices.

He'd broken his bond with Sadie, but he could restitch it and their future.

He walked into his room and pulled the quilt she'd made him out of the chest at the end of his bed. Smoothing it out, he studied the man she'd depicted in the design.

It was time for him to become the hero she saw when she looked at him.

Chapter 36

When Paige texted Sadie to ask if she wanted to meet her and Haley at the park, she decided to take her sister up on the offer. The fall days were starting to lengthen, and the rustle of leaves was growing louder as the trees dropped them in a colorful display. Perhaps she might even find some inspiration for her new quilt.

Her last quilt had sold at the store in a record two hours. She'd stitched the night sky into it, capturing those enormous falling stars that had begged her to wish upon them. The woman who'd bought it had exclaimed she'd never seen anything so beautiful, and somehow her praise had soothed Sadie's heart for a moment. She hadn't forgotten that beautiful night sky or stopped praying for a miracle.

When she pulled up at the park, she caught sight of Paige pushing Haley on the swings. Mark was standing beside her, his hand on her back, and though she loved the quiet affection between them, it made her heart hurt. She wouldn't have that with Riley anymore. She might never have that with anyone again, and right now, she wasn't sure she couldn't find peace in that possibility.

"Sadie," she heard someone say. Her heart leaped into her throat—she would know that voice anywhere—

and she turned to see Riley standing in the middle of the parking lot, holding Jess' hand.

Jess waved and then ran toward her. She wrapped her little arms around her, and Sadie crouched down to hug the little girl. Tears sparked in her eyes when Jess whispered, "I've missed you, Sadie."

"Me too," she said in a hoarse voice. "I'm so sorry about your mom, honey."

"Yeah," Jess said, "it made me really sad and angry. It wasn't okay, what she did. But I have my dad. And Haley. She's the best friend ever. And Mr. and Mrs. Bradshaw. They're my family."

She glanced up to see the Bradshaws watching them. "Yes, they're a good family to be a part of," she said.

"I'm talking to Dr. Kate about things, and she's really nice. She tells me I'm doing great."

"I'm so glad." Her demeanor seemed much older, and it made her think of Rory. The nasty business with his daddy had matured him before his time, but he'd healed with time and love, becoming a much happier boy. She prayed it would be the same way for Jess.

"Thank you for my princess quilt. I know I made you a card, but I'm glad Dad finally got over being silly so I could thank you in person."

Silly? She looked over to where Riley was standing. He hadn't moved from the middle of the parking lot, which didn't seem smart. Why wasn't he coming over?

"I'm going to go swing with Haley," Jess said. "My dad wants to talk to you and say he's sorry."

Her heart picked up its pace.

"I also wanted to tell you…" Jess ducked her head. "I know I said no one else could be my mother, but Dr. Kate said it would be okay to have another one if I wanted. She said a real mother loves her kids and isn't like mine. I know I'm not your kid, but if you wanted to be my mom, it would…I'd be okay with it."

Tears streaked down Sadie's face. "I'd be more than okay with it, Jess. It would make me so happy to be your mama."

"Whew. That was intense." Jess wiped at her tears and hugged her again. "Dad's really sorry he was so stupid. He doesn't know, but I've heard him crying a few times after he put me to sleep."

Hold it together. Don't completely lose it.

"I've cried too," she admitted softly.

"I made him bring your ring," Jess said, finally giving her a smile. "And something else... Dad, come over here. What are you waiting for?"

A mischievous look flashed in the little girl's eyes, much like the old Jess, and then she ran off. Sadie rose to her feet slowly as Riley crossed the distance between them.

He held out his hands awkwardly. "I've gotten it all wrong, and I'm sorry. I thought I was protecting Jess and you and your family and...I meant well. That's the only excuse I have. Sadie, I'm sorry. I can't say it enough."

His sorrow was obvious, as was his contrition. "I am too."

"You have nothing to be sorry for," he said, taking the last steps toward her. "Sadie, I love you, and I hope I haven't ruined things for good. I hope...you can trust me again. That I didn't remind you too much of your father."

That puzzled her. "Why ever would you say that?" He was nothing like her father.

"Because I walked away from you," he said, "and the reasons don't change the hurt I caused. But I want to fix things. Can I show you something?"

She nodded, and he pulled out a large manila envelope and handed it to her.

"All of these sport jackets have finally come in handy."

Opening it, she pulled out the papers inside, captivated by the vibrant colors. "Comics? Wait, she looks like me." And she was wearing all gold, from her breastplate to her short pants.

He sidled up to her. "I told you how much you've inspired me, but I finally got her right. This is how I see you. Courageous. Powerful. Kind. Do you see the needles sticking out of her belt?"

They looked like knitting needles to her. "Yes."

"I couldn't figure out a way to make quilting sexy, but the concepts are there. She's called the Weaver, and she uses the thread her mother gave her to do it. I'll tell you about that another time. The important thing is that she can take a block of time, like one of your quilting blocks, and move it around to create a more just and happier future for the people she helps. Sadie, I want to restitch our future together...if you'll let me. Can you forgive me enough to be with me again?"

She studied the woman he'd drawn. He'd shown her drawings of herself before, but this woman... She could do anything. She was the woman she'd tried to tell Jess she could become. She was...the woman Sadie wanted to be.

The woman Riley already saw when he looked at her.

Leafing through the rest of the pages he'd brought her, some of them complete, some rough sketches, she felt a smile stretch across her face. Did he know Nathaniel Gray resembled him?

"Do you promise to never shut me out again?" she asked. "Riley, we promised to support each other, and while I understand how much you want to protect Jess—"

"We can't let villains win," he said. "I'm sorry I almost allowed that."

"I'm sorry too," she said, finally meeting his eyes. "It hurt me, Riley."

"I know," he said, putting his hand on her arm. "I've been trying to restitch my own heart so I could be brave enough to come after you."

She finally understood how hard his self-imposed isolation had been on him.

"Will you help me restitch my heart the rest of the way and let me work on yours?"

Her heart would be safe with him again, she knew that deep down in her bones. "I like your comic," she said, "but the superhero needs a little more clothes." Goodness, she had long legs, mostly bare.

"We can talk about that," he said, "if you can forgive me and give me another chance?"

"I forgive you," she said, "but I'm feeling a little power-hungry after seeing the comic you created."

His eyes narrowed. "Okay..."

"No iguanas," she said.

It took him a moment, but then he laughed. "All right. If you're going to play hardball."

With that simple teasing exchange, she felt a few pieces of her heart stitch back together on their own. She wiped the tears running down her face. "Jess said you brought my ring."

He sucked in his breath, almost like he was surprised at her response. "Yes, I...didn't want to presume, but she insisted I had to. You know how she likes to boss me around."

That made a laugh sputter out. "Maybe I need to do more of that so you won't do anything... What did Jess say? Silly?"

"Yeah," he said, reaching into his jacket. "Silly works. Of course, Paige said I was stupid, and that seems more accurate. Sadie..."

He extended the ring, and she looked at it. The diamond winked at her, as if celebrating their reunion, but the wedding knots in the band drew her eye most. They looked stronger somehow, resting in his large hand, even though she knew it must be her imagination.

"The thread my superhero carries is in knots like

this," he said. "I don't know if you noticed. I wanted it to be the strongest thread on earth."

That made her heart soar. "Oh, I love you, Riley," she said, holding out her left hand. "Of course I still want to be with you."

He slid the ring on her finger and brought her hand to his mouth, kissing it softly. "I never want to be without you again."

"Then don't," she said, leaning up on her toes. "Now you'd better kiss me or else."

"Ah...here comes the bossiness." He kissed her lightly on the lips. "I think I'm going to like this side of you."

She thought of his female superhero. She had some living up to do for it to be her new normal, but she was up for the task. "Me too," she whispered. "Kiss me again."

And with the Thomsons cheering alongside Jess in the background, they renewed the promise they'd made to love each other.

Forever.

Chapter 37

The chocolate garden seemed richer and more vibrant despite the end of the season as Sadie and the rest of her family gathered for Thanksgiving at J.P. and Tammy's home. The children were situated at their special table decorated with the papier-mâché turkeys Jess and Haley had made at school.

Maybe it was because this was her first holiday with someone beside her—the man she was going to marry—but it struck her that everyone was sitting two by two mostly. As she looked around at her siblings and the members of her extended family, she felt a smile touch her face. Even Me-Mother was with them. Sadie's mama had finally gone to visit her. She'd done the impossible and convinced her to join them for Thanksgiving.

"What?" Riley asked, leaning closer.

"Everything seems so...perfect." She put her napkin on her lap. "I'm so happy, Riley."

"Me too," he said, kissing her on the cheek.

They'd done a lot of talking since that day at the park. She'd also gone to one of Riley and Jess' appointments with Dr. Kate, wanting to be as much of a help as she could. From the first appointment, she'd known Dr. Kate was a miracle worker with kids, much like her mama was with the people she counseled.

Her eyes tracked down the table to where her mama was sitting next to Dale. For so many years, Mama had been their rock. And yet their father's abandonment had left this hole inside all of them. Now that hole was finally filled. Somehow facing down their daddy in person had given them all the closure they'd been seeking, even Paige.

This was her family now, and she was lucky to have them. J.P. had been father and brother to her, and he would be the one to take her down the aisle when she married Riley. He'd stood by her side with love her whole life, and it seemed more than fitting. It seemed right.

Paige had added the final piece of healing by being a beautiful woman and coming into their family at exactly the right time. Funny how that made her think of Riley's superhero who wove time. Now that she and Mark and Haley had joined them, the door to the past had been completely closed for all of them.

There was peace in that.

"Before we begin our dinner, I'd love for everyone to go around the table and share what they're grateful for," J.P. said, standing at the head. "Mama started this tradition for us McGuinesses a long time ago, when we were having a hard time connecting with gratitude."

Sadie remembered. Their daddy had been gone for a few years, and times had been hard. They'd had a honey-baked ham courtesy of a local food bank.

"I'll begin," J.P. said, taking Tammy's hand. "I'm grateful for my beautiful wife and our children, and I know I can speak for everyone when I say I'm also grateful for Paige and her family coming into our life like they did. And for Riley and Jess making our Sadie so happy."

That choked her up, and she could tell Riley felt it too by how red his ears turned.

"I'm grateful to John Parker," Tammy said, "for always knowing how best to support me. And to Rory and

Annabelle, for giving me such joy as their mama."

Sadie's mama was next. "I'm grateful for this beautiful family. We've grown so much these past years with so many wonderful additions. We'd be here all day if I named them all, but I especially want to say I'm grateful to Paige... She knows why. And to Lenore for joining us and helping us all come together anew. Oh, I'm tearing up."

Was it any wonder? Me-Mother was sitting next to Dale, looking radiant in a brand new peach dress. J.P. was still hoping she'd eventually move to Dare River—that she'd let them buy her a small home of her own here—and they all planned to show her how lovely it was while she stayed with them for the holiday.

"I think everyone's entitled to a few tears after the past few months," Dale said. "I'm grateful for Louisa here, who does so much for so many, and to all of you... I know I don't say much, but y'all mean the world to me."

Sadie had to wipe at the tears streaking down her face. She leaned in to Riley.

"It's always like this," she whispered. "We all end up crying."

He looked a little alarmed, but rubbed her back in comfort.

"I'm more than grateful to be here with y'all," Me-Mother said. "I feel blessed beyond words. Thank you, each of you, for welcoming this old woman with open arms. You're a treasure to me." Her lip quivered and then she waved a hand like she was finished.

"I guess I'm next," Susannah said, sniffing. "I'm grateful for my wonderful husband, Jake. And for the baby we're going to have this May."

"That tops my list," Jake said, "along with my beautiful wife here."

Everyone stood up, exclaiming, and started to form a line to hug the happy couple.

"Oh, this is such good news," Sadie told Riley. She remembered how afraid Jake had been to have children, given his recovery from PTSD. He'd worked hard to overcome it, and now they were going to have the family they'd always wanted.

When they were all back in their chairs, Amelia Ann made a show of dabbing a napkin under her eyes. "Are we going to get through this? Well, I'm grateful for my husband here, and for all the people I can help using the law."

Amelia Ann hadn't picked up the new comic series, which hadn't yet gone on sale, but Sadie thought she was a lot like Nathaniel Gray, something she'd told Riley.

"I'm grateful for this woman here," Clayton said, "and for the heart she puts into everything she does."

"I didn't hear you say you're grateful to me for being your boss," Rye joked.

Clayton rolled his eyes. "Like being your manager is any picnic. Mama?"

Georgia was up from Florida, visiting for the holiday. "I can say I was rarely grateful while I was Rye's manager, but that was when he ran wild. Good to see you settling down, son."

Sadie had to laugh. Only Georgia could get away with calling Rye 'son.'

"I'm grateful to see the man my boy has become. Your daddy would be so proud. And for Amelia Ann. You're the perfect partner for Clayton, and I don't worry about him none now."

"How nice," Amelia Ann said, lifting her wine glass. "Cheers to me. Shelby, you're next."

Sadie's middle sister sat back in her chair and patted Vander's knee. "I'm grateful for hot stuff here."

"Nice," he said, shaking his head and laughing. "Classy."

"We need some levity," Shelby said. "And for all of my family, old and new. I love y'all."

Vander handed her his napkin so she could dry the tears leaking from her eyes. "I never imagined having a family like this. I'm grateful. That's all."

"Succinct and to the point," Shelby said, teasing him. "He's so cute when he gets emotional."

"Don't make me—"

"Promises, promises," Shelby said, interrupting.

"It's Hampton's turn," J.P. said, clearly wanting to move things along.

The older man looked around the room, taking his time. "It's been said, but it bears saying again. I'd like to say how thankful I am for this family. We had a lot of holiday celebrations when our children were growing up, but we were missing something. I'm glad we've finally found it. And to my wife here... We went through a lot. I'm glad we found a way to be happy together. It's a good feeling. And to all my grandkids... I love y'all to pieces."

"Me too, Grandpa," Annabelle cried out. "Will everyone go faster? I'm hungry."

"Annabelle," Rory said. "I told you to eat your snack."

"I didn't want a snack," she said. "I wanted dinner."

J.P. was laughing. "We're almost there, honey. Margaret, it's your turn."

Sadie leaned forward. Rye's mama had been a hard woman, but she'd softened tremendously, which was why she and Hampton had found their way to reconciling after a long separation. "I'm grateful for my children. I mean, our children. For them being...kind to me and showing me...there was a better way to be. Thank y'all."

"Nicely put, Mama," Rye said, kissing her cheek. "Sadie, why don't you go next? I'd like to go last."

Tory gave him a look like he was purposefully being difficult, but Rye only shrugged.

Honestly, Rye could be as difficult as he pleased if you asked Sadie, after what he'd done for her and Riley. She'd decided to make him a thank-you quilt, one redolent with all the power, charm, and kindness he now exhibited.

"Okay, I'm happy to go," she said. "I'm especially grateful this year for my wonderful Riley and his beautiful daughter, Jess, who are my new family."

She thought of the other children they would have, and the quilts she would make them as they progressed through their lives. She planned to show each of them what was possible and remind them of who they truly were inside. Superheroes, all of them.

"I'm also so happy and grateful Paige took my quilting class and gave us all a chance to be her family."

"Me too!" Haley said, making everyone chuckle. "What's so funny? I *am* grateful."

"And I'm grateful for you too, Haley," Sadie said. "And for your dad. Y'all are my new neighborhood family. We're going to have a lot of fun living next door to each other."

"Yes, we are," Riley said, clearing his throat. "I guess it's my turn. I'm grateful for Sadie, for having the biggest heart of almost anyone I know. For my daughter, Jess, whom I love so much, for Paige, whom I consider a sister, and for Haley."

"What about me?" Mark asked with a grin.

"I'm thankful for you too, you…silly head," Riley said, making the kids giggle. "Okay, who's next?"

She realized how nervous he'd been when he released a big breath.

"I'll go," Paige said. "I'm…"

She stopped, and tears filled her eyes. Sadie wiped the ones that had started streaming down her face.

"Give me a moment," she said, sniffing and dashing at her tears.

"Take your time," Mark whispered, taking her hand.

She nodded. "All of you know I didn't grow up having Thanksgiving, and when I had my first one with Mark and his family I…I was kinda a mess. Well, I'm a mess here too, but that's only because I'm so grateful for all of you. Sadie, thank you for coming to our door and asking me to be your sister, and to all of the rest of you—J.P., Susannah, and Shelby—I could never have imagined better siblings than you."

J.P. had to grab a napkin, and that made Sadie smile through her own water works.

"I'm taking a while, but I just have so much to be grateful for. Louisa, thank you too. You know why. And Me-Mother...and the rest of y'all. Oh, and Rye, for letting me have your number in my cell phone."

She laughed, and so did everyone else.

"I can send you an autographed poster too, if you'd like, sugar. Would look right good in your parlor," Rye said, giving her a mischievous wink.

"Can we, Mark?" Paige asked. "And, on a more serious note, thank you to Mark. You're the love of my life, and you taught me everything I know about how to love someone. Haley, my precious girl. Thank you for letting me be your mama. And to our little one inside me... Oh, I can't wait to meet you."

Sadie felt Riley lurch against her.

"I'm pregnant," Paige whispered. "Due about the same time as Susannah."

Sadie flew out of her chair and hugged her sister.

"Thank goodness she finally said!" Haley told Jess. "I was going crazy keeping it to myself after they told me this morning."

More hugs were given. More tears shed. Sadie was especially touched when Paige placed Riley's hand on her belly and said, "This is your future niece or nephew."

He had a glazed look on his face, but it turned into a grin. "I'll be ready with his or her superhero outfit."

Paige nodded, and then Riley man-hugged Mark off the floor. Jess did a little dance and hugged Haley.

"Yay, you're gonna have a brother or sister," she said.

"Finally!"

"I know!" the little girl echoed, and they hugged each other tightly.

When everyone settled back into their chairs, Mark took his wife's hand. "I'll be brief. Paige and Haley, I love you with all my heart. To our new family, thank you for welcoming us like you have. And to Riley and Jess—and now Sadie—you're the best neighborhood family in the world."

"I'm grateful for my new brother or sister, and my mama and daddy," Haley said. "And Jess. Okay, and Riley too. And Sadie for moving in next door."

"I'm grateful for Sadie marrying my dad soon and becoming my mama," Jess said, looking straight at her and breaking her heart.

The little girl had embraced her completely as her new mama, and she got choked up every time she thought of it. She was going to do everything she could to live up to it.

"I'm grateful for everybody," Annabelle said. "Rory, be quick. I'm starving."

Her brother gave a half smile. "I'm grateful for everybody too. And our dogs."

"Right," Annabelle said. "Them too. Uncle Rye? You go."

Rye settled back in his chair. "Tory's up. I'm last."

Tory looked down at Boone. "I'm grateful for our son, and for Rye. Most days. The rest of you guys know how much I love you. Okay, Rye, make it quick."

"Honey, I don't do anything quick," he said, standing up. "I wanted to go last not only because I'm grateful for our son, but because it's like Daddy said. We had a bunch of holidays growing up that were different than they are now. A lot of that is because of the people in this room, but most of it is because we all remembered what's really important."

Sadie's eyes blurred when Rye paused and coughed to clear his throat.

"I might have been one of the most pig-headed people in this group, which is why it took me so long to get it, but I get it now. I'm grateful for a family who really loves each other and supports the best in each other. Thank y'all for remaking this family right alongside me."

"It's like y'all stitched it back together," Riley whispered.

"We did indeed," she said, hearing the reverence in his voice.

Hampton raised his wine glass. "Hear, hear."

Everyone followed suit and raised their glasses.

"To the true meaning of family," Rye said, clinking glasses with those around him.

Sadie and the others reached as many glasses as they could and then everyone drank to punctuate the toast.

Dinner came and went with lots of laughter and enough food to make everyone feel well fed and nourished.

Needing to walk off her meal, Sadie stood and took Riley's hand. "How was your first Thanksgiving with us?"

"Perfect," he said, kissing her cheek. "Sadie McGuiness, I love the heck out of you."

Words guaranteed to curl her toes. "I love you back."

Rye put a hand on Riley's shoulder. "I think it's time you and me had a bourbon."

Her fiancé's mouth twitched. "Ah... Right. Your new drinking partner is out of commission for a while."

Rye nodded to Paige. "Couldn't have happened to a better person. Another baby. We're going to be bursting at the seams with all the babies this group will have. Of course, I'm trying to talk Tory into having another right away. Every time I mention it, she threatens to bean me with her favorite cast-iron frying pan. Come on, bubba. Let's drink."

Riley gave Sadie one last look. "Come find me in twenty minutes. I have a feeling Rye can drink me under the table."

"You bet your ass," Rye said. "Wanna come, sugar?"

Sadie shuddered. "No thank you. I'm going to congratulate Paige again."

Riley grinned. "It's the best news ever. A new baby next door..." Rye led him off, and her man gave her an amused shrug before following.

Sadie headed over to her sister. "Oh, Paige," she said. "I'm so happy for y'all."

"I know," Paige said. Her mascara had slightly run, but she'd never looked more beautiful to Sadie. "The news was so surprising, and yet Mark's right—somehow it was all perfect. It was like meeting y'all and becoming part of this family opened us up to a miracle. Sadie...I owe you so much."

"I owe you back," she said, hugging her tight.

"You know the quilt you mentioned wanting us to make together," Paige said, pulling away. "I've been doing some thinking about it."

She'd had the idea they should collaborate on one about their family, and she'd already given thought to the color palette they might want to use. Somehow she had to find a way to use *all* the colors since each of the people around them represented the full spectrum of love in her life. There had to be hearts and chocolate flowers and something that represented music, obviously, or Rye would hem and haw to high heaven.

"I think we should call it the patchwork quilt of happiness," Paige said, "and rotate it from family to family. It feels...important for everyone to have a share of it somehow."

"I love that idea," Sadie said, feeling her heart swell to bursting.

Paige gazed at her steadily. "I also have a suggestion

for the prayer we can sew inside this quilt."

Sadie felt tears gather in her eyes. "Tell me."

"May our family always be happy," Paige said, gesturing to everyone in the room.

Sadie thought about everything they'd all gone through. How Rye and his entire family had found their way back to each other better than ever. How she and her siblings had faced down their father's abandonment and healed, and how they'd found Paige, their new sister. And how they'd welcomed in spouses and a grandmother along the way.

"I have a better idea. How about we change it slightly from a prayer to a promise? Our family will *always* be happy."

A smile crested across Paige's face. "That's perfect!"

As Sadie looked across the expanse of the chocolate garden at all of their loved ones, young and old, current and future generations alike, she affirmed that promise in her own heart and knew it would be so.

Dear Reader,

Dare River has been all about reuniting families since COUNTRY HEAVEN, and we've gone through the beautiful reconnection of both Rye's family and now the McGuinnesses'. It's been a beautiful journey, and this book marks the end of this incredible series, one that has changed my life and so many of yours too from all your messages. I want to thank Rye especially for being the first character to come to life for me. You'll always be in my heart, my friend. I have a feeling you'll manage to make another appearance in our Dare Valley series, won't you?

If you enjoyed this book, I would love for you to post a review since it helps more readers want to pick up this story and enjoy it themselves. When you post one, kindly let me know at ava@avamiles.com so I can personally thank you. Thank you for spreading the word!

Are you wondering what's next? Make sure you join my newsletter to find out. More incredible characters and books are coming...

Once again, thank you for loving this series so much and for being part of this extended family. I wish every one of you your own patchwork quilt of happiness with those you love.

Lots of light and joy,

Ava

About the Author

International Bestselling Author Ava Miles joined the ranks of beloved storytellers with her powerful messages of healing, mystery, and magic. Millions of readers have discovered her fiction and nonfiction books, praised by USA TODAY and Publisher's Weekly. Women's World Magazine has selected a few of her novels for their book clubs while Southwest Airlines featured the #1 National Bestseller NORA ROBERTS LAND (the name used with Ms. Roberts' blessing) in its in-flight entertainment. Ava's books have been chosen as Best Books of the Year and Top Editor's Picks and are translated into multiple languages.

Made in the USA
Columbia, SC
18 September 2020